DEMON DAYS
BOOK FOUR

DEMON DAYS
BOOK FOUR
By Richard Finney
D.L. Snell

ISBN 978-1-938457-12-8
FIRST EDITION 2013

Original publication 2011
as DEMON DAYS – Angel of Light

Printed in the United States of America

DEMON DAYS
BOOK FOUR

BY

RICHARD FINNEY

D.L. SNELL

LONO PUBLISHING
Encino / California

RICHARD FINNEY

For Brooke, who's had to learn over the years how to live with a Demon.

D.L. SNELL

For my brothers, Andy and Zach, who over the years have done a commendable job curbing their urges to kill me.

The Story Thus Far…

In *DEMON DAYS* we met Sandy Travis, a news producer for a network TV show. She and her fiancé, Tom Hansen, are involved in a tragic helicopter crash while vacationing in Hawaii. Tom dies, but returns to the living after a Near-Death Experience. However, Tom is a changed man, his N.D.E. serving as the conduit for a demonic spirit to possess his body and control his future actions.

Father Alan Olsen approaches Sandy soliciting her support in helping him investigate supernatural incidents he believes are part of a worldwide conspiracy to usher in the End Days.

Their investigation uncovers proof of an assassination plot which takes place at a celebratory gathering, viewed by millions on TV. Shockingly it turns out to be Sandy, not Tom, who ends up carrying out a violent act enabling Satan to possess the body of the influential diplomat, John Wolfenson.

DEMON DAYS – BOOK TWO introduces Jenna Grant, an American Archeologist who specializes in Paleography. Her brother, Neal, requests her expertise in authenticating an artifact known throughout history as "the Black Pages."

While fulfilling her sibling obligation, she discovers two secrets -- the artifact Jenna ends up verifying is the key to a worldwide conspiracy to usher in the *End Days;* and her brother Neal is not himself.

Neal's final act on behalf of the doomsday group, "Red Veil," is to steer their car toward a collision course with a speeding commuter train.

Jenna escapes the vehicle seconds before the impact with the train and ends up teaming up with another survivor of the accident, George Wyatt.

DEMON DAYS – BOOK THREE allowed us a peek at international hero, John Wolfenson, who is actually possessed by Satan himself (aka, *the Angel of Light*). The possessed Wolfenson travels to Syria on behalf of the U.S. government as a response to a devastating earthquake. The diplomat's trip to the disaster zone to aid the sick and suffering is really a rendezvous with the dead. It is the fulfillment of a prophecy from the "Black Pages" which will allow him to carry forth his plan for world domination.

Standing in the way of the apocalypse is Father Alan Olsen, the same priest who failed to come to the aid of his friend Sandy Travis. Olsen's relentless pursuit to stop the plot to usher in the End Days leads to an historically holy place where he is brazenly confronted by the Angel of Light.

Their encounter changes the way Father Olsen sees the world.

The Angel of Light hopes that by taking care of Father Olsen, he has removed one of the final obstacles to achieving his ultimate goal.

However, Satan does not suspect the greatest roadblock will arise from within his own ranks. Carl Saracen is one of the founding members of the Red Veil, but as events have unfolded, Carl has developed grave doubts about the Angel of Light. These misgivings have prompted him to offer support to Jenna Grant which she has refused because she doesn't trust Carl.

There is too much at stake for Carl to accept Jenna's initial answer. He's confident that his ace in the hole will motivate Jenna to look at the situation differently. It turns out part of his team opposing the Angel of Light is Jenna's biological father, a man she has not seen in years.

An emotionally broken down priest; fractured family ties; and a challenging partnership between Jenna and George are what is aligned against the source of all evil and his operation, hundreds of years in the making… to rule humankind.

CHAPTER 1

THE TRAILER DOOR OPENED and Carl stepped in, just in time to witness Reitz strapping the envoy into a bullet-proof vest. Even from the table in the dinette area, Patricia noticed the surprise on Carl's face.

"Fantastic, sir. Glad you're taking the extra precaution."

Wolfenson motioned to Patricia. "Thank my wife."

She was watching everything over the steaming rim of her cup. She had made herself instant coffee because she knew she would need the caffeine. "Please, Carl, hold your applause. This is one of the few times I finally got John to listen to me."

"Oh, I'm sure you're just being modest. The upshot is, I now know who to see when the envoy won't do something I need him to do."

"How are the travel arrangements going?" John asked as Reitz continued to suit him up.

Carl said, "The motorcade is ready to go. And we'll have three of our own doctors with us, just in case."

Patricia popped out of her seat, leaving her coffee to cool. She started gathering her things for the trip.

"It feels tight," John said, shrugging to make the Kevlar vest fit. "Is it supposed to feel this stiff?"

"Yes, sir, that's the way it's supposed to feel." Reitz snapped the last clasp.

"Okay, but... does this coat of armor come with a sword?"

Reitz laughed.

Carl chuckled too. "I don't think you'll need the sword tonight, but I'll bring one with us just in case."

His response sounded a bit forced. Patricia had no doubt that Carl's job included flattering his clients, but she had never witnessed obsequious behavior from him before. Maybe she had just gotten to know him better and was more capable of spotting when he wasn't completely sincere.

"What is the status of our flight crew?" John asked.

"They'll be ready to leave the moment we arrive at the airport."

"And how are we doing with our patients?"

"All loaded up. We've got the nineteen split between nine different vehicles. You and your wife will be traveling in the only one without a victim. We wouldn't want anyone compromised if we were forced to respond to an attack." Carl immediately offered Patricia a reassuring look. "Not that there's any reason to believe we'll be attacked."

She tried her best not to fidget with her personal effects. "Come on, Carl, do I look at all nervous?"

He shook his head. "No, certainly not."

If he had asked her the same question, though, Patricia would have to admit—it was Carl who appeared to be, not necessarily nervous, but... intense. He hadn't moved one step from the doorway of the trailer since coming in.

John reached for his cashmere overcoat, but Reitz beat him to the punch. He helped the envoy slip the fine garment on over his body armor.

"Okay then, let's go," John announced. "We've got some lives to save."

Carl grabbed the door handle to let him out.

The envoy stopped. "Wait—who will be driving us?"

Carl said, "Reitz."

"And where will you be?"

"Riding shotgun. Seriously, sir, where else would I be?"

With a smile, John clapped Carl on the shoulder, and the two men locked eyes. Patricia knew they each would do anything to save the other. And each would do even more to save her. Since falling from the night sky onto a dark runway in the Middle East, she had not felt this protected.

The door to the portable trailer flew open, and Carl and Reitz jumped out. They scanned the area.

"Clear," Carl said, motioning for Patricia and John.

Together, all four of them sprinted toward the road.

At the lead vehicle in the caravan, Carl threw open the back passenger door and helped John into the back seat.

Patricia stole one last peek at her surroundings—the main Red Cross tent was almost dark. They had shut down some of the generators to preserve energy, and the conservation effort only made the bonfires in the refugee camp shine brighter. But somehow the figures crowding around the flames seemed to remain in the shadows, as specters, barely visible through the smoke and lingering dust.

A squeal of joy caught Patricia's attention as two middle-aged women locked in an embrace, screaming and crying, as if they had never expected to see each other ever again—as if they would never again be separated. It was beautiful. But only a dozen yards away, Patricia saw a lifeless body that no one had yet noticed or collected.

Death and... reunions: they were running through her mind when she felt a gentle hand on her shoulder.

"Here we go, Patricia," Carl said.

She grabbed his hand, and he helped her into the SUV.

"Watch your head."

She plopped down in the leather back seat across from her husband, and Carl slammed the door.

———

FOR THE ENTIRE ROAD TRIP to the airport, both men looked as if they were manning the phone banks at a pledge drive for public radio.

In the back seat, John, on the sat phone, tried his best to push his agenda. Patricia could tell the stiffness of the flak jacket distracted him.

"Yes, Yoni, I understand your concern. But we're talking about nineteen critically injured people who need medical help, and the conditions here are just not up to the task. Please, I'm begging you, talk to Mier. Convince him this will only end up being a win-win for your government, and your party..."

In the front seat, Carl tapped his contacts to arrange visa clearances for the earthquake victims. By Patricia's count, since leaving the Red Cross, he had made five phone calls.

"Sorry, Hagai, I know, I know it's late. I'm here... in Syria, yes. At ground zero. Of course I'm here with the envoy. Listen, Hagai, I'm calling because we both need your help..."

Patricia could do nothing but sit and listen. She wanted so badly to feed them lines that might help—"Tell them all the work you did to rescue these people. Tell them some of them are barely even adults"—but she resisted. They knew better than she did the art of persuasion.

Eventually, she wondered if John and Carl would concede that there was no chance of getting the earthquake victims into Israel. She knew if that happened, it would be a trip of pregnant silences back to downtown Aleppo.

John finished his conversation and clicked off the phone. He went to update Carl, but he was still on the line.

"Nobody's listening to me," John told Patricia. "It's as if weeks ago I wasn't the one who brokered the most important peace treaty in forty years."

Patricia hated when her husband slipped into self-pity. She instantly thought of John's old high school picture: acne; a severe overbite that only an orthodontist could love; and shoulder-length hair, a rebellion against his successful father who John obviously feared he could never live up to.

"Honey, please don't let any of this frustrate you."

"I'm trying my best. But tell me—is it unrealistic to expect a recent historic accomplishment to get a better reaction than excuses and halfhearted commitments? It's as if I were back in junior high, asking one of these guys to take my sister to the prom."

"I recall something you've said to me on more than one occasion," Patricia replied. "'It rises in the east and sets in the west, but rarely in diplomacy does the sun cast the same shadow.'"

John reached over and took her hand. "Pat, all these years I never thought you were listening to a word I said."

She shook her head, as if no assumption could be more preposterous, but she had already lost her husband's attention—Carl had ended his phone conversation.

"So what happened with Hagai?" John asked.

"Honestly, he wasn't happy I was calling at this late hour. But I trust after reminding him of what I had on him..." He stopped in the middle of his sentence.

Because of me, Patricia thought. Nothing new, really. She had grown accustomed to conversations getting put on hold until she left the room.

"Look, sir, I don't need to get into any details, but let's just say my man Hagai will definitely check in with Interior Minister Kahlon about our request."

"Good work, Carl. Very good news."

"Yes, but, sir—I need to tell you... I've seen Israeli officials deny plane clearance at the slightest whiff of a security issue. You need to be prepared for that outcome."

"I hear you."

"Okay. So how did your call with Mier go?"

"Not well. He asked a lot of questions. And offered zero promises until he had more time to consider the situation."

Carl chuckled cynically. "That just means checking with someone else in the cabinet. Or his party. It seems Interior Minister Mier knows any decision that goes wrong is like manure: it needs to be spread evenly around the garden."

John sighed. "Of course you're right. And that's what worries me."

"Here's what I think we need to do..." Carl said, but trailed off. This time it had nothing to do with Patricia.

Reitz was pulling to a stop.

The rest of the caravan pulled up behind him.

Just ahead, a bluff of broken concrete completely blocked the road. The headlights revealed other debris mixed in: a car door, a wad of red textiles with yellow flower designs, what must have been an inlaid backgammon set.

"Sir, what do you want to do?" Reitz asked.

At first Patricia assumed he was talking to Carl, but Reitz was peering in the rearview at her husband.

John didn't respond. His attention was completely on Carl, who had stopped programming another route into his GPS to look up at the pile of concrete.

"Carl?"

"Sorry, sir, just concerned that a route we travelled on only hours ago is suddenly impassable."

John leaned forward, but only a few inches because of the seatbelt. "Is there something else?"

Carl's eyes shifted between the concrete and the area adjacent to it, where a building once stood. "It's dark out there so... it's impossible to be sure."

"At least give me a hint."

Carl turned toward the back seat. "Well, I'm looking at the obstacle in front of us and I'm comparing it to the foundation where it should have come from..."

"And?"

"And I'm not seeing a match."

Patricia let out an audible gasp. Carl was right. All the busted-up ashlar and concrete and wooden Ottoman balconies had come from various sources. The bricks were different sizes, different shades of sand. It looked like a communal dump.

"Envoy, sir, I don't like the way this is feeling. I think we should head back, regroup, and rethink this entire endeavor."

"That's not possible," John said. He unbuckled his safety harness and moved so close to the front seat that he and Carl were a mere foot apart. "If we turn around, most, if not all, of the victims we're trying to help will die. It's that simple."

Patricia knew her husband had been fundamentally schooled in the art of compromise, so she rarely saw this look on his face. Yet in the space of a few hours, she had seen it twice: once back at the Red Cross tent, and now, even in the dark interior of the SUV, she was certain she was seeing it again.

Obsession.

"We need to get them all out of this city to Tel Aviv. I'm willing to stake my life... and my wife's life on this mission. I know you have men working for you, so you have your own decision to make, but I need you to make it quickly."

Carl looked over at Patricia. She tried her best not to offer any facial expression, tried not to sway him either way. After only a few moments of deliberation, he grabbed a walkie-talkie from his lap.

"Tanaka, do you read me?"

"Loud and clear," Tanaka radioed in from the vehicle behind them.

"Okay, so this rubble has us going on a detour. We're making a U-turn, and then heading back less than a block, where we'll hang a right. We'll take a lateral route for a bit and then cut back and catch the main road to the airport. Just make sure the others follow us, over."

"Roger that."

Reitz made the U-turn, and, as Patricia watched out the back window, Tanaka and the rest of the fleet did the same.

John retreated to the back seat and buckled up. "Sorry for volunteering you there," he said, touching Patricia's hand.

She smiled. "You should have given me a chance. I would have volunteered myself."

They didn't drive very far before Carl motioned to Reitz. "Okay, hang a right."

Reitz steered their vehicle from the main road into what was once a commercial district before the quake. Moving down the main street, he weaved through an obstacle course of spilled ashlar and brick, hydroplaning here and there across streams of running water from busted sanitation lines and severed pipes.

Patricia stared out the car window, saw huge concrete slabs lying almost completely intact on the sidewalk, saw shop front windows that had been blown out in sprays of shattered glass.

What she didn't see was a single soul. Several hours past the curfew, the looters and scavengers had found a place to hide and sleep, leaving a once thriving community a modern ghost town.

Carl said, "Okay, Reitz, we're going to want to grab a left at the next intersection."

But as their SUV approached the spot Carl had earmarked on his GPS, they discovered another roadblock. A church on the street corner had fallen. The spire, along with the stone tower, had buckled into an impregnable wall.

"What the hell?" Carl mumbled to himself.

"Plan C?" Reitz asked.

"No, same plan. Just with a minor adjustment. Keep driving straight. I'm going to need a second."

Carl hit buttons on his GPS so fast his fingers became a blur. By his own admission, he had been in plenty of disaster areas and war zones, and could handle the situation. But something about this place was causing him to look genuinely scared.

"Okay, Reitz, we'll be coming up on another corner any second." He raised his eyes from the GPS. "We'll see if this time we can make a left. If we can, do it. This new route will lead us a little bit out of our way, but we'll eventually connect back to the main road."

They approached the corner where Carl wanted them to turn. This time it appeared to be clear of any fallout from the quake.

Patricia checked out the back windshield. The rest of the caravan followed close behind, as if traveling a parade route.

Then Tanaka flashed his lights.

"Carl," she said, but he already had his walkie-talkie up to his lips.

"Yeah, Tanaka. I know it's a narrow street, but what are we supposed to do?"

"How about just abort?!"

Carl looked at John, who was buried in the shadows of the back seat. Patricia could tell Carl was giving her husband one more chance to change his mind. She wasn't sure Carl could see John shaking his head.

"That's a negative," Carl replied into the walkie-talkie. "Look, Tanaka, just a couple more streets and we'll be back on the original escape line, minutes from our end state. I need you to pass it on—everyone needs to just chill. Over."

They pulled onto the side street, more of an alleyway or service road rather than anything Patricia could properly label a street. Their SUV lurched and rattled and bounced over several potholes and cracks in the cobblestone. The side mirrors came dangerously close to smashing into the towering brick walls that flanked them.

"Why's he so worried about the road being narrow?" Patricia asked.

When Carl didn't respond, Reitz said, "Ma'am, a narrow street will prevent us from turning around if there's trouble."

"And since we're driving in a motorcade," Carl added, "going backwards is not an option."

Patricia blanched. All of a sudden, she could feel the walls closing in, threatening to suffocate her, crush her, as if she were buried under them already and was quickly running out of air. She started to tremble, and then shake uncontrollably.

John must have seen it, felt it, because he pulled her close—as close as their seatbelts would allow. She tried her best to calm down and decided to stop looking out the window, out at those encroaching walls. She decided to fixate on Carl instead.

When she was seven years old, Patricia and her older brother, Glen, had accompanied their father to the movie theater to see a scary film. Shortly after the opening credits Patricia had turned around in her seat, and, for the remainder of the movie, she tried to ignore the violent noises and the non-stop screams, some from the movie, some from the audience. For eighty-nine minutes she stared at Glen's face as he stared at the screen.

Now it was Carl who played her medium to events that she couldn't bear to watch. Patricia wasn't immediately comforted though. It wasn't just the thick layer of sweat glistening on Carl's face, but the sight of his hand holding the walkie-talkie. So much perspiration dripped from his palm it was only a matter of seconds before he electrocuted himself.

Patricia barked out a laugh.

Everyone looked at her, and she covered her mouth.

"Sorry, I'm so sorry..."

Never before had she laughed because of pure nerves, and she couldn't explain why, of all times, it would afflict her now. But, watching Carl, she had realized he had a brand new entry for his scared-shitless list.

She was about to apologize again, but then slowly, calmly, surreptitiously, Carl lowered his walkie-talkie into his lap. Reitz slowed down. They both were staring at something ahead.

Patricia bolted out of John's arms, and he tried to hold her back, as if he didn't want her to lift her head above the windows, but he didn't cling tenaciously enough, and she escaped his grasp. What Patricia saw in front of them almost sent her back to her cocoon.

In the headlights, two figures, about one hundred feet away, dragged a long wooden barrier, which spanned the width of the alley.

Veiled almost entirely in black—black jeans, black t-shirts and black leather jackets; black-and-white-checkered Basij headscarves—the two figures looked like shadows with human eyes. They both packed AK-47s strapped to their backs.

Reitz brought the vehicle to a complete halt about fifty feet from the barrier.

"Oh my God..." Patricia said. "I can't believe this is happening..."

John rested a hand on her shoulder. "Pat, it's all right. Just stay calm."

With the walkie-talkie hidden in his lap, Carl hit the talk button.

"Okay, Tanaka, points to you for smelling the cheese first. But now no one is to make a move on these Jackals. We're the ones holding the package, and I'll be the one issuing the green light. Pass it on, over."

"Roger that," Tanaka said.

Thunk... thunk...

A rifle butt tapped Reitz's window, and everyone in the vehicle jumped. A third terrorist had come to play welcoming party. This one wore dark sunglasses.

Thunk... thunk... thunk...

This time, the noises came from the rear windshield. A fourth shadow stood there with his back to the vehicle, probably tasked with deflecting the rest of the caravan. He held a pistol, a 9mm.

Thunk!

The Jackal at the driver's-side window made a throat-cutting gesture, signaling Reitz to kill the engine. But Reitz hadn't even put the transmission in park, and wasn't making any move to do so. He simply sat there, staring at the Jackal, hands raised off.

The terrorist struck harder, trying to shatter the glass, and everyone's resolve.

Thrack-thrack-thrack!

"Sir," Reitz said, "do we have a game plan?"

"Yes," Carl said, "it begins with you looking terrified. Show him his effort is paying off..."

The Jackal outside his window had started to sweat so profusely from his effort that his sunglasses threatened to slip off the bridge of his nose.

Thrack!

Thrack!

Thrack!

Reitz flinched this time, theatrically, and he clutched at his chest as if having a heart attack.

"I see only four of them," Carl said. "Jackal 1 here by your window, Jackal 2 at our rear. And Jackals 3 and 4 over there at the barricade. You get the same count?"

"Yeah, four here as well. But it's dark. Maybe we're not seeing the entire pack."

"Doubtful," Carl said. "This kind of shakedown is all about intimidation. If they could manage it, there would be a whole row of Jackals baring their teeth. So what we see is, I believe, all they have."

Jackal #3, who had been standing near the wooden barrier, marched over to the driver's side of the vehicle. He went straight to the back window and peered inside.

Still as statues, neither Patricia nor John turned to the animal as he eyed them like they were his next meal. Their disregard must have only frustrated him.

Thrack-thrack-thrack!

Carl unbuckled his seatbelt and reached beneath his seat.

"What are you doing?" Wolfenson asked.

"Envoy, sir, this is no doubt all about money." He pulled out a leather pouch, a money belt. "This probably has some cobwebs on it," he said, dusting it off. "We haven't seen this type of action for a while, thanks to your career moving to more exclusive circles."

He unzipped the money belt and withdrew two large bundles of cash. "Hopefully they'll be satisfied with this one score and knock off for the night."

"John," Patricia said, "you can't let him go out there."

Wolfenson didn't respond. So she looked to Carl, who was focused exclusively on Reitz.

"When I'm out there," Carl said, "if it looks like the bribe is a non-starter, wait for me to go for my piece."

Thunk-thunk!

"Reitz, are you listening to me?"

"Absolutely. Just... keep talking while I stare at this moron who's giving me a headache."

"When I draw, that will be your cue to slam on the accelerator... And I hope you take out every motherfucking thing in front of your grill."

Thrack-thrack!

"The package is in this car, so don't think twice about the rest of the caravan. Just drive to the airport. Absolutely no stops. Are we a roger on that?"

"Yes, understood," Reitz said.

"10k?"

Finally Reitz turned to face him.

Thunk—thrack-thrack-thrack-thrack!

"Yes, sir. Everything's 10k."

The last letter seemed to trigger Carl. With the speed of a lethal projectile, he jumped out of the vehicle and slammed the door. Reitz immediately mashed the console button and locked the Humvee.

"I can't believe this," Patricia said, wiping tears from her eyes and cheeks. She wanted to curl up in her husband's arms again, but she refused to cower and hide from whatever happened next.

Arms raised with a wad of cash in each hand, Carl slowly but deliberately walked toward the wooden barrier, toward Jackal #4.

The terrorist leveled his assault rifle at Carl and said something, to which Carl responded. Inside the airtight vehicle, Patricia might as well have been watching a silent movie.

She couldn't see the terrorist's lips underneath the Basij scarf, but she knew he was shouting at Carl by the way he was thrusting his gun at him, and waving it at the SUV in a nervous, aggressive shuffle.

Carefully, Carl held out one of the bankrolls. The terrorist grabbed it, looked at it, then spit on it and threw it to the ground.

Carl, more hastily this time, offered the second wad of cash. The Jackal struck out with the barrel of his rifle, knocking the money from his hand.

"Reitz," John said, "are you watching this?" His voice seemed so sudden and loud in the silence, Patricia recoiled.

"Yes, sir," Reitz said, "absolutely."

"We need to think seriously about making our move now."

"John!"

"Patricia, please..."

Outside, the terrorist jabbed the butt of his rifle into Carl's stomach, and Carl doubled over, dropped to his knees. He fell to one hand and coughed onto the cobblestones.

"Carl!"

Jackal #3 walked around and briefly eclipsed the headlights briefly. He and Jackal #4 started barking at each other, in some kind of disagreement. Jackal #3 reached for one of the discarded wads of cash, but his hand never touched the roll of money. There was a bright flash and he was flying backwards, as if a bolt of lightning had struck him.

Before Patricia understood what was happening, there was another flash, and the other Jackal staggered back. He tried to aim his rifle, but a third flash sent him stumbling.

It was all Carl.

He stood up, gun in hand. Patricia never saw him draw it. He aimed toward the SUV, unleashed another burst of light, and then Jackal #1 no longer stood at Reitz's window. He simply disappeared.

"What are you waiting for?!" John shouted, shaking the driver's seat. "Go!"

Reitz slammed his foot on the gas, and the SUV surged toward Carl, who was turning to aim at the last terrorist, and as Patricia watched, still an audience to this horrifying silent picture, the camera zoomed in on Carl until he filled her whole window—and then, as if he had been hit with a cannonball, he went flying backwards, and the movie was over.

Patricia screamed.

"He's shot!"

Their SUV smashed through the wooden barrier, and a chunk of it ricocheted off the windshield, but barely made a sound, barely left a smudge.

Patricia whipped her head around to look out the back. The last Jackal advanced on Carl, firing his pistol. And Carl, lying on the ground as chunks of cobblestone and dust kicked up all around him, returned fire, emptied his gun.

The terrorist collapsed.

Patricia tried to get out of her seat, but forgot she was strapped in. So she hit the release.

"We can't leave him there! Stop the car!"

John tried to grab her, but she squirmed away, attempted to wriggle into the front passenger seat, where Carl had once sat.

"Honey..." John released his buckle too and made another attempt to corral her. "It's all right."

"Stop the car!" Patricia screeched, pulling at Reitz's jacket.

But Reitz didn't stop. He didn't even decelerate. John wrapped his arms around Patricia and pulled her back into the seat. She pried at his hands and kicked, but sobs wracked her, turned her into something wobbly and weak, and her kicks were dampened, deadened, blocked by the seatback.

"Ma'am, it's all right," Reitz said, "it's all right! Tanaka has stopped his vehicle. And Carl... it looks like he's walking!"

"Pat, did you hear that... it's all right!"

Her husband's insistence wore away at her like an undertow until she was exhausted, spent, and sobbing as he pulled her in and under and down, where all she could do was cry, all the way to the airport. It felt as if she were drowning.

CHAPTER 2

AS DR. COLIN FINCHER PARKED his SUV on the tarmac, he had every reason to believe things were going according to plan.

The earthquake victims had been loaded onto the private plane. The flight crew was finishing their pre-flight check. And just a few feet from the jet, John Wolfenson stood in a cameraman's light, conducting a live interview with a major U.S. news network.

"The Israeli government lent a huge hand in the relief effort," Wolfenson was saying. "They provided state-of-the-art equipment, and it was only with their aid that we were able to rescue these nineteen people. It should have been enough, but instead I'm requesting that Israel continue with their generous spirit. Their country possesses cutting-edge medical services, which these quake victims need to survive."

Fincher had no doubt the envoy's mix of flattery and worldwide media coverage would increase pressure on the Israeli government to allow the

Syrian nationals into their country. And he had high hopes it would eliminate their dependence on Carl. Such a development would only make re-
moving Carl from a leadership role easier for Fincher to execute.

The doctor was not ashamed to admit he felt optimistic—a rare sensa-
tion. Certainly the peace treaty signing weeks ago did not incite the same
passion. Fincher had been overseeing too many moving parts to feel remotely confident that they would succeed. And after everything he had
experienced in Aleppo, this feeling of optimism felt earned.

"Sir," Reitz said, whispering in the doctor's ear, "there was an incident
on the trip—"

Fincher raised a hand to silence him. Even with the constant noise of
air traffic, he didn't want to take a chance this close to the microphone and
camera. So they walked under the private jet to the other side of the tarmac, where there was no one.

"What happened?" Fincher asked.

"Carl saved the lives of the envoy and his wife."

Immediately, the pool of sanguinity Fincher had been bathing in evaporated.

"Tell me everything. Exactly as it happened."

Reitz nodded. He recounted the terrorist attack on the caravan without a
hint of emotion.

Long ago, Fincher had coined a term for people who were possessed:
he called them snails. It was a private joke, one he never told aloud—
especially not in front of the envoy—and yet he had to remind himself that
Reitz, as any snail, would remain completely expressionless even as he
described traumatic events. Indifference was their default mode.

When Reitz finished, the doctor peppered him with questions. He only
stopped when the light on the news camera switched off.

Always one to schmooze, Wolfenson chatted with the reporter and the other members of the crew. It was a common psychopathic profile—an abnormal lack of empathy combined with strong amoral conduct, masked by irresistible charm. But Fincher still couldn't figure out why the Angel of Light seemed to get the same charge from meeting the commoners as the real John Wolfenson had.

Fincher waved and got the envoy's attention. Wolfenson excused himself and walked over, beneath the nose of the plane.

"Colin! Much has happened in your absence."

"Yes, sir. Why don't we find a place to speak privately?"

They retreated to one of the SUVs and sat in front while Reitz paced outside.

Sitting comfortably in the driver's seat, the envoy shared all of his impressions of the terrorist incident. Dr. Fincher absorbed every word. He paid special attention to any detail that might contradict Reitz's report.

Fincher also waited for, indeed, *anticipated*, the envoy's personal insights into what he had endured earlier. Then, before the doctor could collate his thoughts, and certainly before he could respond, the Angel of Light concluded, not with any insight, but with a declaration.

"I believe my previous decision regarding Carl's loyalty was a bit rash. To be completely candid—I believe I absolutely made a mistake."

Fincher expended every effort not to react. Somehow, and for reasons he could not understand, the Angel of Light had voluntarily descended from his pedestal, as if he were going through a period of soul searching.

"Envoy, sir, Carl has worked diligently for years to ensure your arrival. I'm not surprised to hear about his bold action to save not only your life, but Patricia's as well. I do hope, however, that you will indulge a few... inquiries on my part."

"Yes, of course."

Fincher thought about how to phrase his first question. He knew by challenging the envoy's *mea culpa*, he risked his entire relationship with him.

"Who made the transport arrangements to the airport?" Fincher asked.

"I believe it was Carl."

"And was it Carl who also guided the motorcade from the concrete detour?"

"Yes. But, again, Carl clearly stated that he wanted to return to the Red Cross."

"Mr. Envoy, I assure you, I'm not overlooking Carl's passionate declaration to retreat. But if I may, sir, who chose the street which ended up being blocked? And who chose the alleyway that led to the terrorist roadblock?"

"It was Carl."

"The answer to both of my questions is... Carl?"

"Yes."

Fincher settled into the passenger seat like a district attorney who had satisfactorily proven his case. He still had things he wanted to say, dots he wanted to connect, but he didn't for fear that he would just be rubbing it in.

"Doctor, I take by your silence that you are convinced what happened was not what it appeared to be. And apparently you've raised this issue because you are equally convinced that I'm not capable of seeing through a two-bit hominid con."

"No, sir, that's not true. I apologize for my miscommunication. All that I'm suggesting, Mr. Envoy, is that Carl is a very clever and resourceful... hominid. That's why he's been part of the Red Veil almost since its inception. I humbly ask you to entertain the notion that perhaps he took a page from your play book."

The envoy stared out the windshield. Reitz had stopped pacing and was standing still in front of the SUV. Fincher decided not to say another word, no matter how the envoy eventually responded. He had already said too much.

"Sorry, Colin, I'm convinced the mistake I made was underestimating Carl's loyalty. The man ended up taking a bullet for me. And taking a bullet for me has to stand for something."

Fincher wondered if perhaps the perfect possession of John Wolfenson, along with the other considerable tricks, had begun to tax the Angel of Light. The envoy had already shown a physical vulnerability in the last twenty-four hours. Could the possession and his acts be making him... ?

The doctor abruptly ended that train of thought. Despite the weaknesses Wolfenson had exhibited in recent hours, Fincher feared the Angel of Light might still be hiding some incredible powers.

"Yes, Mr. Envoy, you're right. It should stand for something. What would you like it to stand for?"

"I would like us to trust him again."

Fincher didn't respond. So many thoughts ran through his brain, he didn't feel comfortable voicing any of them.

"Can you still do that, doctor? Can you trust Carl?"

Trust, Fincher thought. Something he only did when he ran out of options. And with Carl, he firmly believed he still had other options.

When Fincher responded to the Angel of Light, he suddenly felt like one of the snails: expressionless.

"Yes, Mr. Envoy, if that is your desire."

———

AFTER BOARDING THE PRIVATE JET, Wolfenson stopped by the plane's cockpit to speak with the pilot about the trip. Fincher continued to the passenger lounge.

Furnished with cushy leather chairs and little coffee tables, equipped with satellite TV and a bar, the cabin looked like someone's formal living room, if not for the curved ceiling and narrow dimensions.

The seating was organized in clusters. The main cluster featured a couch and two chairs. On the sofa, amongst the floral throw pillows, Carl sat, shirtless. A physician sat next to him, tending to him, and Patricia sat in an adjacent chair, staring, obviously shell-shocked from the night's events.

The physician was treating what seemed to be a nasty hematoma on Carl's chest—blunt trauma consistent with the effects of a bullet stopped by a ballistic vest.

"Where does the line to get your autograph begin?" Fincher said, delivering the joke without a trace of sarcasm.

Carl looked up and smiled. "Sorry, no autographs. But I am entertaining offers on my life rights for a movie."

Fincher was relieved to hear Carl respond with a joke of his own. The doctor would hate to undo all of the hard work they had put into Patricia simply because Carl was bold and stupid enough to lower his mask.

"I just heard the news," Fincher said. "Seriously, Carl, how are you?"

"Unfortunately, a huge bruise on my chest will end up being my one souvenir from Aleppo."

"I would have gone for the Citadel T-shirt," Fincher said. He turned to Patricia. "And how are you holding up through all of this?"

"Fine," she said, with her eyes fixed on Carl. "Now that I know he'll be all right."

"I'm sure it will take more than a couple of road bandits to switch off Carl's lights. That's why there's no one better at what he does."

This time Patricia fixed the doctor with an intense gaze. "You weren't there. They weren't 'road bandits.' Carl tried to offer them money, but they refused."

The problem with idiots like Patricia was that when they did have the rare intelligent thought, it fooled them into believing they truly were intelligent. Fincher knew it was one of the main reasons she was so easy to con. He supposed Carl's seemingly heroic response to the terrorist attack explained Patricia's passionate support. But he feared a deeper, more emotional explanation. The plan had called for Carl and Patricia to bond as he led her toward the psychic. Was it possible they had done more than *bond*?

"I apologize," Fincher said. "I certainly wasn't trying to minimize Carl's courageous effort in the least."

He turned to Carl for help, and to his credit, Carl immediately bailed him out.

"Of course you weren't intending any offense, doctor."

The verbal support seemed to do the trick: the condemning expression on Patricia's face dissolved.

"While we're on the subject," Fincher said, "what can you tell me about the men who terrorized the caravan?"

Carl winced as the physician rubbed some antiseptic on his wound. He said, "Hezbollah would be my best guess."

Fincher simply nodded, reluctant to contradict Carl in front of Patricia.

"They obviously wanted to take advantage of the quake," Carl continued. "They knew there was bound to be an international relief effort, and they probably wanted to see if they could obtain a high-value hostage."

"Yes, Carl, I'm sure you're right."

"There's my savior!"

Everyone looked up as the envoy entered the passenger cabin. Reitz followed close behind.

Wolfenson stopped at Fincher's side and laid a hand on the doctor's shoulder, but he clearly was speaking to Carl. "So how are you feeling?"

"Just a scratch, sir, please. No need to worry."

Fincher wanted to burst out laughing. Despite his modest response, Carl clearly was milking the injury for as much sympathy as possible. In fact if Carl bit down any harder, the physician would need to stich his bottom lip.

"You, sir, need to accept the laurel of a hero with less modesty," Wolfenson said.

"Just doing my job."

The envoy nodded, seemingly impressed with his reply.

"Sweetie," he said, turning to his wife, "we're going to be taking off in a few minutes. I have it in my mind to go down and visit the earthquake victims. Would you like to join me?"

"Yes, I would like that very much."

Hand in hand, the two disappeared down a stairwell to the belly of the plane.

Fincher almost sighed with relief, but managed to suppress it. No matter what hold Carl had on Wolfenson's wife, their plan had apparently worked. She was clearly at the envoy's beck and call.

Reitz took a chair in the seating cluster behind the couch, and Dr. Fincher slipped into Patricia's seat, which was still warm.

"Where's the bullet?" he asked.

With a nudge from Carl, the physician reached into his pocket and pulled out a slug.

Fincher examined it with a bemused grin. The head of the projectile had flattened and flared out like a mushroom. The Kevlar fibers had left an imprint in the lead.

"Where's your vest?"

Carl pointed underneath Fincher's seat, and the doctor retrieved the armor.

The approximate location of the bullet hole in the vest matched the injury on Carl's chest. But Fincher knew that was the point of having the evidence conveniently located.

Bullet.

Vest.

Wound.

Match across the board.

Case closed.

The evidence, genuine or not, refuted Fincher's first theory, that the terrorists had been firing blanks.

He dropped the vest to the floor and put a hand on the physician's shoulder. "Doctor, do you mind giving us a few minutes?"

The physician, who had been listening to his patient's inner workings with a stethoscope, turned to Carl for confirmation. Carl nodded, and the medic packed up and left.

Once they were alone, Fincher said, "According to Reitz, three of the four terrorists were armed with AK-47s. The other was brandishing a pistol."

"I believe that's accurate, yes."

"So are you telling me the only player who managed to score a hit is the only one not packing an AK-47? The only one not firing rounds that would have cut through your vest like it was butter?"

"Doctor, since when did you become an expert on firearms?"

"You would be surprised how much you pick up analyzing the files of hundreds of killers. But, Carl, if you don't mind, can we stay on point? Either your prayers were answered and the only terrorist who managed to shoot you was sporting a cap gun, or..."

"Or what?"

"Or we have a stage manager who promoted himself to director."

Carl stared at Fincher, who had no trouble staring right back.

After a few long moments of silence, Fincher said, "Carl, tell me you didn't really mention Hezbollah to the envoy."

"You asked me for my theory and I gave it to you. I haven't said a damn thing to John."

"And why would you? Your heroic action speaks for itself."

Fincher tossed the bullet at him, but Carl didn't lift a hand to catch it. The slug hit the back of the couch and fell between the cushions.

"Listen, doctor, you can accuse me of anything you want. But as Patricia just said, you weren't there. Maybe we should thank God for the fact you missed all the fireworks."

"No, we can thank the envoy. I was tending to his business."

"Well then, lucky for you there's still an available seat at such late notice. The plane is kind of full, seeing as we're flying nineteen Syrians into Tel Aviv."

"Yes, I'm completely aware of the operation."

"Really? Because I thought the envoy made the decision about ninety minutes ago, and you've been out of contact with him for hours."

"Carl, what's your point?"

"Point is, doctor, when the envoy first outlined his plan to us weeks ago, he said, and I quote, 'Each step of the operation will be deliberately paced. The last thing we want to do is raise suspicion by moving too fast with a course dictated by unbridled ambition.' End of quote."

"Wow. That's impressive, Carl. I believe those were the envoy's exact words."

"Then at least we won't be fencing over whether or not my memory's hazy. But, doctor, if you don't mind, let's stay on point—why the change in plans?"

"'Circumstances on the ground often necessitate changes on the fly.' I think you've said something like that in the past, am I right?"

"Close enough. The only problem is you're ignoring the subtext. Even when changes are being made on the fly, everyone in a command position is notified. Standard procedure."

"Well, Carl, as you most certainly know, I'm not military. When the time is right, you'll be brought up to speed."

Fincher stood up to leave, but Carl planted his foot in the doctor's chest and shoved him back into his seat.

"No, we're not through here. Not until I get some answers."

Fincher closed his eyes and took a deep breath. The last thing he wanted was for their conversation to spin further out of control. He had promised the envoy to settle things with Carl.

"I promise you, Carl, when I'm able to let you know the details of the operation, I will do so. Until then, get your foot off my chest."

Carl lowered his foot. "Your promise isn't good enough. If there's a chance I'm going to take another bullet for this so-called plan, I want to know what the hell I'm doing it for."

"I'm sorry, but you're barking at me as if you have leverage." Fincher looked around the plane, then leaned forward toward the couch. "As long as your son is a snail, you'll do exactly as we tell you to."

A second before Carl leapt out of his seat, the doctor knew he planned to attack. Because of the reflexive snarl. They were no longer in civilized society, no longer pretending to be.

Fincher also knew something else—Reitz was standing by.

Before Carl could make contact, the bodyguard detained him in a headlock. The doctor almost laughed at the sight. Here was Reitz, once one of Carl's most trusted employees, letting his old boss know he no longer had his back.

"Gentlemen," the envoy said; he had just returned from below. "Is everything all right?"

"Yes, Mr. Envoy," Fincher said. He nodded to Reitz, and the guard released Carl.

"What was that..." Wolfenson said, but trailed off as the plane's flight attendant entered the lounge.

She smiled, completely oblivious. "Envoy, sir, we're ready to take off. We need all the passengers to buckle up."

"Very good." Wolfenson sat in the leather chair next to Fincher. "I'll see to it that everyone follows your instructions."

Carl and Reitz lowered themselves into their seats as the flight attendant left the cabin.

"Thankfully," Wolfenson said, "Patricia decided to stay below so she could tend to one of the patients. Because if she had seen the both of you fighting like children—that might have ruined the mood we have all worked so diligently to set. Now, gentlemen, let's all fasten our seatbelts, shall we?"

Both Fincher and Carl followed the envoy's orders, and the plane started rolling toward the runway for takeoff.

"Carl," Wolfenson said, "whatever Colin has told you, or not told you, I want to tell you myself—I will never forget what you did for me. Your protection during the attack reaffirmed why we are a team. I need you, and right now I need you to understand that. No, wait, strike what I just said..."

The plane turned and rolled to a stop.

"Carl, I want you to *believe* what I'm saying. Please tell me that you still believe."

Carl stared at the envoy as the engines of the plane began to rev up. He stared long enough that it raised doubts about what he might say, but then, as tears welled up in Carl's eyes, Fincher knew exactly how he would play it.

"Yes," Carl said, "I believe you. And, sir, for the record... I have never stopped."

All Fincher could do was lean back in admiration. Carl possessed what some serial killers counted on as their most valuable weapon—charm. But he had refined it, had taken the superficial personality trait to a much deeper level. When properly motivated, he could radiate charisma, not just

41

with his actions but in the way he spoke. He had a special way of projecting sincerity even when it was clearly by design. And most listeners had no trouble whatsoever falling under his spell. Even ones who should know better.

After hearing Carl's words, Wolfenson, too, began to tear up.

The pilot released the plane's brakes and accelerated, faster and faster down the runway. Moments later, the nose of the plane lifted, and then the wheels left the ground. Throughout the entire takeoff, Fincher stared at Carl, who stared at the envoy, who closed his eyes.

At a certain altitude, their plane started to level off, and it no longer felt as if they were in a rocket ship headed to the moon.

The envoy's eyes flashed open and immediately fixed on Carl. "Have you heard from any of your contacts?"

"Yes, sir, I have, but I have some concerns."

"Of course you do," Fincher chimed in.

The envoy shot him a look, and the doctor felt his insides withering, shriveling up like a salted slug. He bowed his head. It was now perfectly clear—there was nothing he could say that would exclude Carl from the final act of their operation. Nothing at all.

"Please," Wolfenson said to Carl, "continue. You have our ears."

"Envoy, sir, you've asked me to get these earthquake victims into Israel."

"Yes, that's right."

"But we all know it isn't truly for humanitarian reasons."

"Mmm."

"Therefore, when I use my credibility, established over twenty unblemished years, and these... *victims* do anything but simply die... Sir, I will be finished."

"Carl, I understand what I'm asking you to sacrifice. I truly do." The envoy looked over at Fincher, and the doctor, recognizing the cue, nodded, as if in complete sympathy to the envoy's proclamation.

"Thank you, sir, but just so we're clear... I will be ruined in this part of the world. My security company will take a huge hit. I candidly reveal this to you now, not because of my own selfish concerns, but because I will have no influence in the Mideast for the foreseeable future."

"I completely understand, Carl. Truly." The envoy leaned back in his seat as if getting ready to watch the in-flight movie. "But what if I were to tell you that after the next twenty-four hours, none of that will matter?"

Fincher hoped Carl would snub the envoy's assurances. Or at the very least, he hoped Carl would reveal, intentionally or not, his disbelief.

"Sir, as I've reiterated, I believe in you. And I trust you will take care of everything, including the future. Which is why I personally *guarantee*," he said with a confident growl, "that we will make it past customs in Tel Aviv."

The plane's flight attendant appeared with a tray of four glasses sparkling with champagne.

"Oh dear, what perfect timing!" the envoy exclaimed. "Thank you so much." He craned around in his seat to check the stairwell, which was empty. "I wanted my wife to be here for the celebration, but... I don't want to rush her. Whatever she's doing for the victims is a good thing."

The flight attendant set the drinks on the table in front of the men, and after some inquiries and best wishes, she went on her way.

John grabbed one of the glasses. Both Fincher and Carl followed suit.

"This, Carl, is just a small gesture to acknowledge your act of courage today. You protected me better than any armor. Cheers."

He clinked glasses with Carl, and then with Fincher. The doctor held his drink out toward Carl, too, and they touched cups and said cheers. Then they both took a small sip.

The envoy, however, drained his entire glass.

Fincher almost choked on his champagne.

What Wolfenson had said back in D.C., that assuming this possession was a very delicate matter, was all too fresh in the doctor's mind.

Looking again to the stairwell, Wolfenson set his empty glass on the table. When there was still no sign of Patricia, he turned back, with his attention, again, on Carl.

"Were you frightened? I mean when that one terrorist was waving his weapon in your face?"

"Yes, sir, I certainly was."

"I must say, you hid your fear expertly. I honestly could not tell. Okay, here's another question—*why* were you scared?"

Fincher could see that Carl was genuinely confused by the envoy's question, by the apparent simplicity of it. Even Fincher was wondering where the envoy's questions were leading.

"What I mean to say is, were you scared because you were capable of imagining what could happen... that you could die?"

"Yes, I suppose that's accurate," Carl said. "I've imagined myself being killed hundreds of times. I guess the trick is to not think about it during the times where it's a real possibility."

"Ah," the envoy said, "easier said than done. Imagining you are going to die is all part of that third brain... the neo-cortex. That's where the Landlord really screwed up."

He let his words wash over his audience for a few moments before turning to Fincher. "You surely know what I'm talking about, right, doctor?"

"Not exactly, sir," Fincher said, embarrassed.

"Hah!" The envoy clapped him on the back. "I suggest you finish your drink then. It'll help get all three of your brains working so you can follow along."

Fincher nodded and took another sip, reassured that his lack of knowledge wasn't held against him.

"Gentlemen, the neo-cortex: supposedly the Landlord's great innovation. His pride and joy. He started with just one brain for the lizards. Then he added another brain on top of the first. Canines, for instance; they have two brains. And that's why they're your best friend. Very loyal, without any questions asked. But then the Landlord decided to get fancy when he created the hominids. He decided to add a third brain, the neo-cortex. I told him then he should simply improve upon the lizard brain, and leave it at that. But, of course, he did not listen. Big mistake. His design was too simplistic and too complex all at the same time."

He pointed to the wound on Carl's chest, and Fincher noticed something unsettling—the envoy's finger was shaking.

"A lizard brain fired the gun that wounded you," Wolfenson said. "But it was the combination of three brains that orchestrated the elaborate circumstances in which the trigger was pulled. Way back when, the Landlord believed a second brain would endow some of his lower life forms with the capacity for emotional connections. By adding the third brain, he probably planned on having his... higher forms empowered with the ability to not only think before acting, but to feel regret afterwards when their actions were wrong. But that's not what happened, is it?"

His eyes moved back and forth between Fincher and Carl, trying to gauge their reactions.

"All the Landlord managed to accomplish with three brains was that hominids became more inventive about how they go about being lizards. Rather than transcending this sad planet, you're all using your artlessly constructed grey matter to imagine and plan on new ways to destroy yourselves. This, gentlemen, is why I'm here. Someone had to intervene."

Carl's eyes shifted as Patricia emerged from the stairwell.

"Ah!" Wolfenson said, noticing his wife as well. He hit the stewardess call button, then unbuckled his seat belt and moved to greet Patricia. They shared a few words that Fincher could not hear, and then the envoy led her over by the hand.

"Honey, I told you we were going to have a celebration, right?" He motioned to the flight attendant as she entered the cabin. "Can we have four more chilled glasses?"

Patricia sat on the couch next to Carl. She looked disorientated. After spending time with nineteen gravely injured patients, she was clearly finding it difficult to make the transition into the plush, comfortable couch while a flight attendant poured her some cold champagne.

"To our hero," Wolfenson announced. He touched glasses with his wife, and then with Carl, and then was about to take a sip when he realized Fincher was still holding up his glass. After a quick clink with the doctor, the envoy slammed back his drink.

Patricia looked over at Carl.

She also downed her glass.

"Now, dear, I leave you in the secure hands of both my second-in-commands. Please, drink to your heart's content. You deserve to celebrate after the valiant effort you made on behalf of all the earthquake victims."

He rose from his seat.

Patricia scooted to the edge of the couch. "John, where are you going?"

"Well, I'm not going to say this too loudly because I don't want the troops to overhear, but..." He leaned over her and said, "I'm exhausted. I've been told there's a room behind that galley with a queen-size bed. I believe a few minutes' sleep will give me the strength to wrestle with the custom agents who are undoubtedly waiting to tussle in Tel Aviv."

Patricia took his hand. "Let me go with you."

"No, Pat, please. Stay here. Enjoy Carl and Colin's good company."

He kissed his wife's hand before releasing it, and then Patricia watched him leave. She continued to stare down the aisle even after he had disappeared through the door on the other side of the galley.

"Pat, are you all right?" Carl asked.

When she didn't answer, Fincher suspected she was so lost in thought she hadn't heard the question.

"None of those people are going to live," Patricia finally said. She spoke so softly, it seemed as if she were talking to herself.

She abruptly turned to Carl. "What are we doing about it?"

He shook his head. "I understand how you must feel, Pat. But I assure you, your husband is doing all he can do."

She just stared at him, not at all looking convinced.

Fincher stood up, grabbed the bottle of champagne from the ice bucket, and intended to refill Patricia's glass. She waved him away as if he were a pesky fly.

They all sat there in silence for a few moments, listening to the quiet sound of the plane.

"Listen to me, Patricia," Carl said. "Sometimes the hardest journeys are the ones that begin with little hope. But we need to take them anyway."

As Carl talked, Fincher watched Patricia's face flush, her lips quiver. Carl raised his hand to comfort her, but a noise caught her attention and she turned away, back toward the galley and the bedroom behind it. Everyone in the lounge froze as the sound became louder, more apparent.

Melodic, sonorous, but most of all haunting, the violin music drifted, floated, bled in and out.

Fincher wanted to believe Wolfenson was playing a dirge, a hymn, an homage to everything he and the doctor had experienced in the last few hours together. And yet Fincher knew the beautiful sounds were dedicated to only one.

Patricia stared in the direction of the music, seemingly hypnotized. "Almost every day, he and Scotty would... practice this song," she said, again softly enough that she was probably thinking aloud.

Carl sighed and fell back into his seat.

Patricia said something, but mumbled so quietly this time Fincher couldn't be sure exactly what she said.

But as Patricia stood up, she repeated it, and there was no doubt what she had said: "Listen to the music."

As she walked off, Fincher clearly heard her say, "I need to open the door..." She was already reaching out.

"Patricia..." Carl said, grabbing her arm.

Fincher scrambled to unbuckle his seatbelt.

"Are you all right?" Carl asked.

Patricia smiled serenely and patted his hand. "Oh, yes, Carl, I'm just fine."

Gently, kindly, she pried his hand off of her arm, and then, with the music, she drifted across the cabin, as if she were the music, as if she embodied it. She passed through the galley, and then, for a few moments, the violin swelled as she opened the door. And then she shut it.

Fincher had been observing Carl closely during Patricia's slow dance. Carl had forgotten himself, where he was, who he was with. Fincher saw him shuffle his feet a couple times, obviously debating whether or not he should get up and stop her.

"Good work," Fincher told him.

Carl looked back at the doctor, undoubtedly realizing what had occurred. He tried to play it off like it was all part of the act. "What do you think, Colin? Patricia looked ready to close the deal."

The doctor played along as if he had seen nothing. "Yes, Carl, let us hope so."

He motioned to Reitz, and the guard brought a leather briefcase to him. Fincher unzipped it and pulled out a tablet computer. He had planned on using the tablet as a wireless video monitor, but he needed to test whether the camera he had set up was still functioning. He had installed it upon their arrival in Aleppo and hadn't checked it since.

"So what happens now?" Carl asked, sounding nothing like a triumphant grifter who had just steered the mark to the payoff.

"You and I turn our attention to the next step. I know you would never tell the envoy that you could get the cargo through customs if you weren't able to do so. Therefore, I'm assuming you have made the proper arrangements."

"Yes. It's all taken care of."

"Then I would request your help in two other areas."

Before Fincher could explain, the violin music cut off. Carl's eyes flashed toward the bedroom door, and the doctor looked down at the tablet computer in his lap; he hit a few buttons on the screen.

"So, are you willing to help?" he asked Carl.

It took a few seconds, but Carl eventually responded. "Yes, tell me what you need."

"We're going to need explosives."

"Explosives? What kind?"

"Something with a maximum shattering capability. But that's not all. The explosives must be traceable back to the Israeli government."

"Colin, what the hell is going on?"

"Can you do it?"

He didn't answer.

"Carl?"

"I'm not sure. Most of my contacts have access to RDX, which would give you a massive shock wave, but it's used almost exclusively by terrorist groups, not the Israelis."

"Then you need to go beyond your normal contacts."

Carl lowered his head.

"And I need your help with the Black Pages."

"Still no progress?"

"Not enough," the doctor said without a hint of shame. "I will need you to pull out all the stops and help me acquire the pages. Or eliminate those that possess them. What do you say?"

Carl ran his hands through his hair.

"I thought you wanted to be part of the plan, Carl. If I'm going to give you the details, then you had better help with some of the heavy lifting."

Carl turned his attention toward the galley door, and Fincher stole a glance at the tablet computer.

"What are you looking at?" Carl asked.

"Oh, just monitoring the progress of our operation. Here... see for your-self." Fincher handed the tablet computer to him.

As Carl stared at the screen, at the video feed from a hidden camera in the bedroom of the jet, the doctor grabbed his champagne.

"Well, Colin," Carl said, "I guess the envoy has closed the deal."

The doctor had to give him his due: in all the years they had known each other, Carl was the only one who came remotely close to Fincher's own control over his emotions. Carl didn't express even a hint of feeling as he watched the envoy having sex with Patricia on the ten-inch monitor.

"And I bet all he will need is one opportunity," Fincher said as he raised his glass in a toast. Then, like the envoy and Patricia before him, the doctor downed his drink. Though the bubbly was no longer chilled, it was still the perfect complement to the surrounding festivities.

Carl handed the tablet back to Fincher and grabbed his own drink. He threw it back in one sharp motion, then set the glass on the table and pulled his satellite phone from his coat.

Fincher looked at the clock on the tablet. "Carl," he said, "who could you possibly be calling at 4:44 in the morning?"

"You need explosives. And one of my best contacts could be available. Would you rather I wait?"

"Absolutely not," Fincher said. Then he poured himself another glass of champagne and sat back with the tablet propped up on his lap.

CHAPTER 3

A T 4:44 IN THE MORNING, Jenna awoke to a ringing in her ears. She immediately sprang up in bed.

Where the hell... was her first thought; she couldn't remember where she had spent the night.

Her second thought, because of the ringing, was the alarm she had set. She snatched up her phone and flipped it open.

The ringing didn't relent.

Jenna grabbed her coat, which was folded on the floor next to her shoes. Carl's sat phone fell out of the pocket and landed in one of her shoes. It lit up with every ring.

"Aren't you going to answer it?" George asked, sitting up in bed. That was another thing she had forgotten: they had shared a room. He looked perfectly calm and rested; the sleep had done him well. "Aren't you at least curious what he has to say?"

"Not in the least," Jenna said. She put the phone back into her shoe. It rang two more times before finally giving up.

Vaguely, letting her head drop to the pillow, she wondered if Carl had equipped the phone with voicemail. She would have given anything to hear his voice—"Please, Jenna, call me. Please, I need your help..."

———

THEY GOT IMMEDIATELY OUT OF BED, and Jenna used the bathroom. She caught sight of her hair in the mirror, but only in passing. It seemed like those little personal details had all but disappeared. Hygiene? What was that? Comb? She had never heard of such a thing.

It didn't matter, quite honestly. Jenna had never been particularly vain. But she bet anyone on the planet could testify to the ill effects of a bad hair day. So she couldn't deny that when she saw her hair and how decent it looked, she felt better about facing the world.

She and George escaped down one hallway after the next, undetected. The church stood completely silent, except for George's choppy breath. Even though he didn't look quite as ill, he struggled to pace Jenna as they made their way through the purple atmosphere cast by the stained glass in the chapel.

Out on the portico, she noticed a walkway to the right of the steps. It circuited an area adjacent to the church. The Garden of Gethsemane—a garden of gnarled old trees.

Jenna wavered between the steps and the botanical path. Finally, she couldn't resist.

"Why are we going this way?" George asked.

"Sorry, I need to see for myself."

"See what?"

Where a miracle occurred, Jenna thought, but didn't say it.

A metal fence restricted access to the garden. She scaled it. It was shorter on her side. Just a low brick wall topped in metal pickets, easy to climb.

Instead of going over with her, George had read the garden plaque. He stared out at the trees, as if for miles.

"Are you coming?" she asked.

"These trees... the Agony..."

"I wouldn't count on it," Jenna said, cutting off his thoughts. "All the olive trees in Jerusalem were cut down by the Romans in 70 A.D."

He didn't say anything.

"What?" Jenna asked.

"You didn't say *actually*."

"What?"

"When you corrected me. You always do. You always say it."

She shook her head, pretending to be annoyed. "Be careful not to catch yourself on the fence." Then she started off, and could hear George trailing behind.

In the garden, a grid of gravel pathways sectioned the trees into long rows. Jenna walked to the middle of the patch before taking a look around.

Some remnants of night still clung to the dawn, so that stars dimly glowed, and early-morning mist twined between the gnarly trunks with their crowns of limbs and leaves. The trees looked like flora from some foreign planet.

Actually, Jenna thought, pondering what George had said.

Not that long ago, Neal had commented on her favorite word in the dictionary. And now George was noticing that she hadn't used it here, when he had suggested these trees were as old as the Agony.

She had refuted him, and yet she had no definitive evidence that these trees, these specific ones here on the hill, had ever been chopped down. Jenna knew enough about history and religious history to know she couldn't come to that conclusion. Most other olive trees in Jerusalem, sure: the Romans had committed blasphemous deforestation. But even then, records were subject to a degree of unreliability, whether due to inaccuracy or exaggeration.

These old specimens here: maybe the Romans had overlooked them. Or maybe they knew better to chop down their last trees. After all, these limbs bore fruit, and essential oils to anoint kings.

If the olives of the garden did predate the Roman siege... and if Pliny the Elder was to be believed... then olive trees never died but simply sprung new life from their trunks. So it begged the question, how long *had* these trees been growing?

And that's why, Jenna decided, she hadn't said *actually*. Because she didn't know. She honestly didn't. Which made this place as good as any for a miracle.

A sudden alarm made her start.

She pulled out her phone and shut it off.

5 a.m.

Right on schedule.

"Okay, George, let's just go the rest of the way through the garden. I think I remember seeing a gate to the narrow path back to our car."

When she didn't get a reply, Jenna turned.

George wasn't there.

She heard wheezing.

"George?!"

As she rounded one of the olive trees, dashing through the gravel, George came into view.

Several yards away, he was leaning against one of the stone pillars that held up a long, bulky olive branch.

He started coughing, hacking, and his eyes watered and bulged.

Jenna ran to him and tried to grab him, support him, but he pushed her away with surprising force. She slammed against the column, and George, coughing, choking, staggered away.

She looked toward the church. It was only a matter of time before people emerged to check out the commotion.

George fell, grinding his knees into the gravel. He stayed there for a moment, utterly still, and she hoped the worst was over. Then he threw up.

Thick black mucus gushed from his mouth all over the path. And then it gushed from his nose. Wave after wave of it, like an oil well spouting, polluting, smothering everything it touched. His entire body clenched with every retch.

Jenna took a step toward him, then took a step back, covering her mouth and trying not to puke as well.

Even George's sweat had turned black.

When he finally finished, and a few thick dark ropes dangled from his nose and lips, she found it almost impossible to believe the large oil spill had come out of George.

"Are you all right?" she asked, stepping toward him.

He nodded and moved to get to his feet. Jenna thought he would need help, but he stood up without any problem and stared down at the mess he had made. He looked shocked. Like he didn't know how it got there.

Jenna grabbed his arm and pulled him toward the exit.

"I think we need to... stay and explain," he said.

"I hear you, George, but we just can't afford to keep hitting snooze."

They approached a gate in the wall, which opened onto the narrow walkway back to their car.

"Are you sure you're all right, George?"

"I think I'll feel better once we leave."

"Really? I don't... why?"

"Can't you smell him?"

"Smell who? Father Olsen—"

"No, the Beast."

Jenna thought about it, and said, "He was here?"

George looked too exhausted to say any more, and they had reached the gate. She opened it for him.

He stopped and dug a hand into his pocket.

"Come on," Jenna said, glancing once more toward the church. "We need to go..."

He pulled out the car keys and jangled them. "Can I drive?"

Jenna, smirking, snatched the keys from him. She shut the gate behind them, and helped George down from Mount Olivet.

———

"PLEASE, PLEASE," said Jawad Bahar, "you must come in!"

Having visited much of the Middle East, Jenna knew firsthand how hospitable Arabs could be. And yet back home, in the States, she knew people tended to dehumanize them, demonize them. And she always had to say to them, "Well actually..." and then she would educate them.

In her experience with Arab communities, dinner invitations and even invites to intimate family celebrations were always open, even to brand new acquaintances.

Nevertheless, Jenna knew Arabic hospitality had little to do with what was happening here on the porch of Father Olsen's two-story residence in Abu Tor on the hill.

She and George had introduced themselves as friends of Father Olsen, but before she could go into any detail, Jawad Bahar was pulling George by the arm into the house, all the while welcoming them in. Jenna wasn't sure if she should follow or call the police.

"Are you from the church?" Jawad asked, shutting the door behind Jenna.

"Well..." she began.

"It doesn't matter," Jawad said, "you must help. I think Father Olsen is in trouble!"

"So you've seen him?"

"Yes, yes, I was on the Internet when he came home last night. I didn't know what to say about his condition. I told him I thought I was dreaming. Father Olsen was able to see! Did you know about this?"

Jenna nodded. "That's why we're here. We need to speak with him."

"Well, you can't speak with him! He's no longer here! That's what I'm trying to tell you. That's why I need your help."

"So you don't know where he is?" Jenna asked. She tried her best to speak in a low, relaxed voice, hoping to calm Jawad, who was wringing his hands and practically shouting at her.

"No, and that's why I'm so worried. He left early this morning, before I was awake. It wasn't like him to leave so early. We usually have... breakfast. But I could tell he wasn't himself."

"Wasn't himself?" Jenna asked. She took a moment to look around, relieved to find the furniture upright, and the photographs still on the walls. "Are you referring to his eyesight?"

"No, I am speaking of his heart."

Jenna and George both turned to each other, and it was clear neither of them understood.

Jawad frowned, huffed, and turned away, pushing his fist against his lips as if pressed for a way to express himself.

Once he had calmed down a little, he turned back to them. "Father Olsen was not himself. He was very sad. Completely silent most of the night. When he did speak, it was... sad talk. Bitter words. Like my friend had been consumed by a dark cloud."

"I understand," Jenna said, moving closer to Jawad. "What exactly was he saying?" When she asked it, she wasn't expecting him to blurt out his reply as if it had been on the tip of his tongue since last night.

"When we first became friends, we would talk about... our differing views. Personally, I don't believe in..." Jawad's face twitched, but then he nodded to himself and said, "I can now say it aloud, my father has passed. I don't believe in the almighty."

Out of the corner of her eye, Jenna noticed that George had walked over to the fireplace, and was touching what looked like a plaque on the wall nearby.

"Over the years we would still talk about it," Jawad continued. "We genuinely wanted to know the heart of the other. But then, last night... everything was different. Father Olsen said to me, he said, 'Jawad, you were right. My life has been wasted serving a Father who took my eyes, and then the very people I cared about... and then my dignity.' He said, 'When

I needed him most, he was not there. He was gone. Nowhere to be found. And I was alone. And lost..."

"But now he sees," George quietly interjected.

Jawad blinked at him, and frowned.

"George..." Jenna said, but he had already turned away from them, quietly humming "Amazing Grace."

Jawad was preparing to flap his lips again, but Jenna held up a finger. She needed a moment to think.

The ground floor of the house was modest. No wall or solid divider separated the living room from the kitchen, and the living room had no TV. Just a beat-up desk with a computer.

On the kitchen table, a few feet from the stove, Jenna noticed an empty bottle of brandy and two glasses. One of the cups still held a serving of the aged-caramel spirit.

"Mr. Bahar," Jenna said, "did you and Father Olsen drink last night?"

"I—" Jawad began, but then the satellite phone in Jenna's coat started to ring.

George stopped humming and turned to look at her. She simply stared back.

"You're still not going to answer?" he said.

"Is there any reason why I should?"

George walked over to her, stepped right in front of her. "Here's a reason. What if he knows something about Father Olsen?"

Jenna had to admit the thought had never crossed her mind. But when the phone rang again, she said, "Sorry, George," and she looked past him to Jawad. Eventually the ringing cut off. "Did you and Father Olsen drink last night then?"

"Yes. No. I'm sorry. He drank. I didn't drink. This is what I'm saying to you about why I'm concerned. Father Olsen never drinks. Never. He drank the whole bottle himself."

Jenna took another look around and saw nothing of interest. "Do you mind if we check his room?"

"Please, of course. Right this way..."

———

JAWAD LED THEM UPSTAIRS and then left them to look around the modestly decorated chamber. A bit of morning light peered through the balcony door and shined on the pine furniture: a dresser and an armoire, and two nightstands flanking a queen-sized bed. Above the headboard, picture frames of all shapes and sizes cluttered the wall—photographs of Jawad's family over a period of sixty years.

Jenna strode to the dresser and started searching through it while George watched.

"A Braille Bible... some clothes... and not much else." She slammed the last drawer and turned around. "It's almost as if he wasn't even here. But if that's the case, if he didn't take anything or touch anything except maybe the bed... I wonder why he bothered coming back at all."

George just stood there, staring and breathing heavily like usual.

"Did you hear me?" Jenna asked.

He nodded. "Maybe he wanted to see his friend?"

"Yeah, maybe."

She crossed her arms and kept scanning the room, hoping to pick up some lost detail. "I think wherever he went, he couldn't go to last night...

perhaps because it was dark or... some other reason. That's why he came back here and that's why he waited until morning to leave."

She looked to George for his response, but he continued to stare. Jenna shook her head.

She prided herself at being a good detective, a vital skill on archeological digs. Finding clues in bones and the placement of objects in unearthed dwellings took patience, a keen eye for detail, and, most importantly, imagination. Thinking outside the box had often led her to great breakthroughs. But sometimes recent events posed even bigger mysteries than things that had ended a long time ago.

As Jenna was contemplating their next step, she caught sight of the balcony door. She marched over, threw it open, and walked out onto the terrace.

At the railing she surveyed the neighborhood, searching for something, anything that might have been important. Important enough for Father Olsen to wait all night till the crack of dawn just to rush out and see it.

Then she saw it too.

Shining in the sunrise as if still minted in melted coins: Islam's shrine, the golden Dome of the Rock.

And, beneath it, the Temple Mount.

"George!"

She almost ran into him on her way back into the bedroom. She ran into the doorframe instead, striking her shoulder, but barely registering the pain.

"I know where he went!"

"Jenna, wait!" George said, but she was already dashing out of the bedroom, down the stairs, and out the front door.

He tried to keep up. "Jenna!"

She stopped halfway down the front steps and turned with an impatient look. "Sorry, George, I almost forgot. Come on, we need to—"

"No..." He was breathing hard, and was having trouble standing on his own two feet. So he braced himself in the doorway. "I'm afraid not."

He looked horrible.

George, she thought, *don't do this—not now.*

"I think I'll stay here with Mr. Bahar, if that's all right with him."

Jawad shouted from the kitchen stove, "Yes, of course! You are welcome to stay as long as you want!"

Jenna nodded. "Okay. Okay. Stay here. Hopefully I won't be long." She turned to leave and said, "Wish me luck."

"Wait!" George clambered down the steps to her, opening his arms. "You're not even going to say goodbye?"

The look of impatience disappeared from Jenna's face. "George..." She spared him the last few steps and met him halfway in a gentle, yet fierce embrace. He trembled against her, and she could feel the rattle in his chest. Back at Padding Station, she had smelled his breath, and had smelled nothing but air. Now, she expected to smell old puke from the garden, but he simply did not have an odor, and she was glad.

George rested his chin on her shoulder, with his lips near her ear, and he whispered something, spoke it so softly she felt only the faintest breath in her hair.

"Good luck," he said, and then he let her go.

CHAPTER 4

JENNA KNEW THE CLOSER SHE GOT, the more difficult it would be to find parking. So she left the car several blocks away and walked.

In the Western Wall Plaza, the Wailing Wall towered between two major religions. On one side, the Dome of the Rock stood like an ascension chamber to the sky. On the other, Orthodox Jews wearing black clothes and lifelong beards routinely mortared the plaza wall with paper prayers.

The wall was a fragment of Judaism's holiest site, a retaining wall of Herod's Temple Mount. Even the bushes that clung to the bricks were sacred.

A few months ago, in this very plaza, John Wolfenson had staged the historic peace treaty between six Middle Eastern nations. And that was why Jenna believed this was also the place she would find Father Alan Olsen.

She walked slowly through the plaza, scanning the legions of people. Tourists, some of them. But at this early hour, the majority were Jewish worshippers of various ages and sects, wearing either a kippah or a yarmulke, depending on the language; and some of them wore black hats.

They stood at the wall, touching it, rocking their bodies before it, some of them rending their clothes. Jenna knew many of them had probably been there for hours.

She tried to recall the newspaper photographs or footage from the day of Wolfenson's treaty. Where had they set up the stage? And where exactly had Sandy Travis cut the envoy's throat?

For some reason, the details of that day weren't coming to her. Maybe the anxiety of hunting for Father Olsen or the distraction of the crowd preoccupied her.

Then she saw him.

He stood alone, about a hundred yards away from Jenna, staring down at the huge stone tiles of the plaza floor. Olsen was wearing a long wool coat. His priestly garb might have been underneath, but it was impossible to tell.

Jenna looked around to see if anyone was watching him, or her. Almost every day for the last few months, the plaza had played host to some sort of showdown or another, so the place crawled with armed guards, as if this were some maximum-security prison yard.

Fortunately the nearest officer was stationed more than two dozen yards away, and wasn't even looking in their direction. Jenna took a deep breath and started forward.

She kept her eyes on the priest as she crossed the plaza. He never moved, never looked up, not even as she planted herself about six feet away from him. She wanted to move closer, but didn't dare. She had no idea what to expect, how he would react to what she had to say. And the last thing she wanted was to end up like the furniture at the Church of All Nations.

"Father Olsen? Excuse me... Father?"

When he finally looked up, Jenna was astonished to see neither bandages nor the slightest sign that he once was blind. His eyes weren't even bloodshot. What surgeon in the world could have pulled this off without post-surgery recovery time?

"Father Olsen, my name is Jenna Grant. I've been looking for you."

"Why is that?"

He kept his right hand in his coat pocket. It wasn't a cold day, so Jenna suspected the good Father might actually be armed.

"We have some common interests," she said, "interests that only a few people besides you and I truly understand."

He shifted his weight, leaning more toward Jenna rather than toward the patch of ground he had been scrutinizing. "Tell me what you've come to say."

She studied the stone tiles at their feet, the ones he had been inspecting. "I don't see anything," she said, a conclusion that Olsen should have come to as well. But a desperate man, haunted by the past, and a drastically altered future, might not be thinking quite as clearly. "Please, Father, tell me if you see something I'm somehow missing.... Of course I'm looking for blood from Sandy Travis."

He shifted his weight again, this time away from Jenna, and as he moved, his hand accidently pulled out of his coat pocket, revealing what he concealed inside.

A gun.

Jenna couldn't help but inhale sharply as her chest and stomach muscles tightened.

Olsen immediately stuffed the gun back in his coat, then glanced around. No one had noticed.

"This is not intended for anyone," he said. "Just my..." He never finished the thought. He didn't have to.

Jenna tried to compose herself, or at least appear composed. She knew she could just walk away. But a single thought kept her: if she had arrived in the plaza just five minutes later, perhaps there would have been a fresh bloodstain on the plaza stones. Maybe the fact that she had arrived when she did meant something.

"Look," she said, "I know why you came to the plaza. You needed to be here, in person... at the very spot where she died. You needed to... see her blood for yourself."

Olsen stared at her as if she were some prophet gleaning truths from a higher power. Truths she had no way of knowing.

"Who are you?"

"I told you, Father—"

"Tell me again!"

"My name is Jenna Grant. And all I want to do is talk to you. And listen. Actually that's the first step. I just want to listen."

He had started to look older and older the deeper he frowned. But he seemed to have relaxed a bit. "Do you know how I got my eyesight back?"

"I have a pretty good idea," Jenna said, using the opportunity to move toward him. "But I want to hear it from you."

"It was... him."

Father Olsen said the last word with such clear disdain, it confirmed what Jenna already knew. Now the big question was—why? She had been mulling it over since the Garden of Gethsemane.

Why?

"He's here," Father Olsen said, "walking amongst us. Along with the rest of humanity."

"You're talking about... the Angel of Light."

His eyes immediately narrowed, and he took a step away from her, noticing how close she had managed to get.

Jenna held still. She needed to explain herself quickly or risk losing him.

"I know about the Angel of Light only because I've uncovered some things... things his people wanted to keep hidden. I know Satan is not only walking amongst us, he's pretending to be one of us. Because he's on a mission."

She pressed her luck and regained the step he had retracted. "I'm here to tell you that I'm going to stop him."

Father Olsen listened quietly, eyes still narrowed, hand still in his pocket. But he had stopped retreating, and Jenna took his motionlessness as a good sign.

She knelt down and examined the stone floor like a detective at a crime scene. After a moment, she shook her head.

"Nope. Nothing. I thought if I got down on my knees, I might see something, but... I don't even see a faded outline where they might have cleaned up her blood."

She remembered the way Father Olsen had postured himself as he watched Sandy Travis die, and Jenna had intentionally mimicked it.

"You want to know why we're not going to find anything, Father? Because Sandy Travis was killed onstage. On some manmade platform that was quickly put together so some important people could stand on it. And the cynic in me is whispering that the treaty they signed... that thing will be taken apart almost as quickly as the platform where they signed it."

She stood up and took another step toward Father Olsen. She needed to close the physical distance between them, or it wouldn't matter what she had to say. A personal connection was impossible if they had to shout at each other.

She said, "To all the people walking around us, and to the rest of the world, there's no trace at all of what happened that day. It's as if Sandy Travis was never even here."

"What could you possibly know about her?" Olsen asked.

The question almost threw Jenna off balance. She didn't know anything about Sandy Travis, not really. Some facts, sure. But what did she know about who Sandy really was?

"I'll tell you what I know," Jenna said, emboldened by an idea. "And then I hope you'll fill in the rest."

She took yet another step forward. "One day, less than a few months ago, in this very plaza, Sandy Travis committed an act of violence. No, wait... two acts. First she killed a cameraman. Then she brutally attacked an important government official. But we both know her horrible acts were something she never would have done before that day. Not a year prior, or even a few weeks. But she did it. Because she had come in contact with... the Angel of Light."

She got closer and closer, and Father Olsen was letting her in.

"Neal Grant, he was just like Sandy Travis. Successful. Full of life. He was a loving son and... my brother. Then he did a terrible thing. His own unspeakable act of violence..."

Jenna was so close now, she could lower her voice to a more intimate level. A shared secret. A confession just between the two of them.

"That's why I'm here, Father. To find out why. To stop whatever happened to Sandy, and to my brother, from ever happening to anyone ever again. But I need your help."

Face trembling, scowling, and clenching against insurmountable grief, Father Olsen took the initiative this time and stepped toward Jenna. "The last time I *helped* someone, Sandy Travis died. Trust me, you're better off without my help."

Dozens of ideas shot through Jenna's brain, countless ways to rebut. She seized upon the one most likely to get the priest's hand out of his pocket to shake hers. But the approach had its risks.

"Father, you and I both know things have changed. You've got your eyesight."

He stared at her, and she could tell he was suppressing either anger or shame. Probably both.

"I promise I won't call what happened to you a... *miracle*."

"Then what would you call it?"

"I don't know. We'll think about it later and come up with something. But right now, the more important question is—why? Why did he do it?"

She only asked because she felt confident she could supply the answer. And it wasn't enough for her answer to simply make sense. It also had to be convincing.

"Let me tell you what I think. I think he gave you your eyesight because he had to. That's right, I'm calling it a desperation move. Satan knows I'm coming after him. Because of what he did to my brother. He knows I'm hot on his trail, and... look at me, I'm not finished."

Jenna was now inches away from his face, and he had no choice but to listen and meet her gaze.

"Satan gave you back your eyesight... so that you would be blind for the first time in your life."

Father Olsen's eyes filled with tears, and she understood why he had been averting his eyes. Here was the turning point. He would either come with her, or do whatever he had planned to do in the first place.

"He knows I wouldn't be better off without you—no, sir. Just the opposite. He's afraid, very afraid. Because he knows that you and I, together, are going to send his ass straight back to hell."

Jenna put her hand on his... the one holding the gun. "The picture I just painted for you, Father... tell me you don't see it."

His whole face was quaking now, holding back the tears. She felt his grip tighten on the gun, but then it slackened; she felt his jacket jerk as his pocket took on the full weight of the weapon.

"Okay," Jenna said, letting go of his hand. "Okay. But now we need to get started. Because, believe me, there's not another second to lose."

She offered her other hand, and Father Olsen grabbed it. The she turned to lead them both out of the plaza—but stopped when she saw the strangler from Virginia, the man with the one green eye.

He was moving toward them through the crowd, pulling something from his waistband.

A gun.

Jenna let go of the priest and shoved him away.

"Father—run!"

The strangler grinned, and Jenna was sure that he wanted her to flee, wanted her to scream in terror so he could have the pleasure of shooting her in the back like some culled animal that didn't have a high enough consciousness to realize its expiration date had come.

Instead, she clenched her fists and crouched, like a runner waiting for the starting pistol. She planned to rush him, surprise him, and give herself a chance.

He got close enough that Jenna could see the bruises on his face, and that he now had two green eyes instead of one.

"You can thank your friend in London for this!" he said, and, grinning wider, took aim...

CHAPTER 5

ETAN BECAME EXCITED the moment she first noticed him marching toward her. Still, simply executing her would not have been satisfying.

He wanted the knowledge of impending death to radiate fear throughout Jenna Grant's entire body. Then he would feel good about pulling the trigger.

Jenna had been talking to a man when Etan first spotted her. As soon as she saw him approaching, she shoved him aside and implored him to flee. Since this man wasn't the same one who had attacked Etan in the States, he didn't care if he escaped.

Etan pulled out his gun and raised it toward Jenna Grant.

"You can thank your friend in London for this..."

He watched her body tense as her nerves took hold. But instead of running away, she rushed directly at him.

He couldn't believe it.

Oh yes, you stupid bitch. The bullet from my GLOCK doesn't travel very far, so I need you to meet it halfway.

He wanted to laugh, but he was concerned that it might throw off his aim.

Then something stopped him. There was no sound, so he wasn't mentally prepared to have the wind knocked out of him. The adrenaline surging through his veins instantly evaporated. As Etan was trying to figure out what had happened, he heard an echoing voice—"What are you doing, lads! You need to stop..."

———

"STOP IT, LADS—do you hear me?! He's had enough! Stop it!"

The jukebox had gone off in the pub. The only sound now was the shifting of boots, and blood dripping, and Etan's ragged breath.

The beating had stopped.

He tried to reach for the rooster claw around his neck, but couldn't raise his arm; as if there were no strings on which his will could pull.

Then he saw Jimoh Adebayo standing over him, laughing. Etan blinked to clear his eyes, to make sure it really was the Nigerian teenager casting the shadow over him, this impossibly long shadow.

It didn't work. Everything remained a blur.

He could still hear the Nigerian's hyena-like cackle, a sound Etan had heard every day after school when Jimoh and his friends started circling him.

Etan closed his eyes.

Finally, the laughter echoed away.

He opened his eyes again. Now there was a bearded man just a few inches from his face.

————

HE TRIED NOT TO LET ON that the man's reflection in the bathroom mirror had spooked him.

"Looks like you have some nasty cuts and bruises," said the bearded man.

Etan wanted to shut the door so he could finish tending to his battered face, but the man wore a tie and jacket and looked important; there would be hell to pay if Etan slammed the door on one of his father's friends.

"Thank you, sir, but I'm going to be fine."

"That's the spirit. But I think I see steam coming from that sink. I know a hot compress might feel good now, but trust me, only ice will reduce the swelling. Let me fetch you some from the freezer."

Etan rushed from the sink as the stranger left the bathroom doorway. "Thank you very much, sir, but don't trouble yourself!"

The man stopped halfway across the room. Etan stopped too and tried his best to maintain his balance, even though every bone in his body felt ready to snap beneath his skin.

"Suit yourself," the man said. "But tomorrow morning when you look in that same mirror, you will wish you hadn't stopped me."

"Are you here to see my father?"

"Actually, I've come to see you, Etan. My name is Marcus Rhodes."

The stranger moved to the family room couch under a window overlooking the veranda. He took a seat on the edge of a cushion and stared at Etan.

"I understand some Nigerian locals are making your life very difficult. I'm here to help."

"My father didn't send you?"

"No, not your father. It was your mother."

"My mother is dead," Etan told him. "She's been dead—"

"Since you were six, I know. God bless her. When your mother was alive, she had a relationship with a very good friend of mine. They had an understanding, which included looking after you."

"Well, tell your friend I don't need his help. I don't need anyone."

Etan wheeled around and stepped back toward the sink. Since the bearded man was not an associate of his father's, there was nothing preventing the boy from slamming the door in his face.

But when Etan tried, the door would not budge. The bearded man was suddenly blocking it.

"Sorry for the misunderstanding, but looking after you was not an offer. My friend is addressing an obligation."

The man charged forward, backing Etan up against the dripping sink. "From here on out you will call me Mr. Marcus. Understand?"

He inspected the boy, looking over every inch.

"*Dikoros*," he finally said.

"What?"

"It means 'double-pupiled.' Heterochromia is the true medical term. Alexander the Great had it. So did Anastasius, ruler of the Byzantine Empire. It was part of their allure. But in the medieval ages, people who had heterochromia were killed out of fear of sorcery or black magic."

Out of reflex, Etan turned his head to look away, as his mother had taught him, but Marcus grabbed his chin and corrected the direction of his face.

"Ruler of an empire, or burned at the stake as a witch. As any great comedian will tell you... timing is everything."

He let go of Etan's chin, then motioned for him to step aside. The teenager stumbled away from the mirror.

Etan had been using a hand towel to tend to his face. Mr. Marcus stuffed the bloody rag into the drain, then opened one of the faucets.

As the sink filled, he stared at Etan in the mirror. "Something you find embarrassing, and brings you pain, I will make sure people perceive as... special. I'm capable of so much more, but only if you are willing to walk the path with me."

He turned from the mirror and addressed the boy.

"What do you think? Can you make that kind of commitment? Or shall we just allow the Nigerian locals and your father to continue burning you at the stake?"

Etan wasn't clear on what commitment this man was referring to, but feared asking questions; he feared even more uttering the wrong response.

So he simply nodded.

"Well, that slight movement of your head was hardly a blood oath... but it will do as a start." Marcus turned off the faucet and sunk his hands into the sink.

Over the quiet rippling, Etan could hear his own breath. He sounded like he was hyperventilating.

Marcus withdrew his hands and let them drip for a moment. He motioned for the teenager to join him.

Etan took a couple of steps, but stopped on trembling knees, afraid they might fail him. Marcus shook his head, already looking disappointed in the teenager. Then his left arm shot out, and he grabbed Etan by the hair.

"Around now is when you should feel fortunate our paths crossed," he said.

He plunged the boy's face into the sink.

Etan wanted to scream. The water was freezing, biting, numbing against his eyelids and cheeks. How Marcus had turned the water so cold was a question Etan would lie awake all night contemplating.

Just as the boy was about to run out of breath, Marcus raised his head from the water. Etan sprayed the mirror and wall as he struggled to breathe.

"You almost died there," Marcus said. "Did you feel it?"

The boy managed to nod, as cold mucus ran from his nose.

"Good! This time when I put you under, you *will* die! Are you listening? I'm going to kill the boy, and with him, the man he would have become! Which, believe me, would have been a sorry sight. Are you still listening, boy?"

"Please, sir—"

"Listen! We're going to start all over because sometimes for something to truly live... you must kill it."

Etan went to inhale, then scream, but instead of air, he drew in the water of the sink. The icy silence flooded his ears, but he could still hear the words—"In the beginning there was only water..."

———

CLAN CHIEF BABATUNDE raised the teenager's head from the bucket of water on the table. Etan did his best to calmly blink back the droplets while he sucked in air. But he still managed to convey how excited he was about the ritual in front of the whole clan, and Mr. Marcus.

"Only water!" Chief Babatunde exclaimed, and he let go of Etan's head.

Right beside the boy, a Yorùbá diviner used an *iroke Ifa*, a tapping instrument made from ivory, to strike an *opon Ifa*, a divination tray carved out of wood. The *iroke Ifa* resembled a totem, with an African figure whittled in the center, and animal figures whittled in the conical top and hollow base. The diviner struck the tray three times.

Then the chief stepped away from Etan to address the surrounding council and the rest of the clan, who had formed a circle in a corner of the marketplace to watch Etan undergo the divination consultation. The chief's white gown billowed around his feet.

"Then Olodumare sent Obatala to bring land to the water," Babatunde continued. "And so Obatala descended from a long chain, and with him he brought a rooster, some earth, and some iron..."

Etan looked up at Mr. Marcus, whose eyes hid behind dark glasses. The bearded man tapped the boy on the shoulder and directed his attention back to the chief.

"Obatala stacked the iron in the water, the earth on the iron, and the rooster atop the earth. Then the chicken kicked, scattering the earth and... created land."

The end of the story was greeted with solemn silence and one final striking of the *opon Ifa*.

Chief Babatunde, a tall man, once again approached Etan. He had a very dark expression on his face.

"Little man, do you know the reason I am standing here?"

"Yes," Etan said, trying to answer clearly and concisely. He and Mr. Marcus had been practicing for weeks his response to this simple question. "You are standing there because you are the chieftain of this clan."

Babatunde burst out laughing. All the other Yorùbá councilmen and clan laughed as well. The chief clapped Etan on the shoulder.

"No, little man, I am standing here... and *that* is why I am chief."

He laughed harder this time and Etan laughed with him, just as he and Mr. Marcus had rehearsed. Their laughter was quickly drowned out by the roar of laughter all around them.

Mr. Marcus had described Babatunde as a second generation clan chieftain. First generation chieftains controlled the original capitals of the Yorùbá kingdom, whereas second generation chieftains ruled over settlements created by conquest.

"Now, little man, come with me."

As the chieftain turned, with billowing gown, everyone in the circle turned with him. And as he started walking, all in the clan started walking too.

The group of hundreds moved through the marketplace of stalls with rusty aluminum roofing or parasols, past women in colorful buba blouses and matching gele headscarves selling yams, fish, corn, and plantains; past goats eating out of a ditch full of trash; past men standing behind rows of tables, selling everything from radios to DVDs; past all the families who had descended upon the marketplace because it was the cultural center, the lifeblood of daily existence in this part of Togo, Yorùbáland.

At the edge of the marketplace, the procession split. Only the clan councilmen, Etan, and Mr. Marcus continued across the street with Babatunde to the chieftain's palace.

At one point Etan looked up at Mr. Marcus, once again seeking his mentor's reaction. Even behind the beard and sunglasses, Mr. Marcus exuded excitement. It was a very important thing, to be heading toward the chieftain's palace.

They approached the five-story house with its long veranda running across the third floor. The gold columns seemed imposing at first, but as Etan drew in closer across the dirt street, he saw the gold leaf was faded and chipping away.

At the doorway of the palace, Chief Babatunde was greeted by aides waiting to take his shoes, offer him a cold drink, or a cool towel, and because they surrounded him all at once, they apparently hoped to do these tasks at the same time.

Babatunde dismissed them with a mere wave and proceeded down a long hallway toward the back of the palace. Before walking through the open back door, he stopped. As many as thirty aides and clan councilmen stopped with him.

Etan was not impressed. He found the councilmen's childlike obedience almost comical. But he didn't dare laugh or smile. He knew his mentor would make him regret it.

The chieftain looked to Mr. Marcus. The two men must have had an understanding, because all Mr. Marcus needed to do was nod. Babatunde nodded, too, and then exited to the back of the palace.

They walked across a courtyard toward three traditional Taberma houses: mud structures like anthills, only shaped like fortresses, with little turrets and thatched roofs.

As they drew in closer to the cluster of hovels, Etan heard a rooster crowing from somewhere inside.

An aide opened the door to one of the houses, and the chieftain gracefully stepped across the threshold into the cool shade.

Etan followed right behind Babatunde, but after a couple of steps, he halted. His eyes were still adjusting to the darkness of the hut, so at first he could only smell the putrefaction.

Then his eyes caught up.

Hanging upside down from ropes attached to the top of the ceiling were the bloody remains of a teenage Nigerian boy, and an older Nigerian male. Next to them dangled the carcass of a rooster.

Another rooster ran around the interior of the hut, flapping its wings as it avoided the feet of the councilmen.

In a panic, Etan started to back up, but ran into someone... Mr. Marcus. His mentor was neither surprised nor repulsed by the carnage before them.

Chief Babatunde moved next to the hanging body of the teenager. "Little man, is this not the boy who has been tormenting you?"

Etan couldn't answer, afraid that if he tried, he would only vomit.

Babatunde turned the body slowly so that its bloated face could be seen. "Is this not Jimoh Adebayo?"

Marcus tapped Etan on his back, urging him to answer.

"Yes..."

The chief nodded, then turned to stare at the grisly corpse swaying inches from his face.

"His name 'Jimoh' stands for 'born on a Friday.' No longer a very descriptive name since he died on a Tuesday."

The clan councilmen laughed at their chief's joke.

Babatunde tilted his head to look at the face of the dead man beside the murdered teenager.

"The boy's father. He should have raised a son who would know better than to disrespect a very little man who will grow to become a very special man."

Taking one last step, Babatunde gently lifted the rooster. For the first time since entering the Taberma house, he showed some emotion as he lovingly caressed the bird.

"This is the rooster who fought hard against my grandfather. I tell you all who stand here... of the three hanging in this house, this one with feathers put up the best fight."

The chief turned and motioned to one of his aides, who then scrambled after the crowing rooster that had been running around the hut. He caught it, and carefully handed it to Babatunde.

"My grandfather is the diviner and a fighter, and he has never lost," the chieftain said. He held the rooster up for Etan to inspect. "This is my grandfather, Opemipo. Look at my grandfather's feet. Five toes. Roosters always have four toes, but this is my grandfather. He is special. He is rare. Now look at Opemipo's eyes..."

The chief pushed the rooster into Etan's face, and the boy could see: the rooster's right eye was green, the left eye brown.

Opemipo began to kick his feet and flap his wings, so Babatunde released him, and the rooster ruffled its feathers and coolly walked away.

"Mr. Marcus has never lied to me, or my grandfather," the chieftain said. "He has seen the future before, and he sees it again. He says you come to help me and my grandfather work with Odùduwà. Is that what you have come to do?"

Etan was not sure what to say. He and Mr. Marcus had not rehearsed this part. None of what had happened since he crossed the backyard of the chief's palace had been rehearsed.

"Yes, Chief Babatunde. I have come to help you and your grandfather, and the clan." Etan spoke loudly, like he knew it was the right thing to say. He exhausted all of his willpower resisting the urge to consult the expression on his mentor's face.

Babatunde had no expression. He ran his fingers through Etan's hair, then dug his nails into the boy's scalp. Etan wanted to cry out, but remained silent and tried his best to remain still.

"Good *Ori* on this little man," the chieftain said. "Yes, Mr. Marcus, you continue to speak the truth."

"Chieftain Babatunde," Marcus said, "do you feel his *Ashe*?"

The chief dug in his nails deeper into Etan's scalp, then nodded, looking very impressed. Babatunde turned to engage the surrounding clan council. "Yes, very powerful!"

"Great Babatunde," said Mr. Marcus, "with such a powerful life force, will you accept the Yorùbán name brought to me by your grandfather, orated to him from Odùduwà? It is a name that will signify this little man's impressive *Ashe*, and will make clear to all who cross his path what he will achieve with his *Iwa-Pele* as a part of your clan."

"What does Odùduwà desire for this little man?"

"Orisas," Marcus said.

Babatunde smiled serenely. "Orisas."

Etan knew only a few Yorùbán words; he certainly did not know the meaning of names.

"A fine designation for a man with such powerful *Ashe*," the chieftain said.

Mr. Marcus did not smile but looked pleased. "Then it is done. From here on out, this man will be known as Orisas—'owner of heads.'"

Marcus put his hand on one of Etan's shoulders and said his new name again...

———

"ORISAS!"

Etan felt the hand on his shoulder before he heard his name called out over the sound of the trains. He was shocked to see who was standing beside him. Especially here in London.

"Mr. Marcus?! What are you doing here?"

"I'm here to see you."

They both looked down at the man lying on the train platform, gasping for air. Etan had been steps away from kneeling beside him and feigning a resuscitation attempt, then making sure his real effort would achieve the opposite result.

"Orisas, this man is not your concern."

"You know him?"

"Yes, in fact I know about everything. It is you who is in the dark."

Despite his stern words, Etan's old mentor did not look like the same man. He seemed smaller and weathered by age.

"Walk with me."

Etan did not move.

There had been a time when anything and everything Mr. Marcus asked he would do. Even now, Etan stood in London a free man only because of what Mr. Marcus had done for him.

And yet Etan could feel the blood of defiance congealing and cementing his legs.

Marcus squeezed his pupil's shoulder. "Orisas, if you still follow Olodumare, you need to follow me now."

This time Etan did not hesitate. He accompanied Mr. Marcus up the stairwell to the surface.

As they took the stairs, Marcus said, "You are in grave danger."

Etan could not hide his fear as they emerged onto the street. He was sure Marcus could see it in his face, and suddenly Etan felt like the cowardly boy who spent much of his time dodging the Nigerian locals. It was something he had not felt in years.

"We need to go someplace so I can tell you what is happening."

"No, Mr. Marcus. I'm afraid that's not possible."

Marcus ignored him and walked several feet away from the stairwell. After a moment of indecision, Etan went along. He knew that his mentor only wanted to speak without being overheard by the commuters emerging from the station.

"Your *Ori* is out of alignment, can you see that? No, I bet you've deceived yourself. You believe your recent actions have increased your *Ashe*, but I assure you the darkness of your pursuit has only diminished it. Are you telling me that I saved you years ago... so you could become this?!"

Etan looked around the street. He was now quite concerned they were both being watched. Or perhaps only he was under surveillance. Perhaps it was Mr. Marcus who had set this all up, streaming the footage to witnesses who couldn't possibly know how close Etan was to achieving something he had spent years trying to achieve.

"I know it is Carl who is pushing your actions. But that fact will not serve you well when you face Odùduwà to account for the spirit you have become."

Etan stared at his old mentor, refusing to respond to the accusation. After the silence had grown uncomfortable, Marcus looked down at Etan's chest.

"I see you are still relying on Chieftain Opemipo to protect you."

Etan had not realized it, but he had absentmindedly reached up and was caressing the rooster claw around his neck. "As long as he is with me, I am invulnerable. You said so yourself."

Mr. Marcus closed some of the distance between them. "Hear me now and try to remember if I have ever uttered these words before—I was wrong. What is happening now, all around us... it is more powerful than even the Odùduwà. Chieftain Opemipo can no longer protect you."

Etan did not honor him with a response and simply continued to rub his rooster claw. So Marcus grabbed for it, but Etan easily caught his hand. How slow and old his mentor had become. How diminished his *Ashe*.

"Marcus, I don't know what you're really doing here, but none of what I do now concerns you."

"Orisas, you need to let go of my wrist."

Etan squeezed tighter, encouraged when he saw the lines around Marcus's eyes and mouth tremble from poorly managed pain.

"Etan, if you don't step from this path... you will die. You must come with me. There is... someone who can help you. But he must have your absolute obedience, do you understand?"

Etan just stared at his mentor, marveling at how the old lion had wasted away to nothing but his pride.

"Little man, I will ask you only one more time..."

———

"LET GO OF MY WRIST."

In the background Etan could hear a car engine, and a siren, and he could feel the bump and hiss of tires. But for the moment he was utterly blind.

"Where am I?" he asked.

"Nice to hear you speak, mate. Now if you please... let go of my wrist!"

"At least he's conscious," a second man said. "And... would you look at that? He's really got quite a hold on you!"

"Yes, Roland, he does. I guess I'm going to continue to handle the matter myself and risk losing the limb rather than counting on you to help."

Etan finally opened his eyes.

"Where am I?"

"I'll answer your question if you'll let go of my wrist. Will you do that, mate? Will you let go of my wrist? We're only trying to help."

Etan had no idea his hand was gripping another man's arm.

"Thank you, mate—ouch." The paramedic shook off the pain. "To answer your question, you're headed to the Kingsridge Hospital. You've taken quite a beating at a pub. Do you remember anything at all?"

Etan tried to sit up, but both of the paramedics pushed him back down onto the stretcher.

"No, no, mate. Not quite ready to get up. Just work with us and we promise we will get you headed in the right direction..."

Etan remembered something about the wrong path, from a dream or memory, or both, and suddenly he was fumbling around his chest.

"Sir, are you looking for this?" One of the paramedics picked up a large clear plastic bag and waved it in Etan's face. "We got it all bagged up. No worries."

Etan could see his phone in the bag, and his wallet, and his neck chain. All that remained of Chieftain Opemipo's claw was just a bit of scales and bone, no larger than a chicken pellet.

"Was it broken... when you... ?" Etan could barely speak.

"Broken? Yeah, mate, exactly as we found it. But at least you're going to be all right. No, no—you just sit back and enjoy the ride."

As the paramedic was speaking, Etan's phone vibrated, and through the clear plastic bag he could see it was his employer calling.

The phone then started to ring.

———

IT RANG A SECOND TIME before Etan answered.

"Where are you?" Carl asked him. There was a sense of urgency in his voice.

"I can see you driving up," Etan said through his swollen lips. "I'm standing near one of your helicopters."

"Yeah, okay, I see you."

He hung up.

Etan stared at his phone. He thought for a moment about sending one final text message to someone before he was killed. But he didn't know who he would send it to, or even what he would write.

The Humvee screeched to a halt and Carl jumped out of the passenger side. The driver, swarthy, with large pouches beneath his eyes, and a bulletproof vest strapped to his chest, stayed put behind the wheel. So was this the man Carl would use to kill Etan for his mistakes?

"Jesus Christ, look at you," Carl said, "you're a mess."

Etan was fully aware of his ghastly appearance. At the hospital, he had taken a good look at himself and knew he would never pass customs in Tel Aviv. So he had paid dearly to stowaway as part of the cargo in a private jet. From London to a brief stopover in Turkey, the plane made its final destination in Egypt to deliver illegal weapons.

From there, Etan paid yet another considerable travelers fee, this time for a Palestinian chaperone into Israel. They went by tunnel beneath the walls along the Gaza Strip.

"I'm afraid my injuries are much worse on the inside," Etan said to Carl.

"What? You've got some internal injuries?"

The noise of the surrounding airport probably made Etan's attempt to make a subtle, deeper point ill-advised. "No, sir, I was referring to the shame I feel in my failure. Everything you sent me to do I've managed to—"

"Fuck up?"

Etan nodded, then turned away in shame. He caught his own reflection in the tinted glass of the helicopter and immediately looked down.

"Okay, so you screwed up. So what are you going to fix it?"

Before Etan could respond, Carl had his arm wrapped around his shoulders and was whispering into his ear. "We're in the Holy Land. Do you know what that means?"

"Sir... ?"

"It's the place of resurrection... and redemption."

Etan lit up immediately. The only way to describe his survival at the pub was a "resurrection." And he had been seeking redemption ever since the train collision.

"Now listen to me, events are moving quickly. I need you to move just as fast. And there is no more room for error. None."

"I totally understand."

"Good. I need you to track someone down."

"Jenna Grant?"

"Absolutely not." Carl dropped his arm from around Etan's shoulders. "You are to leave Jenna Grant and George Wyatt to me. Are we clear?"

Etan was surprised to hear him mention George Wyatt. That meant George must have survived his medical crisis at Paddington Station. Etan could barely contain his rage.

"I'm sorry, sir, I just assumed when I got your phone call in London to get here immediately."

"Well, you assumed wrong. Which apparently is the direction you've been flying for a few days now."

Etan was about to turn away, but he could see in Carl's eyes he already regretted the remark.

"I need you to locate Marcus Rhodes."

The reaction on Etan's face must have been some sort of reply, because Carl took it as one.

"Yes, I know it will be challenging to carry out because of your history with him. But that's what I need you to do."

Etan thought about whether to lie, but he quickly decided against it. Carl would inevitably discover the truth anyway.

"Sir, I have just seen Mr. Marcus in London."

Instantly Etan could see the fire appear in Carl's eyes. "Why in the hell didn't you tell me this?"

"He asked me to keep our meeting confidential."

"And you decided to do as he requested?"

"No, sir. I'm telling you now. Honestly, I wasn't sure seeing him had anything to do with what we've been working on."

"What did he say to you?"

"He told me I was in danger."

"Was this before or after the pub beating?"

"Before, sir."

"Great. I can only imagine how impressed you are with his gift of prophesy!"

"Sir, I have not given it another thought." Etan tried his best to sound convincing.

Carl laughed to himself. "Okay, wait, don't say anything, let me guess—Marcus also told you that your *Ori* is not in proper alignment. Tell me I nailed it."

"Sir, that's exactly what he said."

"I did that to show you how easy it is to impress the simpleminded."

Though Carl was not a believer in Orisha, he seemed to understand the precepts. And Etan knew firsthand that he and Mr. Marcus had once been very close.

"I know that man very well," Carl said. "Of course he knows a thing or two about me." He seemed to lose focus for a few seconds before marching to the Humvee. He opened the back door and grabbed a leather bag.

"In here are keys to the van. The car's registration matches this passport, with your new name just in case there's trouble." He handed the bag to Etan.

"Sir, what van?"

Carl motioned, and Etan turned to look over his shoulder. A white van was driving up to the tarmac.

"You will also find in the bag a GPS, but this one is a bit different. It has specifically been programmed to receive a signal from Marcus's cell phone. The red dot should bring you within fifty feet of his location. So just follow the dot, and when you see him, call me, or... detain him and then call me. But you cannot harm Marcus under any circumstances. He is the key to my plan. Are we clear?"

The white van screeched to a halt and the driver got out of the vehicle.

"I would never harm Mr. Marcus."

"Then we won't have a problem."

"But, sir, there's something I don't understand. We've both spent years trying to acquire the Black Pages. Now, suddenly, it doesn't even matter?"

"Right now Marcus is the key to acquiring the Black Pages. Just do as I ask, Etan. There are things you don't understand."

Etan wanted to laugh. The two men who mattered to him the most in the world had both told him in the last twenty-four hours that he "didn't understand." He either was a complete moron, or the two people he thought he trusted were keeping him in the dark.

Carl reached over and embraced him, and again whispered something. "He was once there for you, but now he's only out for himself. You need to keep trusting me."

Carl then released him.

"I do trust you, sir."

"Do you have a weapon?"

Etan shook his head.

"He will take care of you then..." Carl motioned to the driver of the white van. "Let him know if you need anything else."

Then he wheeled around and started back to the Hummer. He already had his phone out and was making another call, even before he opened the passenger door and got in. The Hummer pulled away without Carl once looking back.

"What're your feelings about a GLOCK?"

Etan jumped. The driver of the van had come up behind him, and Etan had heard nothing. He turned away, so the man could not see how much he had scared him.

"I have a very reliable one with low mileage. But if you prefer a Makarov I have that with me as well. It might come in handy if you need the authorities to believe it was a Bulgarian or Serb who did the nasty work..."

One final time Etan caught his own reflection in the black-tinted glass of the helicopter. At first he didn't recognize the face, but he didn't look away. He locked eyes with the image and continued to stare at it, thinking that eventually everything would make sense.

"Hey, are you all..."

———

"... RIGHT?"

Etan turned to see a portly American sightseer staring at him through a pair of sunglasses. The balding man was part of a tour group visiting holy sites in Jerusalem. Etan had been using the group as cover while he kept surveillance on Marcus.

"Yes," Etan answered. "Thank you for asking."

"Okay. It's just that... you dropped this." The man was holding out the GPS device from Carl. "You seemed to hit the glass pretty hard. Are you sure you're all right?"

Etan turned to the store window, and sure enough he saw a sweat imprint from his forehead where he must have hit the glass. He had been using the different shop windows to watch Marcus's movements from across the street. For some reason he must have fallen into one, but he couldn't remember at all having done that.

He could remember driving Carl's white van to Jerusalem from the airport in Tel Aviv. The GPS had shown a stationary red dot glowing in Abu

Tor. But when Etan was still a couple miles away, the signal started to move. Marcus appeared to be heading toward the Old City walls.

In just a few minutes, Etan was able to close in on his position. He drove the white van right in front of Marcus, who was now on foot, coming out of the parking lot near the Zion Gate.

Along this road, public parking was prohibited. Etan pulled over anyway and got out. He checked the GPS.

Apparently Marcus was still carrying his cell phone, because the bright little dot was on the move behind the city walls.

The Jewish Quarter, Etan thought, and took off.

The Zion Gate, built for Suleiman the Magnificent in 1540 AD, was badly eroded, not by weather, but by the 1948 Arab-Israeli War. Bullet holes pocked the arch and surrounding brick. Etan walked through it like he was storming the gate.

Down a maze of narrow and winding streets he walked, following the glowing dot. He wondered if Marcus was taking a circuitous route on purpose.

It was in the Hurva Square that Etan finally spotted his mentor, and secreted himself amongst the tourist group. They had just finished taking photos of the synagogue, which had been destroyed and rebuilt many times, and probably would be destroyed once again.

Etan walked with the group, parallel to Mr. Marcus, thinking of a way and a place to approach him that would afford the cleanest getaway. That was the last thing he remembered before waking up to this fat tourist.

"So very kind of you," he told the man as he reclaimed his GPS. "I guess I was feeling a little faint."

The tourist nodded and then rejoined his wife and the rest of the travelers on their walking tour.

Etan scanned the square but couldn't locate Marcus. He turned to the GPS for guidance and started walking.

He ended up in the Western Wall Plaza, and hung back on the upper level. Below, worshippers wailed at the wall and tore at their garments. A long row of wooden barriers separated women from men. And there, over-looking the women, Mr. Marcus stood at the rail.

He was facing the wall, so Etan felt safe staring at his back without fear of detection.

There was a time when they had been so close Etan felt sure he knew exactly what Mr. Marcus was thinking all the time. But now, as he watched him, he wasn't sure what was on the old man's mind.

Marcus stepped away from the railing.

Etan turned just enough to hide his face, but kept watch in his peripheral vision.

Marcus walked toward the back of the upper level, toward a row of canvas awnings covering an excavation. The Israel Antiquities Authority had been hard at work, unearthing a building complex from the Mamluk and Ottoman periods; they had found several vaults.

After a quick look around, Marcus ducked into one of the tents and was gone from sight.

Etan waited for a few moments. Then he took position near a long, tall stone monument put up on wheels. Whatever it was there for, Etan had no clue, but it allowed the perfect vantage point to spy on his old mentor.

Marcus was standing just within the entrance of the canvas awning, peering out at the plaza. He was watching someone.

Etan followed his line of sight to see if he could figure out who his old mentor was observing. It didn't take him long to recognize someone...

Jenna Grant.

Adrenaline started a fire in Etan's blood.

Jenna hadn't noticed him yet, too busy talking to an older man in a long coat.

Etan turned back to the tent, but Marcus seemed lost in his own little world.

"Orisas," his old mentor had once named him. "Owner of heads."

Etan would have loved to collect Jenna's skull. But Carl had told him to leave her alone. So maybe he wouldn't hurt her. Maybe he would just strike the fear of God into her, so she would come with him.

Etan started forward. Slowly at first. He needed the element of surprise.

But then Etan thought about what happened at the pub. What her pretty-boy friend had done to him. What had happened to his rooster claw.

Etan quickened his pace and took out his gun.

It was simple: he could not allow this woman and her friends to continue mocking him with their very existence. Later, when he was forced to explain his thinking to Marcus and Carl, he would get them to understand.

"You can thank your friend in London for this..."

But suddenly blood was flooding into his mouth. Etan realized he wasn't even standing, he was on the ground. He must have lost consciousness. Perhaps another black out.

A figure stood over him, a shadow in the brightening light.

Olodumare, he thought.

It had to be.

Because Etan was dying—he was aware of that now, sucking air through the hole in his lung.

Olodumare—he would lift Etan up, stand him up, and judge him, and then send him back as a rooster, with one green eye and one brown—and two five-toed claws.

Etan tried to reach out to his god—"Olodumare... Olodumare!"—but he was falling, away from the light, and the shadow grew until it was everything, eternal and cold, and all was quiet and dark.

———

JUST INSIDE THE COVERED EXCAVATION, Marcus had been watching his daughter and the priest when Etan caught his eye.

He was moving quickly, determinately across the plaza—and drawing a gun. On Jenna.

Marcus didn't hesitate. He reached into his coat for his own 9mm, a Ruger, and he shot Etan twice.

Marcus waited a few moments, looked around. The gun had a silencer on it, and in the din of the plaza, no one had heard the shot. No one but Jenna and the priest had seen Etan go down.

He stepped out of the tent and took off his gloves, contemplating his next move. Since no one had noticed Etan—at least not yet—there was still a choice: Marcus could walk away; or he could walk out into the plaza. He decided he could not possibly face Esu if he simply walked away.

He put his gloves in his coat and approached Etan's body.

Jenna had stopped in her tracks, confused as to why Etan had simply fallen, and startled now by Marcus's approach.

He and his daughter locked eyes.

Jenna's gaze was intense, yet he refused to turn away—refused to walk away. For so many years he had hidden in the shadows of her life. Now on this morning at the Wailing Wall, though he had not planned it, he felt it was time he emerged from the shadows.

She was the one who broke eye contact, scrambling away, not in a panic but with haste. Marcus smiled as his daughter went first for the priest, then for the exit to the street. He did nothing to stop them. And once they were gone, Marcus stepped up to the body.

Etan stared up at him, at nothing at all. The blood from the two gunshot wounds had puddled beneath him on the polished stone, but with the end of his heart, it had stopped its spread.

Opemipo's rooster claw no longer hung around his neck.

Marcus wanted to cry.

In Etan's coat he found a phone and a GPS, which he was certain had been used to track his movements. Marcus took them both, then stood up and took one final look Etan.

He tried to see if there was anything about the little man that had become a grown man. But he could see or feel nothing.

"Orisas," he whispered.

And then he turned and walked away.

As he went, Marcus scrolled through Etan's contacts and came across a name: Orisha.

Suddenly, a woman screeched behind him. Someone had finally noticed Etan's corpse.

Marcus stepped out of the plaza and took a different direction than the way he had come. For all he knew Etan was not alone. As he walked down Makhase Street toward the Dung Gate, he dialed the preset number on the phone.

An Israeli police officer appeared, running directly toward him. Marcus kept walking, listening as the phone rang. The police officer glanced at him, but sprinted right past.

"Hello."

He recognized Carl's voice.

"Your man... Our little man is dead."

"Marcus?"

"Listen to me—Orisas is dead."

"What?!"

"I killed him."

"Oh, Jesus Christ... You killed Etan? Oh my God, why did you do that?!"

"He was going to kill my daughter."

There was silence.

"Tell me, Carl, and make me believe... you were not the one behind his actions."

"How could you possibly think that? Of course I wasn't behind his actions! Marcus, I sent him to find you. Listen to me, you need to come in—"

Marcus cut off the connection. He moved toward a trashcan, prepared to break the phone apart and discard some of the pieces, but then he thought better of it. He knew the phone contained a blocking device and couldn't be traced anyway.

His own phone was another matter.

He could hear the sound of whistles sounding in the plaza. Then another scream. People from all different directions came dashing past him.

Marcus took out his own phone and smashed it. Threw a few pieces in the trash but kept the rest. Undoubtedly, Carl had used the phone to track him. In fact he confirmed it as he walked out the Dung Gate and the little light on the GPS remained behind the city walls.

Two Israeli military cars swerved in and out of traffic, then cut in front of the rest of the cars. One of the vehicles almost hit Marcus as he was crossing the street. The soldiers didn't bother to apologize as they parked and jumped out. They sprinted toward the plaza the way Marcus had just come.

He shook his head and kept walking.

As he finished crossing, the drivers stuck behind the military cars stared at him, obviously amazed at how coolly he handled his close brush with death.

But Marcus thought of the old Nigerian saying: "The spirit that keeps one going when one has no choice of what else to do must not be mistaken for valor."

CHAPTER 6

Interior Minister Yarin Kahlon would not stop glaring at Carl. Kahlon had brought three physicians to examine the nineteen earthquake victims, and now, a dozen feet from Carl on the tarmac, they were huddled together discussing their findings. No doubt Envoy Wolfenson's jet cast a shadow over them all, parked exactly where it had been ordered to park after the Tel Aviv control tower gave them clearance to land.

The glare from the interior minister was burning a hole in Carl's face, and yet Carl refused to look away. He had decided that enduring the minister's intense, withering gaze would be his punishment, and part of his atonement for his efforts in blowing the envoy's contraband past customs.

And like anyone facing the punishment of a martyr, Carl stood alone. Wolfenson was safe and secure in the lounge of the plane with his wife and Dr. Fincher. Just as Carl had predicted, it would be his face, in an extreme close-up, that the Israeli official would remember when the nineteen did everything but die peaceful deaths. Carl had no doubt he would end up being the poster child for decades to come whenever Israel customs was instructing new recruits on the possible ramifications of trusting previously trustworthy entrants into their country.

Kahlon put a hand on the shoulder of one of the doctors who had been briefing him, obviously thanking him for his effort, then the Minister started toward the plane. Before he mounted the boarding stairs, Carl cut him off.

"Oh come on, Yarin. You really aren't going to walk right past me as if I'm not even standing here."

At first the interior minister would not look at him. But when he finally did, it was with pursed lips and distant eyes, as if their whole previous relationship had already been archived.

"I am not a casino, Carl. Yes, you have twisted the arms of some people who owe you, and they happen to be the same people I've had dealings with in the past. Regardless, I am not a casino. My job is not to cash in your chips. Let me be perfectly clear here—I am granting Envoy Wolfenson his request to have the Syrian earthquake victims admitted into our country for emergency medical care. But I grant his request only because my doctors assure me that your patients all have nine toes in the grave anyway. Therefore, letting them into my country will be no risk to me politically, or to my people."

"Thank you, Yarin, for your—"

"Silence!"

Carl lowered his head.

"Yes, today, for one day only, you have forced me to become a casino. And on this one day, I cash in all of your chips. But now I can close the casino register for good because you have no more chips to play. They were all used this very morning. I'm hoping, Carl, for your sake, you are not expecting a receipt."

The interior minister stepped past him and climbed the stairs to the plane.

Carl whipped out his sat phone and dialed a number. "Okay, we've been given the green light," he said to his man on the other end. "Get those copters on the tarmac immediately for a quick evac to Balshem Medical Center."

Once he saw the medical helicopters appear in the sky, Carl made his way into the plane. In the lounge area, the envoy and interior minister were speaking to a dozen newspaper reporters while photographers captured the moment. Both men looked ebullient and proud.

As Carl walked past them, he heard Kahlon say, "We hope our gesture is something that will help draw Syria and Israel closer together."

Neither Patricia nor Fincher was in the lounge. Carl was surprised the doctor wasn't standing beside Wolfenson, soaking up every moment of success.

He headed for the stairwell to the interior of the plane where the nineteen patients were most likely in the process of being offloaded. Carl figured Patricia was probably sitting vigil with some of the patients. So it surprised him when she emerged from the bedroom of the jet.

They locked eyes, and Patricia smiled. Carl moved to speak with her, but when he crossed the galley kitchen, he was surprised to see Dr. Fincher, leaning against the wall of stainless steel cabinets and refrigerators.

"How did things go with the interior minister?" Fincher asked, stepping between Carl and Patricia.

"Look over my shoulder, doctor. Total lovefest."

Fincher smiled broadly. He couldn't help himself. No matter what animosity he and Carl shared, anything that advanced the envoy's plan made the doctor extremely happy.

"Does this mean the earthquake victims will be allowed into the country for medical care?" asked Patricia.

"Thanks to Carl's efforts it does. You see, Pat, sometimes a hero just can't stop himself; no matter what he does, his actions end up saving lives."

Fincher spoke without the slightest trace of sarcasm, and Patricia received him in that spirit.

"Thank you," she said to Carl. "Thank you for everything you've done."

He responded without hesitation, even though he was puzzled by Fincher's unsolicited and unequivocal praise.

"Please stop, Patricia. It's your husband who deserves all the credit. I'm just the... stage manager."

"Patricia!" the envoy shouted from across the jet's lounge. "Please come and express your gratitude to the interior minister for answering our prayers."

Dr. Fincher backed up into the jet's galley to make room for her. As Patricia walked past Carl, with only inches separating their faces, she looked directly into his eyes. For Carl, the connection felt like it lasted for hours. But it was a fleeting second at best.

Once she was gone, Fincher turned to Carl. "Aren't you curious why I gave you credit?"

"Always curious, doctor, in why you do things. But equally afraid of hearing the answer."

"I gave you credit because you deserved it. My way of letting you know we're still a team."

Even while striking a positive chord, the doctor wore a facial expression not much different than when he had accused Carl of being a traitor.

"So very good to hear, doctor." Carl extended his hand. "To the Red Veil."

"Yes," Fincher said, accepting the handshake. "To the Red Veil..."

———

CARL EMBRACED ETAN.

It was a gesture he rarely indulged in over the years. He had always felt showing too much affection for the young man would leave himself vulnerable to manipulation. He felt confident in his understanding of Etan and believed that a firm hand was always the way to go. Now more than ever.

But Carl committed this show of affection because he hoped Etan could find Marcus. The young man was perfect for the job considering his personal history with Marcus. Or he was perfect for the job *despite* his history with Marcus. Either way, it worked for Carl.

"He was once there for you, but now he's only out for himself. You need to keep trusting me."

Etan started to pull away, but Carl held onto him, pulling him tighter into his bear hug. He wanted the boy to feel his... love.

"I do trust you, sir," said Etan.

Carl finally let him go. "Do you have a weapon?"

Etan shook his head.

"He will take care of you then..." Carl motioned to the driver standing next to the white van. "Let him know if you need anything else."

109

Throughout their meeting, Carl had examined Etan's face, searching for some reassurance that he had made the right move entrusting the young man with such a delicate mission. Specifically he had searched his eyes, but Etan's irises were like specks of brown and green, almost swallowed whole by bruised, swollen flesh from the beating he took in Great Britain.

Carl was also on the lookout for signs of betrayal—the evasion of eye contact; a rebellious smirk; a vacuous fixed look in Etan's eyes. But he couldn't detect any warning signs. Carl wondered what he would have done if he had noticed anything to the contrary. Could he possibly have raised his left arm to signal his employee leaning against the van?

The fact was he cared for the young man, as much as he could possibly care for anyone not of his own blood. Carl had known Etan's biological father when he was alive. He knew how much his father would have cared for the boy if he could have seen the man he had become.

Then there was Marcus to consider. Despite mocking him just minutes ago, Carl had always loved Marcus, more than their oldest brother. They ended up not sharing similar religious passions, but their differences had never once compromised their loving bond. In fact, the only serious problem with their relationship arose on the day of Ami's NDE. When Carl called to tell Marcus the news that his son had been demonically possessed, he certainly expected his brother to follow up with a call to arms. Instead, Marcus disappeared. He vanished overnight, like someone who had joined the witness relocation program. As weeks went on with no contact, Carl began to wonder whether Marcus was hiding from the Angel of Light or his own brother.

Carl turned away from Etan and walked back to his Humvee. He pulled out his phone and dialed a number. While he waited for it to connect, he thought about playing "King of the Hill" when he and his brothers were kids. It was probably the first time he really bonded with Marcus. Sweaty, both out of breath, and staring up at their oldest brother who pounded on his chest like King Kong. They both knew if they had any hope of throwing Rex off the sand dune, they would have to work together to defeat him. Working alone would only mean separate tumbles down the hill. Again. And then at the bottom, they both would have to listen to their oldest brother proclaim his victory with a wild banshee howl, so loud it still rang in Carl's ears.

————

WHEN HIS HUMMER PULLED UP for the meet with the explosives dealer, Carl thought the location coordinates had to be a mistake. His local "fixer" Michael Loder had made the arrangements, and usually Carl had no reason to criticize Loder's choices. But for some reason his fixer had set the meeting on the West Bank, miles beyond the Green Line border, and right in the middle of a construction zone for a new Jewish settlement. A dozen cement foundations and wood skeletons framed Carl's view of the desert.

His phone rang.

"Hello."

"I have a visual on them. It looks like they came alone with no backup. You should see their grey SUV any second."

"Loder, is this your idea of a joke?"

"Well, I don't hear you laughing so I guess I should come up with a better punch line."

"In the middle of nowhere, no cover, no place to even do business. We're completely wide open here. If this is a setup, whatever they're shooting—guns or surveillance—they shouldn't have any problem bagging their target. What were you thinking?"

"It's not a setup. If it were, I would be able to see. Clear vision in all directions for miles. That's why I chose it. Look, all you will be doing is approving the explosives they're selling, making sure it's exactly what you need regarding the Israeli signature. Then you leave. I will be the one following up later with the payment and transporting the package to wherever you designate."

"Okay, got it." Carl put away his phone. He could see the dealers' grey SUV coming up on the dirt road, just as Loder described.

The moment Carl put his phone in his coat pocket, it rang again. He took it out and looked at the caller ID. It was Etan. Was it possible he had already locked in on Marcus?

Carl flipped open his phone. "Hello..."

"Your man... Our little man is dead."

"Marcus?"

"Listen to me—Orisas is dead."

"What?!"

"I killed him."

"Oh, Jesus Christ... You killed Etan? Oh my God, why did you do that?!"

"He was going to kill my daughter."

Carl couldn't catch his breath. How was it possible that Marcus, Etan and Jenna had intersected all at the same location... all at the same time? What was happening?!

"Tell me, Carl, and make me believe... you were not the one behind his actions."

"How could you possibly think that? Of course I wasn't behind his actions! Marcus, I sent him to find you. Listen to me, you need to come in—"

Marcus hung up.

The dealers parked their SUV about twenty yards away from Carl's Hummer. Two men, wearing jeans and linen dress shirts and black leather jackets, got out of the grey vehicle while the driver stayed behind. Both passengers were white, with close-cropped blond hair. They didn't move very far from their SUV as they waited for their client to exit his vehicle.

Carl just stared at them, stared right through them. His mind was racing from the phone call with Marcus.

"Sir, are you all right?" Carl's driver asked.

The phone rang. Carl answered quickly, hoping it was Marcus. "Hello..."

"Carl, what are you doing? They're standing right in front of you."

"Call it off."

"What?"

"Call off the deal, Loder!"

He terminated the call, waited a moment, then speed-dialed the phone he had given to Jenna. He had already tried to reach her twice since leaving Aleppo, but maybe after whatever happened with Etan, she would be scared enough to answer.

After the second ring, someone picked up.

It was George.

"Where's Jenna?" Carl asked.

In front of the Hummer, one of the explosives dealers reached into his leather coat and answered his phone—no doubt a call from Loder.

"She's not here," George said. "But why don't we use this opportunity to speak?"

"Fine, George. I'm calling to see if you and Jenna have changed your mind about working together."

"As a matter of fact I have."

Outside, the dealer on the line with Loder was not taking the last-second cancellation well. He was screaming into his cell phone and pacing back and forth like a caged tiger waiting for a late serving of his meal.

"If you agree to leave Jenna out of this, I will tell you everything you want to know about the Black Pages."

"Agreed," Carl said. "When and where do we meet?"

The explosives dealer snapped his phone shut, then motioned to his partner. They both reached into their leather coats and this time they pulled out automatic pistols. Together they started toward Carl's Humvee.

A gunshot rang out in the desert, and dust leapt up just a few inches from the dealers' feet. They both froze, then quickly dropped to their knees, glancing around for the location of the shooter.

"Not so fast, Carl," George said. "There's one other condition."

A second gunshot echoed in the desert, and it kicked up the dirt even closer to one of the dealers. This latest shot sent them both scampering back to their SUV.

"Go ahead, George. I'm listening."

"I want to meet with Fincher. And I want you to arrange it."

The grey vehicle peeled out of the construction yard, leaving a thick cloud of dust in its wake.

"George, do you mind explaining to me the hard-on you have for the doctor?"

"He has something that doesn't belong to him. Once I get it back, then you can have everything that's in my head. Now do we have a deal?"

Carl's eyes caught something in the Hummer's rearview mirror. It was Loder. He had emerged from his sniper position and was approaching the Humvee from the rear. Carl's fixer was covered in dirt and sand from bald head to Doc Martin boots. Nevertheless, he looked like the same calm and cool associate Carl had been trusting for over a decade.

To George, Carl said, "I'll tell the doctor I have located one of the people who has the Black Pages, and that you want to meet."

"Whatever you need to do to get him in my space."

"Then what, George? What do you plan to do?"

"I plan to take care of my problem. And my solution will take care of your problem as well. Now get back to me with a location for the meeting. And call in the next five minutes. I don't want Jenna to know we've spoken. And I remind you of my other condition—Jenna is to remain out of your plans."

George hung up.

Then Loder tapped his 9mm pistol on the rear window of the Hummer to get Carl's attention.

Thunk... thunk... thunk...

Loder turned his back to the car and waited.

Carl took a deep breath, trying his best to clear his mind. Things were spinning too fast. For the first time in a long time he felt he was in way over his head. Besides his uncertainty of how to proceed, he wasn't sure he could trust his own gut.

Marcus had accused him of sending Etan to kill Jenna. Though he felt confident of convincing his brother otherwise, Marcus still would never forgive him for contributing to the circumstances that led to Etan's death.

Even though Marcus had pulled the trigger, he undoubtedly felt as if his own brother had forced his hand.

Carl unbuckled his seatbelt and got out of the car. Loder stepped toward him, but then backed away when he saw that Carl wanted to be by himself.

Out across the desert, Carl ran. More than a hundred yards from the construction site, he stopped, huffing and puffing, sweating all over. He caught his breath, then looked up into the sky. There was nothing but blue. Not one cloud that he could stare at that might give him a clue of what to do next.

Years ago in his journeys, Carl had discovered something important—a special knowledge of the hidden truths that governed humankind. But this discovery came at great cost. Since his revelation, he had never encountered a single person whom he felt shared his secret.

Until he met George.

In the monastery, Carl had noticed there was something off about George. He seemed absentminded, undisciplined. Whether that was real or just a ruse didn't matter to Carl. He saw something else beneath the bumbling façade—a determined, focused spirit.

Ami's reaction to George had confirmed what Carl had felt standing near the man: a powerful, tangible energy distinctly different than what he felt when in the presence of the envoy. His instincts told him George was on a different side. And Carl was further convinced that George had been put into the mix for a purpose.

The Jerusalem Peace Forest popped into Carl's mind. It would be the perfect meeting place. The various trees and stone structures could be exploited for backup support. And at night, the place was completely deserted, decreasing the chances of civilian collateral. It was the perfect place for

George to meet with Fincher, and for the doctor to finally get what he had coming to him.

Carl pulled out his phone to make the call to George. For the first time in days, he felt confident, because this time... he was betting on God.

CHAPTER 7

THE HELICOPTER CARRYING ENVOY WOLFENSON, Patricia, and Dr. Fincher circled the rooftop of Balshem Medical Center in Jerusalem. The other two helicopters, carrying the nineteen earthquake victims, landed one at a time. Within minutes a swarm of emergency care attendants had offloaded the patients and had rushed them into the hospital. Then the traffic control booth cleared the envoy's helicopter to land.

As the pilot made the descent to the helipad, Dr. Fincher took a moment to look out at the ancient city. The sprawl of Jerusalem had always been modest, as were the heights of the buildings erected over thousands of years. Even the spires, domes, and towers and modern buildings beyond did not reach very high toward the heavens, where the faithful of three major religions aspired to end up as their final destination.

The doctor was no architect, but he presumed that even if some religion was capable of building an impressively tall structure in Jerusalem, the unstable ground would never support it. There were now too many buried civilizations. Too many conquered tribes and squashed religions. All the blood that had been spilled over thousands of years of violent conflict would have made the ground impossible for modern engineers to create a foundation stable enough to bear any one structure that might meet God halfway.

For these reasons, Jerusalem had always reminded Fincher of something much less transcendent. For the doctor the cityscape brought to mind... a cemetery. All of the squat buildings, with their flashy gold baubles here, and marble there, and crumbling ashlar all over, were like mausoleums, not for the dead, but for the living, who had nothing better to do than spend their entire lives preoccupied with the dead.

In the next forty-eight hours, if the envoy's grand plan proved successful, not only would a few buildings fall to the ground, but everything that had been buried for thousands of years would no longer matter. Anything that dared to be erected in the aftermath of all the blood and carnage to come would never claim any ambition of building toward the heavens.

"John, what's wrong?"

Patricia and the envoy sat opposite the doctor in the passenger cabin. She had been holding her husband's hand through the entire flight, but now she looked scared.

"Nothing, honey, I'm perfectly fine."

Fincher had to admit Wolfenson did not sound convincing.

"John, your hand is shaking. And you're sweating up a storm." Patricia pressed her palm to his forehead. "My god, you're burning up!"

"Please, Pat, there's no need for alarm. I'm just nervous about what will happen to all these poor people we're trying to save—whether these doctors will be able to help."

The envoy's excuse seemed to pacify her, at least for the moment. But Fincher was not so easily fooled. He kept an almost unblinking eye on the envoy until they landed.

The doctor's close scrutiny paid off when he saw Wolfenson attempting to unbuckle his seatbelt; the envoy could barely steady his hands.

Patricia had already left the passenger cabin, so she missed her husband's struggle. Fincher intended to keep it that way. He turned in his seat so that his back prevented any witnesses as he unbuckled the envoy's belt.

"Sir, how are you feeling?"

"Electrified! Like I am a lightning bolt touching down in this ancient city. How are you feeling, doctor?"

"Frankly, sir, a little worried."

Wolfenson stood up and grinned. "Don't be." He slapped the doctor on the shoulder, but there seemed to be no weight behind his hand.

Then the Angel of Light exited the helicopter and followed a team of bodyguards toward the entrance of the hospital.

———

AFTER NEARLY TWO HOURS in the visitors lounge of Balshem's critical care unit, Fincher cut short the conversation he was having on his mobile phone. He was the first of the envoy's entourage to see the team of doctors moving down the corridor, almost in lockstep. There were four of them, and they all looked as if they were part of a jury returning to the courtroom after deliberations, just seconds away from entering a death sentence verdict. Their grim findings were written all over their faces, but they also showed signs of a clear conscience, as if they had nothing to do with what they were being asked to decide, nor anything to do with carrying out the sentence, aside from rendering the verdict aloud.

"Okay, everybody, this doesn't look good," said Larry Zepp, Envoy Wolfenson's press agent. Like Fincher, Zepp had picked up on the vibe as the doctors approached. It was obvious there would be no heartwarming, inspiring stories to share with the world.

The press agent stepped over to the envoy, but this time he spoke in a much lower voice, so only the envoy could hear. "Sir, if this is indeed toe-tag news, we'll need one of the doctors to speak at the press conference. The last thing I want is for you to be the one going on live television announcing a body count."

Zepp may have intended to whisper, but Patricia overheard. She had always resented Zepp for replacing the previous press secretary, Rick Walsh, whom she considered a friend, so Fincher was not surprised to see the outrage on her face.

Before Wolfenson could respond to his press secretary, before Patricia could voice her indignation at Zepp's shallow remarks, the Balshem staff doctors began briefing the envoy about the medical status of the nineteen earthquake victims.

Since Fincher had expected nothing but the grim details, which ended up comprising the entire report, he couldn't help but indulge in a mental game: counting how many times certain words or phrases were repeated during the briefing. After excluding the word "blood," which the doctors iterated too many times to make the contest interesting, Fincher wound up with "blunt trauma" being the clear winner at thirty-three mentions. "Contusion" was a close second. And receiving the bronze medal was the word "perforation." At one point Fincher became convinced that one of the doctors might have become wise to his contest, because the resident repeatedly used the term "subcutaneous," almost as if he thought the word had a solid chance of placing in the top three.

Finally, one of the doctors said, "Mr. Envoy, sir, the bottom line is... every one of the nineteen patients you have brought to us will die. Some in minutes, others in hours. None longer than a day or two."

The envoy had absorbed the depressing details without any noticeable reaction, but immediately after the grim medical summation, Wolfenson said, "I'm hoping one of you doctors would be so kind to speak to the media with me. I believe we have a press conference scheduled to begin in a few minutes..." Wolfenson turned to his press secretary for confirmation.

Zepp said, "Sir, to be more precise, the press conference should have begun five minutes ago."

Fincher looked over at Patricia and saw her confusion as she stared at her husband. Confusion and concern.

One of the doctors said, "Envoy, sir, if you would like, I could go ahead and represent Balshem Medical Center and brief the media."

"And what is your name, doctor?"

"Dr. Daniel Diamant, chief resident. Sir, I'm the one who worked on your wound after your attack. Don't you remember?"

Without the slightest sign of embarrassment, the envoy said, "Of course I remember, Dr. Diamant. My question was on behalf of my press secretary, who will need the spelling of your name."

Dr. Diamant turned to Zepp and spelled his name.

"Okay, got it! 'Diamant,' with two A's. Thank you for stepping up, doctor. Now, envoy, sir, if you're ready, and if the chief resident is ready, why don't we all make our way to the seventh floor? I imagine the media is hungry for answers."

Wolfenson's entourage followed Zepp toward the elevators, and Fincher started after the envoy.

Patricia cut him off.

"Dr. Fincher, what is wrong with John?"

"Well, Pat, I'm not sure what you're asking. Have you noticed something that perhaps I'm missing?"

"You would only miss it if you were blind, doctor. Can't you see he is not himself? Clearly this is not the same man I've been married to for years!"

As Fincher listened to Patricia, he realized for the first time that they shared the same concern—Envoy John Wolfenson was not in the right state of mind to hold a press conference televised live worldwide.

"My husband has gone to all the trouble of flying these victims from another country, then twisting the arms of the Israeli government to get them to this hospital, but when he hears the news from the medical staff that they're all going to die... he just segues without emotion to a press conference?" She grabbed the doctor's shoulder. "Colin, you saw him in the helicopter. There's something wrong. Please, help me."

Fincher was startled by the use of his first name, and her attempt at a personal, physical connection. Never before had she directly approached him about anything. Now, her emotionally naked plea for help came as such a shock, the doctor didn't make a move for several seconds.

Then he was scrambling down the hospital hallway after the envoy's entourage like a physician responding to a code-blue alert. He arrived just in time for the elevator doors to shut in his face.

The Angel of Light was headed to the seventh floor.

———

THE MEDICAL CENTER'S CONFERENCE ROOM teemed with reporters and camera crews from all around the world. The last time this many media people had crowded one floor of the hospital was weeks ago, following the assassination attempt on Envoy John Wolfenson.

Worldwide interest in the nineteen earthquake victims had built overnight, spreading from the Aleppo airport where the envoy had publically announced his intention to transport the Syrian survivors to Israel. At first much of the media assumed the angle would be the Israeli government's refusal to admit Envoy Wolfenson into the country, but when all of the major Israeli cabinet officials, including the prime minister, had come forward in favor of allowing the nineteen into the country, the story took on a new spin. It was the American TV networks that had spearheaded this new angle—Envoy Wolfenson's desperate redeye mercy flight, combined with the earthquake victims' courageous struggle to fight off death, epitomized the best of human survival stories. When the network and cable morning shows broadcasted the press conference live, TV audiences would be able to start their day off with a tear in their eye along with their morning coffee.

After a quick introduction by Zepp, Dr. Diamant took to the podium, and, without preamble, launched into the dire prognosis for all nineteen patients. There were audible gasps throughout the media horde as, one by one, the doctor detailed the bleak future of each patient. Clearly no one in the room had been prepared for such devastating news.

On the critical care floor, Fincher had waited several minutes for another elevator, but finally gave up and hit the stairs. He burst through the fire door onto the seventh story and fought his way through a hall packed with media support people, who were servicing the video equipment set up for the press conference in the adjoining room.

The doctor was stunned to see hundreds of long, thick black cables stretching, seemingly for miles, across the carpet, flowing to and from every doorway and window of every room connected to the hall. As he raced to the back entrance of the conference room, he felt as if he were treading across a pit of snakes.

Dr. Fincher arrived at the back of the room just as Zepp was introducing the envoy to the media. Fincher waved his hands in a last-ditch attempt to get the press secretary's attention, but the bright lights cast by all the video cameras made it impossible for Zepp to see more than ten feet in front of the podium.

The doctor bulled, shouldered, and shoved his way toward the front of the crowd. At one point he caught sight of Patricia as she entered the conference room. She looked horrified at the sight of her husband stepping up to the podium.

"Please, everyone, I will answer your questions, but first I have a brief statement. I want to thank the government of Israel and especially Interior Minister Kahlon for allowing me to bring these nineteen earthquake victims into this country. I would also like to commend the staff of Balshem Medical Center for their dedication and topnotch medical care.

"And finally, responding to what we have all just learned from Dr. Diamant... of course it greatly troubles me to hear the astounding odds facing the nineteen earthquake survivors who my wife and I rescued. But that just means we all need to intensify our prayers and hope that these courageous people are somehow granted a miracle. Okay, I will take your questions."

Fincher had finally pushed his way to the front of the room. He got Zepp's attention just as the envoy called upon a U.S. cable TV reporter.

"Envoy Wolfenson, already many in this country and in the United States are calling you a superhero and an international role model for your effort in the last forty-eight hours, what with your delivery of equipment and supplies to the disaster zone, and now your attempt to save critically injured earthquake victims. How do you feel about that kind of acclaim?"

"Humbled," the envoy said, radiating sincerity and thoughtful contemplation. "I am humbled whenever I hear people speaking about me in such glowing terms."

"Doctor," Zepp whispered to Fincher, "is there a problem?"

"First of all," the envoy continued, "I am just doing what my president has asked me to do. But I am also doing what any man in a position to make a difference should be trying to accomplish. I just wish over the course of my career I could have dedicated myself to more humanitarian efforts, so I would feel worthy of the high praise."

Dr. Fincher turned to Zepp and shook his head. His concerns appeared to have been unfounded. The envoy was on top of his game after all.

Fincher looked over at Patricia, and for the first time since her arrival at the conference, they exchanged eye contact. She appeared to be as relieved as he was, seeing the envoy clearly in control of his actions and words.

From the podium, Wolfenson pointed to a female reporter in the middle of the room.

"Envoy, sir, there have been rumors that Syrian officials originally did not want you coming into their country on your rescue mission. One official in the last hour has said, without attribution, that if he knew you were transporting citizens of his country to Israel, he certainly would have stopped you. What are your feelings about those reports?"

"Well, I'm disturbed. I wish anyone who challenges what I have done would go on record so we can all see who they are, and so I can take appropriate measures."

Almost immediately there was the distinct sound of hundreds of reporters scribbling into their notepads. It was followed by a rising murmur in the room as the less attentive reporters asked their neighbors for an instant replay.

All of this was especially audible because the envoy had fallen silent. While the media muttering swept across the room, Wolfenson just stared out into the bright lights of the video cameras, as if in a trance. It only lasted about three seconds, but on live television, three seconds of silence felt like an eternity.

Then the envoy began speaking again, as if he had never stopped.

"However, it is my belief that none of the Syrian officials I have been dealing with are behind that quote, or any of the ill will directed toward me. Everyone I've had contact with accepts that a government's first responsibility in a disaster is to care for its people, not its politics."

Dr. Fincher yanked the arm of Zepp's suit jacket. Had the sleeve been cheaply tailored, the jacket would have ripped. "Get him off camera right now, or I will kill you."

Across the room, Patricia started pushing her way through the media. She had heard enough and was moving determinedly toward her husband.

"You, there in the back row," Wolfenson said, pointing with a steady, confident hand. "You have a question..."

"Mr. Envoy, yes. After hearing Dr. Diamant's medical prognosis for all nineteen victims, are there any second thoughts about your actions? However well-intentioned your rescue attempt may have been, the victims are now in a foreign country, and reportedly all Muslims, which means specialized burial rites. Who will be the one to ensure their religious beliefs are observed?"

"No second thoughts at all," Wolfenson replied. "I did what I thought I should do to save these people's lives. And I say to everyone who might have similar concerns that I will do everything to make sure these victims will not be treated like a tribe of hominids."

Another buzz swept across the room, and Fincher could hear the word echoing: *hominids, hominids*.

"Believe me when I say, I will use all of my power and influence to make sure any of the victims who die here will have a proper Muslim burial. And that is a pr..."

Larry Zepp took over the podium before the envoy had a chance to finish, so that Wolfenson's final word, "promise," was uttered a few inches from the gaggle of podium mics.

"I wish we had more time for questions and answers," Zepp said, "but as you can see Envoy Wolfenson has had a very long and trying tribulation in Aleppo, and after traveling through the night with the earthquake victims, he is clearly very tired. There are a few things the envoy just said that I would now like to clarify..."

Almost simultaneously, Patricia and Dr. Fincher each grabbed a side of the envoy and led him to the conference room exit. They passed through the snake pit in the hallway, and finally came to the elevators, where they were forced to wait.

There, out of earshot of the nearest camera, microphone, or reporter, Patricia addressed her husband point blank. "John, what's going on?"

"Nothing at all, honey. Just a bit tired. But everything is all right. I know Zepp will clean up whatever I may have said that needs cleaning up."

Fincher stabbed the elevator call button repeatedly, desperate to sequester the envoy to a private place.

Patricia pressed her hand to her husband's forehead. "Oh my God, you're boiling! I'm going to get one of the doctors to take a look at you. Can you stay with him, Dr. Fincher?"

"Yes, of course, please get some help..."

Patricia rushed back toward the press conference where she had last seen the chief resident in attendance.

Fincher went to press the elevator's call button again, but before he made contact—

Ding!

—one of four elevators opened. Fincher pulled the envoy into the car, then hit the close button before anyone could join them.

As soon as the elevator doors shut, the envoy said, "So how bad was I?"

"Not good, sir. With all due respect, you need to tell me what is happening so I can help, or there could be problems."

"No need to worry, doctor—it's all over now. I'm sorry I did not better anticipate the toll of keeping nineteen people alive. But now the world knows what John Wolfenson has achieved, and I can finally shed myself of this burden."

"But, sir..."

Wolfenson had already shut his eyes and was mumbling words and phrases, some in English, some in Latin, some in twisted tongues. Fincher tried to make sense of the invocation.

Raising nineteen.

Sleepy eyes.

Beautiful jewels.

Shattered stone.

And Draconem, which Fincher happened to recognize as Latin for "dragon" or "snake."

Ding!

The envoy's eyes sprang open. Dr. Fincher, confused but... not quite as concerned, followed him out of the elevator.

Together they made their way toward the critical care recovery area. As they turned a corner, a sudden flurry of footsteps and the rattle of casters startled them. They hugged the wall as a team of nurses, orderlies and one doctor raced past them with a crash cart, a defibrillator on wheels.

Two of the nineteen patients had gone into cardiac arrest. And by the time Fincher and Wolfenson reached the critical care window, the ER team was tending to yet a third victim.

The envoy stared through the glass at the nineteen patients, and Fincher believed he beamed with joy, as if he were a proud father staring into the maternity ward at his newborn son.

"John, there you are!" Patricia shouted as she and Dr. Diamant rushed into the room.

"Honey, I'm fine," Wolfenson protested, but Diamant steered him into a corner and shined a light into the envoy's eyes. Then he grabbed the envoy's wrist and started counting heartbeats.

Another ER team with a crash cart rushed by, into the critical care unit.

"He seems to be fine," Dr. Diamant told Patricia. "Maybe your husband should check himself in for some tests just to be safe. Now, you'll have to excuse me..."

Before Patricia could ask any questions, or even tell him thank you, Dr. Diamant rushed through the doors of the critical care unit, off to lend a hand with the dying patients.

Patricia drew close to the envoy and scrutinized his appearance. She couldn't believe this was the same man she had seen minutes ago. The John Wolfenson standing before her looked like the picture of health—confident, vibrant, and alive.

"John, what is going on with you?"

"I'm so sorry, Pat. I'm sure this all sounds crazy, but I was standing there at the podium answering questions, and I guess it just hit me... right then and there... the awful, painful truth that these poor people we've been trying to help... they're all going to die."

His voice caught on the last word. And then...

Wolfenson wept.

"Oh honey," Patricia said, pulling her husband into an embrace. "I know... I know."

Out of respect, Fincher stepped away from the envoy and his wife, but he couldn't resist staying to watch the reactions of everyone who walked past the couple. All were moved, some to tears of their own, as they witnessed Envoy Wolfenson weeping for the dead.

CHAPTER 8

THEY DROVE THE ROAD TO ABU TOR without taking in any of the sights. Father Olsen rested his eyes nearly the entire trip, while Jenna kept her eyes on the rearview mirrors.

It didn't matter that she was driving past an archaeological garden with ruin layers dating back to the late first century BC. It didn't matter that Kind David's Tomb was right up the hill. It only mattered that they weren't being tailed. And after the confrontation at the Western Wall Plaza, with a man who had apparently tracked her all the way from the States, she had to assume someone was always following her.

Jenna resisted the urge to speed. The last thing they could afford was a traffic stop by the local police.

As it turned out, Father Olsen said only five words to her the entire ride. He said the first three with his eyes still shut.

"Who was he?"

"He was a killer," Jenna replied. "And that was the third time he and I have crossed paths. I think he's working... excuse me, I think he *was* working for Carl Saracen. Ever heard the name before, Father?"

Olsen's eyes weren't even moving beneath the lids when he responded—"No."

His answer confirmed something to Jenna: that at least on one account, Carl had given her the straight facts; he had stayed away from the entire exorcism.

"Father, what about the second man? The one who appeared out of nowhere? Did you recognize him?"

Olsen's fifth and final word was, again, *no*.

The silence that followed allowed Jenna to dwell on the mystery. She hated to admit it, but the second man from the plaza had seemed vaguely familiar. Yet each time she recalled his face, she also questioned her recollection.

Contrary to popular belief, Jenna knew human memory did not work like some recorded TV show you could play back later verbatim. It worked more like a true-crime show recreation: the brain assembled different layers of its original perception, and then tried to rebuild the memory as close to the actual experience as it could.

This system had its plusses—most humans would never move past the grieving of a loved one if the memories and emotions did not degrade with time. But there was also a downside to this "recreation" system. It could be faulty, even in recalling recent events. Toss other mitigating elements into the mix, like advanced age, alcohol, drugs or disease, and the human memory could not be counted on as a reliable instrument of recollection.

Perhaps, Jenna thought, she had been so frightened of being killed that everything she took in visually at the plaza had been compromised—

including the face of the man she found vaguely familiar. Jenna was rolling that around in her brain as she drove around the base of Mount Zion, and entered Abu Tor.

The priest must have felt some familiar curve in the road because his eyes flashed open as they began their final approach to the two-story stone house he shared with Jawad.

As they drove up to the building, Jenna immediately noticed that the front door stood open. She and the priest stared at it as they drove right on past.

Jenna ended up parking two blocks away and spent at least a full minute examining Jawad's house in the rearview mirror. From what she could see, all of the windows on the second floor were closed, but the drapes were wide open. Perhaps someone was in the bedroom keeping an eye on the street.

"Father," she said, "do you still have that gun?"

Olsen didn't answer immediately, until Jenna took her eyes off the rearview mirror and looked over at him. He was apparently still ashamed of what he possessed.

"Yes. I still have the gun."

"Okay, good. Because I think we need to keep it within easy reach, at least for a while."

The priest raised an eyebrow. An ironic expression, Jenna surmised— less than an hour ago the gun was something that stood between them; now it was an object that could make a difference in their mutual survival.

She was a few steps ahead of Olsen as they walked down the street. All along she kept watch on the house. No movement behind any of the windows. No fluttering of the drapes.

Jenna slowed to a crawl as they closed in on the front door. It was creaking back and forth in the wind.

All she could think about was her decision to leave George behind. He had been so weak the last time she was with him; probably too weak to have survived any sort of home invasion.

Something clanked inside the house. Jenna and Father Olsen stopped just a few feet from the door.

She could hear someone speaking in Arabic.

The priest touched her shoulder, and she turned to see him hunched over, gripping the pistol in his right hand. She had no idea why he tried to get her attention. Then, when the Arabic voice blared again from within the apartment, Olsen stuffed the gun into his coat and went rushing into the building. "Father!" Jenna shouted, running after him.

"Jawad?!"

"Alan?!"

In the kitchen Father Olsen threw his arms around his friend. Jenna didn't have to look very far to see George standing near the sink. She walked over for her own reunion hug.

As they were still in each other's arms, George whispered, "So Father Olsen is no longer lost."

Jenna laughed, then pulled away. "That's right, George, Father Olsen was once lost, but now he is found."

"Oh my, the sandwiches!" Jawad shouted, rushing to a little toaster oven on the counter. He pulled out two overdone pita pockets stuffed with tomato slices and what looked like cubes of chicken, but was actually haloumi cheese.

Jawad turned to the priest with the sandwiches, looking sheepish. "I'm sorry, Alan. When you came up missing, I didn't know what else to do. So

I did what I always have done for our lunch, and I hoped... and I admit, Father, I even prayed that the smell of this pita bread would somehow bring you home."

The priest was so choked up, he couldn't speak.

"But you can see what I've done," Jawad continued. "Like an idiot, I've burnt your pita."

Olsen took the sandwich from the tray and took a big bite out of it, closing his eyes as he chewed. "Mmm. Jawad... I can honestly say... this is the best sandwich I have ever tasted... in my entire life."

Jawad was beside himself with joy. He turned to offer his other guests one of the sandwiches, but Jenna and George were no longer in the kitchen. They were now in the living room, standing transfixed in front of his computer, which was playing a news story, a repeat of Envoy Wolfenson's press conference conducted earlier at the Tel Aviv Airport.

Jenna unmuted the sound.

"The Israeli government has shown both grace and compassion with their decision," Wolfenson was saying. "Their kindness should stand as a shining example, and a great symbol of peace for all other countries to emulate today. By allowing these nineteen earthquake victims into their country for medical treatment is both a humanitarian gesture and an act of spiritual kindness, no matter what god you worship..."

At the word "nineteen," Jenna turned to George, but he was distracted. For some reason he was completely fixated on Father Alan Olsen, who was now standing right beside him.

CHAPTER 9

ANGEL OF LIGHT...

Near-death experience...

Demonic possession...

Father Olsen was telling his story, and in the process he was practically quoting the fifth quatrain. And yet Jenna and George had told him nothing about the Codex Gigas. They never got a chance. Jawad had left for half a day's work, and almost immediately the priest had begun breathlessly relating his personal experience the last few months.

Assassins.

John Wolfenson.

The Restrainer.

Without knowing it, Olsen had quickly moved from the fifth quatrain to the seventh. And if Jenna converted the word *Har Megiddo* to its corrupted version, *Armageddon*, she would practically have the contents of the Black Pages.

"Father," she said, "let me run a few phrases past you so I can get your reaction. The first phrase: 'The Restrainer holds back the star.'"

"Well, you've just used the word 'Restrainer,' but not in the context of the Bible. Other than that, I have no other reaction."

Jenna nodded, and continued. "'But a fatal wound invites his light.'"

"What is this?" Olsen asked.

"Wait, Father, one more. 'An astonished world is a witness / As a messenger of'—"

"What is that you're quoting?"

"—'peace is resurrected.'"

Father Olsen glanced at George. "Is this a poem?"

Jenna looked over at George too, fully expecting him to jump in and explain like he had done for Carl. But this time George remained silent, apparently too interested in what Father Olsen had to say.

"Father, before we answer your questions, let me throw a few more phrases at you. 'His veiled plan calls for raising nineteen.' What does that sound like to you? Does it sound like anything that's happened in recent history?"

Father Olsen took a few moments to think about it, but then shook his head. She hadn't seen him react to the number nineteen earlier in the day either, when they had watched Wolfenson's interview on Jawad's computer.

"All right," Jenna continued, "what about the next couple of lines? 'And they will cast their sleepy eyes / On the most beautiful of jewels.' What about that?"

"Ah," Father Olsen said, "Jerusalem—I believe the 'most beautiful of jewels' to be Jerusalem."

"Good. That's exactly what we thought." Jenna couldn't be more elated. She had done her due diligence; she had taken her theory all the way through the scientific method—and here someone was, recreating her results.

Jenna looked to George for his reaction, but he was busy studying the priest. *Weird*, Jenna thought. She wondered what he was looking at.

"Is it a quatrain you're reciting?" Father Olsen asked. "I'm hoping it's not a crossword puzzle you're asking me to solve. I'd probably have to question your priorities if that was the case."

"Wait, Father, just one more line: 'Rebuilding a house on a shattered sacred stone.' Can you see anything that might relate to that? Maybe a place?"

"Well, in Jerusalem, there are countless sacred stones. But if this were a word association test, the first thing that popped into my mind was the Temple Mount. Obviously I could be thinking of it only because that's where we were today, Jenna, but I don't believe so."

It was the one line she and Raymond had failed to completely decode, whether from the alcohol, the stress, or the lack of sleep. But she had always had a gut feeling about what "sacred stone" was referring to, so it was meaningful to her that Olsen went to the Temple Mount as his first choice.

"It's also the phrase 'rebuilding a house' that I find significant," said Olsen. "It's long been an obsession with apocalyptic prophecy that the Jewish temple be rebuilt on the Temple Mount. Christians believe it will be one of the key signs of the Second Coming."

"Father, you had asked where I got the quotes. What if I were to tell you that the Angel of Light has visited before, beyond any of the other times he's mentioned in the Bible. What if I told you that he possessed a Benedictine monk way back in the thirteenth century? And the method of possession was a near-death experience?"

The priest raised an eyebrow. "Well, if it was simply a 'possession,' I guess I wouldn't be too surprised. But adding the element of an NDE certainly makes it more profound for me. That is how the demons took possession of Tom and... Sandy."

Jenna had purposely steered clear of sensitive topics, such as Sandy Travis, her fiancé, and even Carl's son, Ami. Father Olsen had yet to volunteer any details in those areas, so she didn't press her inquiry, fearful that the priest, in his fragile emotional state, would just shut down on her. But now she could put it off no longer. Jenna needed answers, and dancing around his feelings would only put them all in jeopardy.

"Father," she said, "you just mentioned Tom Hansen and the fact that he was possessed after a near-death experience. It got me wondering... did you ever try to save him?"

Her question affected him much in the way she first feared. He turned away from her, looking sullen, almost ashamed.

Just when it seemed like he wouldn't respond, Olsen said, "Yes, I did recently attempt to save Tom. While visiting him at an Israeli detention center hospital I discovered his health had been severely compromised and I feared that the demon which had been possessing him for weeks would lead him to his death. So without going through any of the church's protocols, I decided to perform an exorcism. Though Tom's demonic possession ended during my session, I would have to classify my efforts as... inconclusive. Only because the demon said it left Tom's body on its own accord. But please understand, one of the main weapons Satan has in his arsenal is subterfuge and obfuscation."

Jenna was formulating a response to what the priest had said when George spoke up.

"So what you are freely admitting, Padre, is that you performed an exorcism on Tom Hansen, but your actions may have been completely ineffectual?"

Jenna was surprised to hear George finally say something. But she was shocked by the tone and content of his question. They had talked to two different priests in the last few days, and George had never used the word "padre." And the way he posed his question made it sound as if he were cross-examining a murder suspect.

Olsen stared at George for a few moments, then closed his eyes. When he opened them again, he had turned to Jenna. "I'm sorry—I hope you understand. I shouldn't be discussing this. Really, it's a violation of my patient's rights."

Inside Jenna cringed. She didn't want to look over at George, but forced herself and saw there was a half-smile on his lips. When she turned back to Olsen, his eyes were closed again. A snide remark ran through her brain—*Hey, if I'd been blind all of my life, I wouldn't be closing my eyes so much. What are you hiding from?*

Jenna got up from her chair and started to pace. She didn't doubt Tom's right to privacy, or Father Olsen's legal discretion as a licensed health professional, but she also knew it wasn't just demons who used subterfuge and obfuscation. She was thinking about the best way to handle the situation when she heard George cough, then clear his throat. It sounded like he was going speak again.

"George, can you let me handle this?"

"Yes, of course, Jenna. After just one more question." George leaned in toward the priest and asked, "Father, do you ever feel like... you're not in control?"

"I'm sorry, but I don't... what do you—"

"I mean of your body? Your emotions? The way that you think? Maybe even the way that you dream?"

While keeping the same tortured expression, Father Olsen answered, "Yes, I feel that way all of the time. I'm Catholic."

Jenna burst out laughing. She tried to stop, but it just invited another round of laughter. She had to give Catholic priests credit: at least they had a great sense of humor about their religion.

George, however, was not laughing. He was still staring at Father Olsen, waiting for a real answer.

"Well, George, in all honesty, I have never, through all of this, felt like I wasn't in control of my thoughts or actions. I wish I could say that it wasn't my own choice to involve Sandy. But it most certainly was my self-appointed quest to uncover the secrets that I thought lay at the heart of a boy's possession—and a plot to usher in the Apocalypse... it was my *obsession* that ultimately led to the death of someone I cared about deeply. Now each day I must live with that choice.

"And, by the way, I do still dream. I'm sure they're my own dreams because, in them, Sandy Travis is still alive."

George began to reply, but then stopped, swallowed, and tried again. This time he started to cough. For a few moments, it looked as if the fit would subside, but it only got worse.

George tried to stand, but his knee hit the table and knocked it to one side. Then he stumbled backward over his chair, which toppled, clattered, so that he had to clamber over it to get to the bathroom.

"George!"

Father Olsen went after him, but Jenna stopped him, then followed him herself.

She entered the bathroom just in time to see George hunch over the toilet and throw up. She could see bits of pita mixed into the mucus—a thick congealed stream of a pure and scentless black.

CHAPTER 10

C ARL STOOD AT THE CRITICAL CARE WINDOW, watching Patricia through the glass. She sat on the edge of the hospital bed, holding the hand of an earthquake victim. Only six were still alive.

Even though Carl had been standing at the window for over thirty minutes, Patricia hadn't noticed him. He wanted to keep it that way. He was more than satisfied staring at her while he contemplated his plan. If she was to look up, and they were to lock eyes, he wasn't sure how he would react.

"Carl, what are you doing here?"

Dr. Fincher approached him in the hallway. The last time the two had spoken, on the phone earlier that day, Fincher had hung up on him with no explanation. Carl knew the doctor did not enjoy being in the position of asking anyone for forgiveness, especially him. So Carl had already lowered his expectations.

"Is there something wrong with your phone?" he asked Fincher. "After you hung up, I tried calling you several times for hours, but kept getting your voicemail. Eventually I felt I had no choice but to drive out here. You know, Colin, I wasn't trying to sell you time shares in Boca. I really needed to speak to you."

"I'm sorry, Carl. You have no idea what has been happening here."

Carl was shocked and gratified to hear the apology, but refused to rest on his laurels. He knew the best time to mine information was when the other party was on the defensive.

Carl lowered his voice. "Fine, doctor. I just hope that whatever it was, it ended up being more important than the explosives you asked me to obtain, or the Black Pages you needed me to locate."

"Yes, Carl, it was at that level of importance, I assure you." Fincher looked around, and, lowering his own voice, he said, "Remember when you told me that perhaps the envoy has limitations? Well, you ended up being right. I was managing those limitations until he bounced back. Now he's fine."

Carl thought Fincher's answer was almost perfect. Not only was it self-serving—meant to showcase his triumph over a trying situation—it was vague. His word choice didn't add up to a single solid detail. But his answer was still *almost perfect* only because he confirmed that the envoy had a vulnerability.

"Now did I hear you right, Carl, you drove here because you have a lead on the explosives?"

He answered Fincher's question with a sly smile.

"And what about the Black Pages?"

Carl's smile turned into a shit-eating grin.

Dr. Fincher looked around one more time, then broke out into his own grin. "Details, Carl, please."

"I will have the explosives in my hands tomorrow morning at 8 a.m. All I need from you is the location and the target, and I can handle the rest."

"You'll get that information at 7:55 and not a minute sooner. Now tell me, do the explosives have an Israeli signature?"

"Yes, absolutely. These bombs were taken by an Israeli supply depot overrun during the war with Hamas a few years ago. After their detonation, anyone who knows the finer points of brisance and explosive train will be able to pin the tail on the Israeli donkey."

"Excellent, Carl. Excellent." Fincher put his hand on his shoulder and squeezed. "Now what about the Black Pages?"

"As you know, I have a source here in the country, and he was able to get close to someone who was in contact with Jenna Grant. She was looking to use the information from the Black Pages as a bargaining chip in order to get to the people behind her brother's death."

"Are you telling me she doesn't believe her brother just freaked out and tried to—"

"I'm afraid not. Apparently she's convinced that Envoy Wolfenson is involved in a conspiracy, and that's why she's here in Jerusalem. After my source touched bases with me, I made contact with one of Ms. Grant's... allies. I arranged a meeting for tonight. This guy is supposed to give us the Black Pages in exchange for names. He wants to know exactly who is behind the plot that drove Jenna Grant's brother to kill himself."

"And you believe this to be completely legitimate?"

"Good question, Colin. It's exactly what I asked this guy during our phone conversation. I told him to prove that they really had the artifact, and he said, 'The Black Pages are full of quatrains. Who else would know that fact except for the person who possesses them?'"

Fincher turned away to contemplate the information. Carl waited to see whether the doctor was buying it. When he didn't see a problem, Carl continued with the flood of information.

"My question to you, Colin, and maybe it's a question best answered by the envoy, but... can we confirm that the Black Pages contain quatrains? If the answer is yes, then I think this is all on the up and up."

The doctor gave the situation some more thought, then turned to Carl. "Where is the meeting, and at what time?"

"Here in East Jerusalem at the Peace Forest, 3 a.m."

The doctor nodded, then looked over at Carl with surprise. Almost as if Fincher were suddenly aware of his presence for the first time. "So, Carl, why are you here?"

"I thought we should run this all by the envoy. I need to know what to do."

"Get the Black Pages," Fincher said, speaking louder than he intended. "I don't understand the confusion."

"Colin, the target probably won't have the Black Pages on him. That's how these things work, right? We need to find out from the envoy what he wants me to do if that's the case. Should I just kill him? Bargain with him? Invite him over for cocktails? I need some guidance here because I don't want to make the wrong move."

"Why don't I go with you?" Fincher blurted out. "I'll be the one who guides you."

Carl feigned surprise, as if he hadn't anticipated the suggestion. "I... I don't know. That could be risky. I think I'd be more comfortable talking to the envoy."

"Tell you what," Fincher said, sounding more and more confident as he spoke, "I will talk to the envoy about contingency plans, and you be here at 2 a.m. to pick me up in front of the hospital. We'll do the meet together. What do you think?"

Carl nodded, but made sure he still looked confused. "Okay, Colin, if you will speak to the envoy about how to handle whatever contingencies might come up, then I'm all for both of us getting the Black Pages. And then we'll both be heroes."

"No," Fincher said, once again putting his hand on Carl's shoulder. "No matter what happens, I will personally make sure you get all the credit."

———

AFTER GEORGE WAS ABLE TO STAND, Jenna helped him from the bathroom to the stairs.

Father Olsen stood near the kitchen table. "Is everything okay?"

"Yes, yes, feeling better all ready," George said as cheerfully as he could.

Jenna caught sight of her coat, slung over the kitchen chair closest to the priest. There was a bulge in one of her pockets that hadn't been there when she first returned from the Western Wall Plaza.

"Let me know if there's anything I can do," the priest said as Jenna and George began to climb the stairs.

In Jawad's bedroom, Jenna eased George into bed and stooped to remove his shoes.

"What was going on down there, George? You were actually nicer to Carl than to Father Olsen."

"Do you really think so? I certainly didn't mean to be. I should apologize."

Just as she finished taking off his second shoe, George tried to sit up.

"No, no," Jenna said, "you lie back down. You can tell Father Olsen in the morning."

George did as he was told and fell back onto the pillow. Jenna doubted he could have gotten out of bed anyway. He seemed incredibly weak, and his skin was sallow, at least where it wasn't black and blue. George's eyes also looked dazed and buried in a thick film.

"I only mentioned it because I'm puzzled by your behavior," Jenna told him. "And, to be honest, a bit concerned. You were like one of those dogs trained to sniff out bombs—you just wouldn't stop barking. Then you end up vomiting the same black crap you threw up at Carl's monastery... and at the Garden of Gethsemane. So I guess I'm a little anxious about how I'm supposed to interpret all of this."

George seemed to make an honest attempt to answer her question. His eyes narrowed and focused for a bit, but then he just shook his head. "I'm not sure," he whispered.

Jenna pulled the covers over him. "Look, why don't you get some sleep—"

He grabbed her hand. "Wait."

She didn't sigh, but needed to. Not out of exasperation, but out of pent-up stress. She still had a few things she needed to discuss with Father Olsen, and she also wanted to investigate the bulge she had seen in her coat. And yet, when she looked down, George looked as frightened as a five-year-old child afraid of the dark.

She plopped herself down on the edge of the bed. "What do you want to talk about?"

He let go of her hand and shrugged. "I don't know. I just don't want you to leave."

Jenna looked away, a little embarrassed, and at a loss for conversation starters. Then something popped into her brain.

"You know, George, you never told me what book you were working on. When we were visiting Father Walton I remember you saying you had visited a lot of churches. But you teach evolutionary psychology, so I'm definitely missing the connection."

"Oh," George said, sitting up in bed as if he had just been given a shot of adrenalin. "I've been writing a book about the evolution of altruism. My approach is to alternate chapters between the title subject and the life and work of George Price. Do you know who he is?"

"Yes, a little bit."

George looked at her with a dubious face. "Oh come on, Jenna, don't start being modest now."

She grinned. "Okay, I know him very well. George R. Price was a pioneer in evolutionary theory, though he began his career as a population geneticist and a physical chemist. His interpretation of Fisher's fundamental theorem of natural selection, now known as the Price equation, has universally been accepted as the most logical, mathematical and biological explanation for the act of human altruism. But besides that impressive accomplishment, he was also the first to consider ritualized animal conduct, game theory, and evolutionary genetics as part of one unified vision of behavioral evolution."

Of course she managed to spit it out in one breath. Then after taking a breath, she said to George, "You still haven't answered the question. Why did you visit a lot of churches?"

"You see, Jenna, altruistic acts which benefit the recipient but harm the actor have perplexed evolutionary scientists for years. If the goal is to get your genes into the next generation, then sacrificing one's self makes no sense. That's where kin selection comes into play."

"Whereas your genes get passed on to the next generation vicariously," Jenna said. "Because an altruistic act that saves someone with fifty percent or more of your genes still allows those genes to carry on into the next generation, even without you reproducing directly. George, I know Hamilton's rule. Now I'm going to give you one more chance to answer my question."

She had made the threat lightheartedly. Jenna loved nothing better than discussing all areas of science, especially with experts in those fields she merely dabbled in. She was intrigued to hear George's answer. More than that, the passionate discourse had revitalized him. Blood had returned to his skin, and his eyes practically twinkled. She refused to be the one to snuff it out.

"Hamilton's rule is really beside the point," George said. "Because somehow as a species, we have grown beyond the genetic motivation of sacrificing ourselves solely for our kin group. We now help other human beings who are not blood relatives at all. That's how the act of altruism has evolved.

"And perhaps organized religion is one of the prime reasons altruistic behavior has taken such an evolutionary path. The whole idea of being a faithful member of a church and helping others in your community, and even people across the world, is something I needed to personally explore if I was to write a book about it. Don't you see, Jenna, we're all animals, but when we behave altruistically, especially for strangers—that very behavior is at the core of why we're special on this planet. Some of the most selfless acts have been made by someone helping another human being whom they have never even met."

Jenna held back her reply. She needed to decide exactly what she wanted to say. To be more precise—she needed to decide exactly what she wasn't going to say.

What she wanted to say is, "Yes, George, we're such a special species that we are the only ones in the animal kingdom who take pleasure in inflicting pain. Doubling down on the concept—we're the only species that gets pleasure from the thought of inflicting pain. Or, splitting the aces and doubling down again, we're the only species who gets pleasure when we remember inflicting pain."

Jenna was also tempted to point out that, both historically and in modern times, organized religion was one of the major motivators for violence worldwide. Moreover, and in direct violation of Hamilton's rule, organized religion had often inspired the mutilation or killing of one's own kin suspected of violating the rituals and rules of worship. That sounded a lot like the opposite of altruistic evolution.

And when George said, "Some of the most selfless acts have been made by someone helping another human being they have never even met," all Jenna could think about was George's wife. Was George singing a philosophical requiem to reconcile the donation of Carri's heart to a man apparently involved with the same people who had corrupted her brother, Neal?

Those were all the things Jenna decided not to say. Because saying them would only have ruined the moment between them.

"I'm sure it's going to be a beautiful book, George."

She stood up.

"Where are you going? I was hoping for another 'one-night stand' with you."

Jenna chuckled. "Don't worry, you certainly will get your one-night stand. Where did you think I was going to sleep, with the priest?"

George laughed, but then immediately started coughing. Jenna thought if there ever was a cure for trying to be funny, it would be where everyone started violently coughing as well as laughing when you told an amusing joke.

Fortunately, George stopped hacking after just a few seconds.

"Here's the thing, George, I'm going to come to bed a bit later. I'm still wound up over what happened today, so I wanted to go downstairs and collect my thoughts. I promise I won't be too long. And then we'll be once again sharing a bed."

What she said was perfect because George didn't laugh; he only smiled.

As Jenna was leaving the room, she couldn't help but reflect on the trajectory of George R. Price's personal life. His marriage had ended in divorce over religious differences; Price's wife was of deep Roman Catholic faith, whereas Price himself was an atheist. But then in 1970, Price underwent a religious conversion mainly because he could find no other explanation for all the extraordinary coincidences which he believed had occurred in his life. He spent his remaining years trying to disprove his own thesis in favor of a new one, that altruism was not evolutionary, but spiritual. His experiments to prove this new hypothesis were not conducted with math theorems like before; rather his laboratory now encompassed his own personal life.

Price opened up his house to the homeless, the lost, and the addicted. Several months into the "experiment," he discovered that the very people he was attempting to help had oftentimes taken advantage of him; they stole his belongings; they disturbed the peace in his neighborhood.

A short time later, in 1975, after becoming homeless himself, Price committed suicide. He was buried in an unmarked grave in North London.

After everything that had happened in the last few days, Jenna was chilled by the prospect that one George, writing about another George, would somehow end up being the first thing she thought about whenever someone asked for the definition of the word "ironic."

She was about to shut the door behind her when George said, "What do you think of this title for my book? *Giving from the Heart: The Evolution of Altruism.*"

Jenna nodded. "I really like it, George."

———

JENNA SHUT THE DOOR to Jawad's room. Across the hall, Father Olsen's door stood open. So did the door to the balcony. He was outside leaning on the railing, gazing out at the night lights.

"Father," Jenna said as she came up behind him.

"How's George?"

"Fine. Resting."

"Oh, good. I was worried."

Jenna stepped up to the railing beside him, and they both looked out at the city. Jerusalem lit up at night, illuminating all the major domes and minarets.

"You know," Jenna said, "for as long as I can remember, I would inevitably look right past this kind of scenery. My mind would always go straight down, which is where I do much of my work, digging, unearthing, and hoping to find clues to what was once aboveground. Now, looking out at all of this, I guess it's kind of crazy searching for something buried and perhaps hidden forever—when it means ignoring what's right in front of my eyes."

At first Olsen had listened to Jenna while staring out at the city, but when he eventually realized there was something on her mind, he turned to her so he could absorb both her words and her face as she spoke. It was a rare experience in his life.

After Jenna was finished, the priest turned back to the city. "I wouldn't be so hard on yourself, Jenna. The secrets of the past are important. And those who seek it, in combination with the present, may discover enlightenment... or they may just be running from the responsibility of living in the present. Even a blind man can see the difference between those two choices."

Jenna chuckled, but it was just for show. She had been closely observing him the moment she stepped out onto the balcony. And her show of amusement would probably be the last concession to social protocols. Time was short, and she didn't know who to trust. And if those she thought she could trust were not worthy, she needed to know now so she could scramble for a replacement.

"Those are very profound words, Father. But I was hoping you could speak to something else. And, to be honest, I'm more interested that your reaction comes, not from a blind man, but from a blind man who just regained his sight."

He stood up to face her, and for the first time she realized exactly how tall and intimidating the priest could be when he actually stood upright.

"Jenna, you sound so paranoid right now. What's troubling you?"

"You know, Father, after everything I've been through, the last thing I'm going to apologize for is my paranoia. Here's my point: you were not able to exorcise Ami. I know that much from the videotapes I saw when I was with his father, Carl Saracen... and from meeting Carl's deranged son in person. Then, just a few weeks after you approach Sandy Travis with suspicions of some worldwide conspiracy, she gets gunned down after seriously wounding an international government official during an assassination attempt. And on that same day, Sandy's fiancé, Tom, who as we both know had previously suffered a near-death experience, just like Ami, gets arrested and has since been held in confinement at an Israeli detention center. After all of those events, something totally unexpected occurs—you regain your eyesight. Obviously it's an event that changes your life profoundly. I'm just wondering, Father, if you were objectively evaluating this chain of events, what would your conclusion be?"

For a very long time, he stared at her. "I think you're asking me to comment on the premise that my eyesight was a reward for my past actions. Am I correct?"

Jenna refused to speak. She was willing to wait until he either supplied a specific answer to her question, or an answer to the provocative question he had posed on his own.

"This is coming from George, right?" Olsen asked. "I could tell he didn't like me."

Before Jenna could answer, Olsen had already turned away from her. He leaned down and rested his arms on the balcony railing as if he were settling in for a while.

"Hmm... that's it, Alan? We're finished after just one pointed question?"

"No, we are not finished. I just need a moment to collect myself before I respond, because I believe my answer will be exactly what you're looking for... and then I believe we might be finished."

Finally, Father Olsen turned and met her eyes. Jenna took a step back—she had no idea what to expect from him.

"Despite my best efforts, there's so much in this world I don't understand. But I never dreamed I would be part of the mystery. For months I've been asking myself why, given many opportunities, I have not been a wall to prevent evil from flowing into this world. And the best answer I have been able to come up with is, perhaps it's because I have failed to put up a wall to stop evil from flowing into myself. Now, Jenna, you take that confession and you do what you think is best."

———

QUIETLY, SHE LET HERSELF back into Jawad's room. George lay asleep, breathing peacefully in bed.

Jenna went to the nightstand and opened the little drawer. She had seen the Bible and pen in there earlier, and had been surprised by the Bible; after all, this was Jawad's room.

Now when she opened it, she understood the reason for its being. It had been personalized by Father Olsen. It simply said, "For your fellowship, and your understanding."

She looked back at the bedroom door, as if she could still see the priest out on the balcony.

The Bible's last few pages were, of course, blank. Jenna picked up the pen and began writing. But then she second-guessed herself and tore out the page, ready to throw it away.

Ultimately something stopped her from crumpling it up—she didn't know what. She stared at the door again. Then she laid out the page and finished what she had to say.

CHAPTER 11

J ENNA HAD ALMOST FALLEN ASLEEP when she heard George's gentle breathing stop.

She had laid there for hours, between reality and a dream, and there came upon a peculiar notion: that the cadences and susurrations of George's respiration seemed to transform into an open channel, a clear wavelength for communication, as if she could tune in and hear a voice.

Then his breathing stopped.

Jenna knew instantly that he was holding it on purpose. She could tell because of the tension on his side of the bed; his muscles were clenched.

He was listening.

With a creak and a crack, George began to move; he waited several minutes between each furtive advance.

Bathroom? Jenna thought, but she knew better.

So she pretended to be asleep and breathed through her mouth, allowing her soft palate to vibrate lightly; she didn't want to overdo the snoring.

George eased himself off the bed. She could hear him putting on his shoes, and then he opened and closed the bedroom door behind him.

Because of the size of the room, and the fact that Jawad slept alone, the bed was arranged against the wall. Jenna had to crawl over George's side to get out of it.

His side was soaked, and reeked of copper or something metallic. She got some of it on her fingers.

Too afraid to snap on the bedside lamp, Jenna parted a curtain. She shined some moonlight where George had lain. A silhouette stained the pillow and sheets. It looked as if he had been sweating something black, but from the smell of it she knew it was blood.

Oh my God, Jenna thought. *George...*

She stuffed her feet into her shoes, threw on her jacket, and opened the bedroom door just a crack.

She didn't see George in the hall. But when she crept out and peered down the staircase... he was there, just now headed for the door.

Jenna glanced back at Father Olsen's room. She put a hand in her pocket and felt the page she had handwritten just hours ago.

Then she heard the front door open and close, and she thought, *Nope, there's no time*, and she hurried downstairs to catch up with George.

She reached out for the door.

"Jenna?" someone said behind her.

She whipped around and saw a shadowy figure moving toward her from the small living room that adjoined the kitchen. Only after she started to get into a protective stance did Jenna recognize who it was approaching her.

"Father Olsen," she said, "what are you doing up?"

"I should ask George the same question," the priest said, stepping into a shaft of moonlight. "So I'll settle for asking you. Where are you going at this hour of the night?"

"Honestly, I don't know. But what I *do* know is that my sat phone went missing right around the time George insisted on giving me a hug good-bye. Then somehow, after you and I returned from the plaza... it magically reappeared in my coat."

Father Olsen shook his head. He still seemed confused. "And now you're just going to get up in the middle of the night and follow him, see wherever it is he goes?"

Despite his castigating tone, the priest looked scared. Even haunted. Why was he not in his bedroom sleeping? Why was he in the living room sitting in the dark?

She glanced at the front door.

"Look, Father, it's something I have to do. It's hard to explain, and I don't have the time to explain even if I could." She turned toward the door.

"Wait."

Jenna actually braced herself, as if she were going to be attacked. That's how on edge she was. Was it the hour of the night? George's sleepwalking? Or just Father Olsen?

He walked to the fireplace, toward the plaque Jenna had seen earlier, even though she could barely see it now in the dark.

"Every day Jawad would tap on this. 'Everything belongs to God.' He probably thought I assumed it was some sort of religious ritual he had worked up to honor his father..."

165

Father Olsen opened the plaque and took something out of it. "I never had the heart to tell my old friend that the oils used to clean a gun have a very distinct smell."

Then he handed the pistol to Jenna, and she saw it was the same gun Father Olsen had been packing back at the plaza.

That's why he had come back to the apartment after regaining his eyesight, she realized. He wanted the gun. To commit suicide.

"I must have been crazy," Father Olsen said. "How would Jawad ever have lived with himself, knowing that I... that I had used his weapon to...?"

Jenna put the gun in her jacket pocket, and her knuckles brushed the delicate paper.

She still didn't know whether to trust Father Olsen. Her nerves were making that very clear. But she was about to go chasing George into a possible trap, and if something happened to them both, it would only matter that she had not ended up trusting anyone.

"Father, I need to give you something. And if I'm correct, it'll be way more powerful than the gun you just gave me."

She handed him the page.

He skimmed it, then looked up at her. "What is this? What's going on?"

"I don't know, Father. I really don't. And nothing I've done for the past few days seems to change that fact. But you need to read the words on that paper. And then memorize them."

"Memorize them?"

"Yes, Father, as if your life depended on it."

On her way out the door, she said, "Because it does..."

———

FROM THE SHADOWS of a Jewish memorial courtyard, Carl watched the main entrance of the Balshem Medical Center across the street. He was watching for any sign that Fincher might be planning something... unexpected for their late-night meeting in the Jerusalem Peace Forest.

Carl watched for over an hour, then slipped out of the shadows and walked down a side street to his Humvee.

At 2 a.m. on the nose he was pulling up in front of the medical center. Less than a minute later, Dr. Fincher stepped through the sliding glass doors. Right behind him was Reitz.

Carl lowered his window. So far, the good doctor had played his hand exactly as predicted.

"Colin, my apologies. I guess I was not clear enough about the rules of the meeting. I'm supposed to show up alone. Now, I may have a way of explaining your presence, but if we go in looking like the Three Musketeers, I think it could spook the target."

Fincher motioned to Reitz, who pulled out his GLOCK and dashed the last dozen feet to the driver's side of the Humvee. He pressed the business end of his gun against Carl's forehead.

"Colin, what's going on?" Carl asked meekly.

The doctor didn't respond as he got into the backseat of the Hummer. He reached over the seat and searched Carl, confiscating a sub-compact GLOCK and a mobile phone.

"Now unhook your seatbelt and slide over to the passenger side," Fincher said.

Carl did exactly as he was told and took shotgun. Reitz opened the driver-side door, still training his pistol on Carl's forehead. The precaution was a redundancy; Fincher had already settled into the back seat and was pointing Carl's own gun at him.

"Doctor, I completely do not understand your move here. I thought we were doing this together."

"We are doing this together. I'm just taking some precautionary measures."

"Look, you obviously don't trust me. So why don't I postpone the meeting and let you handle the whole situation?"

"My friend, you are looking at this all wrong. It's not about distrusting you. It's about keeping an honest man honest. Now, Carl, you need to put on your seatbelt. We wouldn't want anything to happen to you if there was an accident."

Reitz started the engine while Carl snapped on his seatbelt. Then the bodyguard put the Hummer in gear and they pulled away from the medical center.

"Listen to me, Colin, the person we're meeting has no idea what I look like. All you need to do is drop me off up here and you go in my place. Problem solved."

"Everything you're saying is not making me feel any better. In fact, Carl, it's making me more suspicious. I think we're going to stick to my plan."

Carl shook his head as if he couldn't understand anything that was happening. He stole a glance at Reitz and saw that his old friend had come without a bulletproof vest. Rather than looking relieved, Carl closed his eyes and said a prayer.

"How are you doing up there," Fincher asked.

Carl turned around to address the doctor. "As I said already, I don't get your play at all here. I'm getting you the Black Pages, and five hours later I will be delivering the explosives you asked for. So tell me, what did I do wrong? Should I have arranged for them to be gift-wrapped?"

Fincher leaned forward in his seat. "Carl, I'm listening to you; why aren't you listening to me? I already told you not to take this the wrong way. If we go to this meeting and we walk away with the Black Pages, you're a hero. If hours later your contact comes through with the explosives... again, you're a total hero. At that point, I swear to you, I will give Reitz this gun and just stand still while you take a poke at me. Make that two swings. I will deserve it. But until we get there, we're going to play things my way."

Carl took a deep breath, turned back around, and exhaled. Then he didn't say anything for several minutes while they drove toward their meeting.

About ten minutes away from the Peace Forest, Fincher said, "Okay, we're almost there. Do you have anything to say?"

"Yeah," Carl said. "If you have a sweater, you might want to grab it. I hear the forest gets cold at night."

The doctor smiled, not only because he thought it was funny, but because he was gratified to hear that Carl wasn't backing down from where he claimed the meeting would take place.

The phone Fincher had taken from Carl started to ring. The doctor looked at the message window, which read *Unknown*.

"Who is this calling you?"

"Not important," Carl said, sounding bored. "Probably just the guys who are delivering the bombs."

Fincher sneered, and tried to quickly hand the phone to Carl.

"Hello," Carl said. "Hello? Hello!" He clicked the phone off and tossed it back to the doctor, who juggled it a few times before dropping it back into his lap.

"So what does that mean?" Fincher asked, trying his best not to sound panicked.

Carl kept staring straight ahead. "I don't really know. Since I didn't answer after we arranged to speak at 2:30 a.m. sharp for the final green light, they might just move on. You know these arms dealers. They can be extremely paranoid. But knowing the guy who is running this deal, I bet he's going to give it one more—"

The phone rang again. He didn't dare smile. That would have been over the top.

Fincher handed him the phone, and Carl answered.

"Hello... Yes, it's me. Sorry, sorry, I couldn't answer. There was a car swerving in and out of the lane in front of me. Relax, will you? I'm talking to you now... Yes, we have a green light. 8 a.m. just like I said before. Nothing's changed, and there's nothing to get excited about. Yes, I will be there with the plants. You're coming with the fertilizer, right? Great. Sounds like everyone is going to go home happy. What? No, sorry, I don't have the location yet. I know, it's a little bit crazy, but that's the people I'm working with. I find out at 7:55... and I promise to call you then. Well, those are the terms... Look, it's not up to me... Are you listening? There's nothing I can do about it."

Carl turned to Fincher, who was clearly following the conversation because he looked as flustered as Carl was pretending to be.

"Come on, you got to be kidding me," Carl said. "You're bolting over a small detail like this? That's ridic—hello? Hello!"

He clicked off the phone and tossed it toward the doctor in the back seat. This time Fincher was so devastated he let the phone drop to the floor.

"Sorry, Colin. You heard me. I tried my best. We just lost the explosives deal."

In the distance, Carl could see the turn off from Naomi into the Jerusalem Peace Forest.

"Can you get them on the phone again?" Fincher asked.

"No, it doesn't work like that. I go through a contact, who goes through a contact, who then calls me. Everybody has signed off. So now the deal is dead. Besides, without the drop-off point, what would be the... point?"

Fincher leaned forward and shoved the pistol into the back of Carl's head. "Stop fucking with me, Carl. I don't care how it's done. Get these idiots back on the phone. This time we'll give them the location of the drop-off point so there are no more deal breakers."

Carl held his hand out for the phone, and Fincher gave it to him after withdrawing the gun. Carl checked his watch. It was less than twenty minutes before they were supposed to meet George.

He started dialing.

———

PROMENADES AND PATHWAYS ran along the hillside of the Jerusalem Peace Forest. In the daytime from these promenades, all nine measures of Jerusalem could be seen: the Old City, the New City, the City of David; all white, as if all the synagogues, walls, and ashlar houses had been carved from the Judean Desert around Mount Zion and Mount Olivet, and beyond it all the Dead Sea.

But at night, Jenna could discern only the distant lights, and the surrounding darkness of the forest.

Gun drawn, she kept one eye on the black evergreens and terraced plazas, on the strange pyramid constructed from bars and platforms of wood. She kept her other eye on the ghost of George's shirt ahead of her. He seemed to know where he was going as he picked his way down the garden paths.

Jenna tried to ascertain where he was headed. Instantly she recalled all of the biblical landmarks nearby.

According to tradition, Abraham was brought to one of these ridges so that he could see Mount Moriah, and know it as the site for sacrificing his son; the Haas Promenade supposedly ran right along that very ridge.

Also there was the Hill of Evil Counsel, where Judas finalized his covenant with the Pharisees to betray Christ; but the hill was now a base for the United Nations—hardly the best place for a secret meeting, or whatever George was up to.

Just up the hill, Jenna could make out two concrete towers, north and south. The northern tower, farthest from her, looked like a turret. The closest one looked more like a castle keep, albeit decidedly modern and smooth.

George went down the stairs below the turret.

As Jenna hurried closer, she saw that the two towers overlooked an amphitheater of terraced grass. She couldn't see the stage below. Not at this angle. The keep blocked her view.

But she could see that George was headed for it, down the terrace path.

Jenna crept across the little bridge into the castle keep, hoping for a better vantage point, a better idea of what George was getting himself into.

Tall narrow doorways led out to the keep's shallow balconies, but Jenna, fearing she would be too exposed outside, moved to one of the lancet windows where she could see the entire amphitheater.

Standing there, looking down at the bottom, she saw a slab of concrete used as a stage for ceremonies or theatrical presentations. But tonight three men stood there, waiting for the festivities to begin. One she quickly identified as Carl. The other two she didn't recognize.

George emerged from the surrounding shadows, heading directly toward the three men. What Jenna first suspected earlier in the evening now was proven right—George had swiped the phone from her coat when he had hugged her on the stairs... and he had used it to speak with Carl.

Why, George?

Why was he so willing to trust a snake like Carl Saracen? It was a question she intended to ask him herself.

Jenna heard the footstep behind her too late.

She tried to turn.

But the ambusher caught her in a stranglehold and slipped his right hand over her mouth to choke off her scream.

"Shhh," the man whispered in her ear. "If you cry out... they will kill your friend George and then try and kill you. I might not be able to save you this time. Do you understand?"

Jenna nodded calmly, but only to buy herself an opportunity to use Jawad's gun. Her captor must have seen the weapon and anticipated her next move, because he twisted her hand, and forced Jenna to surrender the pistol. With that, he released her, and she turned to face him.

"Jenna," he said, "do you have any idea who I am?"

"Of course I do." He was the same man from the Western Wall Plaza who had killed the strangler from Virginia. But he was also more than that.

"You're my father," she said.

He seemed surprised that she had come to the conclusion so quickly.

"Big deal. Hope you're not expecting an exchange of hugs and tears," she said. "All I care about is the man outside that window. So let me go."

"I wish that were possible, Jenna. But I'm afraid it's not. And you need to prepare yourself—I believe George has stepped into a trap, and he's going to die. This is why I stopped you. If I'm correct and that is his fate, it's imperative you don't share it with him."

She nodded as if taking in everything he was saying. Then she tried to bolt away from him. She covered less than a dozen feet before he caught up with her and wrestled her back into his control.

"Jenna, you've managed to stay alive this long by being very smart. But if you do something stupid now, you will die... and thousands will die with you. Perhaps millions."

At the amphitheater platform with Fincher and Reitz, and with George on the approach, Carl, like a good stage manager, was making sure he kept all three players involved in the production within his range of sight.

George had come stumbling up to the meeting as if he were a homeless bum looking for spare change. Carl hoped to God his fragility was an act, a plan to convince Fincher to lower his guard.

As for the doctor, his face, normally a display of emotion on par with a marble statue, became animated the moment he saw George stumbling up to the meet. Carl noted Fincher's jaw as it unclenched, and watched as his eyes lost that intense, fixed look he had perfectly mannered for previous occasions such as this. The doctor's pupils were now dilated, and continuing to expand like the wide universe he thought he controlled, but which he now realized could also be very small.

"Doctor, are you all right?"

"Yes, I'm fine. It's just that... I recognize this man."

Terrific. You recognize him. Carl wasn't sure he would. Oftentimes the average person who shuttles across the mental radar of a sociopath like Fincher is not necessarily remembered, even if that person's wife donated her heart to extend Fincher's life. It would be similar to expecting the queen bee to remember all of the faces of her drones.

"Recognize him?" Carl asked, doing his best to sound confused. "What to do you mean, doctor?"

From her position in the tower, all Jenna could see was how much George was staggering as he faced off against Carl and the other two men. Her father said George was a dead man, and nothing in George's behavior seemed to contradict it. Jenna knew he was unarmed. When she had helped him into bed earlier that night, she had practically frisked him. Now, knowing that he was about to go up against Carl, she so wished it was George who was packing the priest's pistol.

"I once knew both of those men," Marcus whispered beside her at the window. "Years ago. I'm not claiming to know or trust either of them now. That's why I have you with me. Once things got put in motion, believe me, all the rules changed, and there was nothing I could do."

"Nothing you could do? Are you talking about George and me? Or Neal?"

Marcus turned to her, and for the first time he spoke with some emotion on his face. "There was nothing I could do about your brother. Before I could intervene, they had already possessed him. It caught all of us by surprise."

Jenna shook her head. "Is that what you tell yourself at night when you can't sleep? Instead of counting sheep, you try counting all the ways you tried to save Neal? I'm curious, does it work? Are you able to fall asleep?

If you are, then you should immediately make arrangements to market the method as a sleep aid..."

He just stared at his daughter, without verbally responding. But he also didn't turn away from the fixed accusatory look on her face. The only thing that brought their stare-off to a conclusion was their mutual interest in what was happening outside.

Dr. Fincher was stepping to the edge of the stage to greet George. "Seeing you again, under these circumstances, is both shocking and completely beyond the pale," the doctor said. "I was tempted to immediately regard this situation as paranormal, but as a man of science I've quickly regained my common sense. So now I ask of you, George—can you confirm you are nothing more than a black swan?"

George tried to laugh, but coughed instead. Carl witnessed the man's knees buckle as the hacking shook his entire body.

After a few seconds, George recovered. "Perhaps I am a black swan, doctor. I don't really know myself."

Carl took a deliberate step toward Fincher. "What's going on, Colin?" The purpose of his action wasn't to ask the question, but to gauge Reitz's reaction to his movement. His ex-employee followed Carl's step with two of his own, but Reitz moved laterally, in an attempt to widen his shooting pattern in the event that he had to protect his client against either man.

"Please, Carl, let me handle this," Fincher said, measuring his words emotionally. He did not want to display any sign of temper as he was attempting to ingratiate himself with his target. "George, you and your wife... you gave something up to me that was beautiful and priceless. Somehow, the world being what it is, you have another gift you could share with me. If you choose to make the smart decision and share this second gift, I promise you... Wait, better yet..." Fincher traced an X across his chest. "I cross my heart that I, in return, will give you back the same gift that you and your wife gave to me."

George stared at Fincher's chest where he had drawn the X. Then he said, "When I was growing up, when one of us would do what you just did, we would say, 'Cross my heart and hope to die.' Did you somehow forget to say the last part? Because if that is the case, you could just say the words now... and then die... and we could all go home."

Carl was stunned. None of this was playing out as he had envisioned. Rather than employing a rope-a-dope strategy, this idiot was leading with his wife's heart on his sleeve. And he could barely stay upright. How could George possibly have planned for this to end in Dr. Fincher's death?

George pulled out a knife.

His action not only lacked the element of surprise, he struggled to pull the weapon from his coat. And it wasn't even an impressive knife. It was a steak knife... a rather dull one that looked like it had never been sharpened.

George lunged at Fincher as if the doctor somehow had overlooked all the obvious warning signs preceding the attack.

Reitz did not perform so haphazardly. The moment George reached for his kitchen cutlery, the bodyguard went for his GLOCK. He was moving into a shooter's stance when Fincher stepped out of the way of George's attack while at the same time waving off Reitz's attack.

The doctor's whole response to the attempt on his life made it seem as if he were moving with superhuman speed, which only added to Carl's humiliation. The last thing Dr. Colin Fincher was capable of was super-human anything.

"Please, George, don't do this," Fincher said, trying to sound as com-passionate as possible. Clearly the doctor had the luxury of empathy when the man intending to kill him was staggering around like he was blindfolded, brandishing a knife capable of cutting through meat only if it were dead on a plate and covered in steak sauce. "Just tell me how much you know about the Black Pages and I will take care of you... because of what your wife has done for me."

Again George lurched toward him with the knife. This time, the failed attack took a major toll on him. George's knees were shaking, and water was streaming out of every pore in his body. He continued to cough.

Carl looked over at Reitz, and even for a snail, his ex-employee couldn't hide his embarrassment. He was ashamed to be party to such a pathetic display.

Fincher moved closer to George the moment he stopped hacking. "George, we can't let this go on forever. You either help me with the Black Pages, or my man here will do the honors. For the record, because of what your wife did for me, I won't be the one pulling the trigger. But it will hurt all the same if I have to order it. Come on, George, listen to reason..."

Carl thought he could see in George's eyes that he was saving his strength for one final attack. And indeed Fincher had drawn closer and closer to him as he continued to speak. Maybe, finally, this was the miracle Carl had hoped and prayed would happen.

Suddenly, George leaped at Fincher, catching the doctor completely by surprise... but at the same time Carl could hear the deep, muffled sound of bones cracking in George's legs. The steak knife clattered to the ground, and George dropped to his knees with a thud.

Fincher staggered backward, regained his footing, and then stood upright. He was completely untouched.

In the tower, Jenna gasped at the sight of George falling to his knees. It was the final moment of the drawn-out and painful torture of watching someone she cared about flail hopelessly through a situation he was clearly not meant to survive.

Marcus turned to comfort her, but instead he walked into a punch. She hit him square in the face, not hard enough to really hurt him, but it was a combination punch—surprise and force. She followed up with a powerful shove as she took off running.

With George now on his knees, weaponless and coughing non-stop, Fincher was caught up in his own little drama about what had happened and what he should make of it.

Carl saw an opportunity to perhaps seize the stage, even as Fincher was soaking up the spotlight.

"This is so sad," the doctor said. "Almost gut-wrenching. Both of you were witnesses to how hard I tried to offer this idiot a chance."

George finally stopped coughing. The doctor dropped to his knees, so that he was level with George, able to scream at him while looking into his eyes.

"Idiot! I tried to treat you with respect—a respect I've shown no other victim. But you refused the honor! This is probably why I've never extended it before. You're all cattle to me. Ready for slaughter—look at me when I'm talking to you! Look... the fuck... at me! Your wife obviously had the heart of a lion. But you will go down like another slaughtered cow. And when I die, I will be sure to tell your wife what it was like to use her heart to kill a man who obviously was not worthy of reclaiming any of her organs, especially... her heart!"

The doctor got back up on his feet, then reached for the sub-compact GLOCK he had taken from Carl. But even before he had completely retrieved the weapon from his pocket, he was blindsided from behind.

Carl had timed his action perfectly, hitting Fincher hard enough and early enough in his move for the pistol that he caught both the doctor and Reitz by surprise. The weapon fell out of the doctor's hand, and bounced twice on the concrete before sliding into the shadows.

Reitz raised his gun toward Carl, but then froze.

A second before... traveling through the silent forest air, Michael Loder's sniper bullet—fired from the turret and moving at over eighteen hundred miles per hour—slammed into the bodyguard's chest. The projectile pierced Reitz's "shell" before he could register the noise of its approach, mostly because Reitz was no longer in control of all his senses.

Carl's struggle with Dr. Fincher on the stage had quickly proven to be decisive. He was on top of the doctor, pinning his face to the concrete while carefully shifting his hands to Fincher's throat.

"I knew it was you!" Carl shouted at him. "You were the one who struck my son with the car—you were the cause of his NDE!" His grip slowly tightened around Fincher's neck. "You didn't even have the decency to hire someone else to do it. Because you've always loved doing the dirty work!"

Carl was applying that last bit of pressure to finish him off, but then Fincher stabbed him in the thigh. It took a few seconds for Carl to realize the doctor had somehow gotten ahold of George's steak knife.

Fincher pushed him off and rolled away, gasping, choking, struggling to suck in the air that had been denied him for nearly a minute. Then he saw the GLOCK Carl had knocked out of his hand, just a dozen feet away. He started crawling toward it. But then a bullet whizzed past his head and sparked against the stage inches from the gun.

Fincher leapt to his feet just a moment before another bullet hit the concrete where he had just been lying prone.

He ran, in a straight line at first, but then veering right, then left, only because it was something he saw soldiers do in an old World War II film once. Then the doctor half-vaulted, half-clambered over the brick-and-bar fence at the back of the stage, a moment before a third shot pinged off the railing right where he'd left an imprint of his hand.

Jenna was on a breathless and adrenaline-charged run down the stairs to the amphitheater, allowing the feeling of hope to sweep through her body. She could still hear George's hacking noise as it echoed up the terraced lawn and through the darkness of the surrounding trees.

Then it stopped.

She registered the silence, but kept running. The sudden cessation of the noise Jenna had associated the last few days with George, a noise that had become so horrible that at times she had begged for it to end, no matter the cause, was now indeed... gone.

Moments later, Jenna emerged into the amphitheater and immediately saw a body lying near Carl, who was writhing on the concrete, knife sticking out from the meat of his upper thigh. She started to move toward them, but quickly realized the dead body was one of Carl's men, not George.

Jenna looked all around amphitheater, but couldn't find any sign of George.

Somehow, he had just... vanished.

In the distance, sirens began to sound.

"Where's George?" Jenna said.

Carl was somewhat surprised to see her, but more surprised to hear the question. He looked over to where George had been, but saw only bare concrete.

"He's dead," Carl replied. "I don't know what happened to his body, but... you have to believe me, he's dead."

Jenna took a step toward Carl, but then stopped. She began to back away.

"Jenna, listen to me..." Carl tried to stand, but he might as well have been ramming the knife in deeper for all the pain it caused him. He slipped back down to the stage. He couldn't believe that he was in such a vulnerable state in front of the only person left to save his son, his life, and his strategy for beating the envoy at his own game.

"You can't go," he said. "I'm the only one who can make this right."

Before Jenna could answer his plea, a noise distracted them both. It was Marcus, descending the stairs to the terrace.

Carl turned to say something to Jenna, but she was gone. Unlike George, he saw her disappear into the shadows of the night.

The sirens grew louder, closer.

Marcus stopped his approach about a dozen feet from the stage.

"Great timing, bro," Carl said, wincing. "I was counting on you being an asset with your own daughter."

"Why would you think that? Why, when clearly both Jenna and I despised the way you've handled this situation?"

Carl reached down and dipped his hand in the hot fluid that had formed around the steak knife. "I guess I was counting on blood being thicker than water. Something like that."

Marcus shook his head and started to reach into his coat—a bullet hit the concrete right in front of his feet.

"No!" Carl shouted, frantically waving off Loder, still in the turret, doing his job. Marcus waited a moment, then took a cautious step, then another, and finally moved to help his brother stand.

Leaning against Marcus, Carl looked around the amphitheater. "Reitz..." he said as he saw for the first time Loder's handiwork. "I need to..."

He started toward his fallen comrade, but Marcus jerked him away. "There's no *time*."

Carl took one final look at his dead friend. Then, hobbling, he allowed Marcus to lead him toward the dark forest.

The sirens now sounded like they were right on top of them as Carl whispered to his brother, "You need to help me..."

CHAPTER 12

HIS BROTHER'S MOTEL ROOM WAS TACKY. When Carl pointed this out, Marcus took a quick look around at his accommodations and said, "Maybe we're already both in hell and we don't know it yet."

The Crusader Inn, as it was called, sat just outside the Jaffa gate. Carl couldn't believe the name alone hadn't made the motel a target for Muslim extremists. He knew the moment they pulled into the parking lot it was a tourist trap catering to Christians, because there was a Bible quote on the inn's sign: *We who had sweet fellowship together, Walked in the house of God in the throng—Psalm 55:14.*

While Marcus cleaned and dressed the stab wound in his leg, Carl sat in one of the chairs and entertained himself with a brochure he had found on the room's coffee table, next to a Bible. The brochure listed all of the Christian attractions of the Old City as if it were a map of Disneyland. The street of the Via Dolorosa, which marked Christ's path as he carried the cross to the site of his own crucifixion, merited five stars and was a "must-see" for all "true believers."

"Marcus, if you're hard up for money, why didn't you just say something? I can help you."

"I have money, Carl. That's not the problem. I'm staying here because I'm hoping AOL will never think to look for me at a place like this."

He had first used the acronym AOL for Angel of Light while they were leaving the Jerusalem Peace Forest, shoulder to shoulder.

Marcus said, "I'm not surprised Fincher is the one he chose for his number two. Ever since his arrival, everything AOL has done has been one-dimensional and... befitting of a common thug."

Carl couldn't help but note how drastically his brother's heart and mind had changed. They each had worked tirelessly to ensure the Angel of Light's safe arrival, and throughout all their plans, setbacks, and orchestrations, his brother had always referred to the envoy with nothing short of reverence.

Marcus stepped back to check out his work on Carl's stab wound. "Okay, I think the bleeding has stopped. That bandage should keep it from starting up again, but you'll need to change it every few hours."

Carl looked at his watch and then grabbed the pair of pants Marcus had given him from his suitcase. He put the pants on and tried to stand.

"What are you doing, Carl? You need to rest."

"I wish I could."

"Carl, I'm serious, you better take it easy or you might black out. You lost a lot of blood."

"Yeah, and most of what I lost was in your rental car. I'm sorry. If I thought you still intended to return it, I would ask you to send me the bill."

They both knew Marcus couldn't take the car back with a bloodstain, nor could he safely drive it around the city and risk getting pulled over in it.

"Well, I still plan on sending you a bill. But when I switch motels tonight, I'll just leave the car behind."

"So that means you're sticking around? At least until this thing is over?"

"Over?! How can you even use that word? What's wrong with you? This isn't even close to... over." Marcus sounded as if he were gearing up to a verbal chastisement, a punishing payload that only Marcus could deliver. But then his brother just stopped and shook his head. "What would Howie say right now, if he were with us?"

Carl grinned.

Growing up, they had spent a lot of time with their cousin, Howie, who was the most optimistic person ever. When they were playing sports on the same losing team, Howie would try to cheer on his teammates: "This is nothing! We're just at the beginning of the beginning." Later, when things got even worse, he would say, "Come on, everybody, no need to worry. We're just at the end of the beginning."

"If Howie were here," Carl said, "he would probably call it just the beginning of the middle, still miles away from the end."

Marcus's dour expression never changed, though Carl knew the answer had amused him.

He limped toward the door. "So you'll be here when I get back?"

Marcus didn't answer. Instead he walked over to the nightstand and grabbed the remote to the TV. "Any minute the local news should be covering what happened..."

Just as he switched on the television, someone knocked on the door.

Marcus muted the volume.

Carl held up a hand. "That should be Loder," he said. "I called him when you were out getting the bandages." He hopped over to the peephole and peeked out. Then he nodded to his brother and opened the door.

A 9mm handgun greeted him.

Keeping the gun pressed against Carl's head, Loder stepped into the room and shut the door behind him. Carl, trying to move backwards on his wounded leg, stumbled and fell to the shag carpet.

"You didn't tell me it was Reitz I would be killing," Loder said through gritted teeth.

Carl pushed himself up on one elbow. "I didn't tell you because... I wasn't sure you would back me up."

The sound on the TV set switched on again. Loder changed the direction of his aim, but then lowered the gun. Marcus was just sitting at the edge of the bed, watching the news, apparently not the least bit interested in interfering.

"Hey, sorry about taking a shot at you earlier," Loder told him. "Nothing personal."

Marcus raised his hand to acknowledge the apology, but never looked over.

Once again Loder turned the gun on his original target. "Why, Carl? I thought you liked Reitz. I know I really liked him."

Carl winced at a pain in his leg as he sat all the way up. "Trust me, you were doing him a favor. If he was capable of seeing what he had become, he would have begged you to kill him."

"What the hell are you talking about?" Loder asked, lowering his pistol.

Carl crawled a few feet to his chair and used it to pull himself up. "Look, we really need to get going." He turned to say something to his brother, but Marcus was just disappearing into the bathroom. He shut and locked the door behind him.

"Go where?" Loder asked. "Is there another one of our buddies you want me to kill?"

Carl tried to ignore the remark as he limped past Loder toward the bathroom.

"I know what you want!" Carl shouted through the door. "You want to contact your daughter! And I have a way to do it. Do you hear me? I have a way to do it! Come out here and I'll show you how."

By the time the bathroom door opened, Carl and Loder were gone. Marcus looked down and saw a satellite phone on the floor.

The room door opened and Carl poked his head in from the hall. "Call her. Arrange a meeting. Blame everything on your baby brother. Just get her to meet with us."

He closed the door behind him, not even bothering to wait for Marcus's reaction. Despite how many times he had been wrong in the last seventy-two hours, Carl knew he would be right on this one. Family, if nothing else, was always easy to predict.

———

"IF YOU'RE MAKING THIS SHIT UP, Carl, then I really am going to kill you!"

Carl wished he was the one behind the wheel of the car, because Loder was so upset and focused on making threats, he wasn't driving fast enough. The stab wound probably had cost Carl his opportunity to get the upper hand on Wolfenson, but if they didn't get to the Balshem Medical Center quickly, he might as well toss his latest napkin plan in the trash.

"Look, Loder, don't you think if I was making something up I would go for something more believable?"

"So you're saying Reitz was possessed, is that right?"

"That's exactly what I'm saying."

"And because Reitz had the devil inside him, this is why he would have killed you if I hadn't taken him out?"

"Well technically it was only a demon possessing him. But, yeah, Reitz was no longer working for me. He was working for... the devil."

"You know I've been everywhere in the world, Carl. Everywhere! I've seen yogis in India... the shamans of Tuvan... the Pai de Santo in Brazil. And you know what, they're all fake. Every last one of them! And now, Carl, for the first time since we've known each other, you are sounding like a fake as well."

As a teenager, Michael Loder had backpacked in wild areas of Asia like Thailand, Laos, and Myanmar. He tried going to college, but couldn't stand it and dropped out after his freshmen year. He migrated back to Asia and worked as a travel guide, but after a while his Type A personality urged him into more daring exploits. Repeated scrapes with the law or local drug dealers should have squelched his wild spirit, but it only whetted his appetite for the main meal.

For the next fifteen years, Loder spent time in some pretty nasty areas: Algeria, Yemen, Kurdistan, Kosovo, Palestine, Chechnya. He kept his connections to the Western world minimal, which always helped earn the trust of any number of rebel groups he was more or less keeping an eye on. It was a tough high-wire act; generally he made his money through Western connections—like government agencies and private security firms, but mostly journalists who were more than happy to plagiarize his reports and file them back to their employers while lounging comfortably with a lap-top at the hotel pool.

Carl and Loder's paths crossed twelve years ago when a mining com-pany in Columbia contracted with Carl's security firm. Six of their miners had been kidnapped and were being held captive by the terrorist group FARC. Carl used one of his security teams to free the hostages. As it turned out, Loder was also being held prisoner in the same isolated jungle location, and he was freed along with the other prisoners. Freed personally by team leader Reitz.

Instead of sending flowers, Loder ended up working with Reitz and Carl on various assignments all over the world, wherever Carl needed him; including, more recently... Aleppo.

"Look, Loder, I understand you've been places and seen things, but trust me... this is very real."

"Can you give me any proof?"

"Yeah, after we're done here, I will need you to fly to the monastery and pick up my son, Ami. He'll be the one under restraints, screaming blasphemies at God. That's your proof."

Carl motioned for Loder to turn into the community center across the street from the hospital, and was pleased when Loder did so. Revealing that his son was possessed had the desired effect. Just like that, the soldier he had counted on for years was now back at his side, ready to follow his game plan.

"Wait for my cue on your phone," Carl said as he pulled a pistol, an IMI Jericho 941, from beneath the seat. "Then you'll enter the hospital parking lot across the street and head straight for the back. There is a ser-vice ramp in the middle of the tallest building. I will meet you there."

He opened the door and tried to move his leg, but almost cried out from the pain.

"Why don't you let me do this," Loder said.

"Thanks, but it has to be me. I have a security pass that... hopefully they haven't revoked. And I have to be the one who talks to the contact."

He lifted his leg out of the car and stood up, then wiped his forehead. He was already sweating.

Carl leaned into the car. "If things go well, we'll become a threesome. But if you don't hear from me in, like, twenty minutes, it means it's time to abort. Don't be a fool and wait any longer than that, no matter how safe it seems. If you leave without me, I will need you to drive back to the motel and tell my brother what happened."

"That was your brother back there?"

Carl simply nodded and shut the door.

As he stumbled toward the hospital, he stuffed the pistol in the inner pocket of his coat. He wasn't packing the gun to intimidate Patricia, or even to defend himself against Fincher and his own employees, who were probably now possessed by the envoy, each and every one of them. After seeing George die in such a pathetic way in the Peace Forest, it was clear Carl had lost everything he had betting on God. And since he had already taken sides against Satan, he felt he was a man without any deity to call his own. So he had brought the gun because after everything he had done in his life, if things didn't pan out, there appeared to be only one exit strategy left.

CHAPTER 13

E VER SINCE SHE WAS A TEENAGER, Jenna had started most mornings with a four-mile run.

Even when she moved to England, her routine remained the same, except for the scenery. She had traded the Occoquan for the River Cam.

Other joggers ran with headsets, but Jenna felt listening to music negated one of the sport's main attractions—an hour of silence and mental isolation. It was the best time to work through a problem or flesh out a new idea.

Deep thinking was best accompanied by the soundtrack of her own steady breath.

But her dash from the violent confrontation at the Peace Forest back to Abu Tor forced Jenna to expand the spectrum of what silence, mental isolation, and her own rhythmic breathing could lead to if it was also mixed with the mysterious disappearance of someone she cared about. Deep thinking could give way to feeling absolutely alone in the world.

Jenna opened the door to the two-story stone house and was greeted by darkness. Only the dimmest light shined.

She stepped inside and closed the door, then listened for potential threats. She took a few steps.

Father Olsen suddenly became visible. He sat at the source of light, Jawad's computer screen on the desk. The priest's back was to her. He seemed to be staring at the screen.

Jenna was surprised he hadn't heard her. She was even more surprised he had yet to sense her presence.

"Father?"

He didn't reply.

Jenna took one last look at the shadows. Then she walked over to the priest's side.

His chin rested on his chest, and Jenna was relieved to see that he had simply fallen asleep. Apparently he had been staring at a portrait onscreen.

The artist exercised a great enough command of watercolors that Jenna easily recognized the subject. No doubt the bright-red slash across the man's throat had aided her identification. The gruesome streak looped up to form a crimson halo to crown the graven image of Envoy John Wolfenson.

"Jenna..." Father Olsen said.

She flinched and almost knocked some stuff off the desk.

Not only had her face gotten literally inches from the screen she was so absorbed in the painting, Jenna had been totally mentally engrossed in gaming out all the possible answers to a single horrible question—Why would Father Olsen be looking at such a painting?

"You're back," he said.

"Father, what is this?"

The priest looked over at the monitor and also flinched. It was as if he were seeing the image for the first time. But Jenna knew he was responding more to the fact that *she* was seeing the painting for the first time.

"What you must think! Please, I decided to log onto Tom Hansen's website—let me explain."

"You mean Sandy Travis's fiancé painted this?"

"Yes. As I told you, there was a... let's call it a demonic-induced disturbance affecting the way Tom behaved. Unfortunately because of his detention by the Israeli authorities... he has been unable to take these dreadful paintings down."

It was dark in the house, but as she and Olsen met eyes, Jenna tried to spot any clues of a "demonic-induced disturbance" in the priest.

"Where's George?" Olsen asked.

The sound of the name jarred her. Reminded her why she had run all the way back to Abu Tor in the first place. "George couldn't make it. Listen, we need to leave here immediately."

"What?"

Jenna crossed the living room toward the front door. When she looked back, she couldn't believe Olsen still sat in his seat.

"Alan, I'm not kidding!"

Finally the priest got up and started toward her, but not quickly enough. She noticed his strides were measured. Jenna didn't want to ascribe his behavior to anything beyond a lifelong habit of moving cautiously through the perpetual dark.

"Jenna, first I need you to answer my question. What happened to George?"

"George is gone."

"Gone?"

"Actually, he's dead." Jenna approached the front door and reached for the door handle, but suddenly Olsen's hand was gripping her arm. He had moved so fast, faster than she thought he was capable of.

"Dead?" he asked.

"Yes, I think so." Jenna was ashamed to say the next part while looking him in the eye. "To be honest, I'm not sure."

She let the words resonate before turning back to the priest, who was understandably confused.

"Look, Father, I'll explain when I can. But we need to get going. Now."

"Do you have Jawad's gun?"

"Sorry, no."

He was disappointed, but she wasn't sure whether he was upset that they no longer had a weapon, or that Jawad would come home to discover he no longer had one.

They emerged from the house at a few minutes past 5 a.m. The sun was on the rise.

Jenna felt like, despite her little respite in Jawad's bed, she had been up the entire night. And Olsen looked as if his only bit of sleep was the catnap she had just interrupted.

The priest headed toward the rental car, still parked up the road out of sight.

"No, Father, we can't use that car anymore. I believe someone has applied some sort of tracking device. Let's go this way."

To his credit, Olsen quickly digested her declaration and followed close behind as she turned in the opposite direction.

"Jenna, can you at least tell me where we're going?"

"Honestly, I'm not sure. I'm not even optimistic we'll recognize it when we get there..."

———

THEY WALKED NORTH ALONG HEBRON ROAD, leaving Abu Tor. Keeping a vigilant eye out for anyone following them, Jenna told Father Olsen everything.

Almost everything.

She told him about George's secret meeting in the Peace Forest; his death and mysterious disappearance. She revealed Carl Saracen's relationship to Ami, the very boy Olsen had tried but failed to exorcise; and she described Carl's involvement in ushering Satan into the world.

All that, and she withheld only a single detail: the identity of the man who had held her captive at the Peace Forest. She didn't know when she planned on telling Father Olsen that it was her own father. Maybe after she had digested the ramifications of the connection herself?

Father Olsen took in her whole story without a single comment, though he did display some emotion. At one point he stopped walking to let the news of Carl's relation to Ami wash over him.

And this was just after he had pulled out a handkerchief to dab at his eyes when he heard the details of George's wife and how her harvested heart had wound up saving Dr. Fincher.

Jenna attributed the priest's verbal self-control to his religious profession. Certainly the daily practice of hearing confessions trains a priest to patiently listen until the confessor has completely finished declaring all of their sins.

The walk from Abu Tor took them past a decrepit railway station, rotting, rusting, barely standing in a lot of weeds and trash. Jenna contemplated stopping there to rest, and to come up with a concrete plan. But then they both spotted the Mount Zion Hotel in the near distance.

Jenna checked her watch. It was still early. Yet she noticed signs of activity in the hotel's lobby.

"What do you think, Father? Shall we find out if it isn't too early for a cup of coffee and something to eat?"

THE HOTEL'S TWO RESTAURANTS were still closed, but a handful of employees were scrambling about, preparing the lounge to service guests. One of the employees, still slipping on his hotel-issued jacket, walked across to greet them. Jenna spoke Hebrew as she requested a table, and the waiter sat them next to one of the large arched windows in the lounge.

While Olsen looked over the menu, Jenna gazed out at the Judean Desert. Dry and rugged for miles and miles, and immeasurable years, it had provided refuge for rebels, monks, and hermits alike. During the period of the Great Revolt, Jewish zealots had made their final stand there against the Roman Army. They had died fighting.

Jenna had worked digs in the desert twice in the last ten years. At one of the sites two years ago, she discovered three perfectly preserved Jewish revolt coins dated year 7, which corresponded with 70-75 C.E. Up to that point all previous Jewish revolt coins ended on year 5, the last year of the rebellion against the Roman Empire, which ended when a group of Jewish rebels, holding out in the desert stronghold of Masada, were killed. Jenna's discovery strongly suggested the revolt coins didn't end when Jerusalem and all of its mints fell. Somehow the Jews found a way to mint more coins.

Her finding had made a small splash in the mainstream media, but was written about extensively in several archeological journals. Most likely Carl had seen one of those journals, which explained why he had flown Jenna and George in a blacked-out helicopter out of Tel Aviv. Jenna was certain that if she set her mind to it, she could figure out the exact location of Carl's "monastery."

The waiter returned with coffee and two sufganiyot, the Israeli version of donuts filled with strawberry jelly.

After the waiter left them alone, Olsen said to Jenna, "You've gone through quite an ordeal. And I'm not just referring to this early morning's distressing events. May I ask you a personal question?"

"Yes, Father, I guess so."

"How would you describe your feelings about the... disappearance of your friend George?"

"Well, I'm clearly... devastated."

Olsen sipped at his coffee and remained silent. He apparently was waiting for more details.

Jenna turned away from him, toward the window where the Judean Desert seemed as barren as her response. She didn't want to say anymore. Talking about her feelings had never come natural to her. Growing up, she and Neal were awarded gold stars on a poster board whenever they could demonstrate to their mother their command over nervousness, apprehension, intimidation or any emotions impeding success. Such feelings were to be buried along with their academic competition.

The phone in Jenna's jacket began to ring. She couldn't have been more pleased for the interruption.

"Raymond?" she asked.

"Jenna, what's going on? Is George with you?"

"Why?"

"Because some official from the National Transportation Board just announced it. They've found another body at the scene of the train wreck. Jenna, the reports are claiming the newly discovered body is George Wyatt."

Jenna jumped from her chair. "That's... impossible."

"Well, I'm looking at George's driver's license picture on my computer monitor as we speak! What is going on?"

"Raymond, I'm telling you, George has been with me this whole time..."

"Okay, that's what I wanted to confirm. So the officials back in the States must be mistaken. Obviously George can't be in two places at once, and you're saying he's with you?"

"No, Raymond, that's not what I'm saying."

She couldn't utter the next part without first taking a deep breath.

"I'm sorry I didn't call before, but George is dead. Wait, what I mean is, I don't have my hand on his body at the moment. But I heard him as he was dying, and I almost got there the moment he actually probably did in fact... die. But by the time I got there... Raymond, his body was gone."

Halfway through her explanation Jenna realized she wasn't making any sense at all. She tried to reverse the trend but that only made things worse.

"Apologies if I'm coming off as thick," Raymond said, "but... can you do me a favor? Pretend I've arrived well after the start of the movie and I need to be caught up with the entire plot."

The satellite phone in Jenna's jacket began to ring. "I'm so sorry. I know I'm not being very clear. But now I need to call you back in a few minutes..."

She hung up on him while simultaneously answering the sat phone...

"Carl, you asshole! I can't believe you killed him! I'm coming after—"

"Jenna, this is not Carl."

She recognized the voice.

"Then where is he?" she asked her father.

"He's nearby. And he's fully aware that I'm calling you; I thought it was best if we all meet up and discuss this situation in person..."

"George is dead, *Marcus*. Because of you and Carl. So what are we meeting for—to discuss the details of his funeral?"

"You say George is dead, but none of us actually saw what happened to his body. Right there, that should tell you two things—everything you've grown up believing has obviously inadequately prepared you for this mo- ment. And second, you and I need to set our Daddy and Daughter issues aside; clearly we're facing bigger problems. Now, it may not seem like it, but we all have the same goal in mind."

She noticed he spoke really fast, without taking a breath. As if he was concerned that, at any moment, she would hang up.

Jenna said, "Where do you want to meet?"

"Can you safely make it to the Mahane Yehuda Market?"

"When?"

"In two hours? No, let's say 8 a.m."

Jenna didn't react to the time. All she could think about was how her own father was either baiting her into a trap... or how she would spring her own trap and kill him and Carl both.

"Jenna, are you still there?"

"Yeah, that's fine. 8 a.m. Mahane Yehuda Market."

She was taking the phone away from her ear to hang up when she heard her father say, "Wait, one more thing—you should bring the priest. I want

Carl to meet him. Believe me, it will serve a purpose. There is no doubt we'll all have much to talk about. But I suggest we stay focused on the matter confronting us because—"

Jenna ended the call. She felt like a rebellious teenager doing it, but she couldn't resist. She looked over and saw Olsen staring at her. She sat back down in her chair. Hadn't realized she had gotten up.

"Who was that?"

"Actually, Father, that was my... father. It turns out he knows you and I are a team. And he says he wants to meet you. Before you commit, there are a few things you should know. People refer to him as Marcus, but my father's real name is Gordon Grant. And besides seeing that name on some postcards a few times a year, he's really had no connection whatsoever with me through pretty much all my life. But, in the last twenty-four hours... I've learned that he's completely involved in everything you and I are now up against."

Olsen reached over to grab Jenna's hand, but she snatched it back before he could lay a finger on her.

"Sorry, Father, I'm in no mood for anyone offering me any... comfort. But I *would* like another crack at expanding my original answer to your earlier question."

"Yes, Jenna, please. I'm listening..."

She was about to answer, but found that the words stuck in her throat. Jenna wiped her nose and started again. "I'm devastated by what happened to George. I didn't really know him, but I already miss him terribly."

She turned away from Olsen, once again to the Judean Desert. The whole landscape trembled like a mirage. She wiped her eyes and forced herself to look at Father Olsen.

"Very early in life I settled on an intellectual understanding of the way the world operates, which, over the years, never failed to... comfort me. It goes something like this: we live in a world where birth, life, death and all the small and large details filling in those categories are not guided by a higher power. Therefore, spending any amount of time searching for an explanation about any particular event in your life is not only frustrating, but ultimately meaningless.

"However, in the last few days, extraordinary events—including what happened to my brother and... now what has happened with George—have all ended up challenging my comfortable understanding of the world. In fact, it has become such a challenge I've actually found myself doing something I've never been tempted to do in the past. For the first time in my life, I've been asking the question... why?"

CHAPTER 14

FINCHER KNEW HE COULDN'T GO BACK TO THE CAR. Carl's shooter would be waiting for him there. Besides, it wouldn't have done any good—the keys to the vehicle were on the dead snail, Reitz.

So the doctor ran from the amphitheater, first heading along the hillside, then up it. In the darkness the hill didn't seem as steep and challenging as it proved to be.

Though the climb was taxing, Fincher motivated himself by thinking about how wonderfully his donated heart was performing, rising to the task of helping him escape retribution.

Less than an hour later, the doctor made his way through the woods to the Jewish neighborhood of Arnona, a town of promenades, shopping malls, and nightclubs.

In the distance, he saw the luxury building towers of East Talpiot. So he had his bearings straight... at least geographically.

At one of the shopping malls, he checked his face in the stainless steel of an elevator. Carl had inflicted dozens of abrasions and cuts. More noticeable were the thick, bright-red marks wrapped around Fincher's neck—the outlines of fingertips, as if his throat were some sort of canvas Carl had used to leave an impression.

Newly formed and freshly burst blisters on his heels forced him to walk pigeon-toed across the parking lot of the mall. He tried to ignore the pain long enough to consider how he would handle the call to the envoy. Fincher wished he could mention nothing more about the meeting other than Carl's betrayal. But the doctor knew omission wasn't possible. Back at the amphitheater, after evading Carl's sniper, Fincher had glanced back to the stage before escaping into the forest, and he had seen a startling sight.

The Angel of Light had to be warned.

Standing at the edge of the parking lot, Fincher could see in the far distance the Old City, still alight but dimmed by the slate-blue sky preceding the sun. He took in the view as he held his cell phone gingerly against the side of his head, waiting for the envoy to answer his call.

"Colin?"

"Yes, sir, it's me..."

"Doctor, I'm so pleased you're still alive. I saw and heard all of what happened up until Reitz was killed. You need to get to the Balshem Medical Center immediately so we can talk..."

Then the Angel of Light hung up.

———

ON THE ELEVATOR RIDE UP, the doctor could think about only one thing: it had been decades since he had felt... vulnerable.

He had always been the one standing in a roomful of people who knew the names, backgrounds, and hidden histories of everyone else, except for him. No one knew his past, his secrets. The meeting at the Peace Forest changed everything. Now he was prepared to pay the price, so long as his punishment was death, not possession.

If he saw the slightest hint in the envoy's eyes that his time had come, the doctor would beg for a quick death, with no regard to whatever after-life awaited him. Anything was preferable to becoming a snail. The thought of some other presence sharing his head, running its sticky hands through all of his secrets and seeing him for everything he truly was, sickened him so much that even the possibility of possession almost deterred him from returning to the hospital to face the envoy.

The elevator opened to one of the top floors. The medical center administrators had been kind enough to grant the envoy one of their conference rooms to conduct business, so long as the earthquake victims were patients at the hospital. Fincher wondered how much longer Wolfenson would have the room, since only one of the nineteen remained alive.

He could hear voices from down the hall, which was packed with at least a dozen men wearing traditional Arabic headdresses and black bisht cloaks over white ankle-length thobes. Fincher recognized some of them as members of the Islamic Council. They had been a steady presence in the hospital since the earthquake victims first arrived, and now they were all waiting in the hallway for the Grand Mufti of Jerusalem, Adnan Fayyad, to conclude his meeting with the envoy.

Fincher saw through the open office door that the grand mufti, dressed in a brown business suit and sporting a red and white Fez hat with a black tassel, was embracing John Wolfenson. After they parted, they also exchanged a hearty handshake.

The council, led by the Grand Mufti of Jerusalem, a Sunni Muslim cleric, presided over all Islamic holy places in the country. It was the first time the doctor had a chance to see the grand mufti in person. Unlike the Islamic council members, Fayyad had not come when the victims first arrived. Perhaps he had thought the patients would have more time for him to make his first appearance.

Fincher slipped into another hallway office moments before the grand mufti and his council moved in unison toward the elevators. He did not want anyone in the entourage to raise an eyebrow at his battered appearance. The doctor was fully aware why the envoy was meeting with the Islamic council, and the subject was of great delicacy. The last thing he wanted was to be yet another setback in the envoy's grand plan.

Once the council had left, Fincher walked slowly down the long hallway. Just as he approached the conference room door, it opened. Fincher was surprised to see the envoy happily welcoming him in to take a seat. As Fincher sat down, Tanaka, the bodyguard assigned to the envoy, silently left the room and shut the door behind him.

"Good news, Colin. Adnan and his council have agreed to allow the eighteen deceased earthquake victims to be buried in the Bab Al-Rahma Cemetery." The envoy was talking while he moved around the conference table, and Fincher noticed a spring in his step.

The news from the grand mufti could have explained Wolfenson's upbeat spirit; one of their obstacles had just been eliminated. However, the doctor feared the dynamic energy was coming from a different source.

"That is very good news indeed, sir. What an amazing accomplishment."

"When I made the proposal last night to the grand mufti, he spoke about how Israeli officials might put up a fuss, but I assured him the worldwide focus on the earthquake victims would help those in Tel Aviv to fall in line."

The envoy stopped to drink some water before continuing.

"And I proved to be right. The transfer of the bodies from the hospital to the mortuary will occur in four hours. All that's left will be for us to transfer the bodies for the service when we are ready to make our move."

"Sir, you have worked out that part of the plan to perfection, but..."

"Oh, yes, I know, there are still things left to be done." He paused, as if giving Fincher a chance to say his piece.

"Sir, I just want to first apol—"

"No. I take all the blame. I want to say that at the outset so there are no misunderstandings. I assume all responsibility for the obstacles we're now up against. Not only did I underestimate the Landlord, I was the one who vouched for the loyalty of Carl, even after you warned me very clearly not to."

"Sir, it's not necessary for you to—"

"No, Colin, when I'm wrong, I need to be honest with myself, and especially honest with everyone working for me—I made a mistake."

He dropped his hand onto Fincher's shoulder and squeezed. The doctor felt the strength in his grip and realized the envoy was back to his old self.

"Now don't you worry, I will take care of Carl Saracen. I would love to promise that I will eliminate him with... just these hands." He slapped another hand down on Fincher's other shoulder, then squeezed, his fingers digging into the doctor's shoulder blades. "But these hands don't look like they've ever picked up anything more dangerous than a letter opener. So I better stick to neutralizing those who oppose me with the resources I'm more comfortable with, even though I never feel there's much sport to it."

Just when it felt like Wolfenson's fingers would burst through the fabric of Fincher's clothes and plunge into his flesh, the envoy let go.

Without missing a beat, he resumed his steady cruise around the conference table. "To be honest, I'm still not sure if what Carl did was truly a betrayal. Maybe he was just trying to kill you so he could get closer to me. Maybe it was all just a power play. In hindsight, I can hardly blame the man. It must have galled him every time he eyed his competition..."

"Sir, all I can say is I'm sorry for my—"

The envoy held up his finger, and Fincher knew enough to shut up.

"Doctor, I already told you I'm the one in this room who is going to be making all the apologies. And do you want to know why? It's because I'm the one who ends up proving the old adage; intelligence skips a generation. There's no other conclusion that I can draw when I'm the one who chose you to be my right-hand man, supremely confident that you would never hold back critical information that could jeopardize the contingent time I have here on this planet."

The envoy suddenly threw himself down in the chair right next to Fincher, and then rolled the chair so his face was just inches from the doctor. As he spoke, the envoy's breath steamed up Fincher's face, and the doctor could smell an odor of rot and decay that he had never noticed before.

"Here's a question—do you think the following would be a good topic for conversation? A man in possession of the missing Codex Gigas pages, who also happens to be the husband of the woman who's harvested heart saved your life, ends up coming to visit you on the same night he also survived a train accident... the very same train accident that you and I arranged. Hmmm... What do you think?"

Fincher dropped his head in shame.

"I know what you're thinking. When it's laid out like that it just sounds so obvious, but then imagine how it must sound when some idiot is calling this obvious contrivance a fucking Black Swan!"

Wolfenson grabbed a coffee cup from the table, stood up, and hurled it across the room. It smashed into a large crystal menorah, which shattered so loudly that, seconds later, Tanaka came running through the door, weapon drawn.

Fincher, now standing, motioned to the bodyguard that everything was all right. Wolfenson silently affirmed the same, and the bodyguard retreated from the room.

The doctor was staring at the broken crystal when Wolfenson said, "Don't worry too much about the damage. The menorah was a gift to the hospital from Patricia and me."

The envoy plopped himself back down in his chair. When he spoke again he sounded more conciliatory, like he was ready to move past the whole episode.

"Colin, all you had to do is tell me what happened. Then I would have known the Landlord was engaged, and we could have accelerated our plans."

"Yes, sir, I know you're right. But I was scared I would lose your ear if you knew George Wyatt was more than just what he appeared to be."

The envoy leaned forward. "What do you mean?"

"Sir, last night, he didn't die. At least I didn't see him die. George Wyatt simply vanished."

Wolfenson froze, lost in thought, staring off into space. "What about Carl?" he asked.

"I don't know, sir. I stabbed him in the leg before he could kill me. And then one of his marksmen tried to—"

Wolfenson stood up, and Fincher stopped talking.

"No, doctor, I'm asking, do you think Carl was working with this... George?"

"I don't know. Possibly."

The envoy rushed toward the office door and threw it open. Immediately Tanaka was beside him.

"Get Patricia's guard on the line."

Tanaka whipped out his satellite phone, hit a button, and waited for her guard at the ICU to answer.

But there was no answer.

The envoy fell back against the wall, dejected, as Fincher and Tanaka raced toward the elevators.

———

ALL THE MEDICAL EQUIPMENT in the room was so loud, she didn't hear him approach. He tapped her arm gently, hoping he wouldn't startle her.

"Carl..."

"Hey, Pat, how are you doing?"

She instantly teared up. Then just as quickly, she wiped away the tear as if it were something to be ashamed of.

"He's the last one..."

"Yes, I know."

She turned back to the last remaining earthquake victim. Carl recognized him. This man in the bed was Omar Sheikh Kashmiri, the Face of Destruction, also known as OSK.

"I'm sorry," Carl said.

Patricia might have heard him, but it was hard to tell. She seemed lost in thought as she stared at the man, who had no color to his skin, no muscle around his bones, and a disfigured face from the large stone that had killed him.

"I'm sorry, Patricia. About everything."

His words got her attention.

"Carl, what's wrong... ?"

"Can I possibly speak with you? Not here. But someplace private?"

She looked around for the bodyguard who had been watching over her, but didn't see him.

"I told Taylor to get some coffee," Carl said. "I told him I would take over for a while."

Patricia let go of the patient's hand and started to follow Carl out of the ICU. But under the bright lights of the recovery room, it was impossible for her not to notice his limp... and the blood drops trailing behind.

"Carl, is that... your blood?"

He turned, and intentionally winced. "Yes. That's one of the reasons I need to talk to you." He then turned and started walking again, hoping she would follow.

CARL LED HER TO A SUPPLY CLOSET next to the ICU's scrub sink. He shut the door as soon as she walked in.

"Listen, Patricia, there's not a lot of time, so I have to just come out and say it. And what I have to say is going to be a shock. First of all, your life is in danger..."

She looked confused, but not scared.

"Patricia, you're a target."

Now she took a nervous step toward the door, but Carl reached out and grabbed her hand.

"Let me tell you why. You were smart enough from the very beginning to see through their lies. You should feel proud. I bet some people even tried to make you feel like you were crazy. I'm glad you ignored them, because it turns out you were right. I had the same feelings, but it took me much longer to figure it all out."

"What are you talking about?"

"Pat, everything you originally thought about John was right. He's not your husband."

"What... ?"

"During the peace ceremony at the Western Wall Plaza, your real husband was attacked, and he ended up having a near-death experience. It was during those few seconds between life and death that your husband was possessed by a demonic entity. The man who woke up in the hospital... was not your husband. The man who says he's John Wolfenson is not your husband."

She started to cry, but Carl could tell she was still listening.

"I told you already I was fooled by whatever had taken over the envoy, and that's why I kept doing what I was asked to do. But then last night I started asking questions... and they tried to kill me." Carl tapped his leg. Pat gasped, and Carl gripped her hand and pulled her closer.

"It was Fincher who tried to kill me. He's the one helping whatever has taken over your husband's body. But the most important thing you need to understand is that you are very special to them."

She stopped crying long enough to ask, "Why?"

Carl used his other hand to gently touch her abdomen.

Patricia screamed.

He tried to muffle her, but she lashed out, as if hitting a punching bag her therapist had given to her to vent all her frustrations. He grabbed her, hugged her. Kept her there till all she could do was sob.

"Pat, there's not much time. If you don't do exactly what I say, they won't just kill you, they will keep you alive only long enough for you to give birth to that thing's baby, and then... you will be discarded like a piece of trash."

She was still sobbing hard into his chest. Carl couldn't be sure whether she had heard a word he'd said. But he also knew he was probably running out of time.

"Pat, you want to know how I finally figured out he isn't the real John? Because I mentioned the story about the baseball glove. He didn't know what I was talking about. He knows some things, but he really, truly does not understand the special bond you had with your son."

His words only made her cry harder, but Carl also hoped it was enough to push her off the ledge, right into his arms.

"Pat, you need to trust me now. I'm the only one who can get both of us out of this hell. Will you do that? Will you trust me? Will you let me take you away someplace where you will be safe?"

As soon as he felt her chin nod into his chest, he hit the button on his cell phone and alerted Loder.

———

AS THEY WERE RIDING ON THE ELEVATOR down to Intensive Care, Fincher told Tanaka to give up on getting ahold of Taylor, the bodyguard assigned to Patricia.

"Right now, you need to call hospital security and alert them to shut down all exits."

Tanaka knew the doctor was right and speed-dialed the medical center's security station.

"You need to tell them there is a kidnapping attempt on Envoy Wolfenson's wife, and then you need to give them the description of Carl Saracen. He's the man attempting to kidnap Patricia Wolfenson."

"What?" Tanaka asked. Someone in hospital security picked up his call, but he covered the mouthpiece and ignored it. "Are you serious? My boss is attempting to kidnap the envoy's wife?"

"Tananka, would I say such a thing if it weren't true? Every second you wait could be the difference in losing Patricia."

Tanaka took a deep breath, then began by telling the head of security to shut down all exits of the hospital because someone was attempting to kidnap Envoy Wolfenson's wife. He was about to give the name and description of his boss, but the elevator doors opened. Tanaka sprinted toward the ICU as if he were competing in the Olympics.

The best Fincher could manage was a pigeon-footed jog. By the time he arrived at the ICU, there was no sign of Patricia, Carl, or even Tanaka. But Fincher did spot something unusual as he looked through the glass divider of the ICU.

Blood drops.

More than a few near OSK's bed.

Fincher followed the trail to a supply closet where he found a small red puddle and two sets of footprints. The doctor surmised Carl and Patricia must have talked there.

He followed another trail of blood drops and diminishing tracks, which went from the ICU and ended at the hospital's service elevators. That's where the doctor was standing when Tanaka caught up with him.

"I found Taylor. He was in the men's room, still unconscious. Whoever attacked him knew what he was doing. There were no signs of a struggle."

"What about hospital security?" Fincher asked.

"I just got off the phone with them. They have all the exits sealed, but so far no sign of Ms. Wolfenson... or Mr. Saracen."

The doctor stared at the last drop of blood Carl had left behind before boarding the elevator with Patricia. Fincher had managed to wound the son of a bitch, but not seriously enough to knock him out of the game.

Since Fincher didn't have family, or anyone he really cared about, he had to acknowledge a blind spot when it came to taking seriously the possibility that all of Carl's actions were motivated by the love of his son. And yet, if that was not the motivating factor, Fincher believed there was only one other option—*Carl really thinks he can take down the Angel of Light.*

CHAPTER 15

"ENVOY, SIR, have I made it too restricting?"

Wolfenson attempted to escape from the masking tape binding his ankles and arms.

"No, this feels about right."

"Sir, how long before you take possession?"

"Shortly after you reach the ICU, you'll see the process begin."

Fincher nodded. Since he had no more questions, he slammed shut the trunk of the BMW SUV.

DR. FINCHER STOOD AT THE ICU GLASS, staring in at the nineteenth and final earthquake victim as he opened his eyes.

OSK.

One of the world's deadliest terrorists.

Now host to the Angel of Light.

The sudden change in the patient's vital signs alerted the lone nurse working the floor. She notified the doctor on call, then rushed into the ICU—only to discover the patient standing right next to his bed, disconnected from the monitoring wires and intravenous feed.

OSK smiled in an attempt to calm the traumatized nurse, but his smile looked perverse on a severely bloated and ravaged face.

JOHN OPENED HIS EYES and saw only darkness.

He took a cleansing breath, then released a trembling air of relief. At least this darkness felt tangible, real. Quite different than what he had been experiencing for what seemed like an eternity.

He focused his efforts on breaking through the masking tape shackling his ankles and wrists.

A beeping sound grabbed his attention.

John listened, hoping to determine the source of the noise.

Suddenly, a shaft of bright light caused his eyelids to shut in response. He tried to overcome the instinct, blinking repeatedly until his eyes could adjust. He desperately wanted to identify the man standing above him.

"Where am—"

The man slapped a strip of masking tape over his mouth. Then whoever it was slammed the trunk.

John Wolfenson, once again, was left alone in the dark.

———

DR. FINCHER DROVE the BMW SUV east on Highway 31, heading toward the small township of Arad, seventy miles south of Jerusalem.

He was personally behind the wheel as a result of Carl's actions. Patricia's abduction had prompted the envoy to forego the use of Carl's security team in any capacity. Even turning them into snails was not an option.

Though the Angel of Light did not believe Carl's ultimate aim by kidnapping his wife was to stop his mission, he no longer was willing to take any chances. All it would take was a simple phone call from Carl to Israeli authorities and suddenly all of his men would be security risks, liabilities to their operation.

After the envoy made his decision, Fincher immediately contacted other members of the Red Veil. They all responded faithfully, drawing upon their resources to provide trusted emergency manpower. The problem was reinforcements would not arrive until the next morning, too late to help with the operation the envoy had already put in motion. Everyone Fincher contacted apologized for their inability to react faster, but expressed their shock and concern that their services were necessary so soon after the Angel of Light's arrival.

Arad was located on the border of what is considered a no man's land in the Middle East. Fincher stared out the car window at the passing scenery.

The doctor could not remember a time in his life when the surrounding landscape had ever influenced his mood or thoughts. And yet in this one case, he was forced to admit the harsh, desolate desert he was driving through might be an example of "expressive projection."

In his research he had confirmed a common thread amongst all psychopaths: eventually their world becomes smaller and smaller... and less populated.

Repeated aberrant behavior functions as a strong deterrent to prolonged intimate relationships with psychologically stable people. Compounding the challenge, the pathologically circuitous brain patterns in the psychopath trigger daily compulsive efforts to achieve complete personal isolation.

The doctor tried to tell himself there was a very powerful, intelligent entity sharing the car with him, that even though it was playing musical shells, it was still very much a partner in his journey. But Fincher was finding it hard to nail down the solace contained within the situation.

Outside the car window, the world stretched on for miles and miles of nothing but dust, while inside the vehicle, the interior felt like it was slowly closing in on him, as if the hand-stitched leather would eventually envelop and smother him.

Despite the ragged breathing from two nearby bodies, Fincher began to believe he would die all alone.

———

"SIR, WE'RE CROSSING THE CITY LIMITS of Arad. Is there a specific address we need to go to?"

The doctor's words stirred Omar Sheikh Kashmiri from his slumber in the passenger seat.

"I wish there was, doctor. Our best bet is to drive to the other side of town, and then take the first dirt road heading east. We will be looking for what I believe should be an encampment somewhere adjacent to the Red Sea."

Not only did Fincher find it disconcerting to hear the Angel of Light speak with an entirely different voice, the doctor believed every one of his words sounded tentative and tired.

"You have no more details than that, sir?"

"I'm afraid I don't. I'm drawing from the memories of this sorrowful soul, and he hasn't seen our contact in more than a few years. But I trust the people we seek won't be too far from where I'm directing you."

"Sir, if you don't mind me asking... how can you be so sure?"

"Because, Colin, the man we seek is a Bedouin, not a gypsy."

CHAPTER 16

S HE AND FATHER OLSEN left the Mount Zion Hotel and took the Jerusalem Light Rail to Mahane Yehuda. Jenna's satellite phone rang a few seconds after they stepped off the tram.

"We'll meet you both at Blatts Deli on Eitz Chaim Street..."

Before she could say anything, her father hung up. Jenna wondered if it was payback, but she was more concerned about his use of the word "both." Was he just assuming she had brought Father Olsen?

Or were they being watched?

THEY ENTERED EITZ CHAIM STREET from some other street named Afarsek, Hebrew for *peach*. In the late 1920s, British Mandate authorities had covered this section of the Mahane Yehuda Market with a permanent ceiling.

Jenna knew the shuk's busiest times were on Thursdays and Fridays when shoppers were preparing for Shabbat. But even on a normal afternoon, the hustle and bustle made it almost impossible for someone searching for a particular destination.

After a fruitless search Father Olsen approached a man selling peppers, and asked for directions. Before the vendor could respond, his Labrador started barking at the priest. Olsen tried to lean in and calm the canine, but it only snapped at him, then began to howl. Jenna grabbed Olsen by his sleeve and pulled him away. She could see he was uncomfortable with what had happened, but then his eyes narrowed and he pointed behind her. "I think I see it."

BLATT'S DELI WAS A CORNER ESTABLISHMENT where customers could accommodate their need for food and their hunger to people-watch. On display was a seemingly endless variety of food, from slices of beef shawarma and fish, to thirty different cheeses.

Near the glass display cases, dozens of high tables and bar stools flowed out into the street. Jenna knew Marcus had chosen the place specifically because she and Alan would feel safe in an open area with steady foot traffic.

Her father met them at the entrance of the deli and led the way to a table he had staked out earlier by purchasing a cup of coffee and a sandwich.

"I don't see Carl," Jenna said.

"He'll be here."

"I don't understand. Did he have something more important going on?" She purposely projected combativeness. Not that it wasn't too far off from the way she really felt.

"Of course not," Marcus said. "You know what it can be like moving around in this city. He's just running late."

Jenna made a point of scrutinizing her surroundings. She wanted her father to be fully aware she took nothing for granted.

"If this were a trap, Jenna, you would already be dead. But then, why would I kill you both when I just went to all the trouble of saving your lives?"

Marcus turned to Father Olsen. "Obviously our paths recently intersected, Father, but we haven't been formally introduced. My name is Marcus Spandel." He held out his hand.

The priest didn't hesitate shaking her father's hand enthusiastically, as if Marcus held a donation check to the Catholic Church.

"That was really smooth... Dad. Seriously, I'm impressed with your attempt to come off as a completely open and charming individual. But wouldn't it be far more interesting if you dropped the façade and told Father Olsen your real name?"

Marcus shut his eyes, clearly embarrassed. She took special satisfaction in his response to her remark.

When he opened his eyes, they were directed straight at his daughter. "Jenna, Marcus Spandel *is* my real name. Gordon Grant was a name I created along with a fictitious background prior to meeting your mother."

She was so thrown off by her father's confession that her brain locked up. At least the constant sound of merchants shouting out their prices made her silence less awkward.

"Jenna, I'm sor—"

"No, you need to give me more than a few seconds to process what you just said."

She turned away from the table.

By the time she turned back to face her father, she had no idea how much time had gone by.

"There have been so many mysteries in the last few days it's a relief one of them is finally solved. All my life I've imagined all sorts of reasons why you ran out on us. I always gave you the benefit of the doubt. Told myself... you probably left to accomplish something bigger and better than just being a simple husband and a father of two in little old Occoquan, Virginia."

Father Olsen tried to get her attention, but Jenna brushed his hand away like she was shooing a fly.

"Now it turns out you've been a liar and a fake from the get-go, even before I was born. So the benefit of the doubt I was affording you? It ends now along with the mystery. But I still have questions. I guess I'll always have questions. Like what are you doing here? And where does the name Spandel come from? And what does it mean? I can tell you what it *doesn't* mean—'father who abandons family but comes back later to rescue them all.' It can't mean that because Neal is fucking dead!"

If Marcus had something to say, he chose not to say it. He and Jenna just stared at each other until a familiar voice emerged from the din.

"I trust the reunion is going well."

"Where have you been?" Marcus asked, clearly irritated.

"I'll explain in a moment," Carl replied. "But first there is something I need to say to this man over here..."

He threw his arms around Father Alan Olsen and gave the priest a big old bear-hug. When he eventually let go, Jenna saw tears in Carl's eyes.

"Father, I'm ashamed we've never met. I hope it's not too late to say how much I appreciate your valiant effort to save my son's life."

Jenna saw Olsen tearing up as well. Then the priest threw his arms around Carl.

She couldn't believe it.

Jenna had come to the meeting suspecting it was a trap. Now, looking around the table, she felt like a mouse being carefully lured in. And the three men hovering around her all had the smell of cheese on their fingertips.

CHAPTER 17

BEYOND ARAD LAY A LAND OF DESERT and dusty mountains, and the Red Sea. They drove for several miles on a dirt road until they came upon a dry river bed, what the Arabs called a *wadi*.

Directly in front of them, on the opposite side of the riverbed, was an impressive gathering of goat and camel-hair tents. The mobile village probably housed anywhere from one hundred to two hundred people. The uniformity and organization of the entire settlement ruled out a refugee gathering, but the evident lack of modern necessities, like running water, electrical generators, and even portable toilets, also ruled out a sponsored archeological dig.

Fincher saw a few trucks, but they were outnumbered by several dozen camels and goats in makeshift pens. The doctor was fairly certain he was looking at what the Israeli government referred to as a "dispersal," an illegal settlement by the indigenous Bedouin.

"I'm drawing from this soul that any vehicle not immediately recognizable might be greeted rudely," said the Angel of Light, speaking through OSK.

The doctor parked about a half mile from the tent village and switched off the engine.

"Okay, sir, how do you propose we handle this?"

"I suggest you proceed across the *wadi* on foot. When you locate Hadji Hassanat, do whatever is necessary to make sure he accompanies you back to our car, where I will be waiting."

THE FIRST MAN FINCHER ENCOUNTERED wore a kuffiyeh, and a white, ankle-length Galabia robe more traditional in Egyptian Bedouin. When the camel caretaker alerted the encampment to their visitor, the doctor quickly discovered that more or less all of the people in the tent village wore the Galabia. Within seconds he was surrounded by forty to fifty mostly male Bedouin.

Though Fincher understood this was not a terrorist camp, or even a den of thieves, he knew the camp earned its money in phosphate exploration.

The sea once flowed here, and the terrain, because of its gentle highs and semi-confined lows, had collected nutrient-rich detritus, and microbial mats in suitable redox conditions. Given time, bioturbation, and currents, phosphorite strata had formed. This Bedouin camp made a living scouting the desert for phosphate deposits, which would eventually be mined and used to make everything from agricultural fertilizers, toothpaste, food additives, and even bombs.

So like any other modern commercial company interested in protecting intellectual property, this Bedouin tribe was no doubt sensitive to strangers who might be spying on their activity.

Though it took some time, Fincher convinced the men that he was not there to steal secrets. Although he did not know how he had convinced them, because no one seemed to understand or speak English. All Fincher could do was repeat the name Hadji Hassanat. Everyone seemed to recognize the name, but no one left in an effort to locate the man.

Finally, out of impatience, Fincher withdrew a Beretta pistol from a shoulder holster. The Bedouin men backed up, and the doctor marched to the center of the encampment, where he fired the weapon twice into the air. After a minute, he fired three more times.

Hadji Hassanat did not appear... at least not that instant.

TWENTY MINUTES LATER, a caravan of five trucks sped into the encampment. The lead pick-up stopped a few feet from Fincher. A thick cloud of desert dust swept past the doctor, and by the time he cleared his eyes, Hadji Hassanat stood across from him.

The Bedouin wore a Pakul hat, but he was one of the few people in the tent village not wearing a Galabia. He wore jeans and a black leather jacket. Strapped across his expansive waist, a tool belt accommodated various excavating tools, plus a serrated bowie knife, nearly a foot long.

"Israeli?" Hassanat asked.

"American. My name is Dr. Colin Fincher."

"Were you the one shooting the gun?"

Hassanat spoke English with a thick Arabic accent, but his enunciation was accurate and precise. Fincher knew the Bedouin wasn't formally educated, but Hassanat clearly had not spent his entire life isolated in the desert.

"Yes, I'm sorry," Fincher said. "I've been sent to find you, and I couldn't wait any longer for you to come back."

"You Americans, always slave to the time. Maybe you should pay less for your watch, and then you'll feel more in control."

Fincher made sure to laugh at his joke.

"So who sent you?"

The doctor wiped the smile off his face and cleared his throat. "Your brother, Omar Sheikh Kashmiri."

Immediately, Hassanat began marching back to his truck.

Fincher started after him. "Mr. Hassanat?"

"My half-brother... is dead."

The doctor grabbed him by the arm, which clearly was a mistake. The Bedouin wheeled around so fast it was hard to believe he had time to draw the knife from his tool belt. The blade of it flashed just inches from Fincher's face.

"No, Mr. Hassanat, your half-brother is alive. He has come a long way to see you."

The Bedouin lowered his knife.

"Can I take you to him, sir?"

Hassanat looked down at the doctor's chest. Slowly, Fincher withdrew the gun from the holster underneath his jacket. He then placed the weapon in the mud-encrusted hand of the Bedouin.

———

A LIGHT LAYER OF DUST stuck to the perspiration covering the doctor's skin, creating something he once called a "sweat cake" when he was growing up in Tucson, Arizona. Sixty minutes since he first left the SUV, Dr. Fincher was crossing the *wadi* again, and this time he was not alone.

"You claim my brother has returned from the dead?"

"I don't just claim it, Mr. Hassanat, I swear to it. And he has come back with the sole purpose of showing you his miracle."

They were approaching the BMW when Hassanat decided to stop. "Dr. Fincher, do you know who I am? What I'm still capable of doing, given the right circumstances?"

Fincher assumed the Bedouin was referring to his military background, and his lineage. He knew Hassanat's grandfather had fought with the Turks against the British during World War I. And years later his father, Zayed Hassanat, like most indigenous Bedouins, had fought another battle for citizenship; but after a bitter defeat, Zayed, like his ancestors, was forced to become a nomad. For years he wandered the deserts of the Middle East until his son Hadji Hassanat was born, an official Arab citizen in Israel.

When he was of age, Hadji served proudly in the Israeli military. But after his discharge, and despite his success in phosphate exploration, rumors of his involvement in terrorist activity damaged his reputation. His affiliation with his half-brother, whom Zayed had fathered while living in Egypt, did nothing to help his official denials. The fact that the Israeli government never made a move to imprison or expel Hassanat only led to more unsubstantiated claims; the most popular one detailed how the Mossad came to prove that Hassanat was indeed a terrorist, but did nothing to stop him because they also discovered he was working for their side.

"Yes, sir, I'm very much aware of your... résumé."

His answer seemed to satisfy Hassanat, and the Bedouin followed him the rest of the way to the BMW.

Fincher approached the passenger side of the vehicle, threw open the door, and stepped back as if he had just ripped away the sheet, uncovering a new work of art.

Omar Sheikh Kashmiri waited several moments before stepping out of the car. He was wearing a traditional grey thobe, but a surgeon's cap covered the top of his head and several layers of operating masks served as a veil to the bottom half of his face. Only his eyes were visible for Hassanat to observe.

The big, burly Bedouin was clearly transfixed, and though his heart wanted to believe, his skeptical brain clearly kept him from embracing the figure standing before him as his half-brother.

OSK reached behind his head and untied the masks, revealing the hideous injury that had led to his death.

The Bedouin flinched at the sight, and then gave way to tears.

"Yes, brother," OSK said in Arabic. "You can see with your own eyes what fate has done to my face. But please, don't despair. It is the price I paid to escape death. I am the same man, even the same boy who can still hear the music you played on your rababah. And if need be, I will be able to run quickly like we once did to chase after our father's goatherd, which always fled when they, too, heard your music."

Fincher had no idea what the Angel of Light, speaking through OSK, had said. But his words caused the proud, resilient, and rough Arabic nomad to snatch his Pakul hat from atop his head and toss it aside. Hassanat pulled his half-brother into a hug.

Dr. Fincher was at first thrilled by the success of their deception, but then moved quickly to separate the two. He was concerned that, in his fragile state, the Angel of Light would be smothered if not removed from the fleshy clutches of his half-brother.

CHAPTER 18

THEY HAD BEEN TALKING for over an hour and had gotten nowhere. Carl didn't trust Jenna. And she didn't trust anyone else, especially Carl.

"If you're not willing to reveal the content of the Black Pages, how can we possibly work together?" Carl said.

"Who says we need to work together? One of my fears is that I give you the content I've translated, and all you end up doing is using it to your advantage."

"How is that possible? I'm assuming you sought out Father Olsen because the Black Pages involve some kind of religious rite, or exorcism. Since I'm not a priest, how could I take advantage?"

"Come on, Carl, we both know you have ways of making others do what you're not available to achieve yourself. But just for the sake of argument, let's say you're right and the Black Pages did contain an exorcism. So then why do you care what I know?"

"Because an exorcism is not the only content in the Black Pages, and we both know it. There is coded information about the Angel of Light's plan. And if you were more open about it, we could all work together to formulate a way to stop him."

"Stop him?!" She couldn't help but laugh. "I'm sorry, but from everything I've learned, you and... *Spandel* over here were the ones who embroidered the word 'welcome' in the welcome mat. And just because I haven't broached the subject, don't assume I've dropped the idea that at least one of you, maybe both of you are still working for him."

Marcus stopped Carl just as he was about to retort, and turned to his daughter himself. "Jenna, what would it take for you to believe we have the same goal here?"

"For starters? Some facts. Carl knows way more than he's letting on. When he arrived, the first thing he did was throw his arms around Father Olsen. Which suggests to me he sincerely thinks redemption is right around the corner."

Carl shook his head in disbelief, but didn't offer a word to contradict her.

"Then after that shameless public display of affection, Carl put his phone down on the table and has been monitoring it ever since. Whatever he's waiting for is so important, he didn't want to trust he'd miss the ring over all this noise. Whatever game he's playing, I assure you, he believes he's the only player worthy of playing it. And despite what he has said over the last hour, he wants to keep it that way."

Marcus looked over at Carl to gauge his reaction, but Jenna wasn't finished.

"But I don't care whether either of you believe me because if Carl doesn't start opening up about what he knows, Father Olsen and I are out of here."

Jenna then reached into her coat and pulled out the satellite phone. "And I'm tossing this in the garbage on our way out. Which means the next time we see either one of you, we'll assume it means you've come to kill us. And we'll be prepared to do whatever it takes to survive."

Carl snorted in derision. "If you two think you can go up against him alone, you'll die alone. Is that what you want? Father Olsen, I'm looking at you!"

"Shut up, Carl!" Marcus had been staring at the smartphone on the table when he suddenly spoke up. "The fact is I don't trust you either. Just so you know. If they die, I die with them."

Despite the look of bemusement on his face, Carl was clearly shocked at the direction the meeting had taken. At a certain point Jenna was wondering which was going to last longer: his look of bemusement or his silence.

"Fine. I will give up everything I know if it will establish goodwill and demonstrate my stated goal for all of us to work together as a team."

Carl then took a deep breath and peeked at his smartphone again before launching into an attempt to rally the troops. "Get ready because I'm going to spray it like a lawn sprinkler and hope you can all keep up. First off, eighteen of the nineteen earthquake survivors have died..."

"Please, Carl, tell us something we don't know," Jenna interjected.

"The nineteenth survivor is Omar Sheikh Kashmiri, the terrorist known as OSK." He sneered at Jenna for interrupting, but she maintained a distrustful glare. "I was not with the envoy when he resurrected OSK, so I have no clue why he was chosen."

"Pardon me for interrupting," Father Olsen said. "You meant to say *rescued* rather than *resurrected*, correct?"

"No, Father, I believe OSK was dead and the Angel of Light... resurrected him."

Jenna could see how much the information stunned the priest. Glassy and unfocused, his eyes started drifting away from the table.

"Now whatever the envoy has earmarked as his ultimate target, I'm betting it's manmade because I'm speculating he's either unable or not allowed to destroy anything that wasn't created by humans."

"Wait," Marcus said, "you just said *manmade*, but a second ago you claimed he resurrected a terrorist. A person isn't manmade, so which is it?"

"I can see this is going to be tough giving everyone just the highlights. Look, there are limits to what he can do to achieve his goals, but I never felt I came close to witnessing his best stuff. Using people is far from his best weapon, but it is his weapon of choice. He'd deny what I'm about to claim, but he'd be lying. He believes having humans do his dirty work is especially insulting to God."

"So you're confirming that he can possess human beings, even ones that have died, but he can't directly kill them?"

Jenna was surprised to hear the question coming out of Father Olsen's mouth. She definitely thought the priest had checked out for the rest of the conversation. But then she recognized why the question vexed him. Olsen probably still wondered why Satan hadn't just killed him when he had the chance.

"Correct, he can't directly kill another human being. Even possessing someone has limitations. He can't order a possessed person to do whatever he wants as if he were controlling a robot. However, there is one huge exception..."

"Wait," Jenna said, "are you implying that no one had any direct control over Neal? That somehow Satan, or one of his demons, simply *inspired* my brother to drive a car, with both of us inside it, directly into the path of an oncoming train? He was just... *okay* with killing hundreds of innocent people, is that what you're saying?"

Carl took a few moments to choose his words carefully, since the question had come from Jenna. "Well, I should reaffirm that there is a demonic possession involved in each of these situations, but, yes, there are... constraints, similar to the limits faced during post-hypnotic suggestion. So when Neal drove his car into the train, the action had to be within the host soul's moral capacity. Otherwise Satan would have ended up coloring outside the lines."

Jenna refused to accept Carl's answer. She believed he had cooked up the facts for a reason, but she couldn't figure out his angle. So she bit her tongue. She would wait until Carl was done divulging everything he was willing to reveal, and then she would enjoy going after him with a carving knife.

"Again, I believe there is an exception," Carl continued. "And when the Angel of Light first arrived, this one huge exception ended up dictating his agenda. From the get-go he was focused on becoming an intimate member of the international political and financial hierarchy, which was paramount."

"Sorry," Father Olsen interrupted, "you said there was an exception to the powers you outlined, but then you swerved into talking about his agenda... and I must have missed the segue. Can you please slow down?"

"Father, let me explain it this way—if he is part of the group he seeks to destroy, then he has... let's just say less limits to his powers. I say *less* because I don't want to come off as if I know any specific details to what he can and cannot do."

"I do apologize, but I'm still not following. Forget the word *less*. Let's go with the word *more*, as in... he has *more* powers—and under what circumstances?"

"Alan, it's the difference between being invited to the party and being a party crasher," Jenna said. "Being *invited* allows Satan *more* power. It's why he was able to possess the oldest children of the members of the Red Veil. Because he was invited to the club. Am I correct, gentlemen?" Though her question was directed at both Carl and Marcus, only her father looked away in shame.

Carl didn't show any embarrassment at all. "Yes, that's exactly what I was trying to say. An invitation is a key factor in his level of ability and... the weapons he has available to him."

"Are you finished?" Jenna asked.

"No, I'm not," Carl quickly answered. "When he arrived, the Angel of Light had two primary missions. First, establish a Kingdom on Earth so he could challenge the Kingdom in Heaven." Carl picked up his phone and started to click some of the keys as he continued. "Second, was to produce an... heir to his new Kingdom on Earth. Now I trust you all have been keeping up when I tell you the only acceptable way to keep his effort within the rules was if the recipient of his seed invited him to plant it in her garden."

The words Carl used reminded Jenna of the eleventh quatrain:

From the seed he has planted
A slithering root will grow
The serpent will be watered from oceans of blood
And fertilized by the bones of the beasts

Carl set the phone back down on the table for everyone to see. The screen displayed a digital photograph of Patricia Wolfenson, staring into the lens with a troubled look on her face.

Jenna noticed that Marcus seemed particularly disturbed by the picture... and she had no idea why.

CHAPTER 19

ONCE MORE OVER THE *WADI* Fincher crossed, this time with a frail OSK and his thankful half-brother.

On the other side of the riverbed, the entire tent village—easily more than a hundred children, women, and men—fluttered as robes in a single wind. They seemed relieved to see their Bedouin leader return unharmed.

Hassanat waved, and they all waved back, and then the doctor watched as the people's relief shifted to curiosity and concern for the slight wisp of a man walking in his own veil of masks, and surgical skullcap.

After entering the encampment, Hassanat led Fincher and OSK to the largest tent. He opened the camel-skin flap and welcomed his brother inside.

Fincher tried to follow, but the Bedouin stopped him. He motioned to a couple of female followers standing nearby, and gave them directions in Arabic. They glanced at the doctor, nodded, and then both scuffled away.

Without another word, Hassanat disappeared into the tent, letting the flap fall behind.

Fincher had no choice but to stand embarrassed in front of the entire village. The group's attention was thankfully divided, showing intense concern for the proceedings in the tent, and a more novel interest in how Dr. Fincher fit into the puzzle.

About twenty minutes later, the two women Hassanat had previously tasked returned. They threw a rug down on the dirt in front of the doctor. On the rug, they carefully arranged two cups of hot drinks, a stack of pita bread with some olive oil, and a bowl of soup.

Fincher thanked them and sat down on the rug. Then the whole gathering watched as he drank and ate heartily. He had not eaten since last night and felt dizzy from hunger.

He tried one of the drinks but found the coffee too bitter, so he settled on the sweet herbal tea. He dipped the pita bread in the soup until he discovered meat in the broth.

The doctor eventually took a moment to address the crowd. "Delicious," he said, raising the bowl. "What is this in the soup?"

One of the women quickly replied. Fincher shrugged to show that he didn't understand Arabic. So someone else shouted out that it was goat.

The doctor smiled. "Yes, goat. Very good."

A few minutes after returning to his meal, Fincher looked up. The group's attention had been diverted.

The doctor rose from the rug, curious. Everyone had turned to watch as a woman—wearing no veil to cover her long, silky hair; wearing shorts, to flaunt her ankles and legs—moved toward them.

The woman held hands with a little blond girl, possibly her daughter, probably no more than eleven or twelve years old. The girl didn't wear any sort of veil either, but wore eye shadow and rouge.

The crowd parted for the woman and the girl as they approached, and at first it seemed the people parted out of respect. But then two men broke away from the group and blocked the two females from Hassanat's tent.

The older woman made an attempt to sidestep the guards, but they pushed her back. She immediately launched into a high-volume Arabic attack.

Hassanat poked his head out of the tent, clearly concerned for the woman. He spoke to her, and she spoke back, and suddenly Fincher was caught in the middle of enemy crossfire.

The Bedouin motioned for his guards to let the woman pass. She spoke to the little blond girl sweetly, and then let go of her hand to enter the tent alone.

Dr. Fincher checked the time on his watch and then resumed his seat. He was reaching across the rug for his tea when the young girl dropped down with him to partake of his spread.

"So you are with Omar?" she asked, without any trace of an accent.

"Yes, I am," Fincher said. He was looking around at the reactions of the other Bedouins. No one showed any sign of protest... or any kind of interest that the girl had sat on his rug.

"What is your name?" the doctor asked.

"Darshana."

"That's a pretty name."

"So is Colin."

Fincher was taken aback. But then he remembered giving his first name earlier, when introducing himself to Hassanat.

The girl grabbed the cup of coffee and took a drink.

"Who was the woman you were with? Your mother?"

"Her name is Noora," the girl said.

Having polished off the coffee, she tossed the cup on the rug. She then snatched up the bowl, which still held some soup, and a spoon clinking around the rim.

"She is the one who will decide whether your Omar is really who he says he is."

"I'm not sure what you mean, Darshana."

"I love the way you say my name. It sounds very different. Probably because you are very different from everyone else."

Dr. Fincher didn't know how to respond. The girl no longer looked as young as thirteen. Try as he might, he couldn't decide how old she looked.

"Who are you?"

"Colin, I know we just met, but when Noora swears her allegiance to the one you are calling Omar, we will all be together again very soon."

"Where are you from?"

"I was not born here, if that is what you mean. But I've lived in the desert for years. I think it's so beautiful."

She set the empty soup bowl on the rug and then leaned closer to Fincher. "I love it here because I can fuck or kill anyone I want."

Noise from the surrounding group failed to draw Dr. Fincher's attention. It took the sound of people emerging from the tent to finally pull him away from Darshana's eyes.

OSK, his half-brother, and Noora all stood in front of the tent, facing the inhabitants of the encampment. Fincher glanced at his watch. An hour had gone by... or had disappeared... since that tent had flapped shut.

He looked up.

Darshana had vanished.

Fincher sprang to his feet and searched around. He saw only a wall of expectant faces as Hassanat's people awaited Noora's judgment.

Hassant, before his tent, addressed the crowd in Arabic. They listened anxiously, and then broke out in applause. Hassant seemed very moved.

But then everyone quickly quieted down as OSK stepped up beside his brother. He stood there for several seconds, engaging the congregation with steely, almost condemning eyes.

Fincher had no idea what the Angel of Light was trying to achieve. He could only sense the unease enveloping not only Hassanat's people, but Hassanat himself.

Omar reached behind his head and untied the surgical masks, then removed the cap from his head.

People gasped, and many looked away. A few children began to cry. Omar stood there, almost defiantly forcing them to soak in the injury that had taken his life.

Finally, OSK veiled himself with the cap and surgical masks, and turned his back on everyone. Nobody in the gathering knew what to do. Even Hassanat was confused, and heartbroken to witness what his brother had done.

Only Noora decided to console the broken man. Her hand lit on his back, and she moved closer to see whether he was all right.

Fincher saw Noora's face contort, and the woman backed off. Not in disgust, but in awe.

OSK turned back around, let drop the surgical masks.

Now the gasps that swept through the gathering were of amazement. The children had stopped crying, and grown men started to weep in their place.

Where before OSK had been hideously deformed, he was now perfectly healed. No deep cuts or scars, nor even a scratch.

Hassanat raised his hands to touch his brother's cheeks, at first gently brushing the skin. But then Omar grabbed his hand and pressed it against his face to show that this flesh was real and could not be changed, even by the thick fingers of a nomadic warrior used to digging in the clay.

The Bedouin dropped to his knees before his brother, and in a wave, all of Hassanat's people fell to their knees as well. Except one. Darshana.

Fincher saw her standing in the distance, watching, but then the doctor lost sight of her as he, too, collapsed to his knees.

OSK started to speak, and everyone listened. He spoke in tongue, so the doctor could not understand the sermon, save for one Arabic word, one of the few he recognized from the media. "Shahids." In English it meant "witnesses."

It also meant "martyrs."

Dr. Fincher, dizzied, blacked out on the rug.

CHAPTER 20

HE WOKE UP SITTING in the passenger seat of the BMW SUV and Omar was driving. The terrorist's head was once again covered with medical garb, because, as Fincher could see, his mortal injury had returned.

"Sir, what is going on?"

"You fainted back at the encampment. I would say it was a combination of the heat and lack of sleep. Are you feeling well?"

Fincher sat up and looked out the window and realized where they were. "We've just driving out of Arad."

"Yes, back to Jerusalem. Take a look on the floor behind you."

The doctor turned to the back seat and saw on the floor a small sealed wooden crate, buried underneath a blanket.

"It's ten kilograms of Semtex."

Fincher turned back around, obviously unable to hide his disappointment, because the Angel of Light picked up on it.

"I must admit I was surprised as well. With all of his dealings with the government, you would assume Hassanat would be sitting on explosives bearing an Israeli thumbprint."

"That's not the only problem, sir. Ten kilograms will not be enough for what we discussed."

"Yes, I understand. And that is why I have decided to modify the plan. But I assure you, doctor, everything will still lead to the final outcome I described. We will be getting some help from my half-brother's people. Indeed Hadji seemed so inspired by my... miracle, I believe he will be participating himself in our effort."

OSK steered the SUV off the highway, into the desert. They drove a safe distance from any passing motorist or witness to what they were about to do.

The engine shot off.

Dr. Fincher moved to exit the car and open the trunk, but the Angel of Light stopped him.

"A word of caution, doctor. From here on out... do not underestimate anyone. The Landlord doesn't often take an active role in the events of this world, but when he does, he likes his actions to be worthy of his effort. Do you understand?"

"I think so, sir."

"You don't sound very confident, Colin. Please... speak your mind."

"My concern is... Carl. Because of my mistake, he knows the drop-off for the explosives."

"Don't you worry about Carl. After I reclaim possession of Envoy Wolfenson, *I* will take care of Carl."

"Very good, sir. I will leave it to more capable hands."

Fincher exited the car to give the Angel of Light a few moments alone. And for a few moments by himself as well. The doctor needed a chance to clear his head... and to think about what had happened back there, at the Bedouin dispersal.

———

FROM ALMOST THE FIRST MINUTE since their arrival, all Jenna could think about was walking out of the deli; so she found it ironic that after seeing the picture of Patricia, it was Marcus who grabbed the phone and stormed out.

"Excuse me," Carl said and immediately chased after him.

Jenna turned to Father Olsen for his reaction, but the priest got up, too, and followed closely behind Carl.

Marcus had skulked away to the open-air section of the marketplace. He stood yards away from two acoustic guitarists and a saxophonist playing jazz in front of a crowd of people who had gathered to listen.

The music was loud, but Jenna could distinctly hear Marcus talking to Carl.

"How dare you take her to my motel room without my knowledge? If this is your naked attempt to get me more involved in this battle, I resent that you even felt it was necessary."

"Marcus, I apologize for not getting your permission, but it was all spur of the moment. Your room is within a reasonable distance from where I believe I'll eventually need to take her."

"Take her where, Carl?" Jenna asked.

Marcus was surprised to see her and Father Olsen, but Carl didn't seem to mind their renewed assemblage.

"Look, Patricia is now under my care because I believe she is one of the keys to stopping the envoy."

"How did you get Patricia to come with you?" Marcus asked, as if he already knew the answer.

"What does that have to do with anything?"

Jenna watched as Carl stepped closer to Marcus, not so he could lower his voice, but so his words would have greater impact. The two men, despite the intimate proximity, showed no signs of awkwardness. Either they were lovers, Jenna thought, or family.

"Marcus, we helped cause this mess. If we're to fix it, we need to move right now because it's all going down. I didn't put her in your room to get you more involved. I put her there because I assumed you would demand to be more involved."

He didn't respond visibly or verbally, but Carl must have felt he got through to him because Carl stepped back, once more opening the conversation to include all four of them.

"When we were flying out of Aleppo, Dr. Fincher assigned me to secure a massive amount of explosives." He lowered his voice just below the music and said, "Explosives with an Israeli signature. Surely there could be only one reason for such a request. I bailed before fulfilling their shopping list, but I have no doubt the Angel of Light will find a way to acquire explosives on his own. But I also was betting his search would buy us some time to organize our opposition."

Carl turned to Jenna and Olsen. "He knows the Black Pages are still floating around, so he knows his own words can still be used against him. By this time Dr. Fincher would have felt compelled to inform him of some recent strange events, like a man who mysteriously vanished before his eyes. All of which I'm counting on will pressure him to execute his plan sooner rather than later.

"Why would that be a good thing?" asked Marcus.

"Because in his haste... perhaps he will make a mistake. Otherwise, without a misstep on his part, I assure you, no one will be able to stop him... including the four of us if Jenna decides to join forces."

All three men were now staring at her. Apparently Carl had finished going through everything he knew, and now Jenna was on the spot. They were leaving the decision on how to proceed entirely up to her.

After a few moments of contemplation, she started to voice her decision, but was forced to stop when the saxophonist from the group sauntered up to them, playing a solo. All four had to wait patiently and offer fake smiles until after the musician left. But the interruption had given Jenna an extra minute to reevaluate what she should do.

"He's going after the Temple Mount as his target," she said.

Carl stepped toward her, urgent and intense. "How do you know this?"

Her response was to first recite the tenth quatrain. *"His veiled plan calls for raising nineteen / And they will cast their sleepy eyes / On the most beautiful of jewels / Rebuilding a house on a shattered sacred stone."*

257

"'Beautiful jewel' clearly means the city of Jerusalem," said Father Olsen. "And 'Rebuilding a house on shattered sacred stone' must be referring to the rebuilding of the Jewish temple on the Temple Mount."

"And there are nineteen earthquake victims here in Jerusalem at this very moment, under Envoy Wolfenson's care," Jenna added. "Certainly that specific detail credibly pins the quatrain to present day events."

Carl nodded. "I agree with you both. The quatrain confirms my own theory. By destroying the Temple Mount and framing the Israelis, he is hoping to start a holy war between Jews, Muslims, and Christians."

"But why? What would a worldwide holy war prove?"

"Absolutely nothing," Father Olsen said, answering Marcus's question. "But according to the Bible, leveling everything on the mount clears the way to erect the third Jewish temple. Its completion will herald the Second Coming of Jesus Christ. Which, of course, will set in motion the final confrontation between the forces of the Lord and those who oppose Him."

"A death match between Satan and Jesus Christ, and the winner gets the gold belt while billions with ringside seats get eviscerated? Please, do you all really believe this is going to happen? Alan?"

"Jenna, I don't know," Olsen answered. "But I think it's clear the force we're up against certainly believes it."

Carl shook his head before turning to Marcus. "We always had different reasons for achieving our goals, but none of what we planned was supposed to be about destruction, possession and... death. It was always meant to be about reconciliation, peace, and heaven on Earth. And it still can be."

"How?" Marcus asked.

"By exorcising... AOL from the face of the Earth. When he calls me to get Patricia back, I will agree to meet him and we will do a swap. Then, once we have him within our grasp, we will stop him."

"Did you just say the word *swap*?" Jenna asked.

Carl's phone, which was still in Marcus's hand, began to buzz. He checked the screen, then looked up at Carl, clearly disturbed.

"Is it Ami?"

Marcus gave the phone to him, and Carl looked at the screen. Despite being visibly distraught, he had no trouble addressing everyone: "This is what I have been waiting for. A camera in my son's hospital room sends an alarm to my phone whenever Ami is... active."

He then turned the smartphone around so they could all witness the shocking confrontation back at the Monastery. The medical personnel were trying to deal with Carl's son, who was raging against the bed's leather restraints like a beast caught in the wild—soulless sunken eyes, bared teeth, and a frightening maze of raised veins gyrating like snakes under fine silk.

"This is the leverage AOL has over me. And this is why we will be discussing a *swap*. A discussion I expect shall commence at any moment—"

As if on cue, Carl's phone rang. Jenna was forced to give him credit. He didn't even pretend to hide his arrogance. Indeed, any sign of false modesty would only have made the rest of his moves in the last two hours suspect in her eyes. But if she had any lingering doubts about his sincerity, Carl erased them by putting the call on speakerphone so they all could listen in.

"Carl, I understand your son is having problems," Envoy John Wolfenson said.

"Yes, I'm watching him now. Obviously it is of great distress to see my son this way."

"Please, you're certainly smart enough to know by snatching Patricia you have forced me to respond aggressively."

"John, I want to assure you Pat is being well tended to. I hope my words still have some sway and might persuade you to ease back on whatever is happening to my own son, so that we can talk about the situation in a reasonable manner."

"Yes, I've proven my point and will do as you request... so long as you agree to listen to me, Carl, with an open heart."

"I'm listening, sir."

"Clearly having one of my followers possess your son was a mistake I now regret. Upon reflection I believe if I had simply given you my unconditional, undying loyalty, you would have given me yours. Am I correct?"

"Envoy, sir, I have never been one to buy into the predictive value in combat simulations. I'm of the mind that a lone bird flying over the battlefield can sometimes change everything."

"Are you suggesting it's too late for me to give you my unconditional and undying loyalty?"

Carl took a moment to look at the three people surrounding him. "Let's just say, sir, that the issue you raised is beside the point. Since your arrival most of your actions have revealed what you truly are—a dragon breathing fire over an already scorched earth."

"Really, Carl, is that the way you see me?"

"Don't take offense, sir. It's the very way I now see myself. I helped bring you here because I was convinced my efforts would justify everything I had done over all these years. You ended up being no more disappointing than anything else in my life."

"Yes, I now understand. Expectations can be a bitch."

"Sir, since two people we care about are in jeopardy, do you mind if I push forward to the negotiations?"

"Fine. Let me propose a transaction that I believe will mutually benefit both sides. I release your son from any further possession, and you return Patricia. Is that the deal you envisioned?"

"Indeed it was, sir. Where shall we meet?"

"How about the place you call the monastery? I would be surprised if you believed I wasn't already aware of its existence."

"I am forced to admit that I deluded myself into believing its existence, and certainly its location, remained a secret. However, I agree it is a good place for us to settle our business. When shall we meet?"

"Today. Perhaps 5 p.m.?"

"Yes, perfect. I will be awaiting your arrival, counting the minutes until we can get this disagreement behind us."

Jenna had been pacing back and forth, barely able to withstand the wait. "He's lying to you," she blurted the moment the call ended.

"Of course he is," Carl said. "But now we all know the exact time he's going to launch his grand plan."

CHAPTER 21

"WHY NOT JUST KILL Wolfenson if he's possessed?"

It was one of the last questions Jenna asked in the Mehane Yehunda Market, after they had already gone over the game plan to stop the Angel of Light.

"Because it would not solve the problem. It would only kick the can down the road," Carl replied. "Let's say we took a gun and shot John Wolfenson dead. The Angel of Light would simply possess someone else here on Earth and start the whole process over again. Only this time none of us would know who he possessed. However, if we stick to the plan... performing the specific exorcism rite from the Black Pages will prevent him from coming back for another thousand years, maybe forever."

Jenna accepted the answer, but it meant Plan A, Plan B, and the last ditch effort known as Plan C all ended with... an exorcism. Either she was the only one who saw this as a huge problem or anyone with a similar viewpoint was keeping it to themselves.

As they were splitting up, Olsen turned to Carl. "If it is ever possible, I would very much like to see Ami."

"Yes, of course, Father, I would love for you to see my son again. Right after we're done with all of this." He embraced the priest and said, "I know you can do this."

So the meeting concluded the same way it began, with Jenna feeling like the odd girl out. Unlike the rest of the group, she wasn't entirely convinced Father Olsen could do it.

AFTER THEY SPLIT OFF from Marcus and Carl, Jenna hailed a taxi. "We're going to the Western Wall Plaza," she said to the driver from the back seat.

"Wait, first we need to make another stop," Alan interrupted. To Jenna, he said, "I need my things." When she raised her eyebrow, the priest added, "So I can properly perform the rite."

That's when it hit Jenna how quickly the lack of sleep had caught up with her. Not only was she slow to comprehend the priest, but also her patience was wearing thin. She thought about the silliness of comic book superheroes who needed to dress up in spandex before saving the world, and couldn't help lumping in Catholic priests who needed their cassocks and Bible before performing an exorcism. Jenna had to consciously will her eyes not to roll.

"Father, we can't go back to the condo for the same reason we left." She didn't say the rest because of the taxi driver, but she hoped the priest realized; anyone could have been lying in wait for them back there.

While the taxi driver got more impatient to start the meter, Olsen thought about Jenna's words. He looked at his watch and brightened. "It's the perfect time. He's home right now. I can call Jawad and have him deliver what I need."

Jenna turned to the driver. "I'm sorry we wasted your time."

THEY STOOD NEXT TO EACH OTHER in silence, hiding behind the smoke and stacked crates of a falafel and shawarma stand as they waited for Jawad to arrive with Father Olsen's things. Jenna was paranoid that Jawad would show up with someone tailing him from the condo. She tried her best to memorize everyone in the vicinity so later she could spot who didn't belong.

Father Olsen was caught up watching all the passing people and workers in the marketplace for different reasons, enjoying the visual details of the way they dressed, looked, behaved and interacted with one another. Despite the danger they faced, Jenna couldn't blame him. He was trying to catch up on a lifetime of imagery that she, until now, had taken for granted.

When Olsen did speak, it took Jenna by surprise.

"What made you finally throw in with Carl?"

"You mean throw in with the rest of you guys?"

"Is that what you thought?" Father Olsen shook his head. "You misread the situation. I was waiting to see exactly what you were going to do and then follow your lead."

"Really? I find that so hard to believe. No offense. It just looked like you guys were all set to choose the colors of your team's uniform."

"I'm sorry I wasn't clearer with my intentions," Father Olsen said, looking a little like he had, in fact, taken offense. "But you still haven't answered my question."

Jenna took her time before responding. "I guess it was... a leap of faith."

Father Olsen saw how embarrassed she was by the admission. "Hmmm... if you don't mind me asking, when was the last time you made a decision based on a similar *leap of faith*?"

Jenna grinned. "Probably back in the eighth grade, walking home from school with Bobby Cantrell. At a certain point I leaned in to kiss him, and I had absolutely no evidence to support the belief that he was going to kiss me back."

"Well, did he?"

"Are you kidding? My lips just hung out there... all glossed up with no place to land."

The priest laughed. "And yet despite that experience, you decided today of all days you would try it again?"

"Well, I figured at least a decade between leaps of faith was a track record that even the hardest hardcore agnostic could be proud of."

"And the fact your father was here today... that had nothing to do with your decision?"

"None whatsoever."

She looked at him and knew he didn't believe her.

"Listen, I went into the field of science because the only leaps of faith are the kind you make when you jump across a canyon gap over a thousand-foot abyss. But you do it because on the other side is where the artifacts are buried... along with the truth. Today's decision was not very different. I measured the three of you lying end to end to end, and I decided I couldn't jump over that gap. So I decided to turn the jump into a leap of faith."

Olsen wanted to respond, but Jenna then motioned toward the marketplace corner. She had caught sight of Jawad holding a day bag containing Father Olsen's Bible and clothes.

The priest moved to greet his friend, but Jenna stopped him. "No, Alan, let's give it a minute or two, see if we notice anyone who might have followed."

He nodded and stepped back, and together they scanned their surroundings for any suspicious people.

"JAWAD, OVER HERE..."

He looked relieved to see Father Olsen and Jenna approaching. Relieved because, in the fifteen minutes Jenna and Father Olsen had waited to meet up with him, Jawad had no doubt begun to worry that something terrible had happened.

"I hope everything is good?" he asked.

"Just fine," Father Olsen responded cheerfully. "Thanks for bringing my things. And I apologize for being so late to meet with you."

"Oh, it is not an issue at all. I switched with another guard this morning, and my next shift does not begin until later this evening. I was just concerned when you asked me to bring these things, and you also wanted me to be... cautious. It reminded me of the last time..."

Jawad had lowered his voice, so Jenna knew the "last time" was something significant.

"Oh, yes, right," Father Olsen said. "Again, how can I ever repay you?"

Jawad closed his eyes and nodded. "I am repaid with our friendship, Father Olsen." They exchanged a hug, waved goodbye, and then parted ways.

JENNA AND FATHER OLSEN caught the Red Line heading toward the Western Wall Plaza. Once they were onboard, and sitting away from other passengers, Jenna asked, "Father, what did Jawad mean by 'last time'?"

Olsen slumped a bit. "The exorcism of Ami. On the second day of the rite, I needed a change of clothes. So I called to ask Jawad if he would bring my other cassock and vestment. That's what he was speaking about."

"You didn't hide from him what you were doing—performing an exorcism on a young boy?"

"That was not an issue. It was Jawad who had originally brought the case of the boy's possession to my attention."

"Oh, I didn't realize that."

"Yes, he said he knew the boy's mother. She apparently came to him and asked for his help in finding someone. And he turned to me."

A bell sounded, alerting the passengers that they were approaching the Damascus station. Jenna pulled out her cell phone to check the time. There was nothing to get nervous about. She and Father Olsen would be entering the Western Wall Plaza in plenty of time to meet up with the others.

———

WHEN SHIN BET AGENT ALUF GINSBERG first heard about a shooting in the Western Wall Plaza, he immediately did not want to hear anything more about it. But just a few minutes later, he couldn't help himself—he wanted to know everything about it.

Aluf was due to leave with his wife and their two teenage boys for a trip to the States, where they would visit her family in Los Angeles. He had even packed his bag after hearing the initial report of the killing, as a way of convincing himself that he would not get involved. But his wife, Orali, knew better. She gave him permission to catch a later flight to California if he wanted to check things out.

A few minutes later Ginsberg got a call from one of his military buddies, Shai Parnas, an inspector for the Jerusalem district police. Shai had been assigned to work the shooting at the plaza, and he invited his friend to drop by the crime scene for a visit.

Aluf ended up giving his wife and two boys big kisses before sending them to the airport in a taxi. He then drove to the Western Wall Plaza with a promise to himself: he would be on the next plane to the States as soon as he wrapped up his visit with his buddy.

————

"HOW COULD A MAN GET SHOT right here, die right here, and right here in the middle of the plaza no one notices until the killer is long gone?"

"*Modus vivendi*," Aluf replied to his friend, Shai. It was a Latin phrase, meaning "way of living."

In the ongoing conflict at the Western Wall, Aluf knew most of the daily visitors had reached a *modus vivendi*—an agreement to disagree with each other. And he knew it was more than just an understanding between different religions; it was also an agreement between opposing Jewish sects who had fought for years in defiance of the country's long stated goal of a collective Israeli identity.

"Everybody is usually in their own little world here," Aluf explained. "Everyone is trying not to bother the person nearby, and in turn, they're looking to be left alone to worship without interference. That's how a murder victim can be bleeding out just a few feet away before anyone pays any notice."

The man had been shot twice from behind, both bullets piercing his back just inches apart. The wounds would probably not have killed him immediately, which impressed Aluf more that he still gripped his gun. Amazing muscle control... or an incredibly strong will.

"He never got off a shot. It's a Makarov. Does he look like a Bulgarian to you?"

Aluf shook his head. "Maybe a Serb. So no ID?"

"Not on him."

"You know what that means, Shai?"

"Yeah, I'm probably not dealing with a local. Did you get a look at his face?"

"Yes." Aluf smirked. "I couldn't help thinking about the way Lior looked after he tried to box that Arab guy... what was his name?"

Shai started to laugh. "Faris. We called him 'Faris the horse.'"

"Yeah, what did you say? 'It looks like Faris the horse galloped all over your face, Lior...'"

The other police officers were watching, so Shai caught himself before he burst into hysterics. He shoved Ginsberg toward some canvas tents covering an excavation at the edge of the plaza. There, Shai showed Aluf a plastic bag containing two 9mm shell casings.

270

"They were found just inches apart right here at the entrance of this tent," said Shai.

"If he was using a silencer, no one in the plaza would have heard a thing."

Shai nodded. Ginsberg then started back into the plaza, following the path of the bullets. Every step he took, memories of that day, weeks ago, seeped into his mind.

A gunshot.

Another gunshot.

Screams.

Then the thunderous stampede as thousands of people fled the plaza after John Wolfenson was attacked.

The memories came to him as sounds, because Aluf had not been there in the plaza to see Sandy Travis attack. He had been nearby securing her fiancé, Tom, who Aluf had been led to believe was the real assassin.

He raised his hand and waved to all the buildings overlooking the plaza. "You should have your men check every surrounding—"

"Yes," Shai said, "I have the officers going door to door in the surrounding apartment buildings, and also gathering up video of the Wailing Wall. What did you think, Aluf, that you're the only one who's ever worked a crime scene at the plaza before?"

Ginsberg smiled. He knew Shai was just busting his balls.

"What else? See anything else interesting? Come on..."

Aluf shook his head.

"Are you sure? Because if I don't end up figuring this out, it's a black mark on Egoz."

Both Shai and Aluf had served together on the Egoz Recon Unit, as part of the Golani Brigade stationed in the north. They both ended up working in military intelligence.

Aluf patted Shai on the back. "No, I don't see anything else. Besides, if Egoz can survive what I did here weeks ago, its reputation will survive anything."

He then checked his watch and wondered if it was still possible to catch an evening flight to the States if he drove straight to the airport in Tel Aviv.

———

THE NEXT MORNING, having failed to secure a flight the previous night, Agent Ginsburg was drinking his coffee and speaking to the airline about rebooking for later in the afternoon.

His cell phone buzzed and he saw it was Shai calling.

"Hey, Aluf, one of the department's other detectives Eyal Friedman is out at the Peace Forest, working a killing that happened in the middle of the night. I told him to expect you. You'll recognize Eyal immediately—he'll be the biggest prick working the crime scene.

"A couple of weeks ago he found out one of his suspects in a murder case fled the country with... get this... Eyal's own fiancée. Now not only can't poor Eyal close the file on a two-year-old murder, he's left eating the deposits on a restaurant, a night club, and a lease on a new condo in Savyon."

"Why should a killing in the Peace Forest be something I care enough about to meet your prick friend?" Aluf asked.

"Well, because the victim killed in the Peace Forest was shot from long distance just like our Makarov stiff in the plaza. Come on, Aluf, drive on over and help cheer poor Eyal up..."

————

GINSBERG DECIDED TO DRIVE to the Peace Forest because he had to admit, two shootings from long range in less than twenty-four hours was highly unusual, even for Jerusalem. But when he got there and started to sift through the evidence, the initial tantalizing similarity—two long-range killings—failed to connect the crimes.

Yes, both victims were shot from at least twenty-five yards, but Mr. Makarov at the plaza was killed with a 9mm pistol. The murder victim at the Peace Forest looked to be taken down with a single bullet to the head from a sniper rifle. Aluf saw the size of the entry wound and predicted the shooter had used some kind of SASR firing a .50 caliber round known as a "light fifty."

Detective Friedman and his team were unable to recover a shell casing, but based on the angle of the head wound, they had worked out a scenario where the sniper fired from a concrete tower overlooking the crime scene. There they found two cigarette butts in the tower exactly where the shooter would have been positioned if their scenario was accurate. As he inspected the tower for himself, Agent Ginsburg recognized they were dealing with a total pro—someone more concerned about picking up his shell casing than leaving behind his DNA.

All in all, the Peace Forest shooting looked every bit to be a carefully planned, premeditated professional operation.

Yes, blood had been left from other people at the scene besides the murder victim. And yes, there were signs of a struggle, which signified that the sniper was a backup rather than the point guy in a flat-out assassination. But no matter the original goal of the operation, the killing was still dissimilar to the shooting at the plaza, which was clearly an act of spontaneity. What professional would plan a hit at a world-famous, heavily trafficked religious site like the plaza? Only amateurs would attempt to target a victim, like an internationally renowned diplomat, in such a setting.

GINSBERG ENDED HIS PEACE FOREST visit by requesting that Detective Eyal Friedman call him once they had ID'd the victim. And Friedman was more than happy to agree. It turned out Ginsberg had made the detective's day the moment he introduced himself.

"Wait, are you the same Aluf Ginsberg who let the assassin in the plaza get to Envoy Wolfenson?"

"Yes, detective, you're shaking the hand of that very same shmuck."

They became fast friends because as long as Eyal Friedman, the guy who allowed a murder suspect to steal his fiancée, kept company with Aluf Ginsberg, the police detective wasn't the biggest fuck-up poking around the crime scene.

———

ALUF DROVE AWAY from the Peace Forest and was headed for the airport when Shai called him on his cell phone.

"You have to come down here and see this."

"See what?"

"No, I'm not letting you off that easy. You have to come down to the station if you want to take a look."

Ginsberg ended the call with Shai and put in another call to the airline, requesting a further hold on his flight to the States.

———

BECAUSE OF THE POPULARITY of the Wailing Wall, web cams surrounded the entire plaza for the benefit of people in different countries who wanted to watch, pray, and donate money.

"But then aren't you just praying to a TV set?" Shai joked as he and Aluf waited for one of these recordings to cue up.

Unfortunately the video they planned to watch came from a non-professional camera, positioned on an eighth-floor balcony of an apartment building quite some distance from the site of the killing. But it turned out to be the only camera that early in the morning recording a part of the plaza other than the Wailing Wall.

The footage showed the victim, Mr. Makarov, moving out into the middle of the plaza toward two people, a man and a woman, raising the pistol after which he was named. Before he could pull the trigger, Makarov suddenly collapsed. Fifteen seconds later—exactly—a third man entered the screen, and Makarov's two targets ran away.

"No doubt that is the shooter," said Shai. "Who else would just calmly walk up to a dead body like that, right?"

The suspected murderer bent down and withdrew something from Makarov's coat, then stood over the victim for a few seconds before turning around and walking away.

"Wait a second—back it up," Ginsberg said, suddenly leaning toward the screen.

"You think you know the shooter?"

"No..."

The video was so grainy it was almost impossible to see anyone with clarity. But something struck Ginsberg and he needed to see it again.

"Wait, freeze it! Right there!"

He was pointing at one of Makarov's targets. The man was running away, and for only a few frames he had looked back, so the camera had captured his face.

"This man," said Aluf, "this man I do know!"

———

ALUF COMMANDEERED THE DESK of a police inspector who had called in sick, and he made some calls.

He started by contacting the Israel Prison Service Medical Center to see if Father Olsen had paid a recent visit to Tom Hansen. The officer at the visitors desk informed him that he already knew about the last time the priest had visited, because the agent had met with him.

Ginsberg then called New York to see if perhaps Olsen had flown back to visit his old parish. Nothing like fleeing a murder scene and hiding out in the church you once ran. But the person he talked to at the church said the priest had not been there in weeks.

Aluf then decided to call all the Catholic churches in the Jerusalem area. Short list. On the second call, he got a hit. Someone at the Church of All Nations immediately recognized Olsen's name. She put him on hold.

After listening to choir music for a couple minutes, Aluf hung up and called back. This time he got someone else on the line and was told one of the officials from the church would return his call.

The agent finally did get that callback an hour later. The church administrator confirmed Father Olsen had met with Bishop Bynum three days ago but had not been back since. When Ginsberg asked for Olsen's address, the administrator refused to disclose any further details.

After hanging up, the agent wrote down in his notebook that the administrator seemed skittish, as if hiding something. Aluf planned on visiting the church tomorrow.

AGENT GINSBERG WENT OUT with Shai to discuss the autopsy of Mr. Makarov over an early dinner. The discussion was over even before their artichokes with dip arrived. They both knew there would only be something to talk about after Shai got the ballistics report on the two slugs recovered by the coroner.

They spent the rest of their dinner speculating on the reason for Mr. Makarov's presence in Israel. Aluf put his money on the Mossad; Makarov was probably one of their foreign recruits, and while they were out showing him a good time, the Serb broke free from his handler only to be shot down by someone who had followed him into the country.

Shai, on the other hand, put his money on a homosexual relationship gone bad—an archeologist working one of the excavation sites in the plaza was being squeezed by his undocumented assistant who threatened to talk to the press.

AFTER DINNER THE SHIN BET AGENT decided to go down to the Western Wall Plaza and take another look around. Aluf was standing in the plaza less than two minutes when it finally hit him. It was embarrassing how much he had slipped over the last several weeks.

The murder of Mr. Makarov had taken place just yards away from where Envoy Wolfenson had been attacked.

If Aluf wanted to forgive himself for the oversight, he simply had to acknowledge that the area had looked different that day, taken up by large staging platforms where representatives from the different countries had signed Wolfenson's treaty. But he was more in the mood to wallow in self-disgust.

He had watched the videotape of Makarov's attack dozens of times. How could he have missed it? The very place Father Olsen had been standing was the same place he had performed the last rites on the assassin... Sandy Travis.

His cell phone rang. Aluf saw who was calling and answered.

"Detective Friedman, how are you?"

"Agent Ginsberg, you wanted to know when we got an ID on the Peace Forest victim. Well, we have one. His name is Randall Reitz. Ring any bells?"

"No, it doesn't."

"Well, we ended up matching him with his work visa. Then we cross-referenced his name with our files, and it turns out he was an employee of Saracen Security..."

"Really?"

"You know the company?"

"Yes, of course, they're one of the biggest private security firms in the world. Shin Bet works with them all the time to safeguard foreign dignitaries."

"Okay, that makes sense, because Reitz was checked in by customs the day before Envoy John Wolfenson flew into the country. Do you see any connection at all? Aluf, are you there... hello... Aluf?"

Ginsberg had lowered the phone, stunned by something he just witnessed a few dozen yards away—a couple walking together, hand in hand, crossed in front of a priest, who stopped to let the lovers pass.

"Father Olsen?"

The priest looked over at Aluf and smiled, but only out of courtesy, and not because he recognized him.

"Father, it's me, Agent Ginsberg." He pulled out his heart medication and rattled the pills in the plastic container. "Remember me?"

Olsen was no longer smiling. He started to turn away, but seemed to catch himself.

Aluf looked in the direction the priest was about to turn, but saw only what looked like tourists and regular worshippers.

"Agent Ginsberg, what are you doing here?"

"No, no, Alan, you just stole my opening question. Do you mind if I have a word with you?"

"Well, I'm here to meet someone. Can we do it another time?"

"No, I'm afraid not. Why don't we go over here and talk in one of these police vans?" The agent pointed, but made sure to keep his eyes on the priest. "Father Olsen, you do see where I'm pointing... don't you?"

CHAPTER 22

SECURING A COMPLETELY ISOLATED, soundproof room close to where the envoy would be calling was not the problem. Carl simply turned to one of his contacts and told him what he needed, and the whole deal went down in less than two minutes.

The problem would be transporting Patricia from the motel to what he had written on the napkin at the marketplace as the "call center."

He did not want to go armed because that would just invite the fates to intervene. A traffic ticket or a guard noticing the bulge under his jacket could lead to an arrest. And yet he couldn't be one hundred percent certain that Patricia would continue to cooperate without force.

She had become more withdrawn, quiet, and emotionally fragile. He would be pacing back and forth in his brother's room at the Crusader Inn, making arrangements for the meeting, and she would be staring blankly at the mute television set, then just a moment later, when he looked back, she would be crying hysterically.

If Patricia decided to make a fuss in the few minutes she was exposed in public, everything they had put in motion could end that instant. The envoy would be free to carry through with his plan, and with Carl detained or jailed, AOL would no doubt find a way to get Patricia, and his unborn child, back into his clutches.

———

DR. FINCHER SLID OPEN THE SECRET PANEL in the concrete wall, then let Hadji Hassanat, his girlfriend Noora, and four other Bedouin terrorists enter the cave before him. Then he grabbed the tape-wrapped bundle and carried it into the cave before sliding shut the secret door.

The doctor stood there in silence, letting the group absorb the space they would be waiting in before they launched their assault. More importantly, he let them prepare their psyches. He knew what they were going through.

It took a special energy to pull off an act of premeditated violence. Murdering your wife when you catch her in bed with someone else is for hotheads. Slugging the idiot in the stands who booed your kid for striking out in the ninth inning was for morons without any self-control. However, taking out the slut spouse two years after the divorce, or shooting the loudmouth father from long range while he celebrates his son's graduation... now that requires someone with forethought, discipline, and the ability to delay gratification.

The doctor's phone vibrated. Right on schedule.

"Yes, Omar, we have arrived on time and are ready to work with you to achieve your will. Yes, of course, here is your brother." Fincher handed the satellite phone to Hadji.

The envoy, mimicking OSK in voice and word choice, let his brother know that he was poised to send in his suicide bombers during the first phase of their attack. Then, after Hadji and his band had completed the second part of the mission, the two brothers would both celebrate back in the desert, where OSK insisted on hearing some of his brother's rababah music.

Hassanat looked cheered and suitably pumped after hearing Omar's voice, and he handed the phone back to the doctor.

Fincher spoke some of the few Arabic words he knew, "Hazan saeed"—good luck—and then hung up the phone.

On the floor, the doctor unrolled the bundle and showed them their weapons and masks, and some clothing.

"After Omar sets off the first wave of explosions, it should clear the place out," Fincher explained. "Hopefully not everyone will leave because we will need some hostages, and I certainly don't want to be one of them."

The Bedouins who understood English laughed.

"Afterward, you will come back down here, change into these outfits, and walk back into the tunnel—right under the feet of all those unwitting police above. The van will be waiting to take you home, undetected."

Everyone nodded. Everyone looked confident. Dr. Fincher couldn't have been more pleased.

"Hadji, here is the phone you'll be using. Just hit this number and you'll be talking to the guy who will be handling your hostage negotiations."

Hassanat took the phone and proudly held it up for the others to see.

"And who will you say you are?" Fincher asked.

"Omar Sheikh Kashmiri."

"And who will you say you need to speak with?"

"Envoy John Wolfenson," answered Hadji.

"Outstanding." Fincher looked at his watch, then smiled at the group. "I can already taste more of that goat soup..."

———

THE INTERROGATION had so far lasted thirty minutes.

Ginsberg had asked the same question five times: "Why are you no longer blind?"

Father Olsen's four previous responses were—

"Agent Ginsberg, couldn't you have asked me that back at the plaza?

"I still do not understand why your curiosity is justification for taking me back to this van?

"I will tell you everything you want to know, if you just let me go right now.

"You have no idea what you are doing. You need to let me go this instant."

The fifth time the Shin Bet agent asked the question, Father Olsen answered, "I guess it was a miracle."

The back of the police van was getting hotter and more uncomfortable by the minute, even with the motor running and the air conditioning turned up high. Ginsberg didn't care. He would wait and watch the priest have a stroke right in front of him unless he got some answers.

"So you're now saying it is a miracle you can see?"

"Yes, a miracle. Now can I please leave?"

"Why aren't you jumping up and down with joy? I know I would be if I were blind my entire life but suddenly could see."

"Don't I look happy to you?"

"As a matter of fact, Father, no, you don't."

Olsen looked at his watch.

"Do you need to be somewhere, Alan?"

"I was just looking to see how long I've been here answering questions about issues I can't believe are any concern to the Israeli police."

"I'm not the police."

"Yes, that's right. We're just in one of their vans."

"That's right, I'm borrowing one of their vans. Because that's what a Shin Bet agent can do."

"Well then tell me what a Shin Bet agent wants to hear, so I can leave."

"So you're just telling me what I want to hear?"

"At this point, yes."

"What makes you think telling me your eyesight was caused by a miracle would be something I want to hear? I don't believe in miracles. When someone asks me how it is that my parents have stayed married for fifty years, I don't answer, 'It's a miracle,' even though it's the most likely explanation. I don't answer that way because I don't believe in miracles. So why don't we work together toward a better answer?"

"How about a better question?"

Ginsberg wiped the sweat from his forehead with the back of his sleeve. "Okay, Alan, how about—what are you doing here? After everything that has happened, I can't believe you would come back to this plaza. How's that for a better question?"

"Pardon me for changing the subject, but how is Tom?"

Aluf looked away and shook his head. He didn't know what to make of the situation. Not a clue.

"I hear he is doing better. He might survive his incarceration."

The priest closed his eyes and mumbled softly to himself.

"Come on, Alan, help me out here."

The priest opened his eyes. "I'm trying my best, sir."

"No, you're not. You're working this situation like you've got something to hide. And it's not like you at all. I hope you don't mind if I presume to know you well enough to say—*this is not like you at all*. But I really believe, because of the experiences we've had together, I've gotten to really know you."

There was a knock at the door of the van, and Ginsberg got up from the chair to open it.

"Inspector Friedman asked me to give you this," said Officer Cohen, one of the policemen working with Shai.

"Thank you," Ginsberg said. He took a computer disc from the officer.

"Shall I continue to stand out here?"

"Yes, do not leave that position until you hear from me. Understood?"

Cohen nodded, and then Ginsberg shut and locked the back door of the van.

He popped the disc into a tablet computer, also on loan from the Jerusalem police department. When the video popped up onscreen, the agent pretended to play with it for a few minutes, only because he wanted to see what the priest would do during the wait.

In fact the priest did nothing. He just stared out the windshield of the van, watching the people head for the Western Wall.

"I brought you here because earlier today I was shown a video," Ginsberg said. "You know the whole plaza here has video cameras shooting all the time because of the wall. Now this one video had something that caught my eye, but it was almost impossible to see. So while we've been talking about old times, I've had someone blow the video up."

Ginsberg looked at the footage playing onscreen and pretended to be shocked. "Wait, Alan, you know something? I have to take back what I said. Maybe I really don't know you."

The agent flipped the tablet around so Olsen could see the video. The recording was still grainy, but now it was digitally enhanced and zoomed in on the face of the man who had run from the plaza seconds after witnessing Mr. Makarov's murder.

"That is you in the video, is it not, Father Olsen?"

"Yes, it is."

The agent was impressed. The priest didn't hesitate or look away; he didn't even deny.

"Very, good, Alan. Now next question. As a man of the cloth, why would you not report this terrible killing, which apparently happened right before your very eyes?"

Olsen leaned back in his chair and started to tear up.

"Father?"

The priest once again turned to stare out the windshield of the van. Just in case he was seeing something Ginsberg was not, the agent turned to look too, but saw nothing; just tourists milling about.

"Do you need some Kleenex, Father?"

"No, I'm going to be all right."

"Then what is it, Alan? What are you not telling me?"

"I'm sorry, Agent Ginsberg, I'm just feeling sorry for myself."

"I don't understand."

"I'm just wondering why God would put me in the same place twice just weeks apart, where I would be in a position to stop the worst from happening, but both times I ended up not being able to do anything. I really truly do not understand."

Then tears started to roll down the priest's cheeks.

————

HE SHUT THE DOOR BEHIND THEM and locked it. The place was perfect. Stone walls thick enough to silence whatever happened inside. According to his contact, the WAQF used it to interrogate suspects before handing them over to the Israeli police. Carl quickly turned on the lights.

On the last part of their walk over, he had felt Patricia shaking, but other than that, she seemed perfectly fine as they moved through the crowds. He was confident her jitters were merely a sign of nervousness for what was about to take place.

Four chairs surrounded a table, which was bolted to the ground. They were the only furnishings in the room. Once Carl was confident he had lured the envoy up to the room, he would get rid of the chairs.

"Patricia, why don't you come over here and sit down."

She moved to the table and took a seat, and he was glad to see how responsive she was to his request.

"It should just be a few more minutes and then this will all be over."

Carl reviewed the plan with Patricia. After the envoy called, and she verified she was indeed alive and in his care, they would then verify their true location. After that, Patricia would be finished, and Marcus would come take her away to a safe place.

"What do you think, Pat? Simple enough, right?"

She just stared at him.

He withdrew from his jacket three different satellite phones and set them on the table. Carl was not ashamed to have written on each phone a letter: L, M, and S. He knew to always make it simple. In the middle of negotiations, it was too easy to make a mistake and speak into the wrong phone.

"S" stood for Satan. Carl had spent years ignoring and denying the hoary myths of an evil Angel of Light, a decadent, unscrupulous entity known as "Satan." He knew that "evil" could only have been conceived by the original creator, and that the darker side of humanity's soul was all part of a holistic creation. Yin would not have a purpose, if there wasn't Yang running around begging to be reined in.

But now because of everything that had happened, Carl had to acknowledge that the myths, like old wives' tales, probably held a grain or two of truth.

"Pat, how are you feeling?"

His question seemed to wake her up. She started to look around the room, almost taking in for the first time their dungeon-like setting. Then she looked over at Carl.

"I don't know what's happening."

He moved around the table and bent down on one knee beside her. "You do know what's happening. This is what we need to do to make this right. And when we're done, it's all going to be good. You believe me, right?"

She didn't answer.

"Patricia, tell me you believe..."

"I'm sorry, Carl, I don't know what to believe anymore."

He grabbed her hand and rubbed it, trying to kindle some warmth in it, for it was clammy and cold.

"I know. I don't blame you for feeling that way after everything you've gone through. But unfortunately, this is the moment where confusion must take a back seat to conviction. Pat, you need to believe in something."

Someone knocked on the door. It was Jenna. Carl let her in and quickly locked the door behind her.

"Where's the priest?" Carl asked immediately.

"Father Olsen was... detained."

"What are you talking about?"

"Someone recognized him. A police officer... I don't know. They took him away."

"Took him where?"

"In a police van parked on one of the streets near the Damascus Gate."

Carl picked up one of three satellite phones resting on the table. He didn't need to dial; it was an open line to Marcus. "Are you listening to this?"

"Yes, I heard. Let me see what I can do."

"No!" Jenna shouted, loud enough for her father to hear. "Alan has done nothing wrong. They will let him go. We need to just be patient."

"The meeting is happening in ten minutes, and I'm positive the envoy will be calling any second," Carl said. "We need the priest here now."

Jenna shook her head. "I don't want any more innocent people getting hurt."

Carl pounded on the table.

Patricia flinched and began to weep.

"Oh, Pat," Carl said, scrambling over and wrapping his arms around her. "I'm sorry. Everything's going to be fine."

Still holding Patricia, Carl said, "Jenna, don't be naïve. Millions of people are going to die if we don't get Olsen's ass over here immediately."

The other phone started ringing. The phone with the "S" written on it.

"That's him. Jenna, are you listening to me?"

She nodded, then hurried out of the room.

The phone rang a second time.

"Marcus, your daughter's coming your way. Get the priest back here immediately and I will try to stall."

"I hear you..."

On the third ring, Carl answered the phone.

"Hello..."

"Carl, just checking in before our meeting. I trust your son is doing better."

"Yes, Ami is doing much better. Thank you for taking care of that."

"I'm a man of my word. Now if you don't mind, I'd like to confirm that you're a man of your word. Do you have Patricia with you?"

"Yes, she's sitting right here. Would you like to speak to her?"

"You read my mind, Carl."

Carl handed the phone over to Patricia.

"Patty, are you there?"

"John, I'm very confused... Is what Carl been saying true?"

"Sweetie, first of all... it's just so good to hear your voice. You know I'm coming to get you. That's what this is all about. And when I leave with you, believe me, everything is going to be fine. Now what has Carl been telling you?"

"He's saying you're not really my husband."

"Now listen to me, dear, and try to pick up on all the emotion in my voice as well as the words. I know there's a lot of static on this call, but I still want you to try and hear all the love that's in my voice, because that's way more important than the words I'm now going to say—Pat, I'm the John you always wished your husband had been."

Patricia started to cry. Her chest was heaving and her hand was shaking so hard, Carl was amazed she managed to keep command of the phone. Perhaps only because she was pressing it so hard to her ear.

"Now, Pat, listen to me. You can't trust Carl. He hasn't been telling you the truth. He's been involved in this plan from the very start, no matter what lies he's been telling you. Whatever he said to you back in Aleppo, and whatever he's trying to spin now... all lies. He's the one who planned this whole deception. I just went along with it."

She managed to stop crying long enough to interject. "But even if I believe what you just said, what does that really mean? It doesn't change the fact that you are not my husband, and you've been lying to me from the start!"

"No, wait, Pat, let me explain. I've just been waiting for the right time to tell you the truth. That's where my head was at. Here was my goal: I just wanted to get our son Scotty back, and then I would have told you everything. After our Scotty was brought back to where he belonged, in your loving arms, then I would have told you everything. Now that makes sense, right?"

"But Scotty isn't your son!" Patricia yelled. Then she screamed. It was so loud Carl was thankful to be behind stone walls at least a foot thick.

"He's *my* son... and he's dead. Dead!"

"That's where you're mistaken, Patty. I can bring him back. You'll see. He'll be as good as new..."

Patricia dropped the phone and started choking. She rushed over to a corner of the room and threw up, then fell to her knees, shaken and crying.

She threw up again.

Carl picked up the phone. "Okay, so now you spoke with her. I'm just letting you know ahead of time, sir, your reconciliation with your wife is going to take some time. Now please, sir, when can I expect you?"

"Well, Carl, you should be seeing my helicopter any second approaching your Monastery."

"Okay, let me check with one of my guys near the helipad." Carl muted the phone marked with the "S" and grabbed the third satellite phone sitting on the table.

"Do you see him?"

"Yes, I see him," Loder said over the phone. "He hasn't moved. He's still talking to you from behind the steering wheel of a cargo van. It's definitely him."

Carl put the phone in his pocket. Grabbed the other phone from the table and put that in his pocket too.

He waved to Patricia to stand up. She did, and he led her out of the room. As they started walking across the small courtyard to the stairwell, Carl unmuted the phone.

"John, I just talked to one of my men, and I believe you're lying to me. You're not on a helicopter. You're not on the way to the Monastery at all. And, surprise, you're not a man of your word."

"Yes, Carl, you are absolutely right. I just needed to do this one thing, and then you and I... and let's not forget Patty... we'll all get together soon. And, I promise, I will release your son. But only if you release mine. Please, I hope you understand and forgive my deception."

Carl and Patricia started climbing the stone steps up to the city ramparts.

The gate, like most ancient fortress gates, projected from the Old City wall, looming taller than the ramparts as one huge block composed of smaller bricks. The double archway that had once led into the Noble Sanctuary and Temple Mount had, a long time ago, been walled in, sealed, so that no one, especially a messiah or prophet, could pass through.

Wolfenson wanted to change all that.

"John, as it turns out, there's nothing to forgive. Because I'm right here. We're both here. Sorry, *all three of us* are here... Myself, Patty, and your unborn baby. We're all here on the other side of the Golden Gate.

"I know the prophecy as well as you do, that if you open this gate, you believe the Messiah will come, and you can bring your... feud to a head. So I came here as well. With your family. And now that we have this part of negotiations out of the way, perhaps we can finally get down to business."

Carl waited for a reply, but heard only static. But then it completely cleared up. Apparently John no longer had reason to emulate helicopter sounds.

"You, Carl, are a man I have grown to respect immensely in the short time I've been here. In fact you have shamed me into now admitting how ridiculously dated my take on all of you hominids has been. I have completely underestimated your intelligence, if not from the beginning, certainly in the last five thousand years. Bravo."

"Envoy, sir, thank you for the kind words, but to be clear: Patricia and I are right here, on the other side of the Golden Gate. If you follow through with your plan, you will kill her and your unborn child. That's certainly not part of the grand plan, right, sir?"

"It's not that I don't believe you, Carl. Everything you've done strongly suggests I should believe you. But how do I know you're not miles away talking to me on a phone, while you're watching me with a video camera or having one of your trusty employees sending you smoke signals?"

"Fair enough, sir."

Carl turned to Patricia and motioned for her to rise along with him. They were now standing on the narrow rampart crowning the Golden Gate. Through the crenellations in the parapet, he could see the envoy's white van parked a short distance below the cemetery. Carl started waving. He motioned for Pat to wave too.

"Do you see us, sir?"

"Yes."

"So you now have proof."

Carl put his hand on Pat's shoulder and they both lowered into a sitting position with their backs against the parapet.

"So let's start talking about an alternative plan. Why don't you come up here, and we'll meet in a private room where nobody will disturb us. Let's work out the swap we originally agreed upon. What do you say?"

Carl didn't get an answer. He knew the silence meant the envoy was contemplating his next move, which he totally expected. But the silence went on for more than a minute.

With every passing second, Carl feared the Angel of Light was contemplating something he had not anticipated.

"Are you still there, Carl?"

"Of course I am, sir. We're all here. Pat, say something..."

"Don't do this..."

After Patricia spoke, Carl said, "We're all three just waiting for you. Come on, sir, what's there to think about? I want my son back, and you want your baby to be safe."

The envoy answered with more silence.

Carl now began to believe it was possible Satan had underestimated him, but perhaps he had overestimated the Angel of Light.

"Sorry, Carl, but you don't know him the way I do."

"No, now you hold on." Carl stood up and waved his hand. "Do you see me, Mr. Envoy?"

"Yes."

"Good, because now I want you to listen. You need to stop what you're doing and come up here. Sit down with Pat and me, and let's discuss changing this world together. Your struggle is our struggle. No one understands that concept better than I do. It's the entire reason I worked so hard to bring you here. We both need to reconcile our relationship with Him. And together we can do that, show Him we're worthy of his acceptance despite our fall from grace.

"Sir, are you listening? Come up here and let's work it out, so we can speak with a single voice, one that won't scream, threaten, beg, cry, or cause destruction. One voice, which we both know He'll hear because it'll be coming from all of us. We'll start with these words—'Father, if it's all right with you, we want to come home.'"

There was silence.

Patricia reached out and took Carl's hand.

"I'm sorry, Carl. I hope you understand. The way I see it is that he sacrificed his son, and I'm prepared to do the same."

The Angel of Light ended the call.

CHAPTER 23

FATHER OLSEN STOOD UP for the first time since Ginsberg had brought him into the van. "I demand that you either arrest me or let me go."

The agent stood up as well. "It doesn't work that way, Alan. First off, I'm the one who does the demanding. And secondly, there are a lot of alternatives available to me other than the two you cited. So why don't you just sit down?"

Olsen stepped toward the agent. They were both sweaty and red in the face from the heat. And the priest looked more desperate than ever.

"You don't understand, Aluf."

"So make me understand." The agent had taken his own step forward, so they were now standing just inches apart.

"Things are happening right now, and if you don't let me go, many people will die. Thousands. Perhaps more."

"Well then I better get on that. Just give me the details."

"I would, but you won't believe me."

"Well, Father, you're in the business of making believers out of non-believers, so this should be right up your alley. Besides, we're not leaving this van until you tell me the truth."

Father Olsen closed his eyes and kept them shut as he spoke. "Envoy John Wolfenson is demonically possessed and intends to blow up the Golden Gate, and then attack the Temple Mount." He opened his eyes the moment he had finished.

Normally Ginsberg would have taken Olsen as one of the many zealot idiots running around the city. But the priest's involvement just weeks ago in the assassination attempt on Envoy John Wolfenson, coupled with the dead body at the Peace Forest somehow connected to the envoy's security team, demanded the agent take Olsen seriously.

"As a Catholic priest I'm sure you know how your words sound to someone outside your religion. But I'm still listening to everything you have to say."

Olsen looked at his watch. "Damn it! We've run out of time!"

Ginsberg was more than a little surprised to hear the priest curse.

Bang, bang, bang!

They both jumped at the sudden knocking at the back doors of the van. Ginsberg knew it was probably just Officer Cohen, but after listening to Olsen for the last minute, he withdrew his firearm before opening the door.

"You need to call someone!" a young woman was screaming. "I don't know what happened, but one of your officers just... dropped to the ground!"

Agent Ginsberg looked over and saw Officer Cohen several yards away on the concrete barrier, surrounded by a growing crowd of bystanders. Aluf hopped out of the van.

"Wait here, Father," he said before slamming the doors shut.

By the time the agent arrived at the scene, the group had swelled to at least a dozen people.

"Please, everybody, just back up and give us some room!"

A man was kneeling beside Cohen, holding his fingers to the officer's neck to check his pulse.

Ginsberg knelt beside him. "How is he?"

"I think he's going to be all right," the man said, withdrawing his hand from the officer's neck.

"Do you know what happened?"

The man attempted to stand up, but then stumbled, almost fell. Ginsberg reached out to catch him, and the man latched onto his arm. He pulled himself up and closed ranks on the agent.

"Yes," the man said, "he was tased..."

A jolt of electricity shot through Agent Ginsberg's body, and the surrounding group gasped and stepped back as the agent fell to the cobblestones.

Aluf tried to move, but couldn't. He had no other choice but to stare helplessly up at the man who had tased him. The agent got his first really good look at the attacker's face—a face he had seen just recently, on a TV screen. This was the man who had killed Makarov in the Western Wall Plaza.

And exactly like he had done after that attack, the man calmly walked away.

JENNA THREW OPEN THE DOORS to the police van.

"What's going on?" Olsen asked.

"Not sure," Jenna said. She motioned for the priest to get out of the van, and he hopped out a few seconds before Marcus hopped in.

"What are you doing?" Jenna asked him, noticing the officer's walkie-talkie in his hand.

"Creating a diversion." Marcus tapped his earphone, which enabled him to hear the conversation between Carl and the envoy. "Everything we planned is going up in flames. Once again my brother has screwed up. Just leave. Get the hell out of here! I'll be in touch when we've regrouped and are ready to go after AOL again."

Marcus slammed shut the van's back doors.

Jenna and Father Olsen stepped away from the vehicle and walked casually up the street, discreetly distancing themselves from the whole situation.

Marcus fired up the police van.

Jenna glanced back and saw her father through the windshield. Marcus had unwittingly admitted that Carl was his brother. Or maybe her father had said it intentionally because he wanted Jenna to know. Perhaps he said it because whatever he was going to do now, he didn't think they would see each other again.

The police van roared past them, and this time Jenna didn't look over.

———

"WHAT'S HE DOING?"

"He's just sitting there in the van, staring out the windshield. Do you want me to take him out now?"

"Absolutely not!" Carl's voice rang out over the wireless headset hooked to Loder's ear.

The Bab Al-Rahma Cemetery stretched out before him. From his vantage point, Loder could see anything and everything all along the cemetery, from the Golden Gate ramparts to the road down below, and even farther out... into the palms of the Kidron Valley.

When he had first settled into his nest, Loder had made detailed observations about the Muslim boneyard surrounding him. He always approached a potential field of fire the same way he approached a relationship with a woman. He never minded getting hurt by some weakness or flaw he had previously observed, but he kicked himself when he was blindsided by something he had missed.

The terraces of the cemetery were so staggered and uneven only neglect or 1,400 years of natural erosion could be responsible. Earlier Carl had explained how the graves were pieces of some ancient strategy, to seal the Golden Gate. How the gate hadn't been opened in thousands of years. But now someone was threatening to open it.

Loder had asked Carl why opening the Golden Gate was such a bad thing, and the answer was so convoluted and confusing, Loder totally regretted asking the question.

Now he was staring at Wolfenson's white van parked down on *Derech HaOfel*, down the hill from the nearest burial vaults. He stamped out his cigarette.

"Okay, he just got out and is opening up the back..."

"Of the van?" Carl asked.

"Yes, the van. Apologies." Loder had forgotten that even though *he* could see things clearly, Carl currently could not. He watched Wolfenson step away from the vehicle and now Loder could see through to the cargo area. It was loaded with long shapes wrapped in sheets.

"Maybe you're expecting this, but... I think he's got Alpha Whiskey Romeo on wheels," said Loder.

Carl knew that "Alpha Whiskey Romeo" was U.S. military speak for "Allah's Waiting Room"—dead or soon to be dead Muslims. But since he was on the move, Carl didn't have time to figure out why Loder was invoking the phrase. "Sorry, buddy, I need you to be more specific here."

"Specifically I think he's got all the Syrian earthquake victims piled up in the back of his van."

Through his scope, Loder watched Wolfenson move down the road from the vehicle. The envoy was careful to look all around him, but he moved with confidence. Like no one in the world could stop him.

"Come on, Carl, let's do something. At least let him know we're here."

There was silence on Carl's end, a prolonged period of heavy breathing.

"Come on, Carl..."

"Okay, Loder, you can explain things to him. But he cannot be harmed."

"Roger that."

304

Loder quickly began to integrate himself back into the environment, letting the air that he breathed, that brushed across his cheeks and swept around him, fill his nostrils. Loder always felt more confident in his actions when he felt as one with the energy around him.

In the Peace Forest, he had missed Dr. Fincher. Twice. He knew he failed because his state of harmony had been disrupted when he shot Reitz, someone he cared about... a man for whom he would have sacrificed his own life.

Loder squeezed the trigger, and the silencer on his rifle suppressed the shot. Grit and chunks of pavement kicked up a few inches from the envoy's feet. Wolfenson noticed it and looked like he was running on hot coals as he high-stepped behind the retaining wall of the cemetery.

"Okay, Carl, so at least he knows we're here. He's now taken cover."

"Where?"

"Behind an arched entryway adjacent to the road. You know, the entryway to Bab Al-Rahma's lower promenade."

"You have to bring me up to speed, Loder. I don't really know the layout."

After a decade of knowing one human being in a way you thought you really knew the man, to suddenly hear him say something you never thought you'd hear was disorienting. Loder had never before heard Carl utter the words, "I don't really know the layout."

"He's taken cover in an alcove, like a rock-throw away from the parked van. Wait, I hear something..."

"What?"

"I think it's him. His voice... it's echoing all across the valley."

"Loder, what do you hear?"

"Sounds Latin. You know the kind of words monks sing? But I think this one is going to miss out on winning the Grammy."

As he continued to wait for Wolfenson to pop into view so he could get off another shot, something else caught his eye. Loder redirected the scope.

"Okay, I think we may have a problem. Wait... okay, we definitely have a problem. I think something in the van is *moving*."

Loder watched as the kafan shrouding each body began to unwind at the feet. A bare foot fell out of the kafan and began to flop about. Then Loder noticed the rest of the bodies squirming.

"It looks like Allah is going to be waiting a little bit longer for these people—they're still alive..."

Suddenly, the bodies started tumbling out onto the road. Like white cocoons, they rolled around on the pavement, squirming until more sashes popped off, completely freeing the legs.

Still shrouded, one by one, the bodies got up and began to walk. Like men on their last leg, because their other leg was broken, some of the walking corpses moved slower than the others. But they were all headed in one general direction.

"Loder, what the hell is going on?"

"You tell me, Carl! Your dead earthquake victims are moving from the van toward the cemetery."

After a second, Carl said, "They're headed for the Golden Gate..."

"That's right. So let me take them out. I'm in the perfect position."

"Loder, that's what he *wants*. If you shoot, the whole place goes up..."

Loder examined the contours of the kafans, the bodies underneath. In each case, the chest seemed thicker than it should have been.

"No, wait, I can see the collar bombs under their pajamas. I just need to shoot for the head and we're good."

"Mikey, if you miss... it's game over."

"There's no way I can miss. I'm firing a Barrett XM500 SASR! Come on, Carl, just give me the green light!"

"Are there any that are crawling?"

Most of the bodies were now climbing up the hillside, over the brick walls and burial vaults. Some had gotten tangled up in young eucalyptus trees and brush. The kafans were now stained with grit, no longer white.

"Are there—"

"Yes," Loder said.

"Okay, then try one. Just shoot at *one.*"

Loder picked out the cocoon-shape of the crawler, who had fallen behind. It had gotten stumped at the retaining wall of the cemetery's upper promenade, bumping its head into the bricks, as if the mind knew what to do, but the body didn't.

Loder fired. The kafan blew out on the opposite side of the head, torn wide open by a .50 BMG round. The shrouded head slumped against the brick.

"The crawler is down," he said.

"Is it getting back up?"

"Nope."

After a respectful silence, Carl said, "Okay. Put them all to rest."

Loder didn't waste any time. He targeted the lead figure and put a round in his head. The body rolled down the hill, finally lodging itself against a cemetery marker.

He scoped out the next one and fired. This one dropped in mid-step and didn't move again. Another one of the kafans stepped right over the fallen one and took the lead. This body was shorter than the others. Obviously a child.

Loder took a quick cleansing breath before setting up his third shot. He had the white shroud in his scope and was about to the pull the trigger when the child suddenly went down.

A gunshot echoed throughout the valley.

"What was that?!" Carl said.

Loder looked up toward the Golden Gate and saw two soldiers at the parapet, pointing their weapons through the crenellations. Green pocketed vests; M-16s, set to single shot; funny little dark berets.

"Israeli Defense Force," he said. "Two of them standing at the parapet. They just took out one of the gate crashers with a headshot, but that doesn't mean they know what they're up against. I need to warn them..."

"No! Loder, I'll warn the soldiers. You just finish the job..."

Through his headset, Loder heard a loud rush of air as Carl apparently took off running.

The shrouded bodies had crossed over the upper promenade at the top of the hill and were clambering over the last few rows of tombs and graves. One of them got stuck on the metal fence surrounding the platform. It wriggled, and its cocoon slid completely off, revealing the poor mangled thing underneath.

Loder locked in his next target and fired. The head exploded, and the body fell to its knees and then fell face-first into a marble marker.

One of the soldiers noticed Loder's muzzle flash and tried to get his shooting buddy to look over, but the other soldier was too busy taking aim at one of the kafan bombers.

As Loder got ready to take out another target, he could still hear Carl's heavy breathing through the headset, but now he could also hear his feet slapping the stone steps to the rampart.

He fired again, and his target rolled down the hill, colliding into two others. They all went down in a heap of kafans. But within seconds, the two were back up, climbing on their hands and knees toward the gate.

Carl's heavy breathing paused for a moment as he yelled at the two soldiers. "Hey, you guys, do you know what you're doing?!"

There was a flash in Loder's rifle scope.

The ear-shattering force of the blast followed almost simultaneously, streaking across the cemetery, burning all the eucalyptus trees to charred sticks and setting everything else on fire.

Worshippers at the Western Wall and Dome of the Rock felt the rumble, then heard the sound. Everyone froze as black and white smoke plumed into the air. Many on the mount began to shout and run away. Others just stood there and watched, staring into the sky, completely uncomprehending.

———

THE EXPLOSION SLAMMED CARL against the rampart wall. He might have blacked out, but only for a moment; he was fully conscious as cracks appeared all around him, then widened right before his eyes.

He looked up at the gate, but didn't see the two soldiers. However, he could see the east-facing crenellations, and the wall had sustained heavy damage. The front of the parapet had partially collapsed.

Carl got to his feet, then dizzied and collapsed to one knee. After quickly regrouping, he stood up again and started to walk. He pulled out his telephone.

"Loder, are you there? Mikey, come in!"

Carl moved down the stone staircase to the courtyard and stumbled through a cloud of smoke. Thanks to the sun shining through, he could just make out the huge rugged outline of the new archway blasted into the Golden Gate. After thousands of years, the gate stood open. Carl was surprised the entire structure hadn't crumbled.

A figure ran past Carl, about a dozen feet ahead. He barely caught a glimpse of the person through the smoke.

"Patricia?!"

Before the explosion, he had taken her as far away as he could until he heard Loder's phone message about the soldiers picking off suicide bombers. He had left her on the side of the wooded path up to the Temple Mount before heading back to the east wall.

Carl moved closer to the blasted archway, waving his hand in front of his face to clear away the smoke. He heard something, and immediately saw the figure again, running straight for the new archway of the Golden Gate.

"Patricia!"

She disappeared into a cloud of smoke. Carl followed her.

On the other side of the newly opened gate, the cemetery had been reduced to rubble and flames and noxious smoke. Carl choked on the reek of human death.

He had only been a dozen steps behind Pat, but now he was having trouble finding her as he scanned the cemetery hill. Then he saw her, on her knees choking, her hand on a stone sarcophagus. Carl rushed over and pulled her up.

"Patricia, we need to get out of here."

She didn't respond, but nor did she resist.

As Carl steered her back toward the east wall, he looked in the direction of Loder's sniper nest. The haze made it impossible to see anything that far away. He had no idea whether his friend had escaped the explosion, or had joined the rest of the dead on the hill.

Carl found the sound of sirens in the distance somewhat comforting. As he and Patricia stumbled across the rubble that now lined the Golden Gate, all he could think about was how the silence on this side of the wall was deafening.

———

"I'M PARKED NEAR HEROD'S GATE," Marcus said on the sat phone. "It's relatively a ghost town. I guarantee you, Carl, you will not be detained."

"Why aren't there any police?"

"Because right now half of the initial responders are surrounding a police van I left parked on a cement divider outside of the Lion's Gate. It's the closest gate to the blast site, so they think the van is also wired to explode. I'm listening to the whole thing on a police officer's walkie-talkie. Seriously, we've got the whole boulevard to ourselves."

A few minutes later Carl and Patricia appeared, moving underneath Herod's Gate, and out of the Old City.

Marcus started up the engine, made a U-turn, and pulled up right next to them. Carl helped Patricia into the back seat and climbed in beside her. He hadn't even closed the door before Marcus pulled into traffic.

Carl looked out the rear window to see if they were being followed. On the other side of the divider, a pair of Israeli police cars, sirens blaring, raced past them, heading toward the esplanade.

Finally Carl exhaled and looked over at Patricia. She was just staring at the seat in front of her, expressionless. Carl looked up and could see his brother watching them both through the rearview mirror.

"Whatever happened to Olsen?"

"Taken care of. That's where I got the police van. He's with Jenna."

"And Jenna knows everything went south?"

"Yeah, I updated her before I let them go."

Carl nodded, feeling dejected, not only about the way everything had concluded, but because he knew that in the back of her mind Jenna would wonder whether he had planned this outcome all along.

One of his phones rang. He reached into his pocket. It was the "L" phone.

"Loder?"

"You know that was not my shot that triggered—"

"Shut up, I know it wasn't you. I was there. Where are you now?"

"Heading east just like I was supposed to do after the job.

"Are you well enough to drive?"

"I guess we'll find out."

"Okay, when I get off the phone I will send you the address of the safe house where I've got my wife and younger boy stashed. After you get them, drive to the second set of coordinates I send you. A helicopter will then fly the three of you to the rendezvous point. Understood?"

"Got it."

"Okay, we'll see you."

"Wait. You owe me a new XM500 SASR with a custom-fit suppressor."

"Get my wife and kid to the helicopter, Loder. Then I'll buy you any sniper rifle you want, no matter the cost."

He ended the call.

The car swerved around a slow-moving vehicle, and Carl slid into Patricia. As he pulled the seatbelt over her shoulder to strap her in, Carl said, "Everything's under control, Marcus. Can you please just drive the speed limit?"

———

CARL WAS WATCHING A SECURITY MONITOR of Patricia sitting on a cot. She looked completely shattered, not moving at all and staring blankly into space.

He had put her in one of his hangar offices at the Tel Aviv airport, and was keeping watch on her from the security room, where he had two dozen monitors tied to cameras set up both inside and outside the hangar.

It had been more than an hour after Marcus had dropped them off so he could go dump the escape vehicle. It had been forty-five minutes since Loder last checked in with him.

Carl was feeling paranoid and introspective. He tried not to stare at the monitor, but couldn't help it. Maybe he and Fincher weren't so different after all. The doctor got off on watching Pat have sex on a computer, and Carl was now obsessed with watching her on a slightly larger monitor after she had flirted with death.

If he had not safely transported her from the Temple Mount, there would have been nothing to prevent AOL from hunting him and his own family down and clubbing them all like seals.

Marcus appeared on one of the monitors as he approached the hangar on foot. Carl buzzed him in, then met his brother in the middle of the hangar.

"Any problems?"

He shook his head. "I drove north toward Netanya, and exactly where we planned, I ditched the car, set it on fire, and drove away in the car Loder had waiting for me. I left it in the main terminal's parking lot, and then waited awhile before walking over here."

"Well, the helicopter should be here any minute."

"Helicopter? Where are we going?"

"To a place I call the Monastery. We'll be safe there."

"I'm not looking for safe. And I thought neither were you. I told Jenna and Olsen we were going to regroup and take another run at AOL. What's going on?"

Carl's sat phone rang and he counted the interruption as a blessing.

"Loder, tell me you have my wife and boy?"

"I'm looking at them right now. Your wife is kind of getting on my nerves, asking me why I haven't married. I told her I'm gay, but that doesn't seem to be putting her off."

"Sounds just like Zeinah! What's your ETA?"

"Less than ten minutes."

"Great job. See you in ten."

Carl disconnected and immediately turned back to his brother. "So, Marcus, are you coming with us?"

"Yeah, sure... absolutely. As long as we're all going to be safe."

"Don't worry about that. This place we're going to is like a medieval fortress... a high-tech medieval fortress. Look, I want to do a perimeter check before the chopper lands. Will you keep an eye on Patricia?"

"Yeah, sure. Absolutely. Where is she?"

CARL UNLOCKED THE DOOR and slowly opened it so Patricia wouldn't be startled.

"Hey, Pat, how are you doing? Everything's going great out here. We're about to take a helicopter ride to a special place, and then that's it. It'll be home for a while. Sound good?"

Carl waited, but didn't expect a reaction from Patricia. She met his expectations by just staring at him, then wiping her nose with her hand.

He showed his brother in. "You remember, Marcus, my brother, right? Well, he's back. He's going to look after you while I go away for a few minutes."

Patricia stood up, looking distressed.

"No, no, nothing to worry about. I will be back here in just a few minutes, and Marcus will be here to make sure nothing happens to you. Okay?"

She seemed more calmed after he reached out, grabbed her hand, kissed it, then kissed her cheek.

"Okay, I will be right back, Marcus." Carl shut the door—and sprinted directly to the security office.

He had a hunch. But he had been pretty much ninety-five percent wrong in the last two days... the last two decades. He dearly hoped that, at least this one time, his losing streak would persist.

As it turned out, Marcus didn't waste any time. The moment Carl got back to the security office, he saw on the security monitor that his brother had already yanked a lamp cord from the wall and from the back of a lamp, and was now advancing on Patricia.

The door to the office flew open and Carl rushed in with his gun drawn.

Patricia had obviously fought back because the interior was already a mess, and the furthest Marcus had gotten in his attempt to kill her was to corner her in the room. His brother was still holding the power cord taut between his two hands.

"Marcus!"

"We need to talk about this, Carl!"

"Yeah, we'll talk, but first step away from her!"

"Brother, listen to me. This is another one of your mistakes."

"No, Marcus, you listen to me. Step the fuck away from her, or I will be firing this gun. Are we clear?"

"Carl, don't look at her face. Just focus on what's inside her. Aren't we responsible for ending what we both helped create?"

When he fired the gun, it sounded like a bomb going off in the room. Marcus dropped to his knees in agony, clutching the back of the thigh.

Carl rushed across the room and shoved the gun into his brother's spine.

Patricia was crying and Marcus was laughing. Carl knew it was just a technique he was using to squelch the pain.

"Can't say I didn't warn you, Marcus."

His brother stopped laughing and started sucking in air like a pregnant woman taking a Lamaze class. Marcus stopped his focused breathing long enough to say his piece.

"There's no leverage standing here, Carl. AOL already showed you he doesn't care about her or what she's carrying."

"He didn't care today. But that doesn't mean he won't feel differently in the future."

"I guess you know him best."

"You're bleeding something awful there, Marcus. I suggest you get to your point."

"Listening to the two of you talking on the phone was a real education for me. What was the line from that song the three of us used to sing when we were kids? 'I am he as you are he as you are me and we are all together...'"

"If you keep talking nonsense, big brother, pretty soon I won't know whether you're delirious from the blood loss, or just delirious."

"Why don't we let Rex settle this? He's the one who always accused you of getting carried away with yourself and believing the craziest notions. Wonder what he'd say if I told him I thought you had the grand idea of somehow being the Yoda to the future Antichrist?"

Carl didn't respond. The relentless sound of Patricia sobbing saved the room from silence.

He raised the gun and thrust it into his brother's scalp.

Marcus stiffened. "Do it, Carl! Pull the trigger! Do it!"

Pat started to scream.

"Just do it, because if you don't, I promise you I will not stop until her baby is dead. Come on, if you intend to go down this path anyway, then do yourself a favor and get one obstacle out of the way now. And do me a favor, because I would rather be the brother who is shot than the one having to pull the trigger!"

Before pulling the trigger, Carl had one more question.

"What do you want to do about Jenna?"

———

THE HELICOPTER LANDED ON THE TARMAC in front of Saracen Security's hangar at the Tel Aviv airport.

Patricia ran toward the chopper with Carl shielding her like an umbrella.

Loder hopped down from the passenger compartment of the helicopter, and helped Patricia in first. He turned to Carl with a confused look.

"I thought your brother was coming with us."

Carl shook his head. "He didn't make it." He shoved Loder in, and was preparing to step onto the helicopter himself when he caught sight of his wife and son. Tears filled his eyes as he stepped onboard to join them.

After they were all buckled in, Carl tapped the dividing glass and the pilot pulled back on the stick. The black helicopter lifted from the tarmac toward the sky, and flew off toward the Judean Desert.

CHAPTER 24

IN HER MIND there was never any question that she would ignore her father's advice to "just leave." Jenna had come too far to simply turn back and wait for another opportunity... which may never come. But she needed to know what Olsen wanted to do. She couldn't stop Envoy John Wolfenson by herself.

Then they heard the explosion.

Neither consulted the other. They raced into the Western Wall Plaza while hundreds of people raced in the opposite direction. She tried calling Carl on his phone, but no one answered.

As they stood staring at the black smoke rising from the eastside, Olsen began praying. Jenna began to think.

Carl had obviously failed. From the look of the smoke plume, the explosion was huge. But it wasn't so massive that she and Father Olsen weren't still standing there.

Shattered sacred stone. The phrase continued to haunt her.

"Shouldn't we check it out?" Father Olsen asked.

"No, that's not where we need to be. Alan, no matter what has happened over there, we need to be more concerned with what hasn't happened. Maybe we can still stop him."

"So you think Satan is going to attack again?"

She wanted to answer, but emergency response teams were rushing past them toward the explosion. Jenna worried that whoever had detained the priest earlier could still be running around, so she grabbed Alan and led him toward Wilson's Arch. They stepped into an alcove near the tunnel at the foundation of the Western Wall.

"I know a little something about explosives," she said. "What we just witnessed looked big, but it doesn't match the explosive power Carl had been asked to obtain."

"Okay, so let's say you're right. What would be the envoy's next target?"

"Carl said he can only personally attack manmade creations. So we have a few choices around us, but let's see if I can narrow it down a bit: 'shattered sacred stone.'"

"Ah, we're back to those words again. Okay, how about the Wailing Wall..."

"I agree it's considered sacred," Jenna said, "but it's an entire wall of sacred stones, not just a single sacred stone."

To his credit, Olsen came up with his next answer almost immediately. "The Dome of the Rock. But it's not shattered..."

"Not yet at least. Carl also mentioned that they wanted him to acquire explosives that would have an Israeli signature. If the Dome of Rock were to be destroyed, and the Israeli government were to be blamed..."

"It could trigger a sectarian war," Olsen said, finishing her thought.

"And if everyone follows through with his low expectations, the Devil's work would be done for him."

"So let's get to the Dome of the Rock. We'll just be waiting there when he walks through the doors."

"I love your spirit, Father, but it's not going to be that simple. The Waqf, who guard the mount, restrict access to non-Muslims on a normal day. With the explosion, just getting up there will be impossible."

Olsen suddenly got excited. "I know the perfect person who can help us out. Can I borrow that satellite phone?"

Jenna handed it to him and Olsen dialed a number.

"I just hope he will forgive us for bothering him twice in one day..."

"You're talking about Jawad?"

"Yes! He's been a Waqf guard on the mount for years." The priest abruptly turned his attention to the phone. "Jawad... Yes, it's me again..."

————

DR. FINCHER HAD ALREADY WARNED the group of terrorists a few times that they could not celebrate the explosion at the Golden Gate when they heard it because the people on the floor above them might hear. And when the cave finally did rumble, the doctor was heartened that everyone obeyed his directive.

"Okay, so now we wait. Most of the visitors and staff will have heard the noise, and will leave the building to check it out. We just sit tight and let the place clear out."

His phone rang and he answered it. He sat up when he realized it was the Angel of Light.

"Yes, sir, we heard the explosion... Very good, sir... We're all ready to follow your will. And, sir, once again, it's been a pleasure to serve you."

The doctor hung up.

"That was OSK. Everything went as planned on his side."

Fincher looked over at Hadji. "Your brother says I should kick you in the ass like a goat if you have any second thoughts."

Hassanat smiled.

The doctor checked his watch. It was still too early.

His phone rang again and he assumed it was the envoy.

"Hello..."

It was not the envoy. But the caller had compelling information, and Fincher listened without a word. He began to pace back and forth, but after a few seconds he realized he was panicking the attack team, so he stopped in his tracks.

Fincher covered the phone and addressed the terrorists. "This has nothing to do with the operation. Everything is still good." Then he got back on the line.

"Yes, that's exactly what you need to do. You need to lead them to me, and I will take care of the situation... Listen to me, I do know who she is and I will take care of her. Just lead them the same way you led us. Understood? I will take care of the rest. Call me when you've brought them to the mosque."

He ended the call and looked at his watch. Fincher then turned to Hadji. "Who are you going to ask for?"

"Envoy John Wolfenson."

Fincher nodded and looked back at his watch, counting down the seconds. Then he looked up.

"Go with God..."

Before Hadji led the group upstairs, Noora kissed him. Then the big Bedouin man led the other terrorists upstairs to seize control of the Dome of the Rock.

"You're not going as well?" Fincher asked Noora.

"No, I cannot go up there. Not yet."

The doctor was confused. Then he remembered the desert.

"The little girl I saw with you. Who was she?"

"Search your soul, Colin. You know who she was."

He looked away, hoping that perhaps if he wasn't looking at her, he could clear his mind and figure things out. But nothing came to him. When he turned back, she was standing right in front of him. In her hand was a razor-sharp knife.

"A gunshot might alert those on the outside. You will use this to kill the priest who comes to stop us."

Fincher wondered how she knew.

She placed the knife in his hand.

"Make no mistake as to the purpose of this man's effort. He intends not only to stop us today, but to destroy all that has been planned for thousands of years."

From upstairs, the doctor heard shouts and screams and a demonstrative gunshot, and knew the assault had begun.

"You need not worry about what goes on above. I will see that everything goes well. Colin, Father Olsen intends to rob you of your rightful place at the side of the Angel of Light. What are you going to do about it?"

———

AGENT GINSBERG STILL FELT SORE from the Taser attack, but knew his body would recover. He wasn't so sure about his pride.

"They stole the van," Officer Cohen said once Aluf could move again.

Then it got worse.

After the explosion on the east wall, he and Cohen watched as a bomb team took thirty excruciatingly long minutes to approach the stolen police van, abandoned near the Lion's Gate. Even after it was declared a false alarm, the damage had been done—half of the Israeli police department had been used to set up a perimeter in case of an explosion. The manpower clearly could have been used more efficiently minutes after a massive explosion had blown out the Golden Gate.

And it all happened because Ginsberg was stupid enough to fall for a con that teachers back at the military training center wouldn't even use on recruits because it was too easy to see through.

As he waited on hold to change his plane reservations and get the hell out of the country, Agent Ginsberg watched from a distance as one of the police station's staff sergeants screamed in Officer Cohen's face.

"Agent Gingsberg, maybe you can tell me what's going on?"

It was Interior Minister Mier Kahlon. Apparently he had just arrived and had no clue that the whole mess surrounding him was Ginsberg's fuck up. Aluf knew why the minister approached him—the agent had on numerous occasions guarded Mier.

He hung up with the airline. "Yes, Minister, what can I do for you?"

"You can tell me what's going on. I was getting ready to host a dinner party with my wife and I get this call about an explosion on the east wall. Are there any more details?"

"Sir, what we know is that a bomb attack apparently took out the entire Golden Gate, killing two IDF soldiers. It appears to have been a group of suicide bombers. At least those are the initial reports."

Kahlon lowered his head, truly saddened. The minister's cell phone began to ring in his coat. As he was reaching for it, he said, "Can you stay with me and let me know if you get any more information?"

Aluf nodded, and the minister answered his phone.

"Yes, this is Interior Minister Kahlon... Wait... who is this?"

Ginsberg watched the minster's face pale, and, deciding to give the minister privacy, he started to take a step away. The minster grabbed his arm and forced him to stay put.

After listening silently for at least half a minute, Kahlon finally responded to the caller.

"I understand what you've requested, but how do I know..." The minister stopped speaking. He looked at his phone. Apparently the caller had hung up.

"Sir?"

The minister looked shaken, confused. "That was someone who claimed to be the terrorist OSK, saying he has taken over the Qubbat Al-Sakhra along with nine hostages. He says he will only surrender it if he can first meet and speak with Envoy John Wolfenson."

The Qubbat Al-Sakhra—the Dome of the Rock.

So many thoughts ran through Agent Ginsberg's mind that he didn't know which one to voice first. The minister gave up waiting for a response and was already dialing a number on his phone.

Finally Ginsberg said, "Minster, sir, we need to verify first that the Dome of the Rock has indeed been taken over by terrorists."

"Yes, of course we do. Contact the head of the Yamam immediately and get them down here. And can you also please inform Lev Teyman at the Internal Security Ministry? He should certainly be brought up to speed."

"Sir, should I also ascertain the whereabouts of Envoy Wolfenson?"

"That won't be necessary. As I was just telling you, I was hosting a party when I got the call about the explosion. One of my guests, my God, I passed him in the hallway of my house when I was leaving..."

Kahlon held up a finger to Ginsberg. "John," he said into the phone, "this is Mier... Oh, good, glad to hear you're enjoying yourself. But listen, something has come up and it might need your attention..."

———

JAWAD MET THEM AT WILSON ARCH, looking as if he had good news. "If you need to get into the Qubbat al-Sakhra, I think I might be able to help."

Father Olsen hugged him. "Thank you so much, my friend."

Because of their language differences, Jenna didn't immediately celebrate.

"Jawad, how is it possible in the midst of all this chaos for you to get us into the Dome of the Rock... without being noticed?"

"I've talked to a friend of mine and he just now granted me permission, special permission, to allow us into the Qubbat al-Sakhra. After you both clear inspections at the Temple Mount entrance, I will take you to the Marwani Mosque, which is how we will proceed to the place you seek."

Jenna knew of an underground passageway from the al-Aqsa Mosque to the double gate on the east side of the esplanade, but she had never heard of any secret passageway to the Dome of the Rock. Not even rumors.

"I apologize for being difficult, but I don't understand. I thought the only way into the Dome of the Rock is through four doors, on the arcade level."

Jawad stepped in closer to them. "Yes, that's what most people know. But there is a cave below the arcades."

She looked over at Father Olsen, embarrassed that she was going to once more look a gift horse in the mouth.

"I'm sorry to sound so ungrateful, Jawad, but I know of the cave directly below the Foundation Stone, and I know about the legend that the cave rests atop the Well of Souls. But I'm still confused. Because even in the legend... it's just a cave, with access only through the Dome of the Rock."

"There are no issues, Ms. Grant. I know what you seek, and I'm going to take you there. It is a secret way into the cave."

Jenna nodded, hoping she and Jawad weren't talking past each other. They were running out of time. If the Angel of Light was planning to destroy something else on the Temple Mount this day, he would surely act under the cover of chaos.

JENNA AND FATHER OLSEN followed Jawad up the enclosed ramp to the Mughrabi Gate high up on the Western Wall. The Mughrabi Gate was the only gate to the Temple Mount that the Waqf would allow non-Muslims to enter. As a constant visitor to the area, Jenna knew the controversy all too well.

The Muslims called the Temple Mount *Haram al-Sharif*, or Noble Sanctuary, and *Time Magazine* once referred to it as "the most volatile thirty-five acres on Earth."

Throughout history, the hilltop compound had become the epicenter of the bloody conflict between Israelis and Muslims, and Christians were getting more and more involved in the fighting as well.

As she and Alan were being inspected by the Waqf guards, Jenna stared at what many people felt was the figurative center of the conflict—one of the most beautiful and stunning achievements of Islamic architecture: the Qubbat al-Sakhra, the Dome of the Rock. The intricately tiled octagon with its gold-plated dome was the earliest dated Muslim building in the world, clocking in at 1,300 years old. Jenna knew enough about the construction to understand the irony behind its creation—the inspiration of the Qubbat al-Sakhra came from Christian architecture, in more ways than one.

The Church of the Holy Sepulcher, built on the burial ground of Jesus Christ, had been the religious focus of Jerusalem before the city was conquered by Arabs in 638 A.D. When the Muslims first conceived of the Dome of the Rock, their most important goal was to refocus the attention from the tomb of the Lord to a celebration of Islam.

Even the interior of the building was inspired by classic Christian architecture, such as the House of St. Peter in Capernaum. In the center of the octagonal floor plan is the martyria, which is meant to be highlighted, or enshrined. A circular arcade surrounds the martyria, and an octagonal arcade encloses it, echoing the exterior shape of the building.

In the case of the Dome of the Rock, the martyria enshrined was the Foundation Stone: a mammoth rock representing the zenith of holiness, and considered by Muslims to be the center of the world.

But the rock was also considered by many Jews to be the center of their religion as well.

And therein lay the problem.

WALKING PAST THE FINAL GUARD, Jawad led them to the southeastern corner of the compound.

"Can you both wait here just a few minutes before I take you into the mosque? I must get some keys to the secret passage."

"Of course, my friend," Father Olsen said. "We appreciate you getting us this far."

Jawad nodded and then walked to a small building nearby, entering through a locked door.

As soon as he was out of earshot, Jenna said to Alan, "The Golden Gate was blown open."

"How do you know that, Jenna?"

"I'm fluent in Arabic, Alan. I heard one of the guards speaking about it while we were being searched." She grabbed his arm. "Can we... move away from here so we can talk?"

They walked a dozen yards to some heavy-duty earthmoving equipment and other supplies used in the Waqf's excavations of the Temple Mount.

"Alan, this is your last chance to back out. Yes, Envoy John Wolfenson might be personally involved in destroying the Dome of the Rock. Or I'm wrong and his team somehow got their hands on enough explosives to do the job without the envoy getting his hands dirty. If that's the case, we could be going out of our way to be at ground zero at a massive explosion."

The priest had been staring at the Qubbat Al-Sakhra as she spoke. He turned to her as soon as she was finished. "I've taken into consideration everything you've said, and I want to go forward. I trust that the way you've thought this out is the way it will happen."

"And you base this decision on what, exactly?"

Something caught the priest's eye and he moved toward it. "Isn't this the sort of thing you would be wearing while working a dig?"

Near several containers of dirt, someone had left behind a utility belt full of archeological tools.

"Well, I don't wear a belt—that would be too manly—but, yeah, these are some of the tools I would use." Jenna saw in the belt a hardwood needle point, a nickel-plated soil sampler, and of course a trowel. It wasn't a Marshalltown trowel, her favorite brand, but it was certainly sharp enough to get the job done. Holding the trowel in her hand, Jenna felt homesick. Not for London, or Occoquan, but for a dig site... anywhere in the world that had some unrevealed secrets.

She smiled.

"I saw that," Olsen said playfully.

"Ah, you caught me reacting to something I was thinking."

"Hmm... please share."

"Look, honestly, I was thinking nasty thoughts about how coming across these tools here is... well, I was going to use the word *ironic*, but a more descriptive word would be *bullshit*."

She looked around to make sure there was no one nearby.

"When the Waqf dug out the area to build their underground mosque, they made it a point to dispose of all the excavated dirt like it was radioactive, secretly dumping it wherever they hoped no one was looking. It was meant to be a total middle finger to the Israelis, and to the archeological community."

"Why would they do that?"

"Because they don't want anyone to discover evidence that this mount is the historical place of two Jewish temples."

Jenna couldn't finish because Jawad emerged from the small building and waved for them to follow. "Father Olsen... Ms. Grant... this way. We are all set to go."

Father Olsen immediately followed his friend.

Jenna lingered a bit, then moved quickly to catch up with them both.

As they approached the al-Aqsa Mosque, she looked over at the priest and said, "You never answered my question, Alan."

He smiled and said, "It might surprise you to know even priests can make leaps of faith."

———

GINSBERG LOOKED AT HIS WATCH. The meeting was going too slow.

In response to the hostage situation at the Dome of the Rock, they had set up a crisis center in one of the security offices at the Western Wall Plaza. Present were Ginsberg's Shin Bet division head, Ilan Graff; the top man at the IDF, Moshe Kerem; the top man at the Yamam, Omri Galil; the Interior Minister, Mier Kahlon; and Lev Teyman, the Internal Security Minister, who was running the meeting.

There was also someone in the room standing behind Minister Teyman, a man whom Ginsberg had never seen before. This newcomer had the swagger and confidence of someone who was more than just the security minister's assistant. Ginsberg asked Ilan about the man and cryptically his boss answered, "That's Uriel. He's part of the Duvdevan Unit."

It made sense. Uriel looked every bit Special Forces, from his crew cut and facial scars to his musculature. "'Ureil' what?" Ginsberg asked.

Impatiently, Ilan said, "He has Black Clearance. That's all you need to know."

"MIER, DO YOU MIND going through the phone conversation one more time for those who have just joined us?" Teyman asked.

"Yes, of course. He said he was OSK."

"The rebel without a pause?" Galil asked incredulously.

"OSK is dead," Ilan chimed in.

"Says who?" asked Uriel.

"Says the CIA," Aluf responded, stepping up beside his boss.

"Yeah, okay, well then you have me there," Mr. Black Clearance said with a smirk. "Because we all know they've never been wrong before."

Most of the men in the room laughed.

Minister Teyman raised a hand, prompting Uriel to take a step back. "Mier, please continue."

"Whoever it was on the phone said he wanted to talk to Envoy John Wolfenson and that was the only way they would surrender the Dome of the Rock and let the nine hostages go free."

"Those were his exact words?" asked Galil, the Yamam head.

"Yes, word for word."

"You see, I'm worried about the wording," Galil continued. "He will surrender the dome, and allow the nine hostages to go free. That suggests two different stages, or worse... he's lying. He might let the hostages go and destroy the dome, or kill the hostages before surrendering the dome."

"Okay, noted, Omri," Teyman said. "Anything else, Mier?"

"Yes, he ended with the demand to see Envoy John Wolfenson."

"Thank you, Mier." Minister Teyman looked at his watch. "Gentlemen, the grand mufti should be here with the rest of the Islamic Council any minute. So speak your minds now."

"No surprise, I want to go in heavy and hard," said Galil. "We can't scope the place with our sharp shooters, but our heat analysis is throwing back only six terrorists. There's a hatch on the dome roof. What if we told them the envoy was on his way, then have my men drop down from above while the terrorists' attention is drawn toward the doors?"

No one said a word.

Silence.

"I apologize," said Mier, "I should have repeated that the terrorist spokesperson made it very clear the entire building is wired to explode if we attempt an assault."

Galil waved his hand dismissively. "Of course they're going to say that." The head of the Yamam turned to Minister Teyman. "Sir, you know as well as I do these situations are usually never about what my team can do. It's about what we believe the terrorists are capable of doing. Do you believe they want to blow up the Dome of the Rock?"

"Well, they already blew up the Golden Gate, right?" Uriel said, reclaiming his spot next to the internal security minister. "So this is not someone coming into a room and telling us about how big his dick is and then runs the moment we produce a tape measure. These assholes have already taken out the Golden Gate. Shouldn't we respect that?"

"Yes, we should."

The voice came from the doorway. It was the Grand Mufti of Jerusalem, Adnan Fayyad, backed by half a dozen members of his Islamic Council.

"Gentlemen, I know you want to do the right thing here," the grand mufti said as he entered the room. "But is it all right if we do the 'right' thing after we've tried the peaceful way first?"

Meir said, "Adnan, I've already called Envoy John Wolfenson. It is what the terrorists asked for."

"Well, I have just spoken to Envoy Wolfenson, and we agree he should go to the Dome of the Rock and speak with the terrorists."

The Islamic Council stepped aside and allowed Envoy Wolfenson into the room.

"Mr. Envoy," said Minister Teyman, "thank you for coming."

Kahlon walked over and hugged the envoy. "Yes, thank you for answering the call."

"Mier, Minister Teyman, all of you here, I'm glad that under these circumstances I can make myself available for service. The truth is the grand mufti and I were both forced to park miles away from the plaza. Then we ran into each other and had no choice on the long walk over but to speak to each other."

Everyone in the room laughed politely.

The envoy pointed at a glass of water on the table, and the head of the IDF gave John permission to help himself. Wolfenson snatched the glass and everyone waited and watched as he gulped down the water.

"As I said, it was a 'long walk.'" Everyone in the room laughed again.

But not Ginsberg.

"Omri, you have the best assault team in the world," Wolfenson said. "If I fail, no doubt the worst that will happen is that you now have ten hostages rather than nine."

"Not true, John," said Mier. "The whole point of this terrorist operation could be to kill you."

"Ah, yes, thank you for reminding me." Again, like a standup comedian, the envoy hit his punch line perfectly, and it got a great reaction from everyone crowded into the room. But this time there was nervous laughter as well.

"The truth is, I probably should have died here weeks ago, but somehow I didn't. So I know many of you in this room are probably gamblers... Sorry, looking around the room I can see in your eyes that you're all gamblers..." After the laughter died down, Wolfenson continued. "What would you do when you've just been dealt a winning hand? Walk away just when you're feeling lucky? Or stay at the table and at least play another hand?"

Ginsberg looked around the room. People were actually tearing up. He was tearing up... and he wasn't sure how sincere the whole speech was.

"These bad guys are threatening innocent people." The envoy put a hand on the grand mufti's shoulder. "And they're threatening to destroy a place of worship." Wolfenson turned to Minister Teyman. "Let me go in. You can always get to this other stuff if I fail. Because, gentlemen, this is the time when you need to back another gambler on a hot streak, especially if the only one who could get hurt... is me. What do you say?"

Minister Teyman looked around the room to see if there were any objections. He finally turned back to Envoy John Wolfenson. "Yes. And thank you, sir."

"I'm sorry, Lev, what would you like me to do?"

The minister cleared his throat. "Envoy, sir, I'm requesting you go and meet with the terrorists and see if we can settle things peacefully."

Wolfenson nodded, then turned his attention to the grand mufti.

"And you, Adnan, what are your wishes?"

"It would honor us if you would enter the Qubbat al-Sakhra, representing our hopes of having this matter settled without violence."

The envoy embraced the grand mufti, and the whole room broke out in applause.

"Mier, call them and tell them I'm on my way."

———

AGENT GINSBERG CAUGHT UP with Wolfenson, who was accompanied by only one person, Uriel, Mr. Black Clearance. They were moving across the Western Wall Plaza, headed toward the Temple Mount.

"Envoy, sir, do you mind if I ask you a few questions?"

Wolfenson turned and recognized the agent.

"Agent Ginsberg, isn't it?"

"Yes, sir, but I'm sure you only remember my name because I'm the one who almost got you killed."

The envoy stopped and turned to him. "No, I don't feel that way at all, Agent Ginsberg. What happened that day was the most important day of my life. Do you understand?"

"I think so, sir."

Wolfenson embraced him, then began walking again.

"The question I was hoping you'd answer is why you showed up without any bodyguards."

Ginsberg noticed a slight hitch in the envoy's walk after he asked the question. Uriel turned to look at the agent, assessing whether or not he meant any harm.

"I only ask, sir, because the company that normally runs with you is Saracen Security. Is that right, sir?"

Wolfenson stopped walking. He smiled as he looked over at Uriel, but his expression got sharper around the edges by the time he directed his attention to Agent Ginsberg.

"The reason I ask, Envoy, sir, is that one of Carl Saracen's men was found shot to death early this morning. And as far as we can tell, he was working as one of your bodyguards."

Mr. Black Clearance took two very demonstrative steps toward Aluf. The agent knew the interview had run its course, but he hoped that he could still squeeze in one last question.

"Mr. Envoy, do you know Father Alan Olsen? He says he knows you. He swears you are demonically possessed—"

Ginsberg had to acknowledge that perhaps Uriel had been given Black Clearance for good reasons. Aluf barely saw the man move, and the next thing he knew, he was flat on his back on the plaza stones.

There he lay, watching Envoy Wolfenson walk off with Mr. Black Clearance. Aluf was not sure what was true and what wasn't. But Ginsberg couldn't deny the poetry of everything that had happened to him in the last twenty-four hours. As the agent looked around, he realized that somehow he was lying in the exact spot a man had died, and just a few feet away from where Sandy Travis had died as well.

———

LIKE HOMES IN THE MIDWEST—which were built with cellars to withstand tornadoes—citadels, castles, and forts were often built with a fallback plan: a place to hide or flee if the final line of defense was overrun by invaders.

When Romans conquered Jerusalem and burned the Jewish temple in 70 C.E. Josephus tells of the Jews who fled to the "mines," which was the historian's word for "underground passages." The Temple Mount not only had been the site of two Jewish temples, including the Second Temple, known as Herod's Temple, it was also believed by many to have been the home of Solomon's Palace, described in the Bible. And over hundreds of years, each new grand construction replaced the previous one, probably built on top of one another. That's why the phrase "underground passages" took on an even deeper meaning on the Temple Mount.

As Jawad led Jenna and Father Olsen into the underground Marwani Mosque, Jenna got her first look at the huge underground halls, vaults, and pillars that at one point served as Solomon's Stables. Completed in 1999, and carpeted in red, the mosque was controversial from the very beginning. Ignoring Israeli law, the Waqf had commenced construction without proper archeological supervision.

From the portico, Jawad led them down the main hallway of the mosque. At the end of the hallway, they crossed an interior courtyard, then veered off into one of the many different adjacent corridors. Halfway down the passageway, Jawad stopped at a simple wooden door, and used two keys to unlock and open it.

Once in the room, Jawad locked the door behind them, then didn't waste any time scooting one of the many bookcases aside. The secret wall panel had been treated with a façade meant to mimic the surrounding brick; the camouflage was so seamless Jenna hadn't noticed the panel until Jawad pulled it open, revealing the dark.

He reached his hand into the black opening and must have flipped on a switch because a string of small lights lit up all along the ceiling of a long tunnel.

Jawad waved Jenna and the priest into the secret hall. For a second she almost forgot what they had come to do as her heart raced with the excitement an archeologist feels before entering an ancient passageway.

The tunnel was definitely not a tourist attraction like the other tunnels around the Temple Mount. But it was impressive nonetheless. It began with rock-cut steps, leading to a long corridor about seven feet high and six feet across. The tunnel had been cut out of the limestone; Jenna could see the marks of tools used hundreds of years ago... and more recently.

She was guessing that during the construction of the Marwani Mosque, the Waqf must have stumbled upon the tunnel leading to the Well of Souls under the Dome of the Rock. She imagined the discovery delighted Muslim officials. Jenna had heard their ultimate goal was to cover the entire Temple Mount with mosques or other Muslim buildings, and that they all would be connected.

As they walked an upward slope into the tunnel, Jenna began noticing dozens and dozens of small niches cut into the wall.

"Well, those holes wipe away any doubt that this tunnel was not used as a cistern," she said to Father Olsen. "Hundreds of years ago those niches were used to raise doves."

The priest looked over, but did not seem too impressed with her observation. His reaction caused her to once again worry about Father Olsen. She felt right at home moving through a dark and dank limestone passageway. It was easily the first time in days she had felt so... alive. But the priest looked grim. Maybe this was his game face before performing an exorcism. Or maybe he was having second thoughts about confronting Envoy Wolfenson.

"How are you doing there, Alan?"

"Just fine. I've had a few opportunities to go down into the underground area below the Vatican, and I've always passed. Now I'm beginning to realize why."

"Feeling a little claustrophobic?"

"No, that's not it." He turned back to speak to Jawad. "How much farther, my friend?"

"Not very far to go, Father Olsen. We're almost there."

For the first time Jenna noticed Jawad had been walking behind them. While escorting them through the mosque, he had acted more like a guide, taking the lead.

Jenna turned back to the priest. "What is it then, Father?"

"I don't know, it feels like... *death* down here."

MAYBE IT WAS FROM SPENDING so much time with George that made her sensitive to Olsen's words. Perhaps Jenna had come to realize she was clueless about matters either spiritual or paranormal. A week ago she would have been proud of that insensitivity. Now she believed it could get her killed.

Jenna looked around the narrow corridor more closely. Though every ten feet a light dangled from the electrical wire, the passageway still teemed with shadows. The limestone floor was especially hard to see. Nevertheless, Jenna looked ahead and eventually she noticed something.

"Hey, Jawad, how many times have you been down here before?"

He hesitated. "Just once."

Once? Then why would he hesitate? It couldn't be that he was a little slow on the recall. He would definitely remember walking through a place like this, unless he had done it dozens of times, in which case he could have lost count. But only one time? Could he have paused because he was trying to figure out what his answer should be?

"Jawad, how many people know about this tunnel?"

"As I said, very few. It is a very well-guarded secret."

And yet what she had just noticed was that the tunnel ground showed traces of footprints, several pairs, all recent. She could tell because the older footprints were dry and hardened, but these were still moist in the damp dirt covering the stone floor.

Jenna glanced back at Jawad and noticed he had fallen even farther behind. And he looked nervous, his eyes darting back and forth as if he were waiting for something.

She quickly recalled everything she knew about Jawad. "He's been Waqf for years," Olsen had said. A Waqf guard working the Temple Mount would be the perfect person for the Red Veil to recruit... or possess. Alan had also told her that it was Carl's wife who had turned to Jawad for help in exorcising her son, but perhaps that was a lie. Maybe it was really Carl who enlisted Jawad's aid, because he knew Jawad was keeping surveillance on Father Alan Olsen for the Red Veil. So rather than picking a priest out of the phone book, Carl just reached out to Jawad and asked him to bring in Father Olsen.

But what if it wasn't just Carl who knew about Jawad's connection to the Waqf and the Temple Mount? What if another member of the Red Veil also knew about the connection?

Jenna started to speed up a bit, taking two steps for Olsen's one. By the time she moved around the curve in the passageway, she was at least three yards ahead of the priest. She caught sight of a faint glow at the end of tunnel and was about to tell Alan what she had seen when a noise startled her.

Jenna whipped around.

A figure had landed in a crouched position in the tunnel between them. He had apparently been hiding in a large niche she had simply walked past.

Perhaps the lighting conditions in the tunnel were similar to the previous night in the Peace Forest, because she instantly recognized the figure as Dr. Fincher, the man George had died trying to kill.

———

COLIN FINCHER SAW, not terror in Father Olsen's eyes, but confusion. But it didn't matter whether it was terror or confusion—the priest was frozen, a sitting duck. The doctor advanced on him with the knife.

He glimpsed Jawad behind the priest, raising his hand.

"What are you doing?!" Jawad screamed, suddenly realizing that the target was Father Olsen and not the woman.

Fincher heard footsteps behind him, but he was too close to Olsen not to simply follow through and put an end to the priest's exasperating attempts at intervention. The doctor raised the blade.

A sharp stabbing pain in Fincher's neck stopped him from lunging.

The doctor was suddenly gasping for air. He dropped the knife and reached up, feeling a hard wood needle sticking out from the side of his neck. He turned around.

Then there was another acute, painful jolt radiating throughout his entire body, and he looked down to see the handle of a garden tool sticking out from his chest.

Fincher felt his whole body go numb. He watched as a drop of blood slowly fell from his chest wound and splashed into a puddle of blood that had already formed in front of his left foot.

Another drop fell from his body, but this time he realized it wasn't blood; it was a bead of perspiration.

When the sweat drop hit the ground in front of his feet, it did not splash in the puddle of blood. It hit the dry, cracked surface of a riverbed.

Colin looked up and saw he was standing in a desert. It looked like a place he had been before, but he couldn't decide whether it was Tucson where he grew up, or the desert outside of Arad.

It was hot, that's all he knew. Heat waves shook above the ground all around him and for as far as he could see, out into the great expanse of desert before him.

In the distance, a figure began to emerge from the mirage. Colin blinked, and the figure was now standing inches away from him.

It was Darshana. He knew this, but not because of her appearance. She looked nothing like the beautiful little girl he had met at the Bedouin camp. Fincher did not flinch at the hideous sight before him. It would have been self-defeating, because in her wide black eyes he could see his own reflection. Colin was even more hideous than Darshana.

"Are you ready to get back to work?"

She didn't wait for his answer. Darshana grabbed his hand and led him out into the desert.

———

JENNA STEPPED BACK once she saw Fincher drop to his knees, then to the ground. She had snatched the tools from the utility belt before joining Jawad and Father Olsen. She was not surprised she had stabbed him with such efficiency. On digs, someone once told her she wielded her trowel like a surgeon handled a scalpel.

"He's dead," Father Olsen said, kneeling over him. The priest turned to Jawad, who tried to say something only to stumble on his own words. He gave up and scrambled back down the tunnel toward the mosque.

Jenna stared at the trowel lodged directly in Dr. Fincher's heart and thought about Carri... and George. But only for a moment because her attention was back on the priest. Father Olsen stood up and staggered to the tunnel wall, almost collapsing against it in despair.

"We don't have much time, Father."

"I need a minute."

She walked over to him and put a hand on his shoulder.

"Alan, I'm not sure we have a minute. You need to forget about the attack, and forget about what Jawad did. Because clearly we know we're on the right track."

CHAPTER 25

ENVOY JOHN WOLFENSON entered the Dome of the Rock through the Bab al-Kible, or south gate, stepping past one of the masked terrorists holding an AK-47. Armed sentries guarded the other three gates all around the outer octagon.

In the center of the dome, a fifth terrorist stood at the wood screen that enshrined the giant Foundation Stone. He watched over the nine hostages spread out on the carpet, all lying face-down on the floor.

Though the sixth terrorist wore a mask, the envoy recognized him as OSK's half-brother, Hadji Hassanat. He walked over to greet the Bedouin leader.

"So you're the one who will take it from here?" Hassanat asked.

"Yes. And I want to commend you on a job well done, Hadji."

Wolfenson opened his hand, and Hassanat's rifle flew from his grasp and wound up suspended in midair.

"There will be no need for weapons of any kind," Wolfenson said. He waved his hand in a circle, and the automatic guns leapt from each terrorist's grip and joined Hassanat's weapon in a single pile next to one of the pillars behind him.

The terrorist manning the south gate panicked. He lunged for the exit. But then Wolfenson flicked his wrist and all the doors in the building locked at once.

Scaffolding, standing two stories tall, began to vibrate. It had been erected against one of the eight walls so an artisan could repair one of the stained glass windows. Now the metal framework of the scaffolding broke apart, and the rods shot like missiles across the arcade in five different directions.

Simultaneous screams filled the air as each of the terrorists were impaled where they stood.

Hassanat reached for his long serrated knife, but it was no longer on his belt.

Piercing pain shot through his back, and the rest of his body went numb. He barely managed the strength to turn so he could see his killer.

It was Noora, suddenly standing behind him. She withdrew her hand, which was covered in blood, just like the sleeve of her galabia.

Hassanat's eyes froze open as he slumped to a sitting position, where he continued to bleed out.

On the carpets, several hostages, splattered in the blood from one of the dead terrorists, started to scream.

Envoy Wolfenson walked over to them and lifted an index finger to his mouth. He needed absolute silence.

THE WELL OF SOULS, as the cave was called, had formed naturally in the bedrock of the Foundation Stone. Jenna and Father Olsen stepped out from a secret panel set into one of two manmade walls, next to a shrine supporting a table fan blowing back and forth.

The rest of the cave, carpeted, was of natural, rugged rock. A marble staircase, also carpeted, ascended to the ground floor of the dome.

Jenna stepped beneath a natural hole that opened up to the surface of the Foundation Stone. A lamp hung in the hole, blindingly bright.

At first she couldn't believe what she was seeing, and blamed it on a trick of the lamp: somehow frost was drifting down from above, as if the Dome of the Rock were actually a walk-in freezer. Even the temperature in the cave made Jenna tremble.

"Could it possibly be this cold?"

Father Olsen stared at the frost as he replied. "He's here. Satan is right above us."

Silently, Jenna moved across the room, her footsteps muffled by the red and cream rectangles of carpet. She kept her eyes fixed on the top of the staircase, where she could see a bright light, probably pouring in from the building's stained glass windows.

At the base of the stairwell, Jenna looked up but didn't see anyone standing guard at the top. She started to ascend, but a noise interrupted her—a single voice echoing off all the shrine's mosaics, marble panels and plaques, carrying all the way up to the dome, and down below.

It was not John Wolfenson, but a deeper, more commanding voice. Speaking Latin, Jenna realized. Albeit a very old pre-medieval dialect of Latin.

Then she flinched as the building above her rumbled and shook as if there were an earthquake.

After a dozen seconds the tremors subsided, and the conjuring from some dead language promptly resumed, this time louder, at the volume and strength of a hundred monks chanting.

She took another step upstairs.

"Jenna, what are you doing?"

"Don't you hear that? It sounds like he's going to pull the whole building down himself, Alan."

"But you don't know who's up there with him."

"Well, we'll have to find out, because we've run out of time. We can't just stay down here."

She turned and continued her ascent into the booming, demonic voice all around her, resounding even louder as she neared the surface.

Father Olsen joined her on the same step. "Let me go first. He can't harm me."

Jenna wasn't sure whether this was a religious rule he was citing, or something he heard from Carl. But before she could question him, the priest moved past her.

She followed close behind, stepping through the mist created by Father Olsen's breath.

The Dome of the Rock consisted of an outer octagonal wall and two concentric arcades: an outer octagonal arcade, and an inner circle of pillars. Walkways, or ambulatories, spaced out each of these arcades so worshipers and tourists alike could approach the central stone from all directions.

Jenna realized the light did not, in fact, come from the stained glass windows, but from somewhere else in the dome. Every marble, brass, and tiled surface reflected it, so that the whole place seemed to glow, making it difficult to pinpoint the exact source.

In the outer octagon, at the two gates visible to her—south and east—Jenna saw masked men, speared through the chest with long steel rods. Their puddles of blood had begun to crystallize and freeze.

A third masked terrorist lay beside the prayer niche near the south gate. Jenna saw no rod in this one, just a hole in his back, surrounded by the bloodstained fabric of his robe.

Then she and Father Olsen turned toward the center, the Foundation Stone. They could see it, through the pillars and piers of the central arcade; through the wooden screen around it: the "shattered sacred stone" from the Black Pages.

The faithful believed Muhammad ascended to Allah from this rock, and Abraham had nearly sacrificed his son on this rock. And now the rock was completely covered in frost.

Jenna then turned to a ghastly sight—in the carpeted aisle encircling the Foundation Stone, nine people, probably hostages, all lay dead, their mouths stuffed until they burst with slats broken free of the wooden screen.

She took a deep breath, then stepped past the victims, toward the source of the light, which was on the other side of the rock. There was no chance for her to think about how best to approach the situation—Father Olsen was already moving at a steady pace around the inner arcade.

The light became brighter and brighter as they stepped around the curve. At the core of it, they could see a man, who at the start of the hour had been Envoy John Wolfenson, but here now was just a cracking shell.

Beams of light had punched thousands of exit wounds through his body, and when Jenna's pupils adapted to the intensity, she made out burn rings around each opening, as if the shafts of light were scorching the outer skin.

The Angel of Light must have needed every ounce of his powers to shake down the building; impersonating an internationally renowned diplomat no longer made his list of priorities.

For the first time, Jenna could see for herself that his voice was causing the destruction of the building. His very words were shaking painted plaster from the bed of leather on the ceiling, causing it to rain down to the arcade. Jenna almost threw up on the spot. She watched helplessly as fissures and cracks appeared all around the interior of the building, breaking the mosaics of vegetal scrolls and acanthus heads into powder and grit. Jenna choked, not from the dust, but from the sight itself.

She veered away from Father Olsen, leaving him on his path toward Satan, hoping her aid would not be necessary, hoping that he was right when he said he could not be harmed. She stepped up behind one of four piers supporting the inner arcade and peered around the edge of the marble masonry.

A single tile dropped from the central drum of the dome, and crashed against the rock. The noise got Satan's attention and he looked up.

For the first time Jenna saw his face, crispy with the charred, smoking remnants of John Wolfenson's skin—like a millennia-old mummy with thousands of bad facelifts tightening the cheeks and brow, causing the eyes to bulge and the mouth to stretch from one side of the scalp to the next. His pointed ears had somehow wound up on the crown of his skull, in the far back. But his nose was beautiful, like a Hollywood actor's.

"What an interesting turn of events," he said, spotting Father Olsen, who had climbed over the railing and was now striding across the frosted Foundation Stone.

"Padre, if you just happen to be one of the tourists viewing the shrine today, I will be the first one to compliment the Landlord on his timing."

Olsen knew better than to engage in a verbal exchange with the Beast... but he had known as much back in the Garden of Gethsemane and still had failed.

The priest pulled a green stole out of his cassock and tossed the vestment around his neck. Then he opened his Bible to the traditional exorcism; not for the words written in Braille, but for the golden cross he used as a bookmark.

He raised the cross toward the fallen angel, and though the angel no longer resembled John Wolfenson, Father Olsen sought deliverance on behalf of the real envoy, the man who had aspired toward peace on Earth.

"I adjure you, Angel of Light, to depart forthwith from this servant of God, who Almighty God has made with His love..."

An invisible force swept the Braille Bible out of the priest's hands. Satan flicked his wrist and the book landed near a pillar, on a pile of automatic weapons.

Olsen made no move to retrieve it. Nor did he even look concerned. The priest just kept advancing on the Angel of Light.

"I adjure you, Satan, by the judge of the living and the dead, by your creator, and the creator of all Heaven and Earth, for your unclean spirit to yield back the soul of this servant of God..."

From behind the pier Jenna watched Olsen brave the light, and noticed that, whatever his emotional trauma of the last several weeks... and the last several minutes... none of it was apparent on his face.

As the priest continued to voice the expulsion rite, decoded from the Devil's Bible, a stubborn determination hardened his eyes.

"Satan, begone and stay away from this human frame, you enemy of the faith, you, the foe of the human race, you corrupter of justice, seducer of men, betrayer of all nations..."

Satan dipped his head and resumed his chant in ancient Latin. Jenna was only able to translate a few words—Babhomet; Archangel; Lucifer. She had no idea what would happen next.

Suddenly more than fifty stained glass windows ringing the Dome of the Rock all shattered at once, a sound like crash cymbals, so loud Jenna thought if she were to apply her hands to her ears she would feel dripping blood.

A belt of broken colored glass with shattered Qur'anic verses showered down all around Father Olsen as if he were in the middle of a hailstorm in the Dome of the Rock.

"Do not stand and resist; now knowing that your plan for insurrection will come to nothing against the Almighty God..."

A shard of falling glass glanced off Alan's face, cutting his cheek. Jenna stepped away from the pier to help him.

But then Father Olsen removed a white handkerchief from his cassock and wiped the rivulet of blood from his face as he spoke the words, undeterred: "Depart then, Angel of Light, His favorite son, who took His love and turned it into lies of cunning and sin. Depart from this man who is His creature!"

Jenna heard footsteps and turned, then quickly ducked—a knife swept across the air at neck level.

Stepping forward and whipping around, Jenna screamed and threw all of her weight into her attacker. The assassin slammed against the marble pier and dropped the knife. By the time Jenna had stopped reeling, the attacker had disappeared somewhere behind all the pillars.

"Jenna?!" Father Olsen said. He had heard her cry out.

"Alan, I'm all right—keep going!"

The priest solemnly redoubled his intent on Satan. "I cast you out for-ever and forever from this man..."

Jenna was panting as she searched for a sign of her attacker moving around the arcades. Chunks of molded plaster and hundreds of tiles con-tinued to drop to the carpet all around her. Jenna was heartbroken to see the building in such distress. Some of these tiles were painted with the old-est Arabic handwriting recorded. It was all just one more level of motiva-tion in her fight to save the building.

Glancing all around her, and moving cautiously, Jenna bent down to reach for the knife. A woman in a galabia leapt at her from behind one of the piers.

She tackled Jenna to the floor and began to pound at her with bare fists. Jenna fought back, but the woman assailed her like a banshee, with almost superhuman strength.

Several punches connected with Jenna's temple, and dazed her, almost knocked her out. The banshee reached out and throttled her neck.

Through confusion and blurry, watery vision, Jenna thought she recog-nized the woman: she looked like Kelli Langton, the shop owner from her hometown who had gotten killed by a demon.

But then the illusion cleared and Jenna saw the woman's stretched skin and deep black eyes, and she knew *this* was like the demonically possessed blonde back in Occoquan, who had killed Kelli Langton.

As she lay gasping for air, Jenna flashed on the tiles lying all around her on the carpet. She reached out, grabbed one; slammed it against the banshee's arm. It did nothing through the thick sleeve of the galabia robe.

Jenna slid it down to the back of the demon's hand.

Still nothing.

She dropped the tile and reached out for another one, but was beginning to lose consciousness. Her hand fumbled about absently, scraping her nails futilely against the carpet.

The light, gathered like a cloud in the dome above her, began to darken.

Then one of her fingers brushed against another tile. She grabbed it and used all of her remaining strength to slap it against her attacker's cheek.

The stretched skin sizzled and steamed... and almost caught fire.

Jenna, unable to see anything through the haze, held the tile there until the demon fell off of her.

Hacking, coughing, inhaling the stink of burning flesh, Jenna crawled away and lunged toward the knife. She was forced to wait more than a few seconds before the banshee stopped rolling around on the carpet long enough for Jenna to plunge the knife into her attacker's neck.

Only after the body stopped moving did Jenna drop the tile, which was painted with an Arabic word—"God."

FATHER OLSEN STOPPED a few feet from Satan, who stared at him without any expression. The priest calmly held his golden cross just inches away as thousands of incandescent beams of light continued to flow from the skin of Envoy Wolfenson's body.

Jenna waited breathlessly as Father Olsen recited the few dozen words left to conclude the exorcism. He enunciated them perfectly.

At the last word, the rumbling, the voices, the din of things breaking— it had all stopped. Jenna turned away, bracing herself for a light show.

All she got instead was more silence.

So it seemed incredibly loud when the place filled with a wildly vindictive, bestial laugh.

Jenna knew the laughter wasn't meant for her ears, or the priest's. This was a demonstration meant to reverberate all the way to the heavens.

"You say that you are a god, yet you insult me with your effort!"

Jenna raced toward Father Olsen, hoping she could shield him from what she felt sure was going to happen next.

She vaulted over the wooden screen onto the frozen Foundation Stone and was less than a dozen feet away when an invisible force slammed into the priest, sending him flying. He landed like a swatted bug, sprawled out on the surface of the dome's massive rock.

Satan went back to blaspheming God. "If your heart's not in the game, then just forfeit and let me go about my ways. Don't insult me by sending in your reserves as if you don't care about the outcome!"

Jenna scooped up Olsen's golden cross where he had dropped it, and scrambled toward him.

She had realized something during the exorcism. Satan hadn't shown the slightest sign of fear... or even relief when the rite eventually failed. As if he had no doubt all along that it would, indeed, fail. There was something missing.

No, Jenna thought, unable to stop the tears, but drying them just as fast. Not something missing, but something that *never should have been.*

Satan, beyond paying any attention, struck up his chant again.

Jenna knelt beside Father's Olsen's battered body strewn across the rock. He looked over at her. "Jenna, I said the words exactly as you wrote them..."

She tried her best to look reassuring. "Father, I know you did. But... George threw up after meeting you. Which he'd only done on two other occasions, both times when he sensed something... Evil."

There was a deep cracking sound as one of the nearby pillars began to fracture.

"Alan, please forgive me, but... because of what you received from him... you could perform the rite a million times and it will never work so long as you can still..."

She choked up on the final word, and he just stared at her with a fixed expression. He didn't even blink. Jenna began to worry the priest might have died from being smashed against the rock.

But then Olsen sat up and began to look around.

Slowly he climbed to his feet.

"Alan, wait..." She placed the golden cross in the palm of his hand.

More and more pillars began to crack and shed chips and dust, harried by Satan's chant.

A blue shard of stained glass sparkled on the stone and attracted his attention. The priest staggered toward it, then tried to pick it up. The jagged edge cut his fingers. He watched as his own blood dripped and melted a hole in the frost. The priest reached down again, and this time he snatched up the glass without thinking about what it would do to his fingers. He then raked the shard across his eye.

Father Olsen almost cried out in agony, but swallowed it. His knees buckled, and his hand trembled, and he knew if he waited for the excruciating pain to subside, he might lose his nerve. So he took the serrated blue glass, which he could see was slick with his own blood... and he stabbed it toward his other eye, plunging the rest of his world into complete and utter darkness.

SATAN HAD BEEN WATCHING thousands of tiles drop from the roof like he was watching the heavens fall down all around him. But then he caught sight of a figure wobbling across the rock.

"I adjure you, Angel of Light, to depart forthwith from this servant of God, who almighty God has made with His love..."

"Father Olsen... what have you done?"

"I adjure you, Satan, by the judge of the living and the dead, by your creator, and the creator of all Heaven and Earth, for your unclean spirit to yield back the soul of this servant of God..."

"Alan, I can't respect your choice, but I hope I'm not being insensitive when I tell you... because you can no longer see, you may not be aware the game is over. There is no reason for you to continue this fight."

"He who comes now to the aid of this afflicted man and chooses to be free of your control. It is He who commands you, not me, a weak sinner."

Satan rushed forward and grabbed the priest, wrapping the stole around his neck, as if to choke him with his own vestment. "Now you're blind again and you want me to explain what I'm trying to do?! I tried to save you! I'm trying to save you all! Fine, you're blind again. But you're not stupid. I'm all you have! Each and every one of you, if you ever hope to escape the hell that is all of humanity!"

Olsen held up the golden cross. Jenna could tell that the priest no longer knew which direction to face, but he must have known it didn't matter. Evil was everywhere.

"Satan, begone and stay away from this human frame, you enemy of the faith, you, the foe of the human race, you corrupter of justice, seducer of men, betrayer of all nations..."

Satan was backing up, retreating, for the first time looking genuinely scared. Jenna followed forward in the footsteps of Father Olsen. If Satan attempted to escape the building, she wanted to be right there to stop him.

"Do not stand and resist; now knowing that your plan for insurrection will come to nothing against the Almighty God. He who strips you of your powers here on Earth for the laws you have transgressed!"

Satan turned away and Jenna thought this was the moment he would show some weakness, perhaps collapse to the rock under the power of the rite. But when Satan whipped back around to face Father Olsen, he now was the spitting image of Sandy Travis.

"Alan," Jenna said, "he's trying to—"

Before she could complete the sentence, Sandy Travis was right in front of her, slamming into her like a cannonball. Jenna flew back and over the wooden screen, slamming into one of the piers of the inner arcade. She landed unconscious on the floor.

"Jenna? Jenna?!"

"Alan, don't do this," someone whispered to him, whispered in his ear. "Be with me. I need you. I want you..."

Though he could not see her, he knew the voice was meant to sound like Sandy Travis.

"Please, be with me..."

Father Olsen tightened his grip on the cross and said, "Depart then, Angel of Light, His favorite son, who took His love and turned it into lies of cunning and sin. Depart from this man who is His creature. I cast you out forever and forever from this man, stripping you of your immediate powers on Earth and plunging you once again into darkness!"

The priest took a breath, and when he did, he sucked in the foul stink of the Beast. Without a doubt the Angel of Light shined inches from his face.

"I gave you a miracle so you would no longer be blind to the entity you serve, who only returns your devotion by denying you your grace." Satan had discarded Sandy's voice, and was using his own, an intimate but urgent whisper. "He is the same almighty who has also become deaf. I am the only angel who still listens. I am the only one who bothered to hear you scream for help. Alan, if you silence me now, ask yourself—who will listen to your cries then? Who will listen to any of you ever again?"

Father Olsen made it a point to ignore the specific words, but found that he could not ignore the impassioned tone. He expected nothing less. The Angel of Light's original job was as an accuser appointed by God to test men's faith.

Jenna regained consciousness and sat up. Though she was woozy from the physical blow, when she heard Father Olsen uttering the final few words of the exorcism rite, she knew exactly where she was.

Once again, Alan concentrated on reciting the final words of the exorcism, fully aware that the Devil himself had crafted them: "Angel of Light, as you depart from these earthly confines, these prison walls, He awaits, as He always has, to forgive you, to descend upon you, to shine His love upon you so that you may reconcile your soul with His Light... Amen."

Immediately after Father Olsen's last word, Jenna believed that all time stopped around her, the laws of physics suspended like the tiles from the domed roof, poised in midair.

Then everything happened at once, as if making up for lost time.

A ghostly apparition broke free from Envoy Wolfenson, materializing as a gaseous entity hovering above him. The entity began sucking up all the air in the room, and then burst into a fireball, which shot around the arcade, eventually rushing right toward Jenna at hurricane speed.

She ducked, but felt the intense heat and smelled her singed hair as the fiery meteor raced past her and then rocketed toward the top of the dome. A moment before it hit the roof, it exploded into a million different lights, which all floated to Earth, each one fading away before touching the stone.

The silence and stillness in the shrine meant that the destruction had stopped. Somehow the temperature had also returned to normal, the rock no longer covered in frost.

Jenna slowly got to her feet. Father Olsen was not where she remembered last seeing him. He lay sprawled on the rock once again, cast to the far corner. In her periphery, Jenna saw Envoy John Wolfenson, and had to turn to confirm that he, indeed, looked nothing like Swiss cheese, and was back to his mortal self. She could even see him breathing.

Rushing toward the rock, Jenna had enough presence of mind to grab the satellite phone from a terrorist's belt. It looked exactly like the kind Carl had given her days ago. She redialed the last number, and after the first ring someone answered.

"My name is Jenna Grant, and I'm one of the hostages in the Dome of the Rock. The hostage crisis is over. All the terrorists are dead. You can now send in a rescue team to help us..."

JENNA CLIMBED OVER THE WOODEN SCREEN and tumbled down to the rock, too exhausted to get back on her feet. She crawled over to Father Olsen, but before she could reach out, he reached out instead. They clutched each other's hand, and she hoped it was a good sign when he pulled her toward him the rest of the way. Blood was still running down the blinded priest's cheeks as he stared off into space.

"How is Envoy Wolfenson?" he asked.

"He's gone, Alan. You did it."

"I know—I was asking about John himself. The possessed should never be blamed for being a vessel of evil."

"I saw him and he was breathing... but I didn't check because I came here first."

Loud noises caught both of their attention, but Jenna quickly recognized the source.

"Nothing to worry about. It's just the Yamam, the Israeli SWAT team banging away at the locked doors of the shrine."

The priest nodded and relaxed. While they waited for rescue, Jenna thought of something and figured this was as good a time as ever to ask Father Olsen.

"Is it over?"

The priest didn't hesitate. "The fact that we stopped him means it's not over."

Because of their actions, sectarian violence, and no doubt worldwide conflict, had been averted—or at the very least, if it ended up happening anyway, it could not be blamed on the destruction of the Dome of the Rock. But Jenna knew well enough the world she lived in, and there would be a reaction to the fact that the Golden Gate now stood wide open for the first time in nearly five hundred years.

"So, Father, when will it be over?"

This time he did hesitate before answering, and before he responded he was interrupted by the noise of one of the doors to the shrine swinging open, then another, and another.

Streams of sunshine lit up the arcade.

"What's happening, Jenna?"

"It just got brighter in here. The police have opened up the doors to the shrine."

Father Olsen summoned the last of his remaining strength in an effort to stand up.

"Do you mind helping me, Jenna? Point me in the direction of the light?"

But then Jenna used *her* last remaining strength to pull the priest back down, back beside her on the rock.

"Actually, I do mind. At this very moment there's at least thirty Israeli police running around here." She tightened her grip on his hand. "I don't want anyone mistaking us for one of the bad guys."

CHAPTER 26

Envoy John Wolfenson's eyes flashed open. At first he had no idea where he was or what had happened.

"Oh, envoy, sir—you're back amongst the living!"

The voice sounded familiar, but of the man's face he saw only a silhouette behind the bright beam of a flashlight shining in his eyes.

"Where am I?" John asked.

"No, no, sir, I'm the one who gets to ask questions around here. You tell me where you think you are."

John looked around and suddenly his surroundings were so familiar he couldn't believe he hadn't recognized them immediately.

"I'm in Balshem Medical Center."

The words had just left his lips when John lifted his hand toward his neck. The instinct must have just beaten the memory in a race because he then flashed on a woman rushing toward him with a shard of glass.

Sandy.

Sandy Travis.

She had stabbed him. But his hand didn't touch an open wound, blood, or even a bandage. Just a long, jagged scar.

Then everything he had been through the last few weeks started to flood his brain. Sandy Travis's attack had happened weeks ago, though it felt like a lifetime ago. So much more had happened since then.

Fragments of memory flashed across his mind. He saw himself kissing Pat, but he also remembered her running away from him in fear. He experienced the miraculous resurrection of the dead, and then explosions, destruction. He saw millions of people hanging on his every word while he chased after fleeting glimpses of his dead son Scott.

None of the memories clearly shined. Probably because, while everything had been happening, John had been watching it all through murky water, from the bottom of a lake; he could hear vague voices talking above the surface, never close enough to know for sure who was speaking, but close enough to know the voices were familiar. At some point he had simply stopped watching and listening. It was too painful to lie helplessly in the lake bed while the world he had known was floating above right past him.

"Dr. Diamant?"

"Envoy, sir, that's a good sign. This time you remembered my name. But it's not the only good sign. You seem to be doing quite well. I told everyone this morning at the press conference it would be just a matter of time before you awoke. I told everyone you just needed some rest. You understand that by waking up, you'll probably make everyone think I'm a miracle worker."

"Doctor, there's someone I want to see..."

"Well, sir, there's someone that is very anxious to see you. I think you're doing well enough I can allow a visitor."

Dr. Diamant left the room. John tried to sit up, so he could at least look like he was on the road to recovery. But his body wouldn't respond. He was now sweating just trying to smooth out his hair and make himself somewhat presentable.

The door opened, and John froze.

"Hey, sleepy head. Don't worry, we'll get the hair and make-up in here long before we put you before the cameras."

He barely recognized the face, but the voice was one of the few that had reverberated at the bottom of the lake.

It was Larry Zepp, the man who had replaced John's press secretary and good friend Rick Walsh.

"Where's my wife?" John asked.

"Sir, nobody knows where Pat is. She's been missing for days."

More memories flashed across John's brain. He remembered a private jet, a private serenade in the bedroom, Patricia listening while he played the violin, Patricia coming to him, taking the instrument and setting it aside, and then kissing him. It was beautiful, wonderful, but he couldn't remember what it had felt like, her lips against his; couldn't remember if it was something that had happened, or something that had happened to... him.

"Mr. Envoy, if you're feeling up to it, we could start working on something to say to the media."

"The media?"

"Sir, the parking lot is filled with everyone from across the globe. Now there are two schools of thought on how to handle a situation like this. I'm sure you already know what I want to do—I say we remain above the fray.

You should go out there and just repeat every wonderful detail of your distinguished public record, and simply dare anyone to voice their accusations to your face."

"Accusations?"

"Sorry, but I should have inserted the word 'groundless' before the word 'accusation.' Believe me, I did the best I could in denying these absurd claims, but it was difficult to get on top of the situation while you were in a coma."

"What am I accused of doing... ?"

"Trying to destroy the Dome of the Rock."

"Ridiculous. How could I possibly be capable of destroying one of the most treasured landmarks on Earth?"

"I completely agree. More importantly, what you just said was gold. Let's start with that nugget and build the rest of the press release from there."

John tried to sit up, but, again, he couldn't move. He was too weak, too sore.

So he lay back down. "Let's get on top of these groundless rumors immediately."

Zepp lit up like John had just plugged him into a light socket. "That's the fighting spirit! And I think I have the perfect vehicle for you to give your side of the story. Ben Peters from *24/7* has been calling me non-stop, requesting a one- on-one interview. I'm standing by and ready to negotiate an exclusive U.S. primetime television time slot. Just give me the word."

It started to rain. John could hear the drops hit the ledge outside his window. He sighed, then waved his hand. "Go ahead. Make it happen."

Zepp left, and as soon as the door closed, John took a deep breath. Somehow he needed to clear his head of everything and start all over.

Some of the memories were so painful he had hoped to forget them. But John realized if he planned to rise above what had happened, and also find his wife, he would need to remember.

He would need to remember it all.

———

FOR THE FIRST TIME IN A LONG TIME Carl felt like a family man. Down the hall he could hear shooting; his youngest son, "Rocket," was playing a war game with one of the security guards. Carl could also hear his wife, Zeinah, chatting and giggling with her mother in the room right across from him. Occasionally he would hear Patricia as well. She and his wife were getting along great. In fact, just last night he heard Patricia laugh. He realized it was a sound he had never heard in his life.

If every day flowed like this one, Carl would be happy to stay right where they were for years. And he was prepared to do so if necessary. He just wasn't sure if it would be necessary.

A buzzing noise grabbed Carl's attention. The flashing light indicated someone had entered the medical observation room. He quickly notified the security team that he would handle it. Carl was fairly sure of the visitor's identity.

"PATRICIA, WHAT ARE YOU DOING IN HERE?"

She was staring at the glass partition, which was currently blacked out. "You told me I could go anywhere I wanted."

"Absolutely. I'm just wondering why you would come to this room. There's nothing but medical equipment in here."

"There's something behind the glass. Isn't there?"

"Yes. My son."

Patricia continued to stare at the darkened glass.

"Would you like to see?"

"Yes, Carl, I would."

He walked over to the control panel and hit a button. The glass dissolved from black to clear, revealing Ami, who lay unconscious, strapped to a hospital bed. Wires and tubes connected him to monitoring equipment.

Carl moved to stand beside Patricia.

When he had seen Ami for the first time after the envoy had been cast out of the world, Carl had at least felt relieved to see more color to him, a lot more life. But he also felt distressed to see his son's face stretched tight again, just as it had been before the Angel of Light had made his grand entrance into the world.

"We have him in a medically-induced coma because he's not feeling well," Carl said.

"Can I go in and see him?"

"Pat, that's probably not a good idea."

"Please." She grabbed his hand. "Please, Carl. It would mean so much to me."

CARL BRIGHTENED THE LIGHTS in the room before he waved Patricia in.

She moved slowly but deliberately toward Ami's hospital bed, and then reached out to touch him.

"We should go," Carl said, and he started to lead her back out of the room.

Ami's eyes flashed open. Blacker than the windows in Carl's chopper. Blacker than anything.

Though her back was to the bed, Patricia seemed to somehow sense his presence. She turned around.

"I can see you..." Ami said, though it was not the voice of Carl's son. It wasn't even the voice of the demon who possessed him and often spoke as if his son were nothing more than a hand puppet.

"Yes, I can see you very clearly, Carl."

It was the voice of John Wolfenson, but the words of the Angel of Light.

"What is in her will be my legacy. Don't be foolish enough to challenge my will." Ami turned to Patricia. "Come to me, dear. Be with me..."

She rushed toward the bed.

Carl grabbed her, but Patricia fought back. She screamed and kicked and pried at Carl's hands.

He managed to drag her out of the room, trying his best to ignore the spirit in her resistance. He equated it with the way a drowning, terrified swimmer often lashes out at the very lifeguard trying to save her.

———

THE PRIEST HAD BEEN SITTING in the lobby of the Israel Prison Service Medical Center for hours when he heard the main door in the lobby open.

"Father Olsen."

"Tom, how are you?"

"Much better, Father, thank you."

Despite his positive words, Tom still sounded weary. But at least his voice expressed some emotion.

Tom took Olsen's hand, and the priest returned the friendly squeeze. He was glad to feel the warmth in Tom's fingers. It felt like he was human again. Olsen also noticed that Tom must have reached up to take his hand.

"Tom, are you in a wheelchair?"

"Yeah, still too weak to walk on my own. But they said with some therapy I should eventually be able to get around."

The possession had almost killed him. Lack of food and water and any kind of activity had obviously atrophied his legs and probably the rest of his body.

"It's very nice to see you, Father. I didn't expect you to be out here. How did you know when..."

"Oh, Agent Ginsberg and I have become quite close. He let me know when you would be discharged."

There was silence.

"Tom, are you all right?"

"Yes, I'm fine. I'm just now seeing your eyes. I'm confused. I heard from the agent that you somehow had your eyesight back. What happened?"

Olsen wore dark sunglasses, which he had rarely worn before, the first time he was blind. But the gashes he had inflicted upon himself had not healed. And from everything he gathered, until they did heal, the sight was very shocking.

"It's kind of a long story. There's a botanical garden nearby. How would you like to go there and talk?"

"That sounds fine. But I have to warn you. If there are any hills on the way, I might need you to push me."

The priest laughed. "A blind man pushing another man in a wheelchair. This could be interesting."

THOUGH HE COULDN'T SEE THE GARDEN, Father Olsen could smell the trees, the grass, and the soil. They found a quiet corner in the Japanese section, amongst the bonsai trees.

Tom positioned his wheelchair next to a bench. Olsen sat beside him. And they talked.

The priest told him everything, save for the part about hearing his fiancée's voice at the Basilica of the Agony—or what sounded like his fiancée's voice. Olsen had become convinced it was another of Satan's tricks. Mentioning it now, even if he were to relate his doubts, would only trouble Tom further. No doubt he still struggled with what had happened to Sandy. No doubt Tom still blamed himself. Olsen knew it was a feeling they both had in common.

"So there in the Dome of the Rock, I guess you did what I couldn't do."

"I'm not sure what you mean, Tom."

"You stood up to him. Even when it meant giving back your eyesight."

"Hmm, I understand why you might arrive at that conclusion. But it's not that simple. I believe if you had known at the time of the helicopter crash what was at stake, you would have made a similar choice. You certainly didn't know someone you loved was in jeopardy."

Tom was silent. Olsen didn't want to presume to disturb whatever useful contemplation he might be working through. But after a while, the priest finally went on.

"Tom, can I share something else? It happened in the short time I was able to see. I had the opportunity to use a computer at my friend's house, and I checked out your website. There was one piece I found especially striking."

"The picture of Sandy."

Olsen nodded, but didn't continue, hoping that Tom would keep speaking.

"It was a charcoal drawing I did of her while we were in Hawaii. She posed for me the day before I asked her to marry me." Tom choked on his words and started to cry.

Olsen reached over and rubbed his back. "Tom, the picture was beautiful. You did an amazing job capturing the Sandy I knew."

Then the priest took off his glasses and wiped his own eyes. "I'm really glad I got a chance to see it."

———

HER PLANE FROM TEL AVIV landed, and since she had no luggage to claim, she headed immediately to the Heathrow Express. Just as she was about to board the train, she stopped and found a quiet place to make a phone call. She had been putting it off long enough.

Her mother answered on the first ring. Ruth was in her backyard, repairing the damage all the media people had done to her garden.

Before Jenna could lecture her mother to stay off her feet, Ruth told her the last news crew had left that morning. Apparently Neal's rampage was now part of yesterday's news cycle.

The day after the train collision, a sex scandal had broken out, involving a married, father-of-three congressman; he had used campaign donations to pay for a stripper's silence regarding their relationship and their three-year-old child.

And just the previous evening, a disaster at sea led to the deaths of twenty-five people. Maritime officials were working around the clock, investigating witness accounts that the ship's skipper had been drinking excessively the night before the accident.

The phone conversation eventually circled around to Neal's funeral, and Jenna listened to her mother's unemotional account of the ceremony: how much the casket cost, how pretty the flowers were that their Aunt Dinah sent from North Carolina, even how nice the weather conditions were on the afternoon they lowered Neal's casket into the ground.

She listed for Jenna all of the people who had attended the funeral, and, in equal measure, those who did not. Ruth showed no animosity toward those who were unable to attend, and even those who chose not to pay their respects.

As her mother ran through the long list of names, Jenna was fully aware she was one of the many who had not attended. She further assumed the list of names was her mother's prelude to a discussion about Jenna's absence. But when her mother read off the last name, and then moved on to Neal's life insurance policy, Jenna realized she was wrong—her mother had no intention of pointing out her absence on the day Neal was laid to rest.

Jenna decided to broach the subject herself.

"Mom, I'm sorry I wasn't there. You know how much I loved Neal. I'm going to miss him more than I can possibly describe."

"Honey, you don't need to apologize. I know you had your hands full with what happened at the Temple Mount."

Very few people knew of her involvement in the crisis at Mount Moriah. Even fewer knew the truth of what had happened.

"Mom, how did you hear about the Temple Mount?"

"Andrew called and told me everything."

Now it made sense.

Father Andrew Walton had been the only person Jenna called in the aftermath of the crisis. Then immediately after they ended the call, the priest left his church, drove out to Jerusalem, and gave his support to both her and Father Olsen between marathon interrogation sessions with Israeli and Muslim authorities. Since part of the time Father Olsen was receiving treatment for his eye injuries, Jenna would have been all alone if not for Father Walton's warm and reassuring company.

"I can't believe he called you, Mom. I guess I expected Andrew to wait for me to say something to you myself."

"Honey, you're missing the obvious. Andrew was probably relieving you of the burden. Ask yourself, isn't this conversation already going better than you suspected?"

"Yeah, I guess so."

"Anyway, we talked for hours. He's flying to Occoquan next week just so we can spend some time together."

"How nice. Time to brush up on your Scrabble, right?"

"I resent the implication. I assure you, I'm going to kick that white collar's ass."

Jenna laughed. It was a relief to hear her mother speak in such a spirited way.

She was about to crack a joke about their Scrabble rivalry, but then her mother said, "I'm proud of you, honey."

"Proud? What do you mean?"

"Just what I said, Jenna, I'm proud of you. Why wouldn't I be? According to Andrew, what you did was remarkable. I don't know all the details, but I don't have to. I'm proud of you."

Jenna had a reply to her mother's praise, but swallowed her words. A passerby in the train station saw her tearing up and stopped to gawk. Jenna turned away, toward the wall, so no one could see her.

"Here's the thing, Mother—nothing I did can bring back all those people Neal killed, or the families he's devastated. And they can't bring back my brother either..."

"Perhaps that's true, Jenny. But always remember, you didn't kill any of those people... including your brother. Besides, it would have been a tragedy if the Dome of the Rock had been destroyed. A building with that much history has so much to say to future generations. Do you remember what I always told both of you kids?"

Ever since adolescence, Jenna had often thought of how dearly she did not want to end up like her mother, and yet at times Ruth would say or do something that reminded Jenna of how they were so much alike.

"You dig. And you dig. Because what you end up saving... will end up illuminating what was lost."

"Yeah, Mom, throughout everything that was going on, those were my thoughts exactly."

The next train pulled into the station, and Jenna decided it was as good a time as any to say goodbye.

"Mom, why don't I call you in the next couple days?"

"That sounds good. You take care of yourself now."

"I will. I love you, Mom..."

She waited for a reply, but Ruth had probably thought the phone call was over and had already disconnected. It was just as well. If they had stayed on the phone much longer, Jenna would have grown more and more tempted to disclose her run-in with her father. Now she would have something to discuss with Ruth the next time they talked.

JENNA STEPPED OFF THE HEATHROW EXPRESS in London and was surprised to see a man in a perfectly pressed black suit holding a sign with her name on it.

Jenna looked around, wondering if it was a trap. Then she worried that, for now and forevermore, she might always be this paranoid.

"I'm Jenna Grant," she said to the man holding the sign.

He bowed, then reached into his suit jacket. "This is for you, ma'am." He handed her an envelope with her name typed on the outside, then walked away without saying another word.

Jenna opened the envelope. Inside she discovered a manila card:

> *We had a date planned for the next time you were in London. Will you remember the suite number even though it wasn't part of a medieval quatrain? See you on the balcony!*
>
> *Raymond*
>
> P.S. NO JOKE. SERIOUS HERE.

AFTER SHE KNOCKED ON THE SUITE DOOR, Jenna heard some rustling from inside the room, then a loud pop.

She took a step back.

Try and burst through the door? she thought.

Or run like hell?

Suddenly the door flew open. It was Raymond. This time there was no hesitation—they both jumped into each other's arms and kissed. It lasted long enough for Raymond to drag her into the room.

When they parted, he barely gave her time to breathe before he was handing her a glass of champagne. The glass was chilled.

Raymond raised his glass. "To my esteemed colleague. Who not only writes about history, but is making history with everything she does..."

"No, I refuse to drink to something you stole from a greeting card!"

"To be honest, Jenna, I came up with that years ago, dreaming that someday, somehow, someone would make that toast about me. So now I demand you drink to it!"

Jenna allowed him to put his glass to her lips, and as she drank, they stared into each other's eyes.

Afterwards, she offered Raymond his drink. He happily took a big sip, and then set it down. But not fast enough. By the time he looked up, Jenna's attention had drifted over to the empty chair in the corner of the suite.

Raymond observed her glassy-eyed look for a few moments, then grabbed the glass he had just set down. He tossed back the contents, then touched Jenna on the arm.

"If it's any consolation, I noticed the hotel fixed the smoke alarm."

She tried to smile, and Raymond realized something about the text she had sent him after everything had played out in the Dome of the Rock. It hadn't just been something she had fired off on the run, as he had assumed. No, the cold, unemotional message was more indicative of her state of mind: *Dome saved. Wolf gone. Alan blind again. I am OK.*

———

A WEEK LATER IN CAMBRIDGE, Raymond got his wish—he and Jenna drove in together to work. They didn't even bother hiding the fact they had spent yet another night together. On Jenna's first day back at the radio station, Raymond escorted her with one arm wrapped around her shoulders.

A few people noticed, but none of that mattered. Everyone was just excited to see Jenna, and they let her know with enthusiastic hugs and kisses.

At first she thought Raymond had told them about what she had done to save the Dome of the Rock, but it turned out they had heard different news; they had heard of her involvement in the train collision in Virginia. All the hugs and kisses were about that near-death experience she had survived.

Jenna lingered for quite some time, talking to friends. She was in no rush to approach her desk. But after a while, the kind words and affectionate greetings began to trail off, and the normal sounds of a working radio station began to take over.

As Jenna approached her desk, the first sight that grabbed her attention was the framed photograph of Neal and her mother posing with her at her graduation. She probably would have stared at it forever if she didn't gently lay the frame face-down on her desk. Then she spotted something else on the corner of her desk: a brown package.

It sat on top of the rest of the mail that had arrived while she was away. She casually picked up the box, but then saw the return address and dropped her purse.

With both hands, Jenna tore into the package.

Raymond had walked up just as she was shredding the brown paper that covered the box. Rather than asking questions, he grabbed one of the torn pieces of paper, which had been tossed a few feet from her desk. He saw the return address, and the name *George Wyatt*.

Jenna tore open the box.

"A camera?" Raymond asked. "I don't understand?"

"It's... the one George had with him. On the train the day of the wreck."

"Still confused, Jenna. Are we supposed to believe that in everything you and George went through, he had the presence of mind to send you... his camera?"

Jenna didn't reply. Instead she started swiping up all the brown wrapping she had thrown aside like a five-year-old on Christmas morning.

Raymond realized what she was looking for and handed her the piece of wrapping he had picked up.

The postdate indicated the package had been mailed the same day George had dropped her off to visit with her mother in Occoquan.

One of the radio station managers stepped out of his office and called out to Raymond, who waved to indicate that he would be right there.

"Are you going to be all right?"

"Yes. Sure."

Despite her words, Jenna had the same look on her face he remembered from the hotel in London—driven, intense, focused and... haunted.

She looked up and offered a warm smile. "Ray, I'm totally fine. Thanks for being here for me. You know how much it means to me." Then to convince him she was nothing but sincere, Jenna set the camera down on her desk.

Raymond returned her smile, relieved to see her handling everything so well. "We're still on for dinner tonight?"

She nodded.

He was already walking backwards, toward the radio manager's office. "I'll be at your doorstep at six. Chinese takeout sound all right?"

She nodded again, and Raymond blew her a kiss. Then he turned to meet with the manager.

Jenna began to sort through the other mail on her desk. But even as she was reading about a promotional event at a local pub, all she kept thinking about was why George, or anyone else, would send her the camera.

She was on her fifth piece of mail, a solicitation letter asking her to appear at a media event next month, when it suddenly hit her.

Jenna threw aside the letter and snatched up George's camera. She switched it on, and after a few seconds the first picture appeared on the little screen. It was a photo of Carri, George's wife, walking by herself and... smiling. A smile as big as the Grand Canyon.

Jenna flipped forward through the pictures. She finally came upon the one of the woman who looked like Carri, sitting on the train. It was the same picture Jenna had found while snooping around George's apartment.

The picture count on the camera indicated nineteen of twenty-two. Jenna pushed the button to the next picture.

The image seemed to take forever to materialize on the little monitor, but when it finally did, Jenna gasped.

Two figures, both with their backs to the lens, were moving up the aisle of the train car. One of the figures appeared to be Carri. And the other figure looked very much like... George.

Jenna advanced to the next photograph, second to last. The same two figures stood in the train car, but now they were near the exit. And this time their heads were turned toward the camera. Jenna was sure they were Carri and George.

But then she looked closely, as close as she could look at someone's eyes on a camera's tiny screen. She wanted to see if they were, indeed, George's eyes. And for a moment she wasn't sure. She remembered his eyes being enigmatic, questioning, sometimes confused. The eyes of this man in the photograph seemed happy, confident, and... serene.

Then Jenna noticed a detail in the picture she had missed the first time around—the two figures were holding hands.

She started to tear up, but it didn't stop her from advancing to the last picture.

This time, the train car was empty.

Jenna was sure what that meant—*She waited for him... And then George and Carri exited together.*

Jenna put the camera down and looked around the office. Thank God nobody had noticed her crying at her desk. It would have been embarrassing, something she would never have been able to explain to her mother.

———

THERE WAS A KNOCK ON HER DOOR. Jenna looked at her watch and saw that Raymond was late with their dinner. She would have to give him some shit—she was starving!

Jenna threw open the door. "What happened to 'I'll be at your doorstep at'—" She froze when she saw who was in the doorway.

"Do you mind if I come in?" her father said. "It's rather important."

She stared at him, trying not to look panicked.

"Jenna. I need your help—"

She slammed the door in his face.

Then engaged the chain.

Jenna scrambled over to her telephone and dialed Raymond's number. Voicemail.

She was thinking about whether she should first call the police, or her mother. But then there was another knock on the door...

ACKNOWLEDGEMENTS

D.L. SNELL

Thanks to Dr. Kim Paffenroth for the Latin, and both Zeinah Abunuwar and Ahmad Al-Shakarji for the Arabic. And thanks to Krakenten for the invaluable lesson in firearms. Also, I would like to acknowledge all the fans of the first book: without you... well, without you we'd still go on writing, but it would be a lonely, lonely business.

RICHARD FINNEY

I want to express my appreciation for the feedback and invaluable support of Jay Frasco. Emily Finney was so very helpful with her research. Of course none of this would have been possible without the support of David and the rest of the fine people at Ape Entertainment. And a special thanks to Danuta Skulski, who read the first half of this book overnight. Her enthusiasm for the story and her desire to read the rest of the book kept me writing.

ABOUT THE AUTHORS

RICHARD FINNEY is a Los Angeles based writer and producer.

Visit his website -- richardfinney.blogspot.com

D.L. SNELL is a novelist, a member of the Horror Writers Association, and a freelance editor for Permuted Press. He has sold short stories to anthologies such as Pocket Books' *Blood Lite* series, and his first novel *Roses of Blood on Barbwire Vines* pits zombies against vampires. Author Nicholas Grabowsky has called Snell's work "damn good writing."

WRITTEN BY RICHARD FINNEY

DEMON DAYS
DEMON DAYS – BOOK TWO
DEMON DAYS – BOOK THREE
DEMON DAYS – BOOK FOUR

RELICT
BOOK ONE – DRAWING BLOOD
BOOK TWO – SHADOWS IN THE LIGHT (2013)

BLACK MARIAH
BOOK ONE - A CALLING (2013)

www.ingramcontent.com/pod-product-compliance
Lightning Source LLC
Chambersburg PA
CBHW071159250626
47159CB00001B/132